# BURIED IN SECRET

Also by Viveca Sten in the Sandhamn Murders Series

*Still Waters*
*Closed Circles*
*Guiltless*
*Tonight You're Dead*
*In the Heat of the Moment*
*In Harm's Way*
*In the Shadow of Power*
*In the Name of Truth*
*In Bad Company*

# BURIED IN SECRET

## VIVECA STEN

TRANSLATED BY MARLAINE DELARGY

SANDHAMN MURDERS

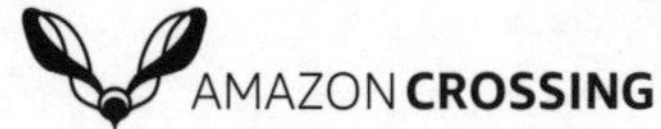

Previously published as *I hemlighet begravd* by Forum in Sweden in 2019. Translated from Swedish by Marlaine Delargy. First published in English by Amazon Crossing in 2022.

Published by Amazon Crossing, Seattle

www.apub.com



ISBN-13: 9781542018524
ISBN-10: 1542018528

Cover design by Damon Freeman

Printed in the United States of America

*To my mother,*
*Lisbeth Bergstedt*
*(1935 to 2019)*

Vindö
Härö
Värmdö
Alskär
Horssten
Styrsvik
Korsö
Stavsnäs
Winter Harbor
RUNMARÖ
Freya's Haven
SANDHAMN
Skanskobb
Grönskär
Svängen
Revengegrundet
Ingarö
Nämdö
Stavsnäs
Sandhamn
STOCKHOLM
Almagrundet
0
2,5
5 km

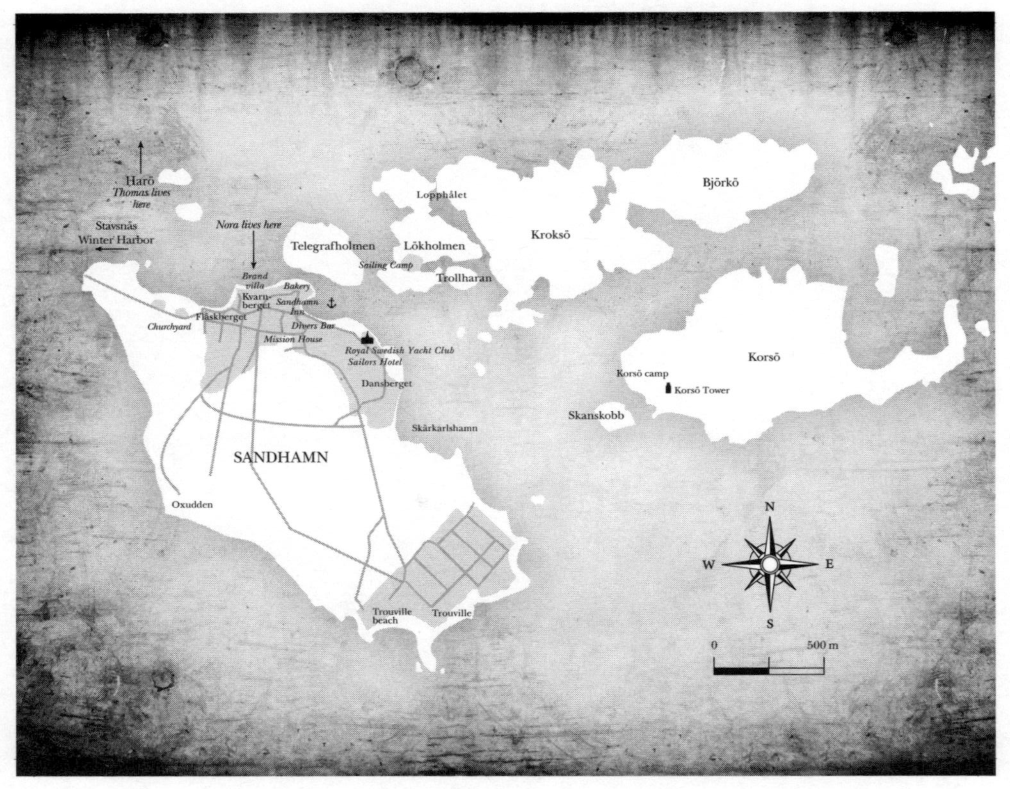
Harö
Thomas lives here
Stavsnäs
Winter Harbor
Nora lives here
Brand villa
Kvarnberget
Bakery
Sandhamn Inn
Flaskberget
Churchyard
Divers Bar
Mission House
Royal Swedish Yacht Club
Sailors Hotel
Dansberget
Telegrafholmen
Sailing Camp
Lökholmen
Trollharan
Lopphålet
Kroksö
Björkö
Korsö
Korsö camp
Korsö Tower
Skanskobb
Skärkarlshamn
SANDHAMN
Oxudden
Trouville beach
Trouville
N
W
E
S
0
500 m

# Prologue

"Blast warning!"

The foreman's voice echoed across Telegrafholmen, and the construction workers hurried to take shelter behind a grove of pine trees.

The yellow excavator stood ready a short distance away. When the dynamite had done its job, the shattered rocks would be removed, and soon, forty elegantly designed homes would take pride of place on the little island opposite Sandhamn. However, at the moment it was nothing more than a building site littered with machinery and rubbish.

The explosion shook the ground beneath the men's feet. The deafening noise bounced off their eardrums before rolling out across the sparkling waters of the Baltic Sea.

A huge cloud of dust hid the sun, and the foreman succumbed to a coughing fit. He waited a few minutes, then straightened up. They were already behind schedule; there was a lot to do before they could lay the foundations and make a start on the walls and roofs.

There was an eerie silence. Micke pushed back his hard hat, staring at something grayish white among the dust and rubble.

"Boss . . . ?" he said, pointing.

The foreman followed his gaze, unable to process what he was seeing. Then the temporary immobility eased and he moved closer.

"What the . . . ?"

The bones on the ground seemed to be glowing at him. Parts of a rib cage, a clawlike hand with two fingers missing. He swallowed hard, determined not to throw up.

"Fucking hell!" someone exclaimed behind him. "There must have been a grave here!"

# Monday,
# August 8, 2016

# CHAPTER 1

The sound of footsteps creeping up to the bedroom door woke Nora Linde. She reached for Jonas, but his side of the bed was empty.

Then she remembered that he was working, and that Julia was staying over with her paternal grandmother. Nora was alone on Sandhamn.

The fear gripped her immediately. *He* had found her.

She'd known for months that he would track her down, that she would never be free. She'd had nightmares about coming face to face with Andreis Kovač's brother, Emir. It had only been a matter of time before he took his revenge.

Nora forced herself to open her eyes and face the darkness.

She could see a blacker shadow in the doorway.

Her instincts were telling her to run, but her muscles refused to obey, even though she knew she would die if she didn't get away.

She couldn't move, couldn't hide, couldn't even call out.

Instead she stared at the door as if in a trance. It slowly swung wide open, and Emir Kovač's ice-cold gaze met hers. The hatred emanating from his muscular frame made her throat close up.

She'd imagined this encounter so often, feared it with every fiber of her being.

Kovač was wearing black leather gloves. He was holding something in one hand, she could see the glint of metal. He was only a couple of feet from the bed now, but Nora was still paralyzed.

As he raised the shining blade, she began to scream.

"Wake up!"

Someone was shaking her by the shoulders.

"Nora, wake up!"

Nora opened her eyes and found herself looking into Jonas's worried face. "You had another nightmare," he said, drawing her close.

"I thought he was here," she murmured into Jonas's shoulder. "It was so real."

He gently stroked her hair until she stopped shaking. Her cheeks were wet with tears.

"It's OK, sweetheart. It was just a bad dream, that's all. No one is going to hurt you. There's nothing to be afraid of."

Nora shook her head. She knew that Jonas was wrong.

The words Emir Kovač had whispered to her the last time they met still resonated in her mind. It was impossible to erase them, no matter how hard she tried.

# Chapter 2

Detective Inspector Thomas Andreasson stared at his screen. His inbox was full of messages. It was the first day back after his vacation, and he ought to be rested and sharp, ready to get down to work. Instead he was finding it hard to gather his thoughts.

His gaze fell on the photograph of Elin next to the computer. It had been taken on the jetty on the island of Harö, down below their summer cottage. His eight-year-old daughter was smiling into the camera, her blond hair blowing in the wind.

He used to have a picture of Pernilla on his desk, too, but it was now in the bottom drawer, the glass cracked—the result of an outburst of rage when things were at their worst, immediately after the separation last year.

However, the situation had improved, he reminded himself. The family counseling that Nora had persuaded him to try had definitely helped; at least he and Pernilla could have a civil conversation these days.

A knock on the door made him look up.

"Welcome back."

Margit Grankvist was standing in the doorway. Thomas's boss had taken very little time off during July, but she still had an impressive tan, which made the lines on her thin face stand out even more.

"I hope you're well rested," she added. "We've got our hands full as usual."

"What's happened?"

"It seems as if human remains have been found on Telegrafholmen. That's out your way, isn't it?"

Thomas nodded. He knew exactly where Telegrafholmen lay; it was the long, narrow island directly opposite Sandhamn, protecting the inlet and the harbor from northerly winds.

An uninhabited island.

"Human remains?"

"A skeleton. The CSIs are already on their way over to investigate. The Royal Swedish Yacht Club is building new houses out there, and the construction workers were blasting to prepare the site. When the dust settled, they found bones lying on the ground."

"How old?"

"I've no idea." Margit spread her hands wide. "I'd like you and Aram to go and take a look. I've spoken to the maritime police—they'll pick you up from Stavsnäs in an hour."

# Chapter 3

Nora leaned over the handbasin. The sight that met her in the bathroom mirror didn't make her feel any better. She looked tired and worn in spite of a whole summer on Sandhamn, and her cheeks were sunken. Her fiftieth birthday was only a few years away; sometimes she felt even older.

It had taken her a long time to get back to sleep after the horrible nightmare about Emir Kovač; she'd been restless all night. It had been the same story for months; sleeping pills were the only way to achieve undisturbed slumber.

The birds were singing outside the window, the sun was shining, but her body felt stiff and slow. She would have liked to go back to bed. Take a pill and pull the covers over her head, but that would have worried Jonas even more. She couldn't cope with his anxious looks and constant concern right now. She couldn't even cope with herself.

He was already in the kitchen chatting with Julia. Nora could hear the clatter of cups and plates, and the aroma of freshly brewed coffee reached her nostrils.

With a sigh, she pulled on a pair of shorts and a T-shirt. She might as well get going. Standing in the bathroom feeling sorry for herself wasn't going to improve things.

Jonas and Julia were sitting at the table having breakfast by the time Nora came downstairs. Julia was busy munching a cheese roll and didn't take much notice of her, but Jonas gave her a searching look.

"How are you feeling?" he asked. "Did you manage to get back to sleep?"

Nora suppressed a sharp response. She didn't want to complain, and Jonas meant well. She mustn't take out her frustration on him, but it was hard to keep up the façade. She would have to go back to work soon; her extended sick leave came to an end on August 31. She didn't want to think about how that would go if she still felt this bad.

"It's been a long time since you were so shaken up by a nightmare," Jonas went on.

"Not now," she said quietly, glancing at Julia. She didn't want to talk about it in front of their daughter.

In broad daylight, everything seemed perfectly normal, but she had spent the whole summer waking up in the middle of the night, drenched in sweat and terrified.

And always with the image of Emir Kovač's hate-filled face in her mind's eye.

She was almost afraid to go to bed these days.

*Why would Kovač take the risk?* she asked herself for the hundredth time. Attacking her would do him no favors. Violence toward a prosecutor would bring down the full force of the law on him.

And yet she couldn't shake off the fear of his revenge.

The implacable look on his face during that final interview had said it all. The hatred had struck her with the force of a physical blow. She was left with no doubt that he blamed her for what had happened to his brother, but there was nothing she could do.

The venomous whisper that had frightened her out of her wits had come when the interview was over and the tape recorder had been switched off.

She'd been so shocked that she hadn't managed to utter a single word, nor had she told anyone about it afterward. She had no proof; it would be her word against his. That was why she hadn't raised the matter with Jonathan, her boss. It was bad enough that she was off sick; she didn't want to be regarded as a victim on top of that, losing what was left of her hard-won professional pride.

She hadn't even been able to tell Thomas, in spite of the effect Kovač's words had had on her.

"Shouldn't you go and see your counselor again?" Jonas suggested. "It's been a few months now, and you're no better."

Her boss had offered to arrange for counseling; Nora had agreed to go twice, then come up with a series of excuses. Everything within her fought against talking about what had happened, because then she would have to admit her guilt, admit that she had failed to protect Mina. Admit that it was all her fault.

She couldn't bear to expose the most catastrophic failure of her career to a total stranger. She knew it wouldn't help, it would simply make her feel even worse.

She took a mug out of the cupboard.

When would she get back to normal? Was there no end to her torment?

She couldn't go on like this.

# Chapter 4

The police launch moored at the concrete quay on Telegrafholmen, and Thomas Andreasson and Aram Gorgis stepped ashore.

Thomas hadn't been here for some time. The island was named after the optical telegraph that had been set up there in the mid-nineteenth century. For many years the residents of Sandhamn had grazed their cattle on Telegrafholmen.

They followed the narrow forest track past the treatment plant; there was a faint smell of drains in the air. Suddenly they heard the sound of voices, and a moment later they saw a treeless plateau littered with excavators and building material.

An area of approximately forty square yards was cordoned off with blue-and-white police tape. A man in his fifties with cropped gray hair was talking agitatedly on his phone.

"Thomas!"

Staffan Nilsson, the forensic technician with whom Thomas had worked long before the district of Nacka was absorbed into South Stockholm, was on his knees a short distance away. His white protective suit was covered in dust, and the ground around him was strewn with rubble and lumps of mud.

Nilsson got to his feet and wiped his gloved hands on his thighs.

"So you finally got here," he said.

Aram gave a wry smile and took out his notebook.

"You're always first on the scene," Thomas conceded. "What can you tell us?"

Nilsson made a face; his idea of a good day at work didn't include picking out fragments of bone with tweezers.

"We've tried to gather together everything that can be seen with the naked eye. It's definitely a human skeleton."

"Male or female?" Aram asked.

"Impossible to say at this stage."

Nilsson pointed to a pile of sealed plastic bags. Most of them were small, indicating that few if any large bones had been found.

"As I said, we've started collecting what we can see, but the remains are scattered over a large area—it was a hell of a blast. If it went off near where the skeleton was buried, then any parts that weren't destroyed on impact will have been hurled in all directions—and they won't be easy to find in this kind of terrain."

He made a sweeping gesture with one hand. Around the construction site, the grass grew tall, studded with clover and yellow vetch.

"I've asked for a search dog," Nilsson added, glancing at his watch. "It should be on its way."

They were almost at the highest point of the island. Across the water lay the summer paradise of Sandhamn, but its busy harbor was hidden by the trees.

Thomas contemplated the plastic bags at Nilsson's feet. He could just make out something that resembled the bones of a human hand. It looked small, but that didn't necessarily mean it belonged to a child or a woman. He knew from experience that size was hard to assess when flesh and skin had disappeared.

"Any idea about the cause of death?" Aram asked. "Natural or unnatural? Are we looking at a crime here? Homicide?"

The look Nilsson gave him answered his questions.

"What about the person's age?" Aram persevered. "Or how long the bones have been buried?"

They could be looking at an ancient burial site, but as far as Thomas was aware, Telegrafholmen had always been uninhabited.

Nilsson shook his head. "Too soon to say."

Thomas glanced around. "Who's in charge of the site?"

Nilsson pointed to the gray-haired man who'd been on his phone when they arrived. "He's the foreman—you could start with him."

# Chapter 5

The foreman introduced himself as Percy Norräng.

"Is there somewhere we could have a few words?" Thomas asked.

Norräng nodded and led the way to a site trailer at the bottom of a slope.

"Coffee?" he said, pointing to a pot on the scratched counter. Without waiting for a response, he poured three mugs. Judging by the smell, the coffee had been sitting there for quite a while, but that didn't appear to matter. Norräng took a swig and sat down. He seemed unmoved, but Thomas noticed a slight tremor as he placed his mug on the table.

"What a way to start the day," Norräng said. "It feels unreal . . . A hand, just lying there . . ." He scratched the back of his neck without looking at the two officers. "I suppose it's part of everyday life to you," he went on, still with his face turned away.

"A situation like this is shocking for everyone," Thomas assured him. "It's perfectly normal to feel upset."

"Can you tell us what happened this morning?" Aram said.

Norräng blinked. "We're clearing the ground for the first batch of houses; they're supposed to be finished by summer next year. We've been working up here for a while, but we've fallen behind, so we're trying to catch up."

"Have you been here all summer?" Thomas asked.

"The guys had some time off after Midsummer, but we've basically kept going."

"But there was a period when no one was on-site?"

Norräng suddenly realized where Thomas was going with his questions.

"You mean someone could have come up and buried . . . the body?"

"We're just trying to establish the facts. Get a clearer idea."

Norräng gazed up at the ceiling. It was white, but there were brown nicotine stains directly above the table.

"What did the area look like before you started blasting?" Aram said.

Norräng shrugged. "The usual. All the trees had been felled, but the ground was uneven and needed leveling. It was a mixture of grass, earth, and stones."

Thomas tried to picture the scene. There must have been enough soil to bury a human body—unless of course they were dealing with a homicide and the corpse had been dismembered.

They mustn't get locked into one particular scenario; anything was possible at this stage.

"Do you have a photograph of the original site?" he asked.

Norräng picked up his phone and flicked through the images with callused fingers. "I took this the other day when we were calculating the force of the blast."

Thomas stared at the photo. It was as he'd expected; the site consisted of a large, irregular surface. He could see the odd stone, but it was mostly grass. In certain places the soil seemed to be deeper, because the vegetation was greener and lusher. At the far end was a rocky slope with grass and yellow moss growing in the crevices.

Thomas pointed to the slope. "Is this where you were blasting today?"

"Exactly. Two houses will be built on that spot."

Thomas took a closer look. The grave must have been pretty near, since the explosion had scattered the bones, and yet someone had dug deep enough to ensure that the body wasn't found by wild animals.

The ground at the bottom of the slope appeared to be untouched, not as if it had been recently dug up or flattened down by human hands. Then again, it didn't take long for nature to reclaim her territory.

The bones gathered so far bore no trace of clothing, skin, or tissue, which meant that the grave had been there for a considerable amount of time.

"You didn't notice anything before you started blasting?"

"What do you mean?"

"Some indication that this was a burial place? Not a headstone, of course, but maybe a cairn, or signs that someone had been digging?"

"It was just the same as the rest of the island," Norräng said, beginning to sound slightly defensive. "There was nothing unusual." He finished off his coffee and stood up to pour himself another cup. "By the way, how long will that area be cordoned off?" he asked over his shoulder.

"Hard to say," Aram replied. "As long as it takes for us to secure the scene and collect evidence."

Norräng frowned. "Can we carry on working in the meantime?"

"No chance," Thomas said.

"My bosses won't be pleased. As I said, we're already behind."

# CHAPTER 6

It was almost five o'clock in the afternoon when Thomas returned to the police station in Flemingsberg. Margit had asked for an update as soon as he arrived; she was at her desk when he stuck his head around the door of her office.

Aram had gone home; one of his daughters was sick, and Sonja, his wife, had a night shift at the hospital.

"I heard that Staffan Nilsson's on the case," Margit said, putting down a folder. "Good news."

Thomas sat down opposite his boss. They'd worked together for over ten years, which included transferring to Flemingsberg when the Nacka police district disappeared in the restructuring. Margit was still only acting head of department, even though almost two years had passed. He knew the situation was taking its toll on her, not least because there were rumors that the post was about to be advertised externally.

"OK, what have we got?" she went on. "Do the bones come from one person, or more than one?"

"I've no idea. There's no indication that the grave was marked in any way; all the witnesses are in agreement on that."

"Is there a crime involved?" Margit asked, resting her chin on her hand.

It was a fair question; Thomas and Aram had discussed the matter on the way back. Why would someone go to the trouble of burying a body on an uninhabited island if it hadn't been done in secret?

"I'd say things are definitely pointing in that direction," he conceded. "I mean, there's a perfectly good graveyard on Sandhamn."

"Could we be looking at a dismembered body?"

"Impossible to say. They haven't found anything yet, plus, of course, the blast will have caused a great deal of damage. Some parts of the skeleton might have been reduced to powder by the explosion."

"How old did Nilsson think the bones might be?"

"He couldn't say."

"Months? Years?"

"He wouldn't commit."

Margit was barking out questions as if Thomas had all the answers at his fingertips.

"So they could be pretty fresh or God knows how old?"

Thomas nodded.

They both knew that bodies began to decompose as soon as they were placed in the ground. Most of the organs were gone in only two or three weeks, as soon as the bodily fluids had evaporated and bacteria and larvae did their work. Within months, little was left apart from the skeleton.

The bones in Nilsson's plastic bags had been dirty, but there were no visible signs of tissue or clothing.

"So we have the bones of someone—male or female—who could have died as recently as last spring," Margit said. "Or decades ago. And we might be dealing with more than one person." She drummed her fingers on the cluttered desk. "How are you intending to move forward?"

Thomas hadn't even started to formulate a plan. He leaned back and thought for a moment. Margit should know better than to ask for clarity at this stage.

Perhaps she read that in his face.

"I've asked Ida Nylén, the new girl, to take a look at missing persons," she said. "It's a start."

She seemed uncharacteristically agitated about the situation.

"Why the urgency?" Thomas asked. If this was a cold case, there was no need to stress.

"The construction work can't be delayed," Margit said wearily. "The company has already brought in its lawyers, and they're leaning on us. It's a highly prestigious project, and large amounts of money have been invested. There are penalty clauses, so if we've cordoned off the site . . ."

She sighed. In recent weeks the police had been heavily criticized for inefficiency and long, drawn-out investigations. The county police chief had publicly promised significant improvements. The pressure from above didn't make life easier for someone who was only acting head of department.

"The company is also worried about negative publicity," Margit continued. "The houses will go on the market for over a hundred thousand kronor per square yard, so they don't want anything to go wrong."

*A hundred thousand kronor per square yard for a summer cottage. Bizarre.*

"It's a crime scene," Thomas pointed out. "They'll just have to put up with it."

He hated this kind of situation, but he wasn't naïve. There were people with influence in every part of society, particularly when big money was involved. It wasn't corruption, just friendly contacts that were used to pass on a discreet but clear message.

"You mean everyone is equal before the law," Margit said wryly. She rubbed her chin. "OK, but you can assume that these people will do everything in their power to make sure our investigation is concluded as quickly as possible. If we want to solve this case, we need to act fast."

# Tuesday, August 9

# CHAPTER 7

It was only seven thirty in the morning, and Nora was sitting down by the jetty. She'd brought her coffee; she needed a little time for herself before the rest of the family woke up.

It was a beautiful day. Wispy clouds caressed the blue sky while the sparkling sunlight danced across the water. She could just see a sailboat in the distance by the island of Eknö, its course set for Sandhamn.

She usually liked to be up early, especially in the summer when the clear air held the promise of another sunny day, but now she could feel the lack of sleep in every part of her body; it had been another bad night. Yesterday evening she'd stood in the bathroom clutching the bottle of sleeping pills; she'd forced herself to put it back in the cabinet. She had to learn to sleep without medication. She would soon be back at work.

Thank God she'd been spared the worst nightmares, but it had taken her forever to get to sleep, and she'd woken up repeatedly, as if her brain couldn't allow itself to relax. Fear was constantly nibbling away at the back of her mind.

Nora took a sip of her coffee. She'd sent yet another text message to Mina but hadn't received a reply. It had been months since she'd heard from her, and she was becoming more and more worried that something terrible had happened to her and little Lukas. Otherwise surely she would have gotten back to Nora? If everything was OK?

Maybe Emir Kovač had tracked Mina down and avenged his brother. In which case, did that mean it was Nora's turn? Was he looking for her right now? She had tried to erase his words from her memory, but they kept on coming back.

She shuddered, even though the sun was still shining.

She heard footsteps approaching and turned around to see Jonas with the newspaper in his hand, the gravel crunching beneath his scruffy deck shoes. As usual he wasn't wearing any socks.

"Good morning," he said. "I thought you'd be down here."

"I didn't want to wake you."

Once again, she felt guilty for wanting to be left alone. She couldn't deal with company, not even Jonas and Julia, her husband and her daughter.

Jonas opened the paper and showed her a headline.

"Have you seen this? They've found human remains on Telegrafholmen."

Nora sat up a little straighter. "What?"

"Yesterday, apparently."

Jonas sat down and spread the paper out on the table. Together they read the article about the bones that had been discovered by the construction workers. A police investigation was underway, but so far the identity of the deceased wasn't known.

Nora looked over toward Telegrafholmen; its western point was almost directly opposite the Brand villa. She had seen the island all her life but hadn't been there for years. She had a vague memory of a covenant stating that no houses could be built there, and yet planning permission had been granted for a significant number of summer cottages.

"How terrible," she said with a shudder.

"It sounds like a bad joke," Jonas said, leaning back. "A body buried on an uninhabited island and dug up by construction workers."

Nora didn't want to hear it. That was exactly the kind of thing Emir Kovač might have done with Mina.

"A joke?" she snapped, turning away so that she didn't have to look at the article. "We're talking about a human being here. Someone's mother or father. Or maybe a child."

Jonas took her hand and gently stroked her palm with two fingers.

"Sorry, sweetheart. I didn't mean to upset you."

Nora tried to smile. She had to pull herself together, stop overreacting.

"It's OK," she murmured.

A young man wearing a red life jacket passed the end of the jetty in a green kayak. He was paddling with long, even strokes, as if the paddle were part of his upper body. The waters quickly closed behind him.

Nora couldn't settle.

"I'm going to the bakery for some fresh rolls," she announced, getting to her feet before Jonas could say anything.

# CHAPTER 8

*Mornings without Elin ought to be stress free,* Thomas thought as he grabbed a mug of tea on his way to the morning briefing.

When his daughter was with him, it took all his time to get her dressed, give her breakfast, and drop her off at school before work, but without her, he was somehow slower, as if he lacked direction, and he often arrived at the police station at the last minute.

Aram was already in the conference room, along with Margit, Staffan Nilsson, and several other colleagues.

Ida Nylén, the new girl, arrived at the same time as Thomas. When they almost collided in the doorway, he noticed how toned her body was. She wasn't particularly tall, but she obviously worked out.

"Sorry," she murmured.

Margit tapped her pen on the table to indicate that she wanted to get started. She handed it over to Staffan Nilsson, who gave a brief summary of the previous day's discovery on Telegrafholmen.

"We'll be treating this as a criminal investigation," Margit said, clearing her throat. "We're under considerable pressure to remove the cordons as soon as possible, because there are significant costs involved when construction is halted. I've had orders from above to act fast."

She made no attempt to hide her irritation, but at the same time she was obviously prepared to give in. One of the major investors in the project on Telegrafholmen must be in a position to influence the police.

"We must try to live up to the expectations of our superiors," she said, turning to Ida. "What can you tell us?"

Ida pushed back a few strands of her long hair, which was colored in various shades of purple and tied back in a scrunchie.

"I've tried to produce lists of all those who've been reported missing, but there are a hell of a lot of them," she began, tugging at the sleeve of her denim jacket. "In the Stockholm district alone, it's over four thousand a year. Over half of these progress to a formal report, so it's a huge task."

Ida was telling everyone in the room something they already knew.

"And there's no crime involved in ninety-seven percent of cases," Aram said. His soft Norrköping accent took the sting out of his words, but Ida was clearly embarrassed.

"Oh . . . I didn't realize the figure was so high . . ." She broke off and looked down at the table, so unmistakably fresh out of the police academy that Thomas couldn't help feeling sorry for her. He'd been in the same position himself once upon a time; he didn't want to count how many years had passed since then.

"Did you check the National Crime Unit's database of missing persons?" he asked in a warm tone. Between twenty-five and thirty-five people remained missing each year and were entered into the national database, which typically contained some nine hundred names.

"I haven't gotten around to that yet."

Margit pressed the tips of her fingers to her temples. "That's your next job, as soon as we're done here. Bring in some of the trainees—tell HR I said so."

Thomas wondered if Ida would have the nerve to pass on Margit's message. He put down his mug.

"Start with the place where the bones were found," he said. "Look for anyone who has some kind of link to Sandhamn and the archipelago, or at least to Värmdö and Nacka. That should make the task more manageable."

"Nacka police district?" Margit said with a hint of longing in her voice.

"Yes."

Margit wasn't the only one who missed the old days. Nacka had had one of the highest clearance rates, and yet it had still disappeared in the restructuring process, which in spite of all the hopes and promises had led to a clear decline in morale within the force.

Politicians could talk all they wanted about priorities and improvements in resources; without efficient organization, decent salaries, and functioning leadership, nothing was going to improve.

"We need to decide how far back we're going to go," Aram said, turning to Staffan Nilsson. "Have you any idea? What's the maximum possible age of the bones? Ten years? Twenty?"

"I told you yesterday—it's impossible to say."

"A wild guess?"

Nilsson shook his head.

"What if we go for twenty-five years?" Thomas suggested. That used to be the statute of limitations for homicide. "Unless anyone has a better idea?"

"We have to start somewhere," Margit agreed.

Thomas stood up, picked up a marker, and wrote *25* on the whiteboard.

"OK. So we're looking for people with a connection to the archipelago who've gone missing during the past twenty-five years."

# CHAPTER 9

By the time Nora reached the bakery, the line started ten yards from the open door. The café area outside, with its white cast-iron chairs, was full. The aroma of freshly brewed coffee filled the air.

A familiar figure was last in the line: Eva Lenander, Nora's best friend on the island. She was absorbed in her phone, but glanced up when Nora arrived.

"Bad night?" she said after a hug.

Was it so obvious? Nora grimaced. Eva was one of the few who knew about Mina.

"Things will get better," Eva said, putting an arm around her shoulder. "None of what happened was your fault."

That wasn't true. If Nora had done her job and persuaded the court that Andreis Kovač should remain in custody until his trial, everything would have been different.

Every time she thought about it, she hated herself.

"Have you heard about Telegrafholmen?" Eva looked a little shaken. "The bones that were found yesterday? Did you see the police launches traveling back and forth?"

Nora really didn't want to talk about it. She fixed her gaze on a mother who had just emerged from the bakery holding her little boy by the hand. They were carrying paper bags that smelled wonderfully fragrant—raisins and cardamom.

Nora decided to buy buns for her family, too. Maybe that would ease her conscience, make her feel less bad about wanting time to herself?

"What if it's that girl who went missing ten years ago?" Eva went on.

"You mean Astrid Forsell? Who lived behind Mangelbacken?"

Astrid had run away from home when she was just seventeen; Nora had sometimes wondered what had become of her. Astrid's pretty face came into her mind's eye.

"Everyone said she left because her mother partied too hard," Eva said. "But what if something happened to her? What if she was murdered?"

Nora shuddered. She remembered Astrid's disappearance with sadness. She'd liked the girl very much; Astrid had looked after Adam and Simon on several occasions. The boys had been ten and six when Astrid left. It was the same summer that Nora's beloved Aunt Signe took her own life, and Nora herself had been in the middle of a growing marital crisis with Henrik. She'd been devastated by the loss of Aunt Signe, and hadn't taken much notice of anything else. That summer had been filled with tragedy.

"You've lived here such a long time—you must know her mother," Eva went on, adjusting the barrette that was holding her blond ponytail in place.

Nora nodded, picturing a thin gray-haired woman. "Monica Forsell. She still lives behind Mangelbacken." She knew exactly where the Forsells' white house lay. The family had lived on the island for generations, and Astrid's father had been a customs officer, like his father and grandfather before him.

"Monica turned to religion after Astrid left," Eva said. "Said the loss of her daughter was God's punishment. Astrid was her only child, of course."

Nora murmured a response, although she really wanted to change the subject. She was trying to think of something to say when Eva glanced meaningfully at a young woman in denim shorts who'd just left the bakery.

"Speak of the devil," she said quietly. "You know who that is?"

Nora recognized the woman but couldn't quite place her.

"Johanna Strand. She was Astrid's best friend back in the day. The police questioned her more than once." Eva was always up to date on the local gossip, and knew exactly what was going on. She watched Johanna until she vanished around the corner of the Sandhamn Inn. "I thought she looked upset," she said, almost sounding pleased. "Maybe the police have already spoken to her. It could be Astrid's body lying in that unmarked grave . . ."

"Don't say that."

Nora knelt down and pretended to retie the laces of one of her sneakers.

Lovely, warm Astrid had made her boys scream with laughter. She'd happily splashed around with them in the little inflatable paddling pool, and was always ready to help out.

*Please don't let it be her in the cold ground on Telegrafholmen for ten long years.*

Nora straightened up.

"I forgot my purse," she mumbled, hurrying away before Eva had the chance to say anything.

# CHAPTER 10

It was almost four o'clock when Ida asked Thomas and Aram to come to the conference room.

There were printouts of lists all over the table, with a pile of documents in the middle. Some had obviously been brought up from the archive, and were still dusty. It seemed as if the computerization of all records had some way to go.

Ida had achieved a considerable amount during the course of the day, and she was in a much better frame of mind. She'd rolled up the sleeves of her pink shirt, and when she gestured toward the papers, Thomas noticed a colorful butterfly tattoo on her wrist.

"So we've checked all persons reported missing during the past twenty-five years who have some kind of link to the archipelago," she began. "Which left us with thirty cases."

They could hear the pride in her voice.

"Well done!" Aram said. Dark stubble was visible on his chin; he always laughed and blamed his strong hair growth on his Assyrian origins.

"I didn't want to exclude any more in case I got it wrong," Ida said. "I thought maybe we could look at them together?"

Thomas took the nearest pile. Thirty cases was a manageable figure, much easier to work with than the anonymous mass on the National Crime Unit's database. However, they needed to eliminate more before they could really get started.

Aram sat down on the other side of the table.

"Shall we take half each?" he said, picking up a file without waiting for an answer. "Let's see what we can find."

Thomas turned his neck from side to side until he heard a crack. Was this yet another unwelcome reminder that he would turn fifty in a few years? His back was horribly stiff, but they'd spent three hours going through all the documents, with the help of countless cups of coffee.

Three unsolved cases that stood out from the rest now lay before them.

Margit came into the room. She was chewing gum, but her expression was grim. Her short gray hair did nothing to soften her appearance.

Aram stood up, went over to the whiteboard, and took the cap off a blue marker.

"OK."

He printed three names neatly:

- *August Marklund*
- *Siri Persson Grandin*
- *Astrid Forsell*

Thomas opened the file labeled "August Marklund."

"Marklund was reported missing just over fourteen years ago. He was seventy-three and lived in Gustavsberg. He disappeared on an unusually cold November day, and despite extensive searches, he was never found. Presumably he got lost in the forest, where he liked to go walking, and froze to death."

"So why do you want to take a closer look at him?" Margit asked.

"He was a sailor and an active member of the Royal Swedish Yacht Club," Aram explained. "He spent a lot of time on Sandhamn, so there's a link to Telegrafholmen, or at least the local area. Plus his wallet was missing, and he always carried a lot of cash, so that could indicate a mugging."

"Or an old man who got lost in the forest with his wallet in his pocket," Margit muttered. Her mood hadn't improved since the morning briefing. "Carry on."

Thomas opened the second file.

"Siri Persson Grandin was thirty-five when she went missing about ten years ago. She worked as a political secretary for the council and was a valued colleague. She was married to Petter Grandin, who was ten years older than her, no children. They lived on the island of Djurö, which is about half an hour by boat from Telegrafholmen."

"What happened?" Margit said.

"According to her husband, she wasn't at home when he returned from a work-related trip; he's a car salesman. He said he never saw her again."

Margit leaned forward.

"That sounds much more interesting than the old guy. If nothing else, statistics tell us that the husband could well be involved."

It was no secret that most women who were murdered were killed by a husband or partner.

"He had an alibi for the time when she disappeared," Ida interjected.

Margit sniffed. "Of course he did."

Ida hastily made a note.

"Actually, I think I remember this case," Margit continued. "There was a major search operation, wasn't there?"

"Absolutely," Thomas said. "This was before Missing People, but police search teams combed the local area and places where Siri Grandin used to go."

The folder was relatively thick and contained transcripts of a large number of interviews with those who'd known the missing woman. Her computer had been checked, as had her credit card—which hadn't been used since she was reported missing—and her travel card for the Stockholm public transport system.

"Officers spoke to colleagues and neighbors, as well as others she'd been in contact with, but her purse and cell phone were missing, so it was impossible to analyze text messages or calls. There was nothing to indicate that she'd been killed."

"So the case was shelved?" Margit said.

"That's right. The theory was that she'd left voluntarily with the intention of taking her own life. She'd also taken sick leave from work a few days earlier."

"Was there a suicide note?"

"A postcard." Thomas took out a photograph of the postcard Siri's husband had found in their mailbox, with the word *SORRY* clumsily printed on the back.

"It's definitely worth taking a closer look," Margit said, turning her attention to the remaining file. "Astrid Forsell?"

"She also disappeared around ten years ago. Astrid was only seventeen when she was reported missing by her mother, who had sole custody. The parents were separated."

"Any suspicion of a crime?"

"Not exactly. There was nothing to suggest that she'd been abducted against her will, so the case was dropped. She had a notoriously poor relationship with her mother, so everyone assumed she'd run away from home. She was due to turn eighteen a month later, and would no longer be regarded as a child in the eyes of the law."

"What's the link to Sandhamn?"

"Her mother lives there," Aram said. "She can practically see Telegrafholmen from her window."

"Is that why you want to pursue the case?"

Thomas nodded. "Plus the fact that she was never heard from again. Ten years is a long time without any contact with your family, if you've run away from home as a teenager."

Margit rested her chin on her hand and thought for a moment.

"Start with the two women," she said. "Leave August Marklund until we're sure whether the bones belong to a man or a woman."

# *Siri*

The hawthorn was blooming at last. Siri hurried to the bus stop, enjoying the fragrant flowers. She loved the feeling when everything began to grow, and the trees were covered in blossoms.

During the fall and winter, she sometimes regretted the decision she and Petter had made to live so far outside Stockholm, but at this time of year it was wonderful.

She got on the bus and found a seat. She had an important meeting this morning, and took out some papers to read through before she arrived at the council offices. The election campaign had just begun, and the next few months would be exciting but intense. In a way it was nice to lose herself in her work, given the atmosphere at home.

A young couple was sitting across the aisle. The girl was pretty, with long, slightly messy brown hair. The boy was wearing a thin blue jacket over a white T-shirt. The girl said something that made him laugh; he leaned over and kissed her on the lips. The kiss turned into something a lot more passionate; when they finally broke apart, the girl happened to catch Siri's eye. She gave an embarrassed little giggle and murmured,

"Sorry," but couldn't help kissing the boy again while looping her fingers through his.

Siri looked away. They were so much in love. It warmed her heart, yet at the same time she felt a lump in her throat. It had been many years since she and Petter had felt that way.

The bus lurched as it took a corner, and Siri grabbed the pole for support.

She'd been young when they married—only twenty-three. Petter was ten years older, and had come across as worldly-wise and sophisticated. He'd been her safe harbor, her rock while she finished studying and considered her future. When they walked down the aisle, she'd been so much in love she was shaking. She could still remember every second of their wedding, the intense joy that had carried her through the day.

And yet she could no longer summon up that same emotion, however hard she tried.

The girl stroked her boyfriend's hand. He put his arm around her back, drew her even closer.

Siri knew she ought to concentrate on her documents, but tears sprang to her eyes. She wanted so much to feel like that about Petter, but she didn't know how to fix things.

When he touched her, she stiffened; the desire just wasn't there. The worst was when he attempted to kiss her; his lips seemed cold, alien, even though his kisses had once set her body on fire.

When had she first begun to feel lonely in her husband's company? She couldn't recall.

She told herself it was just a phase. The last few years had been difficult for them as a couple; they'd been fighting against a headwind for a long time, and it had taken its toll, both emotionally and financially.

She had read that some marriages were made even stronger by such setbacks, which created a deeper relationship between husband and wife—while others were worn down to the ground. She'd been convinced that she and Petter belonged to the first category, but now she wasn't so sure.

The bus driver called out the name of the next stop. Time to get off.

Siri couldn't help glancing at the young couple once more. They didn't even notice as she gathered her things and stood up.

# Chapter 11

Dark clouds had moved in during the course of the afternoon, hiding the sun. The sea was the color of lead, and rain pattered against the windows of the Brand villa as Nora sat down at the dining table.

Jonas had prepared baked fish with new potatoes, dill, and clarified butter. Julia had carefully folded the best napkins, and candles were lit in the antique silver candelabra that Nora had inherited from Aunt Signe, along with the house. The flames flickered in the faint draft from the windows, but they didn't succeed in driving away the shadows.

Nora shuddered. The air was humid and oppressive; a thunderstorm was coming. She wasn't in the least bit hungry, but knew that Jonas had made a real effort. She did her best to hide her lack of appetite by cutting her food up into small pieces and pushing them around her plate. Fortunately, Julia was chattering away happily; otherwise the silence would have taken over.

"Mommy? Mommy?"

Nora gave a start. She'd been lost in thought, not listening to her daughter.

"Sorry, sweetheart. What did you say?"

Julia gave her an irritated look, and Nora put down her knife and fork. What had she missed this time? She had to concentrate hard to keep up.

"Can we go to Alskär tomorrow?"

Julia loved the little island ten minutes to the east of Sandhamn, with its beautiful sandy beaches and shallow offshore waters. Nora had often gone there as a little girl, and enjoyed taking her own children there. It was the perfect place for a summer outing.

"We could have a picnic! Molly's going, too, with her mommy and daddy—please can we go?"

Julia was smiling now, her lips glossy with the clarified butter in which she'd practically drowned her food.

"It's such a long time since we went to Alskär," she went on. "Pleeease, Mommy . . ."

Nora closed her eyes. She would have to pack so many things for a day at the beach. Towels, toys, a change of clothes, coffee, cold drinks, sandwiches. Way too much to think about.

"We'll see, honey."

Julia's head drooped, her shoulder-length blond hair falling forward.

"You never want to do anything anymore," she mumbled.

That hurt. Was that really how her daughter saw her?

"Oh, Julia . . ." Nora said feebly, reaching for her wineglass. It was empty—but hadn't Jonas just refilled it? She drew back her hand as he came to her rescue.

"Let's see what the weather's like tomorrow," he said. "No point in going if it's still raining."

Nora poured herself another glass of wine. "Daddy's right. We'll decide in the morning."

She speared a tiny piece of fish and put it in her mouth. She chewed and chewed. It didn't taste of anything.

# Chapter 12

It was dark by the time Thomas unlocked the front door. He hated coming back to the empty apartment on Östgötagatan. It was better to stay at work in Flemingsberg, then at least he could pretend that someone was waiting for him at home.

He hung up his jacket and went into Elin's room. She'd turned eight in March, and there were dolls all over the place. In spite of repeated efforts to interest her in cars and trains, she loved everything pink. However, in the fall he was determined to take her along to handball, the sport in which he'd competed for many years. She would soon be old enough to play, if she wanted to.

Thomas sank down on her bed and picked up a big pale-brown teddy bear. She couldn't sleep without her white rabbit beside her, so he'd gone to Pernilla's. The rabbit spent alternate weeks with him, as did Elin.

He lay back in the darkness. He couldn't get used to having his daughter on a part-time basis, to the feeling of missing half her childhood.

After all the years they'd spent trying to conceive, without success.

Emily crept into his mind, even though he tried to keep her locked away in his heart, in a place he rarely visited, because it was too painful.

He'd never really gotten over Emily's death at the age of only three months, but he had learned to live with it. Maybe that psychologist, the one he'd hated so much at first, had been right.

It was possible to find a new way to live.

Elin's birth had given him back his life. It had been a miracle when Pernilla became pregnant, against all odds.

And yet they just couldn't make the relationship work.

The fact that they'd separated was his greatest failure. How could they have done this to each other, after all the promises they'd made?

Thomas slammed his fist into the mattress.

Part of him still longed for Pernilla. The problem was that he didn't know how to live with her.

# Wednesday, August 10

# Chapter 13

The front door of Petter Grandin's terraced house was painted black, and was beginning to fade in the sun. He still lived in the home he'd shared with his missing wife, if that meant anything.

Thomas rang the bell while Aram waited on the gravel drive. The door was opened by a suntanned man in his fifties. He had a reddish-brown beard; his hair was the same color, but peppered with gray.

Thomas introduced himself and Aram, and asked if they could come in. Grandin hesitated for a couple of seconds, then waved them through to the kitchen.

"We have a few questions about your missing wife," Thomas explained.

Grandin reached for a half-full coffee cup on the counter.

"She's dead," he said as he sat down at the table.

"She was reported missing," Aram pointed out, taking the chair opposite.

"She was declared dead several years ago—the police must know that? What's the point in talking about it now?"

"Could you tell us what happened when Siri disappeared?" Thomas asked.

"Why? I've already been over this with your colleagues, God knows how many times." Grandin pursed his lips and stared at his coffee cup.

Thomas exchanged a glance with Aram. He would have preferred to hear Grandin's version of events before they told him about the discovery on Telegrafholmen.

"What's this about?" Grandin persisted. He looked at his watch. "I have to get to work."

"We won't stay long," Aram assured him.

Grandin sighed loudly. "OK. I'd been away at a conference for a few days, and when I got back on the Wednesday evening, no one was home. I tried Siri's cell, but she didn't answer, even though I called several times."

"Was anything missing? Her passport? Money? Her favorite clothes?"

"No. Her passport was in the drawer where it was always kept, although I didn't check until later. Her purse and jacket were gone."

"Were you worried?"

"Not at first. I assumed she was out with a girlfriend and would come home eventually. I couldn't even be sure I'd told her exactly when I'd be back."

A droplet of coffee had gotten stuck in Grandin's beard; he wiped it away with his index finger.

"So what did you do?"

"I went to bed. When she still hadn't come home the following morning, I called her sister, Suss. I thought Siri might have stayed over with her. They were very close, and Suss lived in Liljeholmen, closer to the city. Sometimes Siri would stay the night if she didn't want to come all the way out to Djurö."

"But she wasn't with her sister," Thomas said.

"No. I waited for an hour or so, then I contacted the council to check if Siri was at work, but they hadn't seen her. It turned out she hadn't been there since the previous week."

"When did you realize she was missing?"

"I started to get worried during the morning."

Aram glanced at his notes. "You didn't call the police until the afternoon."

"I didn't want to jump to any conclusions."

"So what do you think happened to her?"

Grandin rubbed his forehead and took a deep breath.

"Just like everyone else, I believe she took her own life."

"Why would she have done that?"

For the first time, Grandin showed genuine emotion. He looked over at the window. There was a white orchid in a plastic pot on the sill. There was a flower at the top, but the lower blooms had withered.

"Things between us weren't great that summer. Siri was moody; one minute she was crying, the next she was snapping at me. We argued all the time."

"Was she on any medication?"

"I don't know."

The answer came quickly. Too quickly? It didn't sound like the first time Grandin had uttered those words, but of course he would have had to repeat himself frequently to both the police and others who were concerned about his wife.

And yet . . . Thomas couldn't help feeling that something wasn't right.

"Why all the questions?" Grandin said. "What's going on?"

Time to come clean.

"Human remains have been found in an unmarked grave on Telegrafholmen," Thomas said. "We're investigating all local missing-person cases where we suspect a crime might have been involved."

Grandin stiffened.

"A crime? What are you talking about? Siri wasn't murdered, was she?"

"All we know is that she's missing. Her body was never found, so we can't exclude that possibility."

"Why would anyone want to kill her?"

*Maybe you can tell us that,* Thomas thought, keeping his expression neutral.

"And what the hell would she have been doing on Telegrafholmen?" Grandin went on.

"You know where it is?"

"Of course. It's the island opposite Sandhamn."

"Do you often visit Sandhamn?" Aram asked.

"A few times each summer. It's easy to catch the ferry from Stavsnäs, and I like to eat at the Sandhamn Inn." Grandin tugged at his beard. "Once again—why all the questions? You can't think that I had anything to do with Siri's disappearance! She wasn't feeling good that last summer—I've already told the police all this."

"What do you mean, she wasn't feeling good?"

Grandin shifted position on his chair.

"All the quarreling . . . I hardly recognized her. It was as if everything I did was wrong. Sometimes she looked at me as if she couldn't bear to be living under the same roof." There was bitterness in his voice. "One day she actually said she'd rather die than stay with me. I wasn't enough for her. I assumed that in the end she couldn't stand it any longer." He finished off his coffee. "I've always believed that she decided to put an end to the torment of being my wife."

"Why not get a divorce?"

The answer came without hesitation.

"Only Siri can answer that. Plus she left a postcard with *sorry* on it. Why would she do that if she hadn't taken her own life?"

"If we go with the hypothesis that it is Siri we've found on Telegrafholmen, can you suggest any reason why she might have been there just before she died?" Thomas said.

Grandin frowned. "How would I know?"

Thomas tried to smooth things over. "We're just trying to understand what happened."

"It might not even be Siri, yet you come into my home with your insinuations!" Grandin folded his arms. "I've accepted the idea that Siri killed herself. She did it in a place where no one would find her, presumably out of consideration for others." He shook his head. "For ten years I've lived with the knowledge that my wife preferred to die rather than go on living with me. I've tolerated the gossip and the speculation, the whispering behind my back. The burden of guilt. Now you turn up with a series of allegations and no proof whatsoever. Do you understand how that makes me feel?"

Grandin suddenly got to his feet, walked into the hallway, and threw the door open wide, letting the sunshine in. Thomas and Aram had little choice but to follow him. He stared at the two police officers.

"Thank you for coming," he said stiffly.

# Chapter 14

The ten o'clock ferry from Stavsnäs was pretty full. Thomas and Aram eventually managed to find two spaces on deck, and Thomas went off to buy coffee. When he returned with two paper cups and two cinnamon pastries, it was obvious that Aram had had to defend Thomas's seat with his life; he was surrounded by passengers who were forced to stand, and they weren't happy.

Thomas sank down and held out the tray so that his colleague could help himself.

"Nilsson called while I was waiting in line," he said. "He managed to get priority in Solna, thank goodness. They've already sent everything over."

It would be extremely helpful if the forensic unit could establish the gender of the skeleton. If they were very lucky, the unit might be able to suggest a line of inquiry. In the worst-case scenario, the bones would have to be sent away for further investigation, it which case it could take weeks—or months—before they had a definitive answer.

"I wasn't too keen on Grandin," Aram said, taking a big bite of his pastry.

Thomas glanced around to make sure that no one was listening. The ferry was crowded with tourists on their way to Sandhamn; a surprisingly large number were speaking German or French. None of them seemed to be interested in their conversation.

"That doesn't automatically make him a suspect," he replied, leaning back.

"No. I just didn't like him. And why stay in the house he shared with his late wife?"

"Maybe it's his way of remembering her."

"Did you think he was grieving for her? He seemed to feel sorry for himself more than anything, even though she's the one who died."

Aram had clearly decided that Petter Grandin was on his blacklist. The man hadn't made a good impression on Thomas either, but appearances could be deceptive. It was too soon to form a definitive opinion.

"What would his motive have been?"

"I'm sure we'll find something," Aram said sourly.

Thomas did his best to locate Monica Forsell's house. They'd headed for the old part of the village, within the harbor area. He'd checked the property register before they set off, but that was very different from trying to orient himself among the collection of red and white wooden properties.

There were no street names or house numbers on Sandhamn, so a high level of local knowledge was required. The Forsell place was supposed to be behind Mangelbacken, but there was no sign to tell him where Mangelbacken was. Fortunately an elderly lady was coming toward them with a poodle on a leash. She moved with the assuredness of someone who lived on the island. Thomas swallowed his pride and asked for her help. She explained that they needed to go back a little way.

"It's a white-painted house with red pelargoniums on the gateposts," the woman kindly explained. She looked Thomas up and down, then turned her attention to Aram. Two men in jeans and dark jackets in the middle of summer. Presumably they might as well have had *Police* tattooed on their foreheads.

"Can I ask what it's about? Why are you looking for Monica?"

"Thank you for your help," Thomas said.

The woman drew the dog closer and picked it up.

"Good heavens, is it about her daughter? Is that who you found on Telegrafholmen? You always fear the worst when you see so many police launches . . ."

Thomas knew that rumors spread like wildfire in small communities. Little more than forty-eight hours had passed since the discovery of the bones, yet the neighbors had already drawn their own conclusions.

"It hasn't been easy for Monica over the years," the woman went on. She patted the dog, who wriggled as it tried to get down. "Poor woman. Although of course I don't want to interfere . . ."

*That's exactly what you're doing,* Thomas thought. *Now you've got even more to gossip about.*

"Thank you for your help," he said again, glancing at his watch. "I'm afraid we have to go now."

# Chapter 15

Nora was busy packing the picnic basket. Julia had finally gotten her own way, and they were going on a trip to Alskär with her friend Molly's family.

"I'm just going to the store," Nora called out to Jonas. "We need pastries and coffee."

She cut through the village, and as she was passing Adolf Square, where the Midsummer pole was usually erected, she saw Monica Forsell approaching from the opposite direction.

It was almost too much of a coincidence.

In hindsight, she couldn't understand why she hadn't paid more attention to Astrid's disappearance, but then there had been so much confusion that summer and fall. They'd already moved back to the city by the time Astrid went missing, and when they returned to Sandhamn the following summer, she was long gone.

The years had passed; Nora had been absorbed in her own life. Now she felt ashamed. Astrid had been a lovely, smart, sweet girl. The boys had often asked about her.

Later she'd realized that Astrid hadn't had an easy life at home. A memory came back to her. Astrid had been watching Adam and Simon one afternoon, just a few weeks before she disappeared and the summer came to an end. Nora had come back earlier than planned, and they'd had a coffee together while the boys splashed around in the wading pool. Astrid had asked about Nora's work as a lawyer and whether she knew anything about criminal cases, as if she had something on her mind. However, when Nora told her that she was a legal adviser with a bank, she'd dropped the subject.

Had Astrid wanted to talk about an issue that led to her disappearance, something dark and unpleasant that she couldn't handle on her own?

Had she been looking for someone to confide in?

No, it was too far-fetched. Nora shook her head at her own thoughts. She was letting her imagination run away with her.

And yet . . . What if she'd been more empathetic? Asked questions, persuaded Astrid to open up? Taken the time to listen properly?

It didn't matter—it was too late now. Nora had failed her, just as she'd failed Mina.

She suddenly found it hard to swallow.

Monica was only twenty yards away now. Could Nora do something for her instead? Pay off her debt to Mina by helping Astrid's mother?

Monica had changed. They were almost the same age, but had never been friends. Monica had grown up on the island and had hung out with the slightly more dangerous boys; Nora hadn't been welcome in their gang. They'd partied pretty hard, if Nora remembered correctly.

Ten years ago, Monica had been an attractive woman. Nora remembered her long blond hair, which she liked to back-comb into the eighties style she'd favored as a teenager. She'd shown off her body, wearing the same kind of clothes as Astrid. Many people had taken the two of them for sisters rather than mother and daughter.

The woman coming toward her now had aged twenty years. Her gray hair was cut short, and there wasn't a scrap of makeup on her lined face.

She was getting closer; if Nora was going to say anything, express her sympathy, now was the moment.

She opened her mouth but couldn't utter a single word.

She was too embarrassed.

Ten years had gone by without her bothering about Monica and her loss. Saying something today would just seem stupid or, even worse, patronizing.

Instead she simply nodded as they passed, which was the custom on Sandhamn. Monica gave no sign of recognizing Nora. She simply inclined her head and turned off in the direction of Mangelbacken.

Nora continued to the grocery store, her cheeks flushed red. She wished she could do something to help—but what?

# *Astrid*

Astrid was already wide awake when the alarm clock went off at seven thirty, her body fizzing with anticipation.

It was the Monday before Midsummer, and her first day as a waitress at the Sailors Restaurant. Johanna's mom had managed to get them both a job, even though they were a little too young to work such late nights and weekends. They had to be there at nine to meet their new boss, Lillian Eriksdotter.

Astrid glanced over at the chair in the corner where she'd laid out her clothes the night before. A pink T-shirt, a short denim skirt, and her beloved Converse sneakers. No doubt they'd be given a uniform, but she still wanted to look good when she arrived.

She stretched. The back of her neck was damp with sweat; her room faced east, and was warm in the morning sun.

Everything was going to be fine, she told herself, even if she was going to work all through the summer until she started her final year at high school in the fall.

It didn't matter. She longed to earn a decent amount of money; she'd already done a few shifts in a bar in town during the spring. The

Sailors Restaurant paid well, particularly with the higher hourly wage for unsociable hours. And she knew she could get plenty of tips if she was nice to all the guys who'd had a little too much to drink; she'd learned how to do that at the bar. She didn't really like it when they checked out her breasts and ass; it was kind of creepy, but she needed every krona she could get.

As soon as she turned eighteen at the end of September, she was going to leave home. Only three months to go. She'd already started looking for a sublet. Her mother would no longer be able to tell her what to do; she'd be able to do exactly what she wanted. She would finally escape from her mother's drinking and constant nagging. And her fucking boyfriend.

The thought of Zacharias almost destroyed Astrid's good mood. She rolled onto her side and stared at the wallpaper, traced its faded blue stripes with her index finger. She could still see the mark from a piece of chewing gum she'd stuck on the wall when she was nine years old.

She hated the fact that Zacharias came and went as if he owned the place. He had a place of his own on the island, in the forest behind the tennis courts. Why couldn't Mom see him there, if they absolutely had to be together?

Astrid hadn't minded him too much at first, but the older she got, the more she disliked him. The way he hugged her a little too often, pulled her a little too close.

Mom would do anything for Zacharias as soon as he switched on the charm. In her eyes, he could do nothing wrong; he had her wrapped around his little finger.

She didn't notice him checking out Astrid, just like the drunks at the bar in town.

# Chapter 16

A gray-haired woman was opening the iron gate just as Thomas and Aram arrived at the white-painted house that allegedly belonged to Monica Forsell.

Thomas had seen a photograph of Monica in Astrid's file; according to the notes, she'd been twenty years old when Astrid was born.

He cleared his throat to attract her attention.

"We're police officers," he explained. "Could we have a few words with you? It's about your daughter."

Monica was carrying a bag of groceries, which she put down on the ground.

"It won't take long," Aram said.

Monica picked up the bag. She unlocked the front door and showed them into a living room with a white tiled stove in one corner. The furniture looked as if it had been there for years, maybe even generations. The room would have been light and airy if the heavy, dark curtains had been drawn back.

Monica sat down on a green sofa with brown teak armrests. "You said this was about Astrid?"

A thick book with a black cover lay open on the coffee table. Thomas realized it was a Bible.

"An unmarked grave was discovered on Telegrafholmen last Monday," he began, outlining the situation without going into too much detail. "We're investigating all cases of missing persons with a link to the local area."

"You think it could be my daughter?" Monica said, running her fingertips over the worn velvet fabric of the sofa.

"We don't know yet," Aram said. "We're still analyzing the bones, but we're wondering if Astrid used to spend time on Telegrafholmen."

Monica rubbed her forehead. "She loved the archipelago. We came out here as often as we could, every summer and every school break, all year round."

"Have you lived here long?"

"I grew up in this house. My parents were full-time residents on the island; my father was a customs officer. Unfortunately they died far too young, while Astrid was still a little girl." Her hands were resting on her lap, the nails short and unpainted, the fingers unadorned by rings. "Our family has suffered many tragedies."

"I'm sorry to hear that."

Thomas stepped in. "Could you tell us about the period leading up to Astrid's disappearance?"

Monica seemed to shrink a little.

"It was late summer 2006, shortly before her eighteenth birthday. She had a job as a waitress at the Sailors Restaurant. I hardly saw her; she came home late at night and slept until it was time to go back to work."

"That must have been difficult," Aram said sympathetically.

"I didn't like it at all."

"Did the two of you argue about it?"

Monica looked up. "Why do you ask? What are you accusing me of?"

Thomas made an effort to smooth things over.

"We're just trying to form a picture of Astrid and her routine."

That seemed to do the trick; Monica nodded.

"I kept telling her how important it was to be careful, but she wouldn't listen."

"When you say careful . . ." Aram said in a more conciliatory tone.

"Astrid was young and pretty. She . . . dressed accordingly. She didn't realize how provocative she looked, or how that might be interpreted. She liked it when men looked at her. She wouldn't even leave my boyfriend in peace." Monica's cheeks were flushed now. "I was very young when I had Astrid. It was just the two of us right from the start. It wasn't always easy, bringing up a child on my own. I did my best . . ." She touched the gold cross on a fine chain around her neck. "But the Lord called her to Him."

"I'm sorry?"

"Astrid is in good hands; she's with our Holy Father."

Aram was a Christian; he, too, wore a small cross around his neck and went to Mass on holy days, but even he was taken aback.

"What exactly do you mean by that?"

"The Lord called her to Him," Monica repeated, as if she were revealing a secret she'd kept for many years.

"So you believe she's dead?" Thomas said. "How can you be so sure? Her body was never found."

"I'm her mother. I'd know if she was still alive."

Had Astrid been declared dead? Thomas didn't think so. He made a note to check.

Monica gave an enigmatic smile. "My daughter is happy—that's my great consolation."

Aram tried again.

"Is there any concrete evidence that she's no longer alive? Anything you can share with us?"

The air in the gloomy room stood still. The odd sunbeam that had somehow found its way in between the curtains lit up the hovering dust motes.

"He told me." Monica slowly ran her index finger over the gold cross. "I speak to Him every day."

It took a few seconds for Thomas to realize that she was referring to God. If they were going to get anything out of this interview, they were going to have to find a different angle. He shifted position in the sagging armchair.

"Can you tell us about the last time you saw your daughter? We'd really like to hear what happened in your own words. I understand she was reported missing on Saturday, August 19."

The faraway look left Monica's eyes. "That's right. I'd been in the city, working; it was my first week back after the vacation. Astrid had stayed on the island because she wasn't due to finish at the restaurant until the twentieth—the day before the school semester began."

Astrid had vanished when she was about to start her final year at high school. She was specializing in sciences, and her grades were good.

"When I came over on the evening ferry on the Friday, she wasn't home, but I assumed she had a late shift at the Sailors—that was often the case on the weekends. But she didn't come home that night or the following day, and she wasn't answering her phone. I went to the restaurant, and they told me she hadn't been there all week—she'd called in sick."

Monica's voice broke. She took a deep breath and continued: "I looked everywhere, I asked all her friends and colleagues, but no one had seen her."

"So you contacted the police."

"Yes, on Saturday evening." The answer was so quiet it was barely audible. "No one could find her. Even Johanna, her best friend, didn't know where she'd gone. She said they hadn't seen each other for several days."

"You hadn't spoken to her during the week?"

Monica shook her head. "We . . . we didn't really speak on the phone."

She leaned forward and adjusted a cushion without looking at the two officers.

Thomas hesitated before asking the next question.

"You said just now that you believe Astrid is dead. In which case, what do you think became of her?"

"It was an accident, of course." The response was instant. "I dreamed about it—I saw exactly what happened. She slipped on a rock and fell into the water. That's why they never found her body—it was carried away by the waves." Monica's eyes shone with conviction. "The sea became my daughter's grave. I often think about that when I'm walking along the shore. I know she's out there somewhere, sleeping at the bottom of the Baltic."

Aram cleared his throat.

"She couldn't possibly have . . ."

Monica's eyes flashed with anger. "Astrid would never have taken her own life! Why would she do such a thing? It's a mortal sin. She had her faults, but she would never have done that."

"That's not what I meant," Aram assured her. "I wondered if she might have gone away, maybe with someone else?"

"Don't be ridiculous."

In spite of Monica's strong reaction, it wasn't unreasonable to ask whether Astrid might have run away or killed herself. However, her mother had clearly settled on a different explanation—one that could well be correct.

Unless, of course, Astrid Forsell had been lying in an unmarked grave on Telegrafholmen for the past ten years.

Monica's tone softened. "My daughter could talk to me about anything. I was her mother. She wasn't keeping bad company, and she had no plans to leave home."

"I understand."

"It was a tragic accident." Monica clasped her hands together. "An accident killed my little girl. That's the truth."

# CHAPTER 17

As Nora was leaving the grocery store, she saw Thomas's familiar figure rounding the corner. He was heading for the steamboat jetty where one of the smaller ferries, *Madam*, was waiting.

"Thomas!"

He didn't hear her. She hurried down the steep steps and ran to catch up with him and his colleague.

"Thomas!"

This time he stopped, turned, and saw her. "Morning!" he said with a smile. "I thought I might bump into you at some point."

Nora gave him a hug and said hello to Aram. Then she grew serious.

"Are you here because of . . . ?" She glanced in the direction of Telegrafholmen, where a tall crane was visible above the trees.

Thomas hesitated. Nora suddenly registered the fact that they were coming from the direction of the village.

"You've been to see Monica Forsell, haven't you? Astrid's mother?"

Thomas instinctively nodded, then held up his hands.

"So you think it's her?" Nora went on. "You think it's Astrid?"

Thomas glanced at Aram. "You know I can't discuss it."

Aram gently touched his arm and pointed to the jetty, where *Madam* was about to cast off.

"We have to go," Thomas said to Nora. "I'll call you later."

Nora remained where she was, watching them go.

So Thomas had visited Monica Forsell to talk about her missing daughter. *Poor woman.* Ten years of uncertainty and grief, and now this. Astrid could have been lying in an unmarked grave just a short distance across the water.

Like everyone else, Nora had assumed that Astrid had run away from home. She really didn't want to believe that the girl had been dead all this time, but why else would Thomas and Aram have come to Sandhamn to talk to Monica? Particularly as the discovery was so recent . . .

The need to do something, to help, came flooding back.

Ten years ago, Nora had been too absorbed in her own problems to worry about Astrid. There had been rumors about Monica's partying and the wild life she led; Nora had gone along with the general consensus that Astrid had simply had enough.

She stared at the jetty, where *Madam* was in the process of reversing. Could the truth about Astrid's disappearance be so much worse? It was hard to interpret Thomas and Aram's visit in any other way.

Monica must be devastated. Should she go and see her? Offer her support?

However, the memory of their brief encounter earlier still made her cringe. She didn't know how to approach her without being intrusive. She didn't want to seem as if she were poking her nose in, eager for the latest gossip.

Yesterday, Eva had referred to Johanna Strand as Astrid's best friend. The Strand family lived in Seglarstaden, just above the Sailors Hotel; Nora had a passing acquaintance with the parents.

Maybe Johanna had heard something? If Nora spoke to her, it might make the situation clearer.

Without really knowing why, Nora set off toward Johanna's house.

# Chapter 18

The ferry had just left Gatan, the final stop on north Runmarö, when Thomas's phone rang.

It was Margit.

"We've found out something interesting about Grandin," she said as soon as Thomas answered.

He and Aram were out on deck again, but this time it had been much easier to find a seat. He lowered his voice to be on the safe side. "Go on."

"He tried to have his wife formally declared dead after only thirteen months."

"Seriously?"

Relatives had the right to apply for such a declaration, but many—most, in fact—took their time. As a general rule they didn't want to discuss it at all, and certainly not during the first year or so. On the contrary, they clung to the hope that the missing person was still alive and would turn up again one day.

Having someone declared dead meant accepting the unthinkable: that a loved one was no longer alive.

"It's amazing what you can find when you start poking around in old cases," Margit said smugly. Thomas heard a knock, then murmuring in the background. "Hang on a minute."

Someone started talking to Margit, which gave Thomas the chance to think.

Missing persons were normally declared dead after ten years. The application couldn't even be filed until five years had passed, unless the disappearance was associated with a natural disaster such as the tsunami in Thailand in 2004, which claimed the lives of many hundreds of Swedes.

A high degree of probability and a thorough investigation would be required to have someone declared dead after only a year.

Or personal certainty that the individual in question really was deceased.

It was unusual behavior under any circumstances—the kind of behavior guaranteed to arouse the suspicions of the police.

Margit came back on the line. "Apparently Grandin had a major argument with the insurance company about his wife's life insurance. He tried to get ahold of the money as soon as he could."

"She had life insurance? Why wasn't that in the file?"

"Why aren't all investigations perfect?" Margit responded with a sigh. "I guess the case was shelved before the question of having Siri declared dead came up. Grandin wasn't suspected of anything, so there would have been no red flag when he applied for the payout, even though there should have been a note in the file. Insurance companies usually contact the police if something like this happens, but I guess it slipped through the cracks."

Thomas nodded to himself. Margit was right; it had been a missing-person investigation, not a suspected homicide. He heard the sound of rustling papers, then Margit continued: "If it had been private insurance, it might have been different, but this was a special policy through her job—so no warning bells rang."

They should have, but there was no point in saying so. It was still a very interesting piece of information.

"Any more details?"

"Apparently Grandin demanded the money about thirteen months after Siri was reported missing. When the company refused to pay, on the grounds that she hadn't been declared dead, he immediately applied to the tax office for a formal declaration."

The engines thrummed as the ferry slowed down. It was about to pull into Styrsvik, the last stop before Stavsnäs.

"So what happened?" Thomas asked.

"The tax office turned down his application on the grounds that Siri's disappearance hadn't been fully investigated. This led to an angry exchange of letters—you and Aram can take a look at them when you get back."

"So he didn't get any money?"

"Nope. He tried several times, but the tax office refused to consider declaring Siri dead until five years had passed, since there was no body and no natural disaster involved around the time of her disappearance."

The ferry swung around; Thomas was dazzled by the sun, and had to shade his eyes with his hand.

"And after five years?"

"The insurance paid out in the end. The second Siri was declared dead, Grandin contacted the company."

"How much are we talking about?"

"A lot." Margit paused for dramatic effect, then said: "Four million kronor."

Thomas let out a whistle. That was a fortune for just about anyone. Suddenly there were four million good reasons for Siri Grandin's disappearance.

# *Siri*

Petter's car was on the drive when Siri got back from work on Wednesday evening. She put down her heavy briefcase on the sidewalk and gave herself a couple of minutes' breathing space.

What mood would he be in tonight?

The spring had been difficult, and on Midsummer Eve he'd gotten very drunk, staggering around at Anton and Mia's party in a way that made her both angry and sad. In the end she'd gone home alone.

She sighed. She shouldn't get mad at him. He'd apologized the next day, mortified and full of regret.

If only they could talk to each other like they used to . . . Instead they grieved alone, Siri crying into her pillow and Petter with a glass in his hand.

She picked up her briefcase and headed for the door.

"Oh, so you've decided to come home, have you?" he shouted as soon as she walked in. She was immediately on her guard. Admittedly she was late, but not too late. She should probably have called, but she didn't even want to do that these days.

She took off her coat and glanced into the kitchen. It was a disaster zone; he'd made no attempt to clean up after himself. She went into the living room and found Petter sitting on the sofa with an almost empty bottle of Merlot beside him. His gaze was unfocused, and her heart sank when she saw the red wine around the corners of his mouth. She really wanted them to find their way back to each other, to what they used to share, but nothing about Petter's behavior made that easy.

"Anton came by," he muttered. "He wants you to call him."

Siri automatically glanced through the window. Anton and Mia lived across the street, a few hundred yards away in a single-story house; they had two young sons. Siri and Anton had danced a little too close together on Midsummer Eve, and Petter hadn't been happy.

She'd promised herself she'd be more careful from then on.

"OK," she said, trying to sound indifferent. "It's probably about those minutes I wrote up for the golf club."

She couldn't face another argument, not tonight. It had been a long, stressful day, but the least thing could make Petter lose his temper when he was drunk.

She bent down and picked up a newspaper off the floor.

It wasn't entirely Petter's fault that he drank too much; disappointment had sunk its claws into both of them. They were equally unhappy, and incapable of consoling each other.

The last visit to the fertility clinic had almost broken them. If only they could have had a child, everything would have been different.

How many times had she had that thought?

Siri couldn't help looking down at her flat stomach, where nothing would grow in spite of hormone treatment and several rounds of IVF. She had even tried acupuncture, but to no avail. She'd merely ended up feeling guilty because she was so tense.

A lump came into her throat, and she swallowed hard. There was no point in crying. She had to accept that she was never going to be a mother.

If she let out her bottomless grief, she would never stop weeping.

Petter emptied his glass and reached for the bottle.

Siri muttered something about needing the bathroom, and fled.

# CHAPTER 19

A little voice in Nora's head whispered that going to see Johanna Strand was a crazy idea. The case was none of her business; it was a police matter. She couldn't even be sure that it was Astrid's body they'd found.

And yet she was heading for Seglarstaden.

She hadn't been able to help Mina, but maybe there was something she could do for Astrid?

The image of Astrid's face blended with Mina's. They both had long fair hair that curled around their faces. Beautiful smiles, tinged with melancholy.

Nora carried her own failure and Mina's tragic fate like a constant weight on her shoulders, an invisible companion that had been with her all through this difficult summer. Maybe the burden would ease if she made an effort on Astrid's behalf, if she focused on someone else instead of her own troubles?

At least she ought to try. She couldn't simply turn her back.

Seglarstaden was on the hill above the Sailors Hotel, no more than thirty small pale-green wooden houses built in the 1930s. The idea had been to provide accommodation for participants in the Royal Swedish Yacht Club's regattas, because at that time it wasn't possible to sleep on board the competing boats. These days, every single property had been renovated and extended, with the most ingenious approaches to creating extra room where there was no space.

Nora knew roughly where the Strand family lived—on the third row looking from the direction of the harbor. Thanks to the summer heat, the front door was wide open when she arrived. Like everyone else, they had an extension and a small patio, adorned with pots of yellow and white flowers. There was also a hammock in the shade of a tree growing in the sand.

Nora stepped up onto the wooden decking.

"Hello? Anyone home?"

Part of her hoped that no one would answer, then she could go home again, quash the impulse to get involved. Go home and finish preparing the picnic for the trip to Alskär.

Push aside the thought of Astrid. Again.

She knocked on the door. After a few seconds, Johanna Strand appeared. Today her long hair was piled up in a messy bun. In her cutoff shorts, Johanna still looked like the young girl she must have been when Astrid disappeared, but her face was drawn, and there were fine lines around her eyes.

"Hi," Nora said. The words stuck in her throat. How was she going to explain to Johanna why she was here? She shouldn't have come.

"Yes?" Johanna frowned, waiting for Nora to continue.

She either had to come up with something, or walk away.

"I have some questions about Astrid Forsell," she said hesitantly.

"Astrid?" Johanna stiffened. "Is this to do with . . . Telegrafholmen?" She pointed to the island.

Nora nodded.

"I'm sorry, but what's your name? I recognize you, but . . ."

"Nora Linde. I'm . . . I'm a prosecutor with the Economic Crimes Authority." She would leave Johanna to draw her own conclusions.

"Is it definitely Astrid they've found?" Johanna whispered, sinking down onto one of the wicker chairs.

Nora sat down opposite her. "It's too early to say." At least that was the truth. "If it's OK with you, I'd like to ask one or two questions about Astrid."

Johanna nodded. "She was my best friend. We got to know each other when we were little—we were both in the same class at the swimming club." Her voice grew thick with tears. "We were only four when we first met."

Nora patted her hand. "I realize this will be difficult for you. I promise I won't stay long. How did Astrid seem to you that last summer? She disappeared just before school began, if I've understood correctly?"

Johanna pushed back a strand of hair and took a deep breath.

"That's right—it was the last week before the autumn semester. We were due to finish our summer jobs a few days after she went missing."

"So you worked together?"

"Yes, as waitresses at the Sailors Restaurant. My mom knew the boss, Lillian Eriksdotter, and managed to get us in."

Johanna glanced at the Sailors Hotel, just a few hundred yards below the house. The black roof was visible through the trees; it wouldn't take more than a few minutes to walk there.

"It was a good job," Johanna continued. "The place was busy, but the tips were generous. We both enjoyed it, in spite of the occasional guy who couldn't keep his hands to himself."

Johanna sounded honest. Nora wanted to find out more.

"Do you remember anyone who didn't like Astrid? Anyone who might have harmed her?"

She didn't want to scare Johanna unnecessarily, but if it was Astrid in that grave, then it was an important question. Johanna unpinned her bun and redid it before answering.

"Astrid was the kind of person everyone liked. She got along with almost everyone. She could even handle drunk customers who weren't allowed another drink. That's just how she was, smart and witty. She wanted to be an architect when she finished school."

That fit with Nora's memories of Astrid.

"Did she have a boyfriend?"

Johanna hesitated. "She thought the boys on the island were dumb—way too childish." Her eyes filled with tears. "We used to joke about the fact that the 'local selection' was pretty poor. She couldn't even be bothered to flirt with them, even though plenty of them were interested. She could have had anyone she wanted—you know how it is."

Nora had no idea. She'd never been one of those popular girls. For a while she'd been so badly bullied by the "in crowd" on the island that she'd come to hate summers on Sandhamn. Salvation had come the year she'd turned fourteen. She'd gotten to know a few people during confirmation classes at the local chapel. Thomas and a couple girls from neighboring islands had saved her during the worst of her teenage years, and they'd also built up her self-esteem.

"Have you ever thought about what might have happened to her?" she asked, brushing pale-brown pine needles off the table.

Johanna looked away. "She just vanished. Went up in smoke without a word, even though we were best friends. She didn't say anything to me."

"So what do you think happened?" Nora persisted.

Johanna gazed at an elderly couple making their way up the road. The woman was using a colorful walking stick that was beautifully decorated with flowers.

"I thought . . . it might be something to do with her useless mom."

"Monica Forsell? What kind of relationship did they have?"

Johanna let out a joyless laugh. "She was a terrible woman."

"You mean she was strict?"

"She had no . . . filter. She was loud and volatile, she always had to be the center of attention. The house was always completely chaotic. Monica drank too much and so did her boyfriend, Zacharias. Astrid hated the partying and she hated him. He's vile. She often slept over with me just to avoid being there." Johanna broke off and wiped her nose.

"But would she really have left without telling you?" Nora asked.

A little bird had landed a few feet away, and was pecking eagerly at some bread crumbs.

"She knew that Monica would come straight to me as soon as she realized Astrid was gone," Johanna said in a subdued voice. "Maybe she didn't trust me to keep quiet, but I would never have given her away to either Monica or Zacharias."

Nora wished she'd had a pen and paper with her so that she could take notes. She didn't want to take out her phone halfway through the conversation.

Actually, what time was it? Jonas and Julia must be wondering where she was. It had been more than an hour since she'd left to go to the store.

"So who is this Zacharias?" she asked instead of getting to her feet.

"Monica's boyfriend—the carpenter. Or rather her ex. It ended after Astrid went missing, but it was too late by then."

Johanna bit the fingernail of her right index finger. Nora noticed that all her nails were so badly bitten that the skin around them was swollen.

"I miss her all the time," Johanna said.

## *Astrid*

Her feet felt like two footballs as Astrid walked home through the June night. The sun would be up in an hour, but the sky had already begun to lighten in the east over Korsö.

There were still plenty of people around in the harbor area even though it was late. She passed a group of kids who'd had too much to drink hanging out on the promenade. They yelled at her as she went by; she did her best to ignore them but couldn't resist giving them the finger over her shoulder.

She was so sick of drunken men and their wandering hands.

The old part of the village was quieter. Most of the houses were in darkness, and she took a shortcut behind the Divers Bar.

This was her second late shift in a row, because the Sailors didn't close until two in the morning on Fridays and Saturdays. The place had been packed all night, and her arms and legs were aching after running back and forth nonstop with heavy trays.

She was so looking forward to her day off. She was planning on staying in bed until at least noon. This first week had been much harder than she'd expected, and she was exhausted.

She couldn't wait to get to bed.

She heard the music from some distance away, far too loud given the time. Astrid really, really hoped it was coming from another house, not hers, but as she drew nearer she could see that all the lights were on downstairs. People were dancing and drinking in there.

Mom was partying again.

*Shit.* She'd prayed that Mom would be in bed by now. She needed peace and quiet. She stopped by the gate.

If she went inside, Mom would start in on her in front of everyone as she always did when Astrid got home late; it was even worse when Mom had had a few drinks.

*No.*

All she wanted was to go to her room and get into bed. Crawl under the covers and rest her aching muscles.

A drunken laugh reached her ears. She knew exactly what it meant. Mom was in full swing, with a glass in her hand and a cigarette in the corner of her mouth. It would be hours before she ran out of energy and the guests finally left. The kitchen and the rest of the house would look like a garbage dump. Astrid would have to clean the whole place when she woke up. She hated mess, and Mom just didn't care.

Astrid dropped to her knees and rested her forehead on the white fence. The rails were damp with dew, the grass was cold against her bare legs.

She thought about the money she'd earned tonight, all the tips she'd been given. Every krona was one step closer to freedom. Soon she would be able to escape from all this.

She got to her feet, gritted her teeth, and set off for Seglarstaden. Johanna had left the restaurant at the same time as her; she wouldn't be asleep yet. If Astrid hurried, she'd be able to stay over with her friend.

It wasn't the first time. She was pretty sure it wouldn't be the last.

# Chapter 20

Johanna headed straight for the forest. She had to be alone for a while, get away from all the curious looks. She felt as if everyone were staring at her, even though she knew she was imagining it.

She walked as fast as she could, her heartbeat pounding in her ears, in among the pine trees where neither joggers nor dog owners ventured. The silence made her feel a little better. The soughing of the wind and the distant rush of the sea calmed her.

After ten minutes the stress began to fade. She was still in shock following Nora Linde's visit, but at least she was able to think more clearly.

The pines thinned out as Johanna reached the southern side of the island. The sandy shore wasn't as good as in Trouville, but that meant fewer people found their way here. Today there wasn't a soul in sight.

She'd been caught off guard. When Nora Linde said she was a prosecutor, Johanna didn't have the nerve to refuse to talk to her. She wished she hadn't answered all those questions. The whole thing had brought up too many difficult memories, thoughts she didn't want to think.

The secret she'd carried for ten years.

The crime that must never be exposed.

Johanna had been envious of Astrid's pretty face and stunning figure, but she'd never wanted to swap places with her. She was grateful for her ordinary parents. OK, so her mom could be strict sometimes, but she would never get drunk in front of her kids.

Astrid had often slept over at Johanna's, especially when Monica was partying. The amount of time Astrid spent with the Strand family was one of the few things Monica hadn't complained about.

Johanna still missed her friend every single day. She couldn't allow herself to remember all the dreams they'd had, the plans they'd made.

She'd gone back to school, but had dropped out after only one semester. As soon as she sat down with her books, she lost focus. Her concentration was shot; the forbidden thoughts came creeping in, the guilt that refused to loosen its grip.

The shame.

If only she'd stepped in before it was too late, or told an adult who could have done something.

The fact that a criminal had gone unpunished and Astrid was no longer around was almost unbearable.

Whenever she tried to study, she always finished up in some late-night bar where she could talk crap with strangers and avoid thinking about the dark secret that haunted her.

In the end she'd stopped pretending to work. She had no student aid or scholarship, and had to support herself. Waitressing was the only job she knew. She'd done casual stints here and there without really bothering about the future. The hustle and bustle of a restaurant allowed her to numb her emotions. She smoked weed to help her relax, and when things got too tough, she turned to other substances.

She'd spent the last ten years trying to push thoughts of Astrid aside, but the discovery on Telegrafholmen brought tears to her eyes.

Johanna kicked at the sand. She couldn't allow herself to speculate about what might have happened; that would send her over the edge. She ought to leave Sandhamn; staying on the island wasn't doing her any good at all.

Unfortunately, she couldn't afford to get away. If she'd had any money, she'd have gone to Greece with her girlfriends. Instead she'd spent the whole summer in the archipelago with nothing to do. At least she didn't have to pay for her food here, and Dad gave her some money now and again when Mom wasn't looking. Otherwise Mom would launch into yet another lecture.

Johanna hated having no money; it ruined everything. She'd tried to find a job on the island, but everywhere was fully staffed for the summer.

Or they just weren't prepared to be honest; she didn't exactly have the best reputation. She'd already been fired from most of the cafés and restaurants on Sandhamn.

Her T-shirt was sticking to her back. Her stomach was hot and sweaty after her fast walk. A faint breeze blowing from the south brought no relief.

The only glimmer of light was that her parents were working in town all week and wouldn't be back until Friday. She had the house to herself for a few more days.

She made her way to the water's edge, took off her shoes, and waded out into the waves. The water was cool and refreshing, so clear that she could see the pebbles on the seabed. Walking on the uneven surface was a little painful.

She picked up a small stone and threw it as far as she could. It disappeared beneath the surface and vanished with a faint plop. In a second there was no trace.

Just like Astrid.

If Nora Linde wanted to find out more, she would have to talk to someone else. Johanna had no intention of speaking to her again. She'd already come close to giving herself away.

She mustn't break her promise and reveal what had happened that night, regardless of what had been found on Telegrafholmen.

# Chapter 21

The call from forensic pathologist Oscar-Henrik Sachsen came just as Thomas and Aram were pulling out of the parking lot at Stavsnäs. It was shortly after two o'clock, and lunch had consisted of a sandwich on board the ferry. Thomas was already wishing he'd had two.

He was driving, so Aram took the call and switched to speakerphone.

"Sachsen here. We've started looking at the bones you sent over from Telegrafholmen. You'd have made life easier for us if you'd found some bigger pieces."

"I'm sorry we weren't able to let the construction workers who detonated the blast know that in advance," Thomas said drily.

"A pelvis would have been useful."

It was no secret that the easiest way to determine the gender of a skeleton was by looking at the pelvis; in the female, it was larger and more rounded.

"Or at least a skull," Sachsen went on. "We have too little to go on to establish age or gender. At the moment we have mainly fragments, plus half a hand with a couple of fingers still attached."

"And some ribs," Thomas pointed out, increasing his speed as he left the twenty-mile-per-hour limit.

"That's not enough for a visual assessment, plus there's very little difference between male and female ribs. Could you do another search? See if anything was missed the first time?"

Nilsson had spent two days going over the area with a fine-tooth comb. Thomas found it difficult to believe that someone with his experience would have overlooked something.

"I can't really make progress unless you find more bones."

They ended the call as Thomas drove across the bridge by the Strömma Canal.

"We'll have to ask Nilsson to go back," Aram said. "It's the only way."

"He won't like that. He was in a filthy temper the other day, just like Margit."

Aram rested his elbow on the window. "I can't understand why her promotion hasn't been confirmed."

Thomas had to agree. With every month that passed, Margit's mood worsened, which was beginning to affect the whole department.

Maybe the fact that she was paying so much attention to solving the Telegrafholmen case quickly wasn't so surprising after all.

## *Siri*

Siri was due to meet Suss for coffee at three o'clock, and she was already late when she got in the car to drive to the café.

She parked carelessly and hurried toward the square. Suss was sitting at a table on the sidewalk. Her hair was loose, and she was wearing a tight floral dress that emphasized her pregnancy. There was a slice of princess cake in front of her.

Siri gave her sister a hug and sat down opposite her. She tried to avoid looking at Suss's huge belly, which was touching the edge of the table.

"How are you?" Siri asked, although part of her didn't want to know.

"It's hard work! He's a lively little guy."

Suss embarked on a lengthy account of heartburn and swollen ankles. She was almost eight months along; the baby was due on August 20. Siri tried to smile in the right places as she ordered coffee and a Danish. Suddenly Suss seized her hand.

"He's kicking!" she exclaimed. She placed Siri's palm on her belly before Siri could protest. Something fluttered beneath her fingertips, barely perceptible bird's wings. Then came the clear movement of a tiny foot kicking out beneath the skin.

Siri inhaled sharply; she wanted to laugh and cry at the same time. She was happy for her sister, she really was, but her heart was breaking because she knew she would never experience the same thing.

"It's fantastic," she murmured, reaching for her pastry. The yellow vanilla cream grew as she chewed. She even pointed to her mouth to indicate that it was too full for her to say anything else for a while.

Suss barely noticed. She'd already moved on to her latest visit to the prenatal clinic, the discussions about the birth itself, and the various pain-relief options. She'd always been kind of self-obsessed, but over the past few months, everything else had ceased to exist. All she could think about or talk about was the child who would soon be born.

Siri had long ago stopped telling her sister about her own failed attempts to get pregnant. She loved Suss, but being with her was painful this spring. It was hard to see her growing bump, hard to deal with what could have been if only she'd managed to get pregnant.

She hadn't mentioned the atmosphere at home either. Suss and Petter had never really gotten along; Suss couldn't understand why Siri had married Petter when she was so young. The last thing Siri needed to hear right now was, "What did I tell you?"

"I don't know how I'm going to get through the summer if it stays this hot," Suss said, patting her stomach and rolling her eyes before finishing off her cake. "By the way, when are you two going on vacation?"

"In a few weeks—at the end of July." Siri bit her lip. Petter had insisted that they must go away. He'd even booked a cottage in the Saint Anna archipelago in Östergötland, without asking what she'd like to do. He'd told her the other day, as if it were a surprise that should make her feel happy and grateful.

Time together so that they could recover from this difficult spring, as he'd put it. Siri had fought to keep a smile on her face and seem pleased, even though the idea made her shudder.

Two weeks all alone on a tiny island. The way things were at the moment, they'd drive each other crazy.

And the truth was that she would be longing for another man.

A delicious shiver ran down her spine.

She pictured his face, felt his gentle hands touching her in a way that Petter hadn't done for years. In his eyes she became beautiful and desirable again. She'd almost forgotten what that was like.

They'd only been seeing each other like this for a few months, but she was already deeply in love. Ecstatically happy, in spite of all the pangs of guilt tearing her apart.

Yet another secret that she hadn't shared with her sister.

"I'm going to order another piece of cake," Suss announced, smacking her lips. "Would you like anything?"

Siri shook her head.

She knew it was wrong to cheat on her husband, but right now it was the only thing keeping her going.

# Chapter 22

When Thomas got back to Flemingsberg, he found a note from Ida on his desk. She was in the conference room—could he stop in?

She'd parked herself at the table and was surrounded by piles of papers.

"What's this about?" Thomas asked, his hand resting on the door handle.

"Thanks for coming—I hope it was OK to leave the note?" Ida blushed slightly. She somehow managed to be both sassy and unsure of herself at the same time. Like many colleagues fresh out of the academy, she lapped up praise, but then she shouldn't expect a round of applause for ordinary police work. "I checked out Siri Grandin's sister, as you requested," she went on.

To save time, Thomas had texted her on the way back from Sandhamn.

"Great," he said, pulling out a chair. "Anything interesting?"

"She's known as Suss, but her real name is Susanna—Susanna Alptegen. She's a single mom with a ten-year-old son. She works as an administrator with a construction company and lives in an apartment in Liljeholmen." Ida handed him a piece of paper. "Address and phone number."

"Excellent."

"I also have information about Monica Forsell. As it said in the file, she's a qualified pharmacist and was working at a pharmacy in Gustavsberg before her daughter went missing. After that, she was given long-term sick leave, and six years ago, she received her state pension early on the grounds of ill health." Ida glanced at her notes. "Monica's very active in a free church group known as the Holy Days of Christ. She donates a percentage of her pension to them each month, and she also carries out missionary work to recruit new members. They have a revivalist meeting in their church each week, with sermons that go on for hours—kind of in the American style, with the congregation singing and weeping and shouting out that they've been saved."

Thomas could picture the scene. It didn't surprise him that Monica Forsell had needed to seek consolation, although he didn't like the idea of a religious group exploiting a vulnerable woman. However, it was none of his business to judge how she dealt with her grief.

"One more thing," Ida added as if she'd saved the best until last. "I thought we ought to speak to Astrid Forsell's father, Olav Hansen."

There had been no record of an interview with the father. If Thomas remembered correctly, he'd had little contact with his daughter while she was growing up.

Olav Hansen came from Norway and worked as a mechanical engineer. He'd never lived in Sweden. When the investigation into Astrid's disappearance began, he was on a Norwegian oil platform. Apparently it had been difficult to get ahold of him.

"Absolutely. So where is he now?"

Ida leaned back on her chair and winked at him. "I tracked him down."

"How did you do that?"

She pushed back a strand of purple hair that had escaped from her ponytail. "It took a while, but it was pretty straightforward." She pointed to the laptop in front of her. "I used Facebook. There are ninety-six Olav Hansens on Facebook, but only one of them has an oil platform as his profile picture. He also gives Bergen as his hometown. The more I looked at his photos, the more certain I became. Astrid looks a lot like him—they have the same eyes and nose."

"Well done," Thomas said.

Ida smiled. "His mother, Elise Ingemo Hansen, is one of his friends, so I checked the Norwegian telephone directory. Fortunately, Elise Hansen is a much less common name than Olav Hansen, particularly in Bergen. I called each one that was listed, and eventually I got lucky. I explained the situation, and she gave me his cell phone number."

"Did you speak to him?"

"Yes, and he was very surprised. Said it had been a long time. Here's his number. He didn't really want to talk to me about his daughter, so I thought it might be better if you called—made it more official."

# CHAPTER 23

The good weather had attracted lots of people to Alskär. The little sandy shore was filled with children playing in the sunshine, and several small motorboats were moored farther along.

When Nora felt the water, it was warmer than it had been for a long time.

Julia was so happy. She was busy building a sandcastle with her friend Molly. Nora was keeping an eye on them from her beach towel a few yards away. Jonas lay beside her, absorbed in a book, black Ray-Bans protecting him from the sun.

Nora leafed through a magazine, thinking about what Johanna had told her. If Thomas found out about her visit, he would no doubt think she was interfering in an ongoing police investigation, but it was hard to push aside the memory of Astrid. Her catastrophic failure in Mina's case had weighed her down all summer—so many things she should have done differently, so many bad decisions she'd made. Her self-loathing had grown as the same narrative played out over and over again in her mind.

For the first time in months, she felt a sense of commitment, a belief that she might be able to make a contribution.

Fight for someone.

In a strange way she almost thought she owed it to Astrid. If she'd listened to her during that last summer, maybe she could have helped.

She should have done more for Mina.

She turned the page and found an article about how to lose weight after the summer vacation.

Needless to say, it didn't hold her attention.

Johanna had mentioned Monica's boyfriend, Zacharias. It was an unusual name; it had to be Zacharias Fahlman, one of the carpenters on the island. Nora had never employed him, but people said he did an excellent job—when he finally showed up.

He was a tall man in his early fifties who liked to work out; he still looked good. According to the gossip, he drank too much, just like Astrid's mom had done back in the day. He was just the type Monica would have fallen for ten years ago—cool and a little dangerous. No doubt they'd made an attractive couple.

Jonas's shoulders were beginning to redden. Nora was about to take out the sunscreen when he pushed up his sunglasses and looked at her.

"By the way, where did you go before we came over here?"

"What do you mean?" Nora played dumb, even though she knew exactly what he meant.

"You said you were going to the store for coffee and pastries, but you were gone for over an hour. What happened?"

Nora hadn't told him she'd been to see Johanna. The fact that she'd gone off to speak to a potential witness in a police investigation was almost inexplicable. Instead she'd brushed aside his questions and busied herself with the preparations for their trip. Fortunately, Julia had been with her in the kitchen, bursting with impatience, so it had been easy to put Jonas off.

She'd hoped he'd forgotten about it.

"I bumped into Thomas," she said. Which was true.

Jonas propped himself up on one elbow, still looking a little unsure. His brown hair was slightly sun bleached.

"What was he doing here? I thought his vacation was over. We talked about it the other day—Elin was going to Pernilla's, because he was due back at work."

Like other pilots, Jonas was good at remembering details. Thomas and Elin had stopped by on Sunday before they headed back to town after their stay on Harö. Elin and Julia were like cousins and often played together. They'd been allowed to use the little rowboat, and had practiced with the oars for hours.

Nora turned the page; she hadn't read a single word of the article.

"He was here with a colleague to see Monica Forsell. She's the mother of that girl who went missing ten years ago. They think she might be the one they found on Telegrafholmen."

She was talking too fast.

"OK . . ." Jonas sounded far from convinced. "And you talked to him for almost an hour, when we'd arranged to come to Alskär?"

"We went for coffee."

Now she was lying; she hated not being honest with her husband, but she couldn't tell him about her visit to Johanna.

"Sorry I didn't call," she went on, trying to sound both apologetic and truthful. "I just don't know where the time went."

She stood up and brushed the sand from her legs and feet.

"Come on, we'd better go and admire Julia's sandcastle. The girls have done a wonderful job." She pointed to a splendid construction with impressive towers and battlements.

Jonas hesitated for a couple of seconds too long, then nodded and put down his book.

Nora couldn't look him in the eye as they went to join the children.

# Chapter 24

Olav Hansen's phone number was written in a rounded, childish style. It reminded Thomas that he was almost twice Ida's age. When he was in school, they'd had to practice cursive by writing the same sentence over and over again in their black handwriting books.

Ida was born at the beginning of the nineties—not so young that she'd used a tablet in school, but young enough to jot down most things on her cell phone these days.

He pushed aside a couple of piles of papers and called the number.

*"Hei!"* said a breathless voice just as he was about to hang up. *"Vente lite."*

As always, the Norwegian language sounded lilting and musical to his ears, but Thomas had no problem in understanding what he said. *Wait a moment.*

"Hello?" Olav Hansen said after a while. He seemed to be standing outside; Thomas could hear the wind blowing in the background.

Thomas introduced himself.

"I've already spoken to your colleague."

The terse response wasn't encouraging. A door slammed, and the sound of the wind stopped.

"I know that, but I'd really appreciate it if I could ask you a couple of questions. We've reopened the investigation into your daughter's disappearance, and we're doing our best to understand what happened."

Why was Hansen on his guard? They were on the same side.

"We could really use your help," he added.

"Make it quick. I have to do something in ten minutes."

Ida had already told Hansen about the discovery of the bones, so there was no need for Thomas to go over it again, but he wondered if there might have been someone around Astrid who wished her harm. Expecting a father who'd had hardly any contact with her to answer that question was a long shot, but Thomas wanted to ask him anyway. Sometimes information came from the most unexpected places.

Hansen had barely featured in the original investigation.

"Can you tell me about your relationship with your daughter?" he began. "I believe she spent most of her time with her mother in Sweden?"

"That was Monica's choice."

Was there a hint of bitterness in his voice? Thomas thought it was worth digging a little deeper. "What do you mean?"

"It doesn't matter—forget it."

Hansen was trying to shut him down, but Thomas had a feeling that this could be important.

"I'd really like to know."

Hansen seemed to be going up or down a metal staircase; a dull clank accompanied each step. Presumably he was still working on an oil rig; for many people it became a lifestyle.

"Right now every piece of information is of interest to us," Thomas went on. "As I said, we'd really appreciate your help."

"You need to talk to Monica. She didn't want me to be involved in Astrid's life. She made that clear from the start."

There was a conversation going on in the corridor outside Thomas's office. He got up and quietly closed the door.

"Would you have liked to be involved?"

"I'll be honest with you—Astrid wasn't planned. I was taking part in a yacht race on Sandhamn the summer she was conceived. I was on the crew of a Norwegian boat competing in the Round Gotland Race."

Thomas was familiar with the race—the oldest and largest in northern Europe. Back in the eighties, five hundred boats participated each year, and there were huge public celebrations on Sandhamn at both the start and finish. These days the race began in Stockholm, and the numbers had dropped dramatically.

"Is that how you met Monica Forsell?"

"It was the night before the start—we had a few beers together. Our class did very well; we came second, and partied like crazy when we finished. Monica joined in, and I stayed on for a few more days because of her." Hansen cleared his throat. "And—well, you know what happened."

"That must have been difficult."

"We were both so young. I was twenty-four and Monica was only twenty. Plus we hardly knew each other."

Thomas didn't say anything; he hoped Hansen would keep talking now he'd gotten going.

"When I'd recovered from the shock, I tried to take my share of the responsibility, but Monica said no. She didn't want me to have anything to do with the pregnancy." He snorted. "It was a battle to get my name on the birth certificate."

"How much contact did you have with Astrid while she was growing up?"

"Not much." Hansen suddenly sounded weary. "Far too little, to tell you the truth. I tried now and again, but Monica constantly put obstacles in my way. I offered many times to fly to Stockholm, just for the day if necessary, so that I could see Astrid, but there was always a problem. Astrid got sick, or there was an issue with the school, or some other excuse."

Thomas was taking notes as Hansen talked.

"Of course I should have fought harder for my daughter; I have no other children. But it was too difficult. I withdrew and told myself it was for the best."

Having met Monica, Thomas could easily imagine the situation. He suddenly longed to see Elin. He hated the weeks she spent with Pernilla; the apartment was empty and depressing. However angry he'd been with Pernilla, he had to admit that she'd never tried to sabotage their relationship with their child. In spite of all the arguing, they'd taken great care not to badmouth each other in front of Elin.

"Hello?" Hansen said, bringing Thomas back to reality. "I'm afraid I have to go."

"Sorry," Thomas said. "Just a couple of brief questions. What happened when Astrid was old enough to start asking about her daddy? And when she became a teenager? Surely she must have had her own view of the situation?"

"Funny you should say that. Things did actually improve when she started high school. She called me now and again, and we'd meet up a few times each year."

"Did she ever come to visit you in Norway?"

Hansen let out a bitter laugh. "Monica would never have allowed that."

"When was the last time you saw her in Sweden?"

"I was in Stockholm that April, shortly before Easter. We had dinner in a restaurant one evening."

"Was that the last time you spoke to her?"

"No, we spoke on the phone pretty regularly after that."

"Do you remember your final conversation?"

"I think it was in early August."

"What did you talk about? Was she scared of anyone?"

"Scared?" Hansen sounded as if the question made him uncomfortable.

"Or worried? Had she had a problem with someone, been threatened maybe?"

"No."

"Are you absolutely certain of that?"

"Yes."

"So what did you talk about in that last call?"

"She didn't want to continue living with Monica."

"Did she say why?"

"She didn't have time—she had to go. She said she'd call me back the following day, but she never did."

# *Astrid*

It was still dark outside when Astrid woke up. She blinked and looked at the clock radio: quarter to two. The middle of the night.

The sound of loud voices penetrated through the wall. That was what had woken her. She couldn't help listening, even though she didn't want to.

Mom was in her bedroom with Zacharias. They seemed to be quarreling; Mom often blew up when she was drunk.

Astrid started up at the ceiling, her eyes burning. She had an early shift in the morning; she needed to sleep, but the yelling from the next room made her heart race. She heard a groan, then a thud. Were they fighting, or had they moved on to makeup sex?

Impossible to tell.

Her mouth went dry. Should she go in and see if her mom was OK?

She didn't dare. If she was wrong, Mom would be furious. And if Zacharias was drunk as well, she didn't want to see him.

The bitter taste of self-loathing filled her mouth. She curled up under the covers and pulled the pillow over her head to shut out the noise.

Silence descended on the house. She was desperate to go back to sleep but couldn't interpret the quietness. After a while she decided to count to a thousand. If she didn't hear anything during that time, then Mom was fine. She'd just had a drunken outburst, then crashed. If there were any more weird sounds before Astrid had finished counting, then she would get up and check.

The thought made her stomach contract.

A door opened. Footsteps in the corridor, then her own door slowly swung open. Someone walked in. The smell of tobacco and aftershave reached Astrid's nostrils.

The room spun.

What the hell was Zacharias doing here?

"Astrid," a voice whispered in the darkness.

She didn't answer.

"Astrid? Can we talk?"

She pretended to be asleep, as stiff as a board, acutely aware that she was virtually naked. If only she'd been wearing more than her panties. She normally slept in a T-shirt as well, but she'd been so hot and tired when she got home that she'd simply dropped her clothes on the floor and collapsed into bed.

She pressed the sheet to her body, every muscle tensed. She had a lump in her throat. She wanted to shout for Mom, but that would give away the fact that she was awake.

She could hear Zacharias breathing. A floorboard creaked beneath his feet, which was an ominous sign.

The endless seconds ticked by.

"Are you asleep?"

Astrid screwed her eyes tightly shut, fervently praying that he'd go away and leave her alone.

The door closed. He'd gone. Astrid let out a long breath; her body was drenched in cold sweat.

She waited for a little while, then slid out of bed and jammed a chair under the door handle.

She went back to bed, her heart pounding.

# Chapter 25

The couples' counselor was in the Söder district, just behind Medborgarplatsen. Thomas had been there three times with Pernilla back in June before they took a break for the summer. She was already waiting in the doorway when he arrived.

Was it a good sign that she hadn't gone up to the office on her own? That they were going in together? Or was he seeing signals that didn't exist?

She had her back to him. Her strawberry-blond hair shone in the late-afternoon sun.

They usually booked the last slot, at five o'clock, which gave him time to drive up from Flemingsberg. It didn't make much difference to Pernilla, because she could start and finish work whenever she wished. In Thomas's opinion, that was one of the few advantages of her position. The rest of it—the constant traveling, the nonstop flow of emails and conference calls that encroached on family life—those were the factors that had destroyed their relationship.

It was the feeling of always coming second that had finally made Thomas suggest that they separate; Pernilla had been deeply shocked, in spite of their frequent arguments on the subject.

Her sorrow had quickly been replaced by anger and bitterness until, in the end, they could barely speak to each other, and communicated mainly by brief text messages where every single word was misinterpreted in the worst possible way.

Nora had persuaded Thomas that it was worth trying couples' counseling, and much to his surprise, Pernilla had immediately agreed to try.

"Hi there," he said.

Pernilla gave a start and turned around. Needless to say, she had her phone in her hand. Looking guilty, she slipped it into her purse, but not quickly enough to stop the familiar surge of frustration. *Why can't she leave that goddamn phone alone?*

However, her smile was so disarming that Thomas managed to push aside his anger. There was no point in starting the session in a bad mood. He'd promised both Nora and himself that he'd give it his best shot.

Pernilla gave him a cautious hug.

"You look well rested," she said, brushing a hair off his shoulder. "And tanned. Did you and Elin have a lovely time on Harö over the summer?"

Thomas knew she was being less than honest. He looked worn out, and didn't feel particularly rested in spite of his vacation. But he still liked hearing her say it.

"It's always good to be out there," he said. "Shall we go up?"

Pernilla nodded and tucked her arm under his. "Thank you for doing this, Thomas. I think it's useful for both of us."

Her choice of the word *useful* bothered him, but he knew she meant well. She'd tried to say something positive, and yet his reaction was negative. It was so easy to fall back into the old pattern, to misconstrue what had been said.

He opened the door and allowed her to go first.

They had to stop this destructive behavior for Elin's sake. She had a right to a mom and a dad. It was their duty to be good parents, even if they could hardly bear to be in the same room.

Nobody was going to force Elin to take sides, as Monica Forsell had done with Astrid.

They couldn't allow their relationship to become a war zone.

# Chapter 26

The sun was setting, a huge, fiery ball just above the treetops on Harö. Nora was sitting on the glassed-in veranda with a glass of wine, gazing out across the inlet. The last ferry of the day had just passed by, its swell making the rowboat bob up and down by the jetty, tugging at its moorings.

Astrid used to take the boys out in the boat when they were little. They would sit in the stern laughing as they waved the oars around, splashing each other with water.

Nora couldn't really explain why Astrid had become so important right now, why she felt this overwhelming urge to help out. She couldn't let it go; her mind kept coming back to Telegrafholmen, whether it was Astrid's bones the construction workers had found, and what had happened to her.

Nora shuddered. Murdered and buried in the ground. How could anyone be so cruel?

*Emir Kovač is capable of doing something like that.*

The thought came unbidden. What if Mina had been murdered, too, and was lying in a grave somewhere? If that were the case, where was Lukas? Had Emir kidnapped his nephew? Or was Lukas dead, too?

*If only you'd done your job properly . . .*

Her inner voice was dripping with contempt. When would it leave her in peace? Would she feel better if she stepped back from her role as prosecutor? Maybe that was the price she had to pay—openly admit her failure by leaving the Economic Crimes Authority. A more experienced lawyer would never have put a terrified and vulnerable woman in mortal danger, as she had done.

Nora closed her eyes and took a deep breath, but the guilt was squeezing her chest. She took a gulp of her wine, then another, but it didn't help.

She heard footsteps from the dining room. Jonas came in and sat down on the wicker chair opposite her.

"Julia's asleep," he said. "She went out like a light—I only managed two pages of her bedtime story."

Nora felt even more guilty for slipping away instead of reading to her daughter. Then again, they'd been together all day. She needed a few minutes to herself.

Jonas yawned. "I'm pretty tired, too—aren't you?"

Nora wished she could have said yes, but she didn't feel in the least bit sleepy, in spite of all those hours of sunshine and fresh air on the beach.

She just felt kind of wrung out.

That seemed to be her fate this summer—to be exhausted yet wide awake. Her body couldn't cope, while her brain was working overtime. Hopelessness overwhelmed her; would she ever get back to normal?

She shouldn't have lied to Jonas earlier on. Had he realized she wasn't being honest with him? He'd been a little abrupt with her all evening. She stole a glance at him. *Please don't let him start talking about that psychologist again . . .* She couldn't face the discussion, not tonight. Jonas refused to accept that she wasn't interested in exposing her innermost thoughts. It wouldn't help. All she needed was sleep, a few nights of uninterrupted sleep. Simple.

She tried to suppress her irritation and brought her glass to her lips. It was empty.

"Would you like some wine?" she said, getting up to go into the kitchen for a refill.

"I'm flying tomorrow. You know I can't drink alcohol the day before."

Of course she knew, but it somehow sounded better if she made the offer.

"Sorry, I didn't think."

The silence became uncomfortable, as if Jonas was deliberately not saying anything in order to make a point. She didn't want to overreact, but she didn't like the idea that he was trying to chastise her.

"Can I get you something else? Tea?"

"That would be good." Jonas glanced at her glass. "Maybe you'd like a cup of tea, too?"

Nora stiffened. "What do you mean by that?"

He looked as if he was about to say something, then changed his mind at the last second.

"Nothing. Forget it."

"That's clearly not true. What did you mean?" Nora knew she was picking a fight, but she couldn't stop herself. "Do you think I drink too much?"

"Come on, Nora. Drop it."

Jonas ran a hand through his brown hair and sank back in his chair.

The sun had disappeared now, leaving only a few deep-pink streaks in the dark-blue sky. The Getholmen Lighthouse had begun to flash in the twilight.

Nora had no intention of dropping anything. She'd struggled all summer, and now he was starting on her just because she liked a glass of wine in the evenings! They always had a drink when they were on Sandhamn—it was part of their life on the island.

"Say what you want to say."

Jonas grimaced. "Don't take this the wrong way; I'm just worried about you. We've gone through a hell of a lot of wine this summer—far more than usual."

"And you don't have wine with dinner?"

"It's not about that."

"So it's OK for you to drink wine, but not me?" She knew she'd slurred her words, which made her even madder. She hadn't drunk that much, she was sure of it.

"I'm not happy about going back to work and leaving you and Julia alone out here . . ." Jonas began, but Nora interrupted him.

"I get it!" She put the glass down on the table in front of him with an exaggerated movement. "There you go! No more for me tonight!" She gave him a challenging stare. "Would you like me to go into the kitchen and pour the rest of the bottle down the sink? So I won't be tempted to drink myself into a stupor, since you clearly think I have no self-control?"

Jonas sighed. It was no secret that he hated conflict, but tonight he had only himself to blame. He was the one who'd started it.

"Please, Nora."

The conciliatory tone just made it worse.

"Shall I pour the rest down the sink?" she said again. "I mean, you can't have a wife who drinks! That's not a good look for a hotshot pilot, is it?"

"Lower your voice—you're going to wake Julia."

Jesus, was he trying to guilt-trip her over Julia, too? What the hell was wrong with him?

"Don't drag Julia into this!"

Jonas stood up so that they were standing eye to eye; they were almost the same height. She could see the tension in his jawline.

"For fuck's sake, Nora. Do you have to make a scene every time I'm going to be away for four days? I'm already worried." He was breathing heavily. After a few seconds he went on, in a voice that was far from his usual calm tone: "This is getting us nowhere. Can't we let it go?"

"Maybe you should have thought of that before you started flinging accusations around," Nora snapped. "I'm going to bed."

# Thursday, August 11

# Chapter 27

Thomas yawned at the wheel of the car. It was a beautiful morning. They'd set off early in order to speak to Susanna Alptegen, Siri Grandin's sister, before she left for work.

The information about Siri's life insurance had changed things. Aram had thought from the start that it was only a matter of time before they found a motive that might have led to Petter Grandin getting rid of his wife; there was no doubt that the insurance payout fulfilled that criterion.

"There," Aram said, pointing to a sign that read "Liljeholmstorget."

Thomas turned in and found a parking space. He looked up at the white apartment block; Susanna lived on the third floor of six. It was a pleasant area, with colorful flower beds laid out between the buildings, all of which appeared to date from the beginning of the twentieth century.

"Let's go," Aram said.

The woman who opened the door bore no resemblance to Siri Grandin.

Susanna was in her forties, small and neat, with her fair hair cut into a bob. Siri had had lighter hair, deep-set eyes, and clearly marked features. They were both attractive, but in completely different ways.

"Sorry to disturb you," Aram began, holding up his police ID. "We'd like to ask you a few questions about your sister, Siri."

Susanna reached for the doorframe for support. "Siri? Why?"

"If we could come in, we'll explain," Thomas said. "I think that would be better than discussing things in the stairway."

"Of course—come on in."

Susanna led the way into the airy three-room apartment. A white sofa and armchairs dominated the living room, and there was a large flat-screen TV on the wall adjoining the kitchen.

"Would you like a cup of coffee?"

That was probably the phrase Thomas heard most often when he visited someone's home; the instinct to offer hospitality always kicked in.

"We're OK, thanks," he said. "No need to go to any trouble."

Susanna smiled. "It's a Nespresso—all I have to do is insert a pod and press the button."

"We're fine, but thanks anyway."

Susanna's smile disappeared. "You said this was about Siri?"

Aram explained the situation, and Susanna's growing concern was clear to see.

"You think she was murdered!" she exclaimed.

"It's much too early to draw that conclusion," Thomas assured her. "But we have reopened the investigation into her disappearance."

"Do you have a suspect?"

That wasn't the question Thomas had anticipated. "Why do you ask?"

The sorrow in Susanna's eyes was replaced by another emotion. She gripped the fingers of her left hand with her right hand.

"Have you spoken to Siri's husband?"

"Do you think we should?" Aram asked.

"He tried to have her declared dead only a year after she went missing." She broke off and took a deep breath. "I know it's a terrible thing to say about someone, especially as he's my brother-in-law, but I have wondered . . ."

"What have you wondered?"

"Whether he was involved in her disappearance."

The conversation had quickly taken an unexpected turn.

"Could you tell us a little about your sister and her marriage?" Thomas prompted her.

Susanna's eyes shone with unshed tears. "I'm sorry, it's just so upsetting. Siri was my only sister. I was devastated. The whole thing was unreal—how could she just vanish without saying a word to anyone? There wasn't even a proper suicide note, just a stupid postcard." Her mouth twisted with anger. "Anyone could have written *sorry*. What if Petter did it to cover up the murder?"

Thomas hadn't given much thought to the postcard. He made a note to check the handwriting.

"How did he react when Siri went missing?" he asked.

"At first he seemed upset, shattered, but then, when I heard about the application to have her declared dead . . ."

She looked directly at Thomas and Aram.

"I didn't understand how he could do something like that after such a short time. It was terrible—like losing her all over again. Every day I kept on hoping she'd come back. Whenever the phone rang, I thought it might be her."

Susanna's antipathy toward Petter Grandin hadn't come through in the original inquiry, but his actions had clearly evoked a strong reaction in her.

"What can you tell us about their marriage?" Aram said. "Did they have a good relationship?"

Susanna shook her head. "Not particularly. They'd had problems for quite some time before Siri went missing." She looked down for a few seconds, spotted a blue toy car on the rug beneath the table, and picked it up. "They'd been trying for a baby for a long time, without success."

Thomas leaned forward.

"They were struggling with IVF. The county council paid for three attempts, but they all failed." Susanna turned the car over and over in her fingers. Thomas could see into a bedroom with cars and other toys on the floor, and a shabby teddy bear on the bed.

"Siri wanted them to keep trying, even though they'd have to pay. Petter refused. It took its toll on their relationship. She was considering adoption, but he was against that, too."

"Do you know if they'd talked about divorce?"

"Siri hinted at it, but I don't know if she'd brought it up with Petter."

"What exactly did she say?"

"She didn't want to lose the chance to have a child. She mentioned the possibility of meeting someone else before it was too late."

"Have you any idea what Petter thought?" Aram asked.

"As I said, I don't know if they'd discussed it. If she'd . . . gotten around to it."

"If Petter had found out, how do you think he'd have reacted?" Thomas didn't want to ask leading questions; spontaneous answers were better, but he could feel the tension as he waited for her response.

"I mostly saw Siri on her own. We'd go out from time to time, then she'd sleep over here." Susanna's voice became unsteady. "I very rarely went to visit them on Djurö. I didn't enjoy Petter's company. I didn't like the tone he took with my sister, and when he drank too much, he could be pretty unpleasant."

"What was his problem?"

"Siri worked long hours. She enjoyed her job with the council, and she was very committed. To be honest, she was much brighter than Petter, and he couldn't handle it."

Thomas felt as if the comment was aimed at him, even though Susanna had no way of knowing that he, too, had lived with a woman who was always working. However, it had never bothered him that

Pernilla was smart and successful—on the contrary, he'd been proud of her. It was the sense of being dismissed, of always coming second, that had finally made him walk away.

At least that's what he told himself.

"We understood from your brother-in-law that Siri was moody and tearful when she went missing," Aram said. "Had she been like that for a long time?"

Susanna sat up a little straighter on the sofa. "She wasn't depressed, if that's what you're suggesting."

Aram exchanged a glance with Thomas, then checked his notes from the interview with Grandin.

"According to Petter, Siri was suffering from mood swings that summer. He said she seemed unhappy and discontented with their life."

"Siri was not depressed," Susanna repeated firmly. "I'm her sister—I ought to know. She was sad because they couldn't have children, nothing else."

There was a glint of something in Susanna's eyes. Was it guilt because she hadn't pushed harder in the original police inquiry, or loathing for her brother-in-law?

"I assume you know that the original case was shelved because it was assumed that Siri had taken her own life," Thomas said.

Susanna's grip on the toy car tightened.

"I've never believed that Siri killed herself. Never."

"Didn't our colleagues speak to you ten years ago?"

Susanna's cheeks flushed red.

"Everything was so confused back then. I was just about to give birth when Siri disappeared. My own relationship collapsed after that. I had a lot of reasons to be upset, plus I had a baby who needed me. It was as if I was surrounded by a thick fog."

Susanna shifted uncomfortably on the sofa. Thomas had a strong feeling that she was reluctant to go on; was she hiding something?

"I was suffering from postpartum depression," she went on without looking at either Thomas or Aram. "It wasn't Siri who was depressed, it was me. When the police told me she'd killed herself, I simply accepted it, even though I should have known better."

Susanna rubbed her forehead as if she could erase all those dark memories.

"I'm not sure if you know anyone who's been affected by postpartum depression, but it's a terrible thing. You turn into a different person, you can't sleep or concentrate. Life seems utterly hopeless. Guilt was eating me up, while at the same time I was panicking because I was such a bad mother. I couldn't handle Siri's disappearance on top of all that. I had my hands full fighting all the terrible thoughts that were going around and around in my head. It got so bad that I was afraid I might harm my own child."

Susanna paused, trying to regain control of her voice.

"It took me over a year to get back on my feet. My partner left me. When I found out that Petter had applied to have Siri declared dead, I didn't know what to do. Maybe I should have spoken to the police about my suspicions, but I had no evidence. Plus I was so tired and so low after everything that had happened. I let it go, pushed aside my concerns. It was easier that way."

Susanna stood up and fetched some tissues from the kitchen. She wiped her eyes and blew her nose before sitting down again.

"Sorry," she murmured.

"It's OK," Thomas said. "I can see that things have been difficult."

Susanna placed her hand on Thomas's arm and squeezed hard.

"You have to find out if it was Petter who murdered my sister. Promise!"

## *Siri*

The Friday traffic was crawling along, but it didn't matter. She had plenty of time; they weren't due to meet until later. It was nice to have a breathing space, without anyone demanding her attention.

This would be their first night together. Almost twenty-four blissful hours all to themselves. She felt a tingle of excitement. They'd booked a romantic little country hotel, far away from the city. They'd be able to relax—no one would recognize them.

She had dreamed for so long of falling asleep and waking up together, lying in the same bed, kissing and cuddling with no stress. Not having to shower and rush home, her body still aching with longing.

Each time they parted, she wanted more. It was becoming harder and harder to keep up a façade in front of Petter. She avoided him as much as she could, stayed late at work. When he asked why she was so quiet and withdrawn, she'd blamed it on the failed IVF treatment.

It was better that he thought she was miserable and grieving rather than finding out she was in love with someone else.

This morning she'd told him she was going out with Suss tonight, then staying over at her place in Liljeholmen. They wanted to spend some time together before the baby arrived. He'd barely glanced up from his newspaper.

There was no danger of Petter figuring out what was going on. Suss would never reveal that she wasn't there, if he happened to call her.

She really wanted everyone to know how happy she was, but she realized they had to be careful. It wouldn't look good if their relationship came out. She would never be able to explain it away. She didn't dare think about how many people would be hurt.

Siri still hadn't said anything to Suss, although the words had been on the tip of her tongue several times.

She pushed the thought of Petter's reaction out of her mind. He would be furious.

Her cell phone buzzed as the car in front of her began to move. She checked the display; the brief message made her smile foolishly at herself in the rearview mirror.

What would happen if she left Petter?

Would they move in together?

Siri shook her head. It was way too early for that kind of speculation. She mustn't start planning a future with a man she'd just embarked on an affair with, even if they had known each other for a long time.

However, it was a tempting idea.

She'd been miserable with Petter for years. Someone up there seemed to have taken pity on her at last.

Maybe it was her turn to be happy now?

# Chapter 28

The bed rocked. A little hand tugged at the covers. Seconds later, a warm body scrambled up onto the bed and thudded down next to her aching head.

"Mommy, I'm hungry," Julia chirruped in Nora's ear.

"Mmm."

"Are we going to have breakfast?"

Nora didn't want to wake up; she certainly didn't want to get up. Her head was pounding and her mouth tasted of dust. She was desperately thirsty, but the long trek to the bathroom to fetch a glass of water seemed like an impossible task.

She must have fallen asleep as soon as her head hit the pillow. She didn't even remember getting undressed or brushing her teeth. She'd drunk way too much wine.

Slowly the memory of the previous evening came back with devastating clarity.

Oh God, what had she said to Jonas? He'd been so good to her all summer; he'd really taken care of her.

Last night she'd turned into a vicious bitch, spitting one vile accusation after another at him. She'd made a huge effort to start an argument.

Nora closed her eyes tightly. Why had she done that? They hardly ever quarreled. That was one of the things she'd liked most about Jonas when they became a couple—the fact that he didn't stir up trouble to get his own way, as her ex-husband, Henrik, used to do.

She didn't want raised voices in front of the children. They shouldn't have to see their parents yelling at each other.

Thank God Julia had already been asleep by the time Nora turned on Jonas.

But still. What had made her so angry? How could she have said such terrible things? There had been a blackness inside her that had to come out, and the person she loved most had taken the brunt of her fury.

With some difficulty, she suppressed a groan.

"Mommy!"

Julia shook her shoulder. The pain in Nora's head made her gasp.

"Can we have breakfast soon? I want to go to the bakery for fresh rolls!"

"In a minute."

Nora forced herself to open her eyes, but the bright sunlight caused her so much pain that she immediately closed them again.

However, she did register that the other side of the bed was empty. Slowly she opened her eyes again. Jonas's side was undisturbed. He must have used one of the boys' rooms.

"Where's Daddy?" she mumbled. Every word was agony. She felt as if she had an iron band around her head. If someone had driven a metal spike into her ear, it couldn't have hurt more.

"Daddy's working," Julia announced cheerfully.

"What?"

"He kissed me and said good-bye before he went to catch the ferry."

*Oh no.* Jonas had already left. He was going to be away for four days, but she couldn't remember where he was flying to. Los Angeles? Or was it Hong Kong?

She wouldn't be able to apologize face to face. She'd have to call him as soon as she could manage to get out of bed.

What the hell had she done?

It was the wine. Too much booze turned her into a person she didn't like.

The truth was that she'd drunk at least a bottle yesterday, probably more. Considerably more than she usually drank, and a whole lot more than she could tolerate.

She had to pull herself together. She was going to be alone with Julia until Jonas came back; no way could she drink that much.

*No wine tonight,* she promised herself. *No wine for the rest of the week.*

# Chapter 29

Thomas and Aram were driving to the car showroom in Nacka where Petter Grandin worked. The conversation with Susanna Alptegen had left them with more questions than answers.

Thomas turned into the parking lot and was confronted by rows and rows of shiny new cars. He couldn't help comparing them with his old Volvo, which had definitely seen better days. Still, no point in dreaming of a new car; that wasn't something a cop on his pay grade could afford.

The restructuring had failed to improve salary levels in spite of all the promises the politicians had made, which merely added to the discontent among his colleagues.

They waited while the receptionist contacted Petter Grandin. He emerged from one of the offices set aside for client consultations at the far end of the showroom; his smile faded as soon as he saw the two detectives.

"What is it this time?" he said, buttoning his dark-blue jacket.

"Is there somewhere we can talk?" Aram asked politely.

"This way."

Petter led them into the room he'd just left. There was a model of a brand-new electric car on the desk—presumably the company's pride and joy. This was the future, gleaming "green" cars instead of gas-guzzling vehicles that were destroying the environment.

"What do you want?" Grandin snapped, sitting down behind the desk.

Aram got straight to the point. "We've discovered that you put a considerable amount of effort into having your wife declared dead so that you could make a claim on her life insurance."

"Who told you that?"

"That's the information we've been given," Aram replied, his face expressionless. "We'd like to hear what you have to say."

"I haven't done anything illegal, if that's what you're suggesting."

"It's unusual to request a formal declaration after such a short time," Thomas said.

Grandin stared at him. "It's unusual for a man's wife to disappear without a trace. Was there anything else?"

Thomas met his gaze and didn't speak for a few seconds. Sometimes silence was a good countermeasure.

"I was just trying to get on with my life," Grandin said. "Am I not allowed to do that?"

He suddenly seemed to realize that he had nothing to gain by provoking the two officers. He stopped scowling and produced a disarming smile.

"Sorry, I didn't mean to sound rude," he went on in a completely different tone. "I was just so taken aback when you came to see me the other day. Then you turn up here at my place of work. I didn't quite know how to behave."

Was this what Grandin sounded like when he was trying to sell a car to a new client? Reassuring and competent, with hints of something that was presumably supposed to be humility.

It came across as insincerity.

"As I've already told you, people whispered all kinds of things behind my back," he continued. "That's why I was on my guard when you came to the house. I apologize if I was a little . . . brusque."

No doubt Grandin was a good car salesman, the kind who made women feel valued and persuaded men to buy a more expensive model than they'd intended. He probably also knew a thing or two about psychology; that was what modern sales technique was based on, after all.

Perhaps he'd decided to try that technique on his unwelcome visitors? Thomas couldn't see any other explanation for the sudden change of heart.

"You had quite a payout from the insurance," he said.

Aram nodded. "Four million, if I remember correctly. People can do all kinds of things for that amount of money."

Grandin maintained his pleasant expression.

"Some would call it blood money," Aram added.

Grandin didn't bite back, in spite of the obvious provocation.

"Let me explain," he said, spreading his hands wide. "I had no idea that Siri had life insurance through her job. I only found out when almost a year had passed—the insurance company contacted me." He gave a little smile, as if to say, *What was I supposed to do?*

"When I asked what documentation I needed to provide, they said I had to supply an application to have Siri declared dead. They told me how to go about it. I had no idea it was unusually early to make such an application—I just followed their recommendations."

"You didn't consider the possibility that she might come back?" Aram's tone made his opinion of the situation pretty clear.

"You mean did I think Siri could still be alive?" Grandin sounded genuinely surprised. "I was convinced that she was dead, that she'd taken her own life. She didn't want to go on living, especially not with me. We were hardly speaking to each other over those last few weeks. She avoided my company, and sometimes I noticed her crying when she thought I'd fallen asleep." His voice was a little hoarse. He looked down and traced a pattern on the surface of the desk with his index finger. "We couldn't have children."

On the other side of the glass wall, an elderly couple was studying a used Renault Mégane. A saleswoman was circling the car, pointing out its many features.

"It was a great source of sorrow to both of us," Grandin continued. "We'd gone through three rounds of IVF, and it hadn't worked. The county council refused to pay for any further attempts. Siri found it very difficult to come to terms with the reality."

"Did you consider adoption?" Thomas asked.

"We talked about it, but by that stage our relationship wasn't in a good place. Starting the adoption process felt completely wrong."

He turned to Aram as if he instinctively knew that Aram was the more cynical of the two.

"Siri wasn't well during that last summer. In hindsight, I've realized that she must have been deeply unhappy, and that I was the cause." He tugged at one sleeve. "I wasn't too good either. I was drinking way too much, and it made me short-tempered. We quarreled often, and I said things that I regretted afterward. But I had no idea she was planning to kill herself. If I'd had any idea what Siri had in mind, of course I'd have behaved differently."

Grandin had succeeded in refuting all of Susanna Alptegen's accusations, delivering one reasonable explanation after another. The admission that he'd been drinking too much came across as genuine and honest. Unless, of course, it was a way of forestalling police inquiries so that his alcohol consumption couldn't be used against him.

Who to believe—the husband or the sister?

"You must understand that I could never have imagined that she'd simply disappear," Grandin said. "But in a strange way, I wasn't surprised, even though it was a terrible shock. That summer was terrible, the worst period in my life. I was completely broken afterward."

Aram had listened without interrupting, but he still didn't seem convinced.

"We've been told that Siri's family opposed the application to have her declared dead," he said now. "Apparently her sister was extremely upset."

"Suss? Have you spoken to her?"

Aram nodded.

"I don't want to speak ill of Siri's sister," Grandin said with a barely perceptible shift in his tone, "but Susanna isn't a stable person. She never has been."

"Oh?"

"She's very . . . highly strung. She got worse when her son was born. She suffered from postpartum depression, and it took a long time for her to recover. Her partner couldn't handle it; he walked out before the baby's first birthday." Grandin grimaced. It was impossible to tell whether he really cared about his former sister-in-law or not. "Maybe she didn't mention that little detail to you?"

"We're more interested in Siri's state of mind than her sister's," Thomas informed him.

"Do you mind if we contact the insurance company to verify the information you've given us?" Aram said. "Who got in touch with whom and when?"

Grandin frowned. "As I've already told you, I've tried to move on. Siri's been dead for ten years, for God's sake!"

Thomas was unmoved. "We're aware of that, but as I'm sure you understand, we have to do our job."

Grandin didn't attempt to hide his irritation. "You're stirring everything up again! Haven't you got better things to do?"

"Do you mind if we contact the insurance company?" Aram repeated.

The last trace of Petter Grandin's professional charm disappeared.

"Do whatever the hell you want," he muttered.

# Chapter 30

It was ten thirty. The pool was full of children, and the swimming lesson was about to begin. Nora had made a huge effort and managed to get Julia there on time. Two painkillers and a large cup of coffee had got her moving, but she still needed wraparound shades if she was going to appear in public.

She had dragged herself to the bakery with Julia to buy fresh breakfast rolls; the smell had almost made her throw up.

Some of the other parents were chatting in the shade of a parasol. Nora kept her distance; there was no way she could make small talk in her current condition, and she didn't want anyone to realize how ill she was feeling. Becoming the subject of the latest gossip was the last thing she needed.

The argument with Jonas was still going around and around in her head, all the terrible things she'd said to him thanks to the wine. Why had she drunk so much last night? Why hadn't she had the sense to stop?

Nora didn't recognize herself, and that scared her.

Jonas hadn't even left her a note in the kitchen as he usually did when he left early.

She could hardly blame him.

She went into the girls' changing room and drank some water straight from the faucet. The place was empty, thank goodness, and blissfully quiet. She sank down on a bench and rested her head against the wall. Closed her eyes and tried to ignore the smell of dampness. She'd already checked her phone at least a dozen times to see if Jonas had texted her, but she took it out again. Nothing.

She had to stop brooding over Jonas, it was too difficult. She tried to focus on other things instead, like the previous day's conversation with Johanna Strand. She'd mentioned Monica Forsell's boyfriend, Zacharias. It had to be Zacharias Fahlman, she thought again; who else could it be?

If she could find out something about Astrid's disappearance, she might be able to make a difference in a way she hadn't done in Mina's case. Maybe she would be able to stop feeling worthless all the time.

Nora glanced at her watch. The swimming lesson lasted for an hour. She could easily hurry over to Zacharias's house, see if he was home. He lived in the forest just beyond the tennis courts, if she remembered correctly.

If she stayed here worrying about yesterday evening, she would go crazy. She left the changing room and went out into the sunshine.

Julia was totally focused on practicing her backstroke. She wouldn't notice if Nora disappeared for a little while. There was no requirement for parents to stay; it was more of a habit. Under normal circumstances, it was nice to hang out and chat.

Before Nora could change her mind, she slipped out through the half-open gate and set off toward the forest at a brisk pace.

# CHAPTER 31

The meeting began a few minutes after Aram and Thomas returned to Flemingsberg. Margit had called everyone together at one o'clock.

Thomas sat down next to Staffan Nilsson, who had already undone the top buttons of his white shirt. Several windows were wide open, but there wasn't the slightest breeze. The conference room felt like a sauna.

Margit tapped her pen on the table. "Shall we begin? I hope you've got something for me; there's a lot of pressure in this investigation."

She clearly wasn't happy about the situation.

Thomas summarized the interviews he and Aram had conducted.

"Grandin obviously had a motive for getting rid of his wife," Margit said. "But that's also the only concrete piece of information we have to go on. The fact that there are unresolved issues between him and his sister-in-law doesn't necessarily mean anything."

"I just think it's too much of a coincidence," Aram said, frowning. "The wife vanishes without a trace. The case is written off as a presumed suicide, which the sister disputes. Then four million kronor drops into the husband's bank account."

Aram's antipathy toward Grandin hadn't diminished in the slightest. Thomas hoped his feelings weren't compromising his ability to remain objective, yet at the same time it was hard to disagree. There was a suppressed rage within Grandin that was impossible to ignore. So far he couldn't tell if it had been directed at Siri, but he could understand why Susanna blamed her brother-in-law for Siri's disappearance.

"We ought to tap his phone," Aram continued. "If we're in luck, we've frightened him into doing something that will give him away."

Ida nodded but didn't say anything.

"We don't have enough," Margit said firmly. "No prosecutor will give us permission unless we have concrete evidence. And why would he chat on the phone about a murder he might possibly have committed ten years ago?"

"We don't even know if the remains are those of Siri Grandin," Nilsson pointed out.

"And that's the next problem," Margit said. "Nor do we have confirmation of the gender yet."

"The National Forensics Lab called me this morning," Nilsson informed her. "They're sending the bones to the National Board of Forensic Medicine for genetic forensic examination to see if it's possible to obtain any DNA."

Thomas sighed. That was disappointing; he'd hoped that Sachsen would be able to help them, even though he had so little to go on.

"How does that work?" Ida said almost to herself, as if she didn't quite dare to ask the question.

Nilsson heard her. "They use a technique that involves grinding the bones down to powder; they can extract enough DNA from that powder to create a profile, which can then be compared with existing data or profiles from blood relatives. It's pretty successful."

Ida nodded and made a note.

"Does it matter which parts of a skeleton have been found?" Thomas asked. He was thinking about the collection of tiny fragments he'd seen lying on the ground in evidence bags on Telegrafholmen. Sachsen had said he needed something larger, like a pelvis or cranium, in order to move forward.

"Not really—it's the condition of the bones that's important. If they've been in the ground for a long time, or exposed to moisture or strong sunshine, it's more difficult."

There was probably a low risk of such exposure, since the bones seemed to have been buried on the island for years.

"How long until we hear from them?" Margit wanted to know.

Nilsson grimaced. "Well, it depends—it usually takes about a week, but of course some of their technicians will be on vacation . . ."

Aram sighed.

"Try and push them," Margit said.

Thomas rolled up his shirtsleeves; the heat in the room was unbearable. The victim's DNA wouldn't give them a cause of death, but hopefully it would lead to an identity, because DNA from both Siri Grandin and Astrid Forsell was on file. Since the beginning of the twenty-first century, a sample had automatically been taken whenever someone went missing.

Margit turned to Thomas. "What did you find out about Astrid Forsell? Anything that struck you as interesting?"

"Her mother has turned to religion. She's convinced that her daughter is dead, even though there's been no formal declaration." He'd asked Ida to check. "Monica believes that Astrid slipped on a rock and drowned, and that her body was carried out to sea. She insists it was an accident."

"Does she have any evidence?"

"None at all," Aram said. "Except that *the Lord* has confirmed her theory."

The fact that Aram himself was a practicing Christian didn't seem to affect his view of Monica Forsell's piety.

"There is one thing that doesn't fit," Thomas said. He quickly recounted his conversation with Astrid's father, Olav Hansen. "It doesn't necessarily mean anything. Astrid might simply have quarreled with her mother, but I'd like to take a closer look before we shelve the case."

"I can help," Ida offered. "It was me who found Hansen on Facebook."

To her palpable disappointment, no one around the table reacted.

Margit nodded. "Good. I took a look at the mother's background, and she seems to have lived a pretty wild life before her daughter disappeared. Kind of white trash, if you know what I mean."

Ida stiffened. "I'm sorry, what did you say?"

Margit raised her eyebrows. "What?"

"You called her white trash." Ida shuffled uncomfortably. "I'm sorry, but I don't think it's OK to use that kind of language. It's a very offensive expression, particularly from someone in authority, like you." There was a flash of anger in her blue eyes. "Class contempt like that doesn't sit well with me."

Thomas had worked with Margit for long enough to know how taken aback she was, even though her expression remained neutral.

A rookie officer didn't correct an inspector, especially not in front of other people. At the same time, Ida had a point. Internal jargon was probably a little too raw occasionally; it was easy to forget how it came across to someone who wasn't used to it. Society had changed, and many of the expressions in common usage ten years ago were no longer acceptable.

It was brave of Ida to challenge her boss in front of their colleagues, but her timing wasn't great.

However, Margit decided not to hit back at Ida's criticism.

"You're right, of course," she said. "Sometimes we need to be reminded to watch our language." She smiled and shook her head. "Monica Forsell's lifestyle left a great deal to be desired, but there's no need to use disparaging terminology."

Time to get back to the matter at hand. Thomas caught Margit's eye. "So what did you find out about Monica's background?"

She gave him an almost imperceptible nod of thanks.

"At the beginning of the nineties, she was hanging out in circles where both alcohol and drugs were plentiful. She partied hard even though she was a single mom with a young daughter."

"Was she ever arrested?" Aram asked.

"No, but Astrid's school contacted social services to express their concern when she was about fifteen. Nothing was done."

Aram got up to throw open another window, letting in warmer air. "What was it about? Had Astrid come to any harm?"

"The school was worried about her chaotic home life," Margit explained. "Social services called Monica in for an interview and made a home visit, but concluded that there was no reason to act, in spite of the fact that they found several empty bottles on the kitchen counter. Monica also had a boyfriend who'd been convicted of common assault."

"If Astrid was fifteen, then this must have happened about three years before she went missing," Thomas said. "Do we know if the boyfriend was still in the picture?"

"The answer is yes," Margit said. "He was interviewed, but nothing of interest came up."

"What was his name?"

Margit leafed through her notes.

"Here we are. He lives on Sandhamn, and his name is Zacharias Fahlman."

# Astrid

Astrid would never have believed it was possible to be so desperate for a five-minute cigarette break. She closed her eyes and leaned back against the sun-warmed white wooden wall. She was standing at the back of the Sailors Restaurant with Johanna, just by the staff entrance.

Johanna took a deep drag and blew a perfect smoke ring.

"My feet are killing me," she said. "I don't know how I'm going to get through the rest of the day. Do you think they'd let me go home early because of swollen toes?"

Astrid laughed and tapped the ash from her cigarette.

"Get yourself some different shoes," she suggested.

Johanna was wearing heels; Astrid usually went for sneakers. Her friend had always been the vainer of the two. She worried that her legs were too short, and claimed that she looked like a dachshund. The heels were her attempt to compensate. Maybe there was something in Johanna's assertion, but Astrid would never say so. Instead she reassured her each time Johanna mentioned it.

The sound of angry shouting came from an open window on the floor above them.

"Haven't you got anything better to do than to stand around gobbling food? You're here to work!"

Astrid looked up. She didn't recognize the voice, but someone was getting bawled out. Her stomach instinctively contracted, as it always did when someone yelled or became aggressive.

"You need to fix this!" the man snapped. "I'm sick of cleaning up after you. This is your last chance—understand?"

The other person mumbled an inaudible response. It sounded like a young boy.

Johanna glanced at the window. "What's going on up there?"

"I've no idea."

Johanna stubbed out her cigarette on the ground and dropped the butt in the ashtray on the steps. "Who's yelling? It's not Lillian."

"I don't know."

Astrid didn't like the man's dictatorial tone; it reminded her of Zacharias and the way he spoke to his horrible dog. Astrid hated the big black Rottweiler who followed Zacharias wherever he went.

Zacharias liked to boast about how well trained the dog was, how it obeyed the smallest gesture. More than once, Astrid had seen him let the dog hurl itself at someone, only to recall it at the very last second. When people got mad or scared, he would laugh and say that it only wanted to play. But what might happen if it decided not to obey him one day?

The voices upstairs had fallen silent. Johanna checked her watch. "We need to get back."

Astrid nodded. Her heart was beating a little too fast as they went in, even though she hadn't been involved in the fight.

# Chapter 32

Nora made her way quickly along the narrow duckboard that led through Seglarstaden. She turned left into the pine forest.

In minutes she was surrounded by thick tree trunks. Thousands of needles covered the ground, muting the sound of her footsteps. The treetops absorbed the sunshine, and the atmosphere of the archipelago disappeared as moss and low-growing blueberries gave the ground a green shimmer. If she hadn't been able to hear the crashing of the waves in the background, she could just as easily have been in the deep forests of Dalsland.

Zacharias Fahlman lived farther away than Nora had thought. She'd been walking for quite a while now. She had less than an hour; she would soon have to turn back.

*There.*

She could see the black roof of Fahlman's house up ahead. The place was completely isolated. Most homes on Sandhamn were either in the village or in the vacation complex at Trouville on the eastern side of the island. Few lived alone in the forest, with no neighbors in sight.

Nora was beginning to feel uncomfortably aware of how far she'd come, but she was almost there now. She glanced over her shoulder, half hoping that someone else out for a walk would appear.

She reached the scruffy wooden fence surrounding the property. The black wrought-iron gate was rusty, and wind and weather had taken their toll on the house itself.

There wasn't a sound, and Nora couldn't see any signs of life. Not even a window was open to let in some fresh air. An old moped with a flatbed trailer was parked a short distance away; did that mean Fahlman was home?

She placed her hand on the latch, then hesitated.

The yard was littered with scrap—rusty machinery, a battered metal wheelbarrow, a couple of broken buoys, and a pile of gray roof tiles covered in brown needles.

A few purple pansies were wilting in a cracked pot on the patio.

Should she forget the whole thing? It wasn't too late to change her mind. She could turn around, head back to the pool.

But she was here now.

Nora took a deep breath, opened the gate, and stepped into the yard.

Suddenly she heard loud, aggressive barking from behind the house. She stopped dead, sweat breaking out on her upper lip. She wasn't comfortable with dogs, especially the bigger ones that the owners found hard to control. She'd been bitten by a German shepherd when she was a child, which had made her wary of dogs ever since.

Another bark. Nora began to back away. She caught a movement out of the corner of her eye, and a dark shape came hurtling toward her.

She had nowhere to go.

# Chapter 33

Johanna poured herself a fresh cup of coffee and sat down at the kitchen table. She pushed away her empty breakfast plate and opened up her laptop, then keyed in her Internet banking code.

The balance stared back at her. Less than nine hundred kronor.

Even though she'd tried to cut back, there was hardly anything left in her account. The rent on her apartment in Vallentuna was due soon, and she'd need thousands for that.

She had no idea where she was going to get the money.

Being broke sucked. Plus it wasn't her fault she'd had to leave the restaurant in June. Anyway, she was glad to get away from the creep who owned the place. Hands everywhere whenever he got the chance, and he thought he was so funny when he commented on her breasts.

It was hardly surprising that she'd helped herself to the odd shot now and again, just to be able to put up with him, but he'd had the nerve to accuse her of stealing from him.

She'd left the same day.

Johanna took a sip of her coffee. It was still too hot and scalded her tongue, but she didn't let that stop her.

She had to find money from somewhere.

She hated the thought of looking for another waitressing job. It was hard work, and she was tired of whining customers and bad-tempered bosses. And college wasn't a viable alternative. She'd never be able to handle all those hours of study and thousands of pages of reading, however much her mom nagged her about working toward a decent profession.

A dream had taken root over the past few months: training to be a hairdresser. She'd always liked playing around with her own hair, trying out different styles and colors. She'd done Astrid's hair a thousand different ways when they were growing up.

There were plenty of jobs for hairdressers, according to an article she'd read about the future employment market.

Unfortunately, the training cost almost a hundred thousand. Even if she found herself a waitressing job and studied part-time, she wouldn't be able to afford the first payment, let alone anything else.

She couldn't pay her rent, and she'd never get away from the daily grind.

Johanna stared gloomily at the screen. Eight hundred and ninety-seven kronor, that was all she had. It was like a summary of her life: almost broke, and a failure.

Somehow she had to get ahold of some money.

# CHAPTER 34

The big black Rottweiler was making straight for Nora, teeth bared, saliva dripping from its jaws. Its ears were flattened against its head. It was even more terrifying at close quarters. It probably weighed the same as her, but seemed to consist entirely of muscle, sharp claws, and teeth.

Nora was panting. What was she going to do? In seconds it would bury its teeth in her arms and legs.

Her heart was pounding as if it were about to burst.

She wanted to scream, but fear had paralyzed her vocal cords.

She could see its eyes now, staring angrily at her. Sand whirled up around its black claws as it ran faster and faster.

Time slowed down.

The dog was about to attack when a piercing whistle split the air. The animal stopped dead and stood at her feet as if it were made of stone, mouth open, showing those powerful teeth.

She could smell its acrid breath, and a low growl was coming from its throat, but at least it wasn't moving.

Nora couldn't move either.

The Rottweiler growled again, muscles tensed. The short black coat gleamed in the sun peeking through the trees.

Nora's entire body was shaking. She had to fight not to lose control. Every instinct told her to run, but she didn't dare risk provoking the dog into a fresh onslaught.

Endless seconds passed, then a man in shabby dungarees appeared from the back of the house. His hair was gray and lank, and a little too long.

Zacharias Fahlman stopped and stared at her.

"I hope you didn't let Mason scare you?" he said, even though it was obvious what had happened. He grinned, making no attempt to recall the animal.

Nora was still incapable of moving. Mason kept his eyes fixed on her.

"Can't you put him on a leash?" she called out. The fear in her voice didn't help.

"He only attacks when someone comes onto my land without permission," Fahlman said. He came forward and took hold of the dog's collar. "Good boy. Lie down."

The dog obeyed instantly.

"He's dangerous!" Nora said, backing away.

"What are you doing in my yard?"

Nora wanted to sound calm, but tripped over her words. "Dogs h-have to be o-on a l-leash on the island."

"Not on private property." Fahlman patted Mason's head. "You only have yourself to blame if you ignore the warning." He pointed to a sign Nora hadn't noticed: "BEWARE OF THE DOG."

Her fear was quickly replaced by anger.

"You can't have an aggressive dog running loose! What if he'd gone for a small child?"

"A child can't open the gate—it's too heavy. I'll ask you again: What are you doing in my yard?"

Nora made an effort to pull herself together. Did she have the nerve to bring up the subject of Astrid Forsell's disappearance? Fahlman was already irritated; she didn't want him to become aggressive, too.

The horrible Rottweiler was still lying at her feet. Presumably his master only had to click his fingers for Mason to turn on her again. She searched for something to say.

"My name is Nora Linde. I'm a prosecutor. It's about Astrid Forsell."

Fahlman's eyes narrowed.

Nora's courage failed her. She couldn't ask him about Astrid's disappearance, it was too risky. She had no idea how he'd react. Her mouth was so dry that her tongue was sticking to her palate. She scrabbled around for a reasonable explanation, something that would sound convincing.

He stood there with his legs apart, hands on his hips, waiting for her to continue. He was a big man, tall and muscular. She could see his impressive biceps beneath the sleeves of his T-shirt.

The dog let out a faint growl.

Suddenly Nora's phone began to ring in her pocket. She dug it out and muttered, "Sorry," in Fahlman's direction. The display showed *Julia*.

"Hi, sweetheart."

"Mommy, where are you?"

Only now did Nora realize that she'd completely lost track of time. The swimming lesson must have finished long ago.

"Everyone's left," Julia went on, her voice trembling. "There's only me and the instructor left."

"Darling, I'm so sorry. I'm coming now."

Nora held up her phone as proof that she was in a hurry.

"Sorry. The whole thing was a misunderstanding. That was my daughter. I have to go."

She turned and scuttled away with her tail between her legs.

## *Siri*

It sounded as if Petter had fallen asleep. He was breathing slowly and evenly behind Siri's back, and from time to time he let out a snore.

She ought to try to get some sleep as well; it was almost midnight. Instead she was lying awake, her head spinning with thoughts that gave her no peace. On top of that, the heartburn she'd had all evening was getting worse.

Next weekend she was going on vacation with her husband, despite the fact that she wanted to be with someone else.

The idea of spending two weeks with Petter on a small island was unbearable.

Two weeks when she wouldn't hear that voice she loved so much, because Petter would be around all the time.

She didn't know how she was going to be able to pretend everything was fine. Sit with him day after day, night after night, like a good wife.

Siri couldn't suppress a sob.

She felt so guilty. She'd never pictured herself in this situation, never imagined she'd have an affair behind her husband's back.

When she'd said yes to Petter, promised to stay with him for better or worse, she'd been convinced that they would be together for the rest of their lives. The love between them had been so strong; it had seemed impossible that it could fade.

Now she could hardly bear it when he tried to touch her. She pushed him away, blaming a migraine or period pains.

On vacation she wouldn't be able to come up with excuses every day.

The last time they'd had sex had been terrible. She'd gritted her teeth so hard that her jaws ached. She'd had to steel herself, hang on in there until he was done. She'd tried to tell herself that other fingers were caressing her, other lips kissing her, when all she really wanted to do was push him off her and get out of bed.

Afterward she'd felt cheap and dirty, and spent an eternity in the shower, weeping beneath the cascade of hot water and wishing she were miles away.

It was as if she'd betrayed her lover with Petter instead of vice versa.

The moon shone in through the gap between the roller blind and the window ledge.

Petter would be so mad if she canceled their vacation plans at this late stage. They'd already paid for the cottage in advance, and he was careful with money. But she just couldn't face going to the island with him; it was out of the question.

Siri curled up on her side, staring out into the darkness. She had to find a reason why she couldn't go. Something that wouldn't make him suspicious.

Or furious.

# Chapter 35

Nora's heart was still pounding when she left the pool, holding Julia by the hand.

That horrible dog had really frightened her, and Zacharias Fahlman hadn't been much better. The way he'd looked at her had been extremely unpleasant, as if he were evaluating the balance of power between them.

He was horrible, although his rugged looks probably meant he was used to charming those around him. It was hardly surprising that Astrid had hated him, or that Johanna had described him as vile.

Nora and Julia passed the mini-golf course and came out by the harbor. Behind the Sailors Restaurant, the glass-recycling containers were being emptied.

"Why didn't you come for me?" Julia said.

Nora had already apologized several times, both to her daughter and to Fia, the swimming instructor. Thank goodness Jonas was away and wouldn't find out that she'd turned up late.

"Sorry, sweetheart," she said yet again. "Maybe an ice cream will make you feel better?"

Julia's face lit up. She pointed to the ice-cream kiosk on the other side of the little play area, where several children were already enjoying themselves on the pirate ship and the swings.

"From over there? Three scoops?"

"Absolutely."

This wasn't a day for holding back. Julia could have her three scoops in a cone, even if it was twice as expensive as an ordinary ice pop.

As they set off for the kiosk, Johanna came cycling along the track. Nora called out and waved to her to stop. She bent down to Julia. "Why don't you go and decide which flavors you want, and I'll be there in a minute."

Julia looked uncertain.

"Honestly, this won't take long," Nora assured her. "Off you go."

Julia ran off as Johanna reluctantly dismounted from her bicycle.

"Hi," Nora said. "Thanks for the other day. Do you have a minute?"

Today, Johanna had swapped her shorts and T-shirt for a short pale-gray summer dress. She had a livid bruise on one calf.

"Why? I'm kind of in a rush."

Nora positioned herself in front of the bicycle to stop Johanna from leaving.

"I happened to see Zacharias Fahlman today. He was pretty unpleasant. I can see what you meant."

Johanna looked horrified. "You didn't tell him I'd been talking about him?"

"Absolutely not."

Johanna started chewing her thumbnail. Was she so frightened of Fahlman?

"I just wanted to say you were right," Nora went on. "That vicious dog nearly bit me."

The explanation seemed to reassure Johanna. Her shoulders dropped and she relaxed a little. "He always has Rottweilers. He had a different one when he was with Monica, but it was just the same—big and aggressive. Astrid was scared of it. So was I." She shuddered.

"How long was Zacharias with Astrid's mom?" Nora asked, hoping the question wouldn't put Johanna on her guard again.

"Three or four years, I think. It ended after Astrid disappeared. Monica blamed herself."

"I believe she sought solace in the church."

"She found religion and changed her lifestyle completely." Johanna's expression hardened. "Pity she didn't do it earlier, while Astrid was still around." She put one foot on the pedal. "I really have to go."

"Can I just ask you one more question? You said that Astrid didn't have a boyfriend, but that she was popular."

The sound of a horn came from behind them, and they had to move to one side to let the forklift truck from the Sailors Restaurant get by.

"Was there anyone who seemed particularly fond of her?" Nora ventured. "Maybe a little more than was healthy?"

"I don't really remember . . ." Johanna leaned on her bicycle; it was a real Sandhamn bike, a faithful old friend painted blue, with no gears. Johanna looked as if she'd rather be anywhere else.

"Surely there must have been someone who really liked her?" Nora prompted.

"There was a guy she spent time with," Johanna admitted reluctantly. "But he was sweet. He'd never have done anything to hurt her."

"What was his name?"

Johanna gazed out across the water. A beautiful old wooden yacht, a Mälar 30, was just mooring at one of the jetties.

"Niklas." She frowned. "I don't remember his surname, but it was a fairly common one, I think."

"Was he an islander?"

"No."

"So how did they meet?"

"He had a summer job at the restaurant, just like us."

Johanna swung her leg over the bike, and out of the corner of her eye, Nora saw Julia waving at her. Johanna set off toward Seglarstaden.

*Niklas.* If Nora was going to get anywhere with this, she had to find out his family name. And where she could contact him.

# Chapter 36

It was almost three o'clock when Thomas stuck his head around Aram's door. His colleague was studying his computer screen, a half-eaten apple in his hand.

"Are you busy? Can we talk?"

"Come on in."

Thomas sank down in the visitor's chair and stretched out his long legs.

"I'm getting bad vibes from both cases," he began. "We're getting nowhere."

Aram gave a half smile. "I'd still bet on Petter Grandin."

Thomas grimaced. "I think I'd figured that out."

Aram turned the screen so that Thomas could see. "Look at this. Grandin's made the most of the insurance payout. Expensive vacations and a share portfolio with Handelsbanken. He also bought an apartment in southern Spain. None of that would have been possible without the insurance." He took another bite of his apple, a contented gleam in his eye as he sat back.

"The question is how we prove he committed a crime," Thomas said. "Otherwise everything you've found is perfectly legitimate. It's not illegal to receive a payment after someone dies."

His cell phone rang. He glanced at the display but didn't recognize the number. He decided to take the call.

"Andreasson."

"Hi . . . it's Susanna."

It took him a couple of seconds to realize who it was. Siri's sister, of course. It was only a few hours since they'd spoken to her.

"Sorry to bother you," she added.

"No problem," Thomas said, and mouthed "Susanna Alptegen" to Aram.

"There's something I didn't tell you when you came to see me . . ." She sounded so hesitant that he wondered if she was about to hang up. "Maybe it's dumb, but I can't get it out of my head. I've never mentioned this to the police, but you said I should contact you if I thought of anything . . ."

"I'm pleased to hear from you," Thomas reassured her. "That's why I gave you my card."

Aram pointed to the phone and whispered: "Speakerphone."

"Do you mind if I put you on speaker?" Thomas said. "I'm here with my colleague Aram Gorgis, whom you also met this morning."

Silence. Had it been a mistake to tell Susanna he wasn't alone?

"OK," she said eventually.

Thomas pressed the icon and placed the phone on the desk. "Great. What did you want to tell us?"

"It's because of what you said about Siri being depressed during those last weeks. That just isn't true."

"You already told us that."

"In fact, she seemed happier than she'd been for a long time, and I think I know why." Susanna paused. "I think she'd met someone."

Aram joined in the conversation. "Met someone?"

"I'm pretty sure Siri was having an affair."

A secret lover. That strengthened Aram's theory.

"What makes you think that?" Thomas asked.

"Siri was different, beautiful in a new way. She'd put on a little weight, and it suited her. There was a kind of glow about her, as there often is when someone's just fallen in love. I noticed it a few times."

Aram was scribbling notes as Susanna talked. "You've no idea who it might be?"

"She never mentioned it, and to be honest, I never came straight out and asked her. I got the feeling she wanted to keep it to herself."

"Weren't you close?"

"We were."

"So isn't it strange that she didn't tell you?"

A few seconds passed before Susanna answered.

"Yes," she said unhappily. "But as I told you earlier, I was heavily pregnant that summer, and I had too many other things on my mind. In hindsight, I wish I'd spoken to Siri, of course, but at the time my entire focus was on the baby." Her voice almost broke. "I was in a world of my own. If I'd known she was going to disappear, then of course I'd have asked. I've regretted it so many times."

Aram cleared his throat. "Can you think of anyone in her circle of acquaintances that she might have been seeing?"

"I have given it some thought, and . . ."

Aram unconsciously leaned closer to the phone.

"There was a neighbor she really liked."

"What do you know about him?" Thomas asked.

"Not much. There was a group of friends who used to hang out on Djurö. They played golf on the course at Värmdö, celebrated Midsummer together, that kind of thing. I remember her talking about him after a spring party at the golf club; she seemed smitten."

"Did you ever meet him?"

"I'm afraid not."

"Do you remember any other details?"

*Try,* Thomas thought. *You must have picked up something—a name, where he worked, anything that could help us identify him.*

"His name might have been Anders or Albert, I'm not sure. I'm sorry, it was a long time ago."

"That's great. Thank you so much for calling—this information could be very useful," Thomas said warmly.

Susanna's voice was thick with tears. "I'm wondering if Petter found out about the affair? If that's why Siri . . . disappeared?"

# CHAPTER 37

Siri Grandin's file lay open in front of Thomas on the table in the conference room. All the transcripts of interviews with neighbors, friends, colleagues. Conversations with her husband, Siri's medical notes, background checks.

They'd decided to go over everything again. If Susanna's suspicions about an affair were correct, then surely someone else would have picked up on it ten years ago.

However, there was nothing in the original files to suggest a secret lover. Aram returned from the kitchen with two cups of coffee.

"Sorry for the delay," he said. "I had to take a call. Anything of interest?"

Thomas was shaking his head when Ida came into the room.

"What are you doing?" she asked.

Thomas gestured toward the papers.

"Siri Grandin's sister Susanna just called us. She thinks Siri might have been having an affair, but I can't find any evidence to support her theory."

Ida sat down and stared intently at the documents.

"Was it a man or a woman? Do we know that Siri was straight?"

Thomas had to admit that he hadn't even asked the question. Ida had a way of challenging accepted truths. Just because Siri was married to a man, it didn't mean she couldn't have been attracted to a woman. It was easy to follow the same well-worn track; a fresh perspective was exactly what was needed.

"The sister thought it was a man," Aram said, "but she didn't know much apart from that."

"Hardly surprising if he was a *secret* lover," Ida pointed out.

She was right, of course. Susanna had said that Siri didn't want to talk about it.

"Siri didn't even tell her sister, and they had a close relationship," Thomas said.

"Maybe she was afraid that the sister would give her away?"

"Hardly. Susanna has never liked Petter Grandin, and it seems to be mutual," Aram said.

"The lover must have been someone who had a lot to lose if it came out," Ida mused. "I mean, she didn't meet him on Tinder, did she?"

Thomas didn't bother explaining that Tinder didn't exist back then. Nor was he about to admit that he himself had used the app in a moment of weakness, but had quickly deleted it. Searching for a new woman in that way just felt depressing, plus he wasn't really interested in anyone else. He still missed Pernilla—the old Pernilla, the woman who had wanted *him* more than anything else, the woman who would never have thought of putting her job before her husband.

"Maybe he was married, too?" Ida went on. "They both wanted to keep it a secret, at least until they'd decided to leave their respective partners."

Sounded logical.

"Susanna mentioned a neighbor," Aram recalled. "She thought his name was Anders or Albert, something like that. If he was part of their circle of friends, they certainly wouldn't have wanted the affair to become common knowledge."

"What if it was a neighbor's son?" Ida was on a roll now. "Someone who was way too young for Siri. That would have caused a real scandal!"

She tapped the side of her nose with her index finger, as if she had a secret. Aram tried to give her a skeptical look but couldn't help laughing.

"Can you do some digging?" Thomas suggested. "See what you can find out? Local gossip at the golf club, maybe."

"You realize what this means for Grandin's position as the grieving husband? The insurance payout might have been a lucky break, but if he'd found out that his wife was betraying him with another man . . ." Aram linked his fingers together and pulled until the knuckles cracked.

"That's a horrible noise," Ida said. Aram grinned and did it again, then grew serious. "I think we've found our motive. We know why Grandin wanted to kill his wife."

# Chapter 38

Nora was lying at the very edge of Julia's bed, trying to get her to go to sleep. She wanted to be the kind of mom who read bedtime stories and liked to stay until her daughter was sleeping peacefully. Reading to children was important. It was wrong to replace closeness with electronic gadgets and the Internet.

And yet she was sorely tempted to put on an audiobook and creep out of the room. She'd already been curled up on the coverlet for half an hour. She longed for some time to herself; it had been a long, confusing day.

She felt a pang of guilt; how could she be so selfish? Julia had to come first. How could she think that staying a few minutes longer was a chore?

She wasn't just a useless prosecutor who'd failed to do her job properly, she was a crap mother as well.

She was so tired of messing up.

At long last, Julia closed her eyes. The little body relaxed and grew heavy. Nora gently withdrew the arm on which Julia's head was resting; needless to say, her daughter's eyes immediately flew open.

"Mommy?"

"Go to sleep, sweetheart."

When the boys were little, she'd done exactly the same thing, lying beside them reading stories until they nodded off. Adam and Simon had shared a room for the first few years. The family had lived in the house across the street before Nora inherited the Brand villa. That was where Astrid had taken care of them.

Once again, she pictured Astrid's face, and questions filled her mind. Where did the mysterious Niklas fit in? Nora wanted to find out as much as possible about him. Johanna had also mentioned Lillian, the restaurant manager. Maybe she had some vital information?

Dusk had fallen, and the room was in semidarkness now. The window was ajar to let in the evening air, but Nora was still sweaty from lying so close to Julia.

She must be asleep by now. Nora longed to go and sit on the veranda and enjoy the last moments of the sunset. She could feel the anxiety coming back; the only way to keep it at bay was to focus on something else.

She really wanted to call Mina and make sure she was OK, that Emir Kovač hadn't gotten ahold of her and Lukas. Maybe she would answer eventually if Nora tried often enough?

She gently attempted to withdraw her arm again, and this time her daughter didn't move. Silently she crept out of the room and went down to the kitchen to make herself a cup of tea.

Jonas hadn't responded to any of her calls during the day. He hadn't even sent her a text message, which he usually did before the plane took off.

*He was probably too busy,* she reassured herself. She couldn't remember an argument like this. Yelling at each other just wasn't their style, and the fact that she'd started it made her feel so much worse.

Her glance fell on the half-empty wine bottle from yesterday, which was still on the counter. She hadn't carried out her threat to pour it down the sink when she'd stormed out. There were at least two glasses left. Best to get rid of it now. She hadn't drunk all day, just as she'd promised herself when she woke up.

She'd try Mina first. Everything would seem so much better if she knew that Mina and her son were safe and well.

She took her phone out of her back pocket and scrolled down to Mina's name. Listened to the signals ringing out, one after another.

*Please, please pick up.*

The call ended without going to voice mail. As usual. She hadn't expected anything else, but disappointment still overwhelmed her. What had happened to Mina? Why didn't she get in touch if she was all right?

Almost two months had passed since they'd spoken, and Nora couldn't stop worrying. What if Kovač had tracked down Mina and Lukas . . .

She remembered her latest nightmare about him, and shuddered. It still felt way too real. Her skin was covered in goose bumps, and she had to swallow hard to keep control.

She put away her phone and reached for the bottle. Her head drooped, her body was weighed down by despair. What good would it do if she poured the wine down the drain? Jonas was already mad at her, and he obviously didn't care since he wasn't answering his phone. The boys were in town; they had their own lives these days.

Nobody would know if she had a small glass. If she didn't allow herself sleeping pills or wine, she'd be lying awake for hours, with all those terrible thoughts filling her head.

She took a deep breath; she couldn't bear it.

Today had been terrible. The fear when the dog came rushing toward her was still there; she'd been convinced that he was going to attack. Even worse, she'd gotten nowhere with Astrid's case. She wasn't much wiser than the previous day.

Nothing was going her way right now.

She couldn't resist the urge any longer. Tomorrow, she swore to herself. Tomorrow, she would drink nothing but water.

Nora opened the cupboard and reached for a glass. One glass of wine couldn't do any harm. Just one, to help her sleep.

The crystal sparkled in the lamplight. It was too obvious. If anyone happened to stop by, she didn't want them to know she was drinking on her own.

She put back the glass and chose a mug instead. She filled it with red wine, then went and sat in the wicker chair on the veranda. The sea was calm and shining; the sky in the west was still pale blue.

The first sip tasted delicious.

She took another and felt her body relax. At last she could breathe again. Her shoulders dropped.

*This is the last time,* she told herself. *I won't drink a drop tomorrow.*

But tonight she needed this.

# *Astrid*

Astrid ran down the stairs for a quick cigarette break. She'd been working for hours; the place was full as usual. The Sailors was having a good summer.

It was an overcast evening, with heavy rain clouds over the mainland, but Astrid longed for some fresh air. The restaurant was hot and stuffy.

When she opened the door, she saw that someone was already out there smoking. She recognized him—Niklas, that was his name. He was pretty cute—she'd already noticed him. Unusually tall, but with fine features. He wasn't really her type; he was way too shy and quiet, plus she didn't like boys her own age, she never had. Especially on Sandhamn, where everyone knew everyone else.

Her shoes crunched on the gravel as she stepped outside. Niklas turned and raised a hand in greeting.

"Hi. I guess you needed a smoke, too."

Astrid took out a packet of Princes and nodded. "Mmm."

Niklas offered his lighter like a true gentleman. Astrid placed the cigarette between her lips and leaned forward.

They'd never had a conversation. He was working as a busboy in the restaurant, while she ran herself into the ground as a waitress. She'd heard this was his first summer, too.

"Busy night?"

Astrid shrugged and took a deep drag. A few weeks had passed, and she'd begun to get used to it. Her arms didn't ache as much, and she'd learned to take tiny breaks whenever she had the chance.

Niklas didn't say a great deal, but somehow it didn't matter. The silence was restful rather than uncomfortable. Astrid liked the fact that they could stand there smoking quietly together. Most people talked too much anyway. Her mother never shut up.

Niklas cleared his throat. "Do you like swimming?" he asked, eyes fixed firmly on the ground.

"It's OK."

He swallowed, his Adam's apple clearly visible. He was obviously summoning up his courage to ask her something, and Astrid couldn't help smiling. She took another drag while she waited for him to continue.

"Are you doing anything tomorrow?" Niklas said, a little too quickly. "We could go over to one of the islands if you want. I've got a Jet Ski." He blushed slightly; Astrid thought it was kind of sweet. She was free tomorrow, but Johanna wasn't. They were on different shifts this week, for some reason.

Niklas pushed his light-brown hair behind his ears in a way that was quite cool. He was actually very cute close-up. He had unusually thick eyelashes for a boy.

"Why not?" Astrid said, surprising herself.

Niklas looked so relieved; she realized he'd hardly dared to ask. She liked that; he wasn't cocky, and he hadn't assumed she'd say yes.

"What time?" she added with a smile.

# Chapter 39

The corridor outside Thomas's office was in darkness. He was the only one left in the department; everyone else had gone home long ago. He stretched and yawned. He'd finished going through the additional background material gathered by his colleagues on Petter Grandin.

He stared at a photograph of Siri's farewell postcard. One single word: *Sorry.*

No address or stamp. It had been left in the mailbox, according to Grandin; he'd assumed Siri had put it there. It was written with a thick felt-tip pen; impossible to tell if it was Siri's handwriting or not. Ten years ago, no one had checked whether Grandin himself might have been responsible. It would have to be sent for analysis.

They'd decided to focus on Siri's disappearance, even though they were still waiting to hear from the National Board of Forensic Medicine. There were too many things that didn't fit. The more they dug into the case, the more question marks popped up.

They hadn't forgotten about Astrid Forsell, however. Thomas still wanted to check out what her father had said, and Monica's boyfriend, but as usual there was a shortage of resources.

It was a matter of prioritizing, as Margit often said with an ironic smile.

His phone rang, shattering the restful silence.

"Hi, it's Susanna Alptegen," a voice said tentatively. "Am I disturbing you?"

Thomas looked around the room, which was in semidarkness beyond the glow of the lamp. An empty Coca-Cola can and the remains of a greasy burger lay in front of him.

He was a walking, talking cliché. The lonely, divorced cop eating junk food at his desk, working late into the night because he had no one to go home to.

"No problem," he said, glad that she couldn't see his face or where he was. "What can I do for you?"

"I was just wondering how things are going?"

It was less than six hours since their last conversation.

"I'm afraid we haven't had time to get much further since we spoke earlier."

"Oh, I'm sorry. I didn't think." Susanna sounded exhausted. Maybe she, too, was sitting there longing for something else? A child who was with his dad? Thomas remembered the empty bedroom in her apartment.

"I wanted to ask if you'd arrested him yet," she added. She didn't need to mention Petter Grandin by name. "It must have been him. Who else could it be?"

Thomas wished he could give her reassuring news, but it was far too early. They'd only just started work. He got up and went over to the window. The sun was setting, turning the sky pink and orange. It was exactly the kind of warm summer's evening he used to enjoy on Harö, with Pernilla and Elin.

"We're doing our best, Susanna, but I'm afraid it takes time. We can't arrest someone until we've completed our investigation."

"I thought I'd gotten over it," Susanna whispered. "I thought I'd gotten used to the idea that Siri's dead, but now it's starting all over again."

"I realize it's not an easy situation."

"You read about things like this, how difficult it is for the relatives when someone goes missing. There's no real closure, because there's no body to bury. I didn't understand it until it affected my own family."

Thomas wanted to make her feel better, but he'd never been good at this kind of conversation. He couldn't find the right words; everything he said came out as banal and clumsy instead of sympathetic and comforting.

"How are you feeling?" he said. *Stupid question.*

"Not so good." Susanna let out a sob. "I'm so ashamed of myself. If only I'd talked to Siri more during those last few weeks, asked her how she was doing. Maybe I could have helped her."

"I understand."

"I was totally self-obsessed; I was only interested in my pregnancy, my baby." She was crying now. "I don't even have a proper grave to visit, just a memorial stone. But she's not there."

Thomas tried to mumble something appropriate, but Susanna wasn't listening.

"That's been the worst thing, not knowing how she died. Sometimes I've thought it would have been better if she'd hanged herself at home, however terrible that sounds. At least we'd have known what happened."

"We can't be sure it's Siri we've found," Thomas pointed out. It was meant as a positive comment, but as soon as the words left his mouth, he realized how harsh they sounded.

"Don't say that! I'll be devastated if it's someone else. I'm not sure if I want it to be her after all these years, or if it's better not to know. Then at least there's still hope . . ."

"I understand," Thomas said again, cursing his own ineptitude.

"If it's someone else, you're stirring everything up for no reason."

"We're doing our best to get to the truth," he assured her.

"Promise me one thing . . ." The breaking voice fell silent, and Thomas waited until Susanna was able to continue. "Promise you'll call me as soon as you've arrested Petter."

# Chapter 40

What time was it? The veranda was in darkness; Nora had to peer at her watch to see it properly.

She'd only intended to sit here for a little while, but several hours had passed.

However, she felt much better. She wasn't so stressed, or so upset about the quarrel with Jonas. She hadn't been the only one at fault. He ought to realize that his nagging about her drinking didn't help, particularly after everything that had happened in the spring. He knew how it had affected her.

If he hadn't upset her, she would never have lost her self-control.

He should have been more considerate.

Nora tried to rest her elbow on the arm of the chair, but missed. Her upper body lurched to the side. *Oops!* She giggled. The arm was very slippery. Why hadn't she noticed it before?

She picked up her mug and discovered that it was almost empty. She reached for the bottle, the second one she'd opened that evening; it was unexpectedly light.

She couldn't possibly have drunk it all. No way. She'd been very careful not to drink too much. She had no intention of repeating yesterday's mistake.

She switched on the little lamp on the side table in order to check the contents of the bottle, but changed her mind and switched it off again. She didn't need to look, she always knew exactly how much she'd had to drink, in spite of what Jonas thought.

*Time for bed.* Julia had another swimming lesson in the morning.

Nora got to her feet but swayed and had to lean on the doorpost for support. The mug fell to the floor with a thud, but fortunately it didn't break. Nora was very pleased with herself. It had been a smart move, using a mug instead of a glass. She should have used that trick yesterday, then Jonas wouldn't have noticed she was drinking wine instead of tea, and they wouldn't have had that stupid quarrel.

She smiled. From now on, she would always drink wine from a mug.

Maybe she'd call Jonas again, fix things so they weren't both sulking in different countries.

She took out her phone and keyed in the code, but it wouldn't unlock. She tried again, without success.

Oh well, he'd just have to wait. Maybe she wasn't the one who should be apologizing anyway.

# Chapter 41

The bar at the Sandhamn Inn was only half full when Johanna walked in at about ten o'clock.

As usual, the three tables by the window were occupied, but it didn't matter; she had no desire to look at the view. She preferred to sit in a corner by herself. She didn't need company this evening; she just wanted to be around other people.

She'd sat in the kitchen staring at nothing until the walls began to close in on her. Eventually she'd grabbed her jacket and left the house. Before she knew it, she was standing outside the yellow-painted wooden façade of the inn.

"What can I get you?" asked the barman, whose name badge informed her that he was called Mille.

She didn't know what to say. She needed something strong, that was why she'd come here. Her mind was racing; she couldn't stop thinking about the encounter with Nora Linde. A line of coke was the ideal solution, but the supply she'd brought with her to the island had run out long ago. There wasn't even anything decent to drink in the house—her parents' sparse summer pantry contained very little booze.

"Can you mix me a cocktail?"

Mille gave her a thumbs-up. "No problem. Do you like vodka?"

"Yes—make it strong," she said, not caring if he raised his eyebrows.

Within a couple of minutes she was holding a glass containing an orange-yellow concoction in her hand. When she turned to find a seat, she saw Zacharias Fahlman at one of the far tables by the window.

Her stomach contracted, and she hurried off in the opposite direction.

She hoped he hadn't seen her. She still went out of her way to avoid bumping into him, even though so many years had passed.

Keeping her back to Zacharias, she headed for the other section of the bar. She found a table for two in the corner and sat down, making sure her face couldn't be seen from where he was sitting.

She took a swig of her cocktail. It was strong, just as she'd requested. She took another gulp, hoping the alcohol would soon settle her nerves. She wanted to stop thinking, but her nerves were still jangling. If she'd known Zacharias was going to be here, she'd have stayed home, but it was too late now.

Suddenly she felt a heavy hand on her shoulder. She looked up and saw him standing right next to her chair. His eyes were bloodshot, and his breath told her that he'd been drinking for quite some time.

"Was it you who set that lawyer bitch on me?"

The accusation in his hoarse voice made Johanna feel sick, but she did her best to sound unmoved.

"What are you talking about?"

"The prosecutor. You know who I mean."

"Nora Linde?"

"Did you tell her to come and see me?"

Johanna tried to increase the distance between them by leaning back toward the wall. She was the only one in this part of the bar. She turned her head to try to make eye contact with Mille, but he was busy pouring beer for another customer. Her mouth was dry.

"Why would I have done that?"

"You were talking to her on the promenade earlier today. Do you think I'm stupid? I saw you."

Johanna had been nervous when Nora stopped her; she'd started babbling about all kinds of things she should have kept to herself. She'd even mentioned Niklas's name, and regretted it immediately.

"I didn't say anything about you," she said through stiff lips.

That was true—she hadn't said a word about him today. It was when Nora had come to see her that she hadn't been able to stop herself from slinging a little mud at Zacharias.

He deserved it after everything he'd done. The thought gave her courage.

"Leave me alone," she said.

The courage disappeared when he leaned forward and gripped the back of her neck.

"You don't want to be talking about me behind my back," he hissed in her ear. She didn't dare move. No one else seemed to have noticed anything; it probably looked as if he'd just come over for a chat.

"You have no idea what happened that night," he went on, increasing the pressure so that Johanna let out a little cry of pain. "Keep your fucking mouth shut! Got it?"

"Got it."

He squeezed again, then let go and straightened up.

"Have a nice evening," he said loudly, then walked away as if everything were fine.

# Friday, August 12

# Chapter 42

The bedroom was filled with light when Johanna woke up. The sheets were drenched in sweat, and her heart was pounding.

She'd dreamed that Zacharias was chasing her. She ran and ran but couldn't get away. She shouldn't have gone to the bar last night. Zacharias still frightened her, after all these years.

She curled up into a little ball and pulled the covers over her head. Astrid's face came into her mind, how sad she'd looked those last few days.

Johanna screwed her eyes tight shut, hoping to get rid of the image.

She didn't want to stay on the island. If she left, she would escape both Zacharias and all the painful memories that had come flooding back. But Mom and Dad were coming over this evening. She needed to borrow money for the rent, which meant talking to Mom face to face. Otherwise she'd get nothing.

She opened her eyes. The sun was shining in through the gap between the window and the blue roller blind. She reached out and pulled it up a little way. She felt as if the beautiful weather was mocking her.

It was too late to change anything now. Why did Nora Linde have to come looking for her, stirring up the past? Why couldn't she have left well enough alone?

Nora had almost made Johanna say something she shouldn't. In the end she'd blurted out Niklas's name just to get rid of her.

Should she talk to Mom, tell her everything? No, it was impossible. She would never be able to explain. There were no excuses. Too much time had passed. She had to live with this for the rest of her life. There was nothing she could do about it now.

Once again, she wished she'd never spoken to Nora, but it had all happened so fast. Johanna hadn't even asked any questions. She should have been more alert, not let herself be railroaded like that.

Johanna sat up in bed. Nora Linde had said she was a prosecutor, but something didn't feel right. She'd been dressed in shorts and a T-shirt—not exactly appropriate clothing for an official police visit. Where did she say she worked? The Economic Crimes Authority—what did that have to do with Astrid?

Johanna was no lawyer, but she'd studied some aspects of the law before she'd dropped out of college.

The discovery on Telegrafholmen had to be a police matter—a criminal investigation that had nothing to do with financial irregularities.

She picked her laptop up off the floor and switched it on. Typed in *Nora Linde* and *prosecutor*. The Economic Crimes Authority's website immediately came up. So it was true, Nora was a prosecutor with the ECA.

On an impulse, Johanna reached for her phone and called the main switchboard number. A polite voice answered almost immediately: "Economic Crimes Authority."

Johanna hesitated briefly. "Could I speak to Nora Linde, please?"

There was a pause—long enough for Johanna to wish she hadn't called. Maybe she should hang up? What would she say if Nora came on the line?

"I'm afraid she's off sick," the voice informed her.

"Sorry?"

"She's not available at present. Would you like me to put you through to one of her colleagues?"

"No."

Johanna ended the call and sat there with the phone in her hand. Nora was off sick. So why had she come to see her, asking questions about Astrid? None of it made sense.

Then she had an idea: Could she use this new information to make Nora leave her in peace?

# Chapter 43

Nora was heading toward Sandhamnshöjden. She'd taken two painkillers, but her head was still pounding. She didn't want to think about how much wine she'd drunk yesterday evening. Why had she opened a fresh bottle when she'd fully intended to pour the first one down the drain?

What had come over her?

She'd agreed with Molly's mom that Nora would pick up Molly and Julia after their swimming lesson. That gave her a couple of hours, which should be enough time to talk to Lillian Eriksdotter. She was clutching at straws. Johanna had only mentioned her in passing, but maybe Lillian would be able to give her more information about Niklas.

She passed the Sands Hotel and waved half-heartedly at the receptionist, who was busy watering the plants outside the elegant gray building. The business had originally been founded by Theodor Sand at the end of the nineteenth century. Today it was a popular boutique hotel. Sometimes she and Jonas would go there for the special seafood menu.

*Jonas.*

Her stomach turned over. She still hadn't managed to get ahold of him, and he hadn't called her. Thank God she hadn't left a message last night; he'd have realized straightaway that she wasn't sober. She'd almost locked herself out of her phone. She had a vague memory of fumbling with the code, but had stopped herself from entering the wrong numbers at the last minute.

This couldn't go on—she had to pull herself together.

When she reached the top of the hill, she continued straight in among the newly built houses, ignoring the magnificent view. This was one of the highest points on the island, and the archipelago was spread before her in all directions. Today she just wasn't interested. Lillian lived in one of the first sections to be developed. This had been a major project, with the intention of providing rental properties to permanent residents who couldn't afford the sky-high prices on the island, which had rocketed. As interest rates fell, the cost of summer cottages increased.

Lillian's home stood out from the rest. It was surrounded by beautiful flowers, with climbing roses scrambling up the wall, and lots of pots filled with petunias, pelargoniums, and sweet peas.

The door was wide open; she must be in. Nora longed to focus on something other than her own problems. The only way to get rid of all the oppressive thoughts in her head was to replace them with something else.

She stepped up onto the porch and knocked on the doorframe.

"Hello?" she called out into the house.

# *Siri*

The little Italian restaurant smelled of tomato sauce and herbs when Siri walked in. She'd called Petter from work and suggested they eat out. It was a beautiful, warm summer evening. She'd pointed out that they were due to leave for the archipelago in three days; there weren't many restaurants out there, so they ought to make the most of the opportunity now.

She kept the real reason to herself—the fact that she wanted to postpone the vacation.

She decided to sit outside. The place was almost full, but she found a table for two with a checked cloth and a small vase of daisies.

It was five past seven, but Petter was often late after work. She ordered two glasses of red wine. Hopefully he'd be in a better mood if he had something to drink as soon as he arrived.

"You're here already."

Petter was standing before her in his dark-blue jacket. He always dressed formally for the office; he insisted it gave his clients more confidence in him. She couldn't help noticing a stain on his tie.

Once upon a time she'd have offered to take it to the dry cleaner's for him.

She pointed to the wine. "There you go."

While they were waiting to order, she wondered how she was going to raise the issue without Petter losing his temper. She planned to suggest that they should take a couple of weeks in the fall.

Or never?

Siri couldn't help hoping for a future without Petter. It was early days in her new relationship, but she'd never been so happy, even though she was aware of all the challenges.

She was head over heels in love.

She sipped her wine, then took a deep breath.

"I'm afraid I have some bad news."

Petter looked up from the menu. He was starting to develop a double chin, and Siri felt a stab of irritation. Why couldn't he take better care of himself? OK, so he was ten years older than she, but was it so difficult to keep an eye on the calories?

She was instantly ashamed of her critical thoughts. What right did she have to judge her husband when she was betraying him with another man? She had to stop finding fault the whole time. It might be easy to justify her own failings by listing his shortcomings, but it wasn't fair. Petter deserved better.

"I'm really sorry," she went on, "but I can't take time off next week. With the way things are at work at the moment, it's out of the question."

She reached out and placed her hand over his. She'd never felt so false in her whole life. "I know you've rented that beautiful cottage, but I can't get away."

Petter pulled away. His lips narrowed to a thin line.

"Are you kidding me? I've already paid ten thousand for two weeks!"

"I know. I'm so sorry." She tried to inject her words with a mixture of pathos and sincerity.

Petter was careful with money—almost stingy. It had been a recurring source of arguments between them; he didn't like spending unnecessarily. She couldn't get over his refusal to pay for one last round of IVF when the council funding ran out.

"Maybe you could ask your brother to go with you instead?" she suggested. "Or ask if you could get a refund, say half?"

"For fuck's sake, Siri! You can't do this!" He knocked back the wine and slammed the glass down on the table. "You can't cancel now! What's wrong with you?"

"I'm afraid it can't be helped." She ought to have stopped there, but for some reason she had to add: "If you'd asked me before you booked, I'd have told you then."

Petter threw down the menu, which landed on the floor.

"I've lost my appetite. I'll see you at home!"

# Chapter 44

Aram and Thomas were in Thomas's office when footsteps in the corridor announced Ida's arrival. She'd obviously swapped her usual sneakers for heels. She appeared in the doorway wearing a pair of impressive wedges with yellow straps, and sat down in one of the visitors' chairs.

"I think I've found the name of Siri's secret lover," she began.

Aram sat up a little straighter. "Go on."

"I went through the old transcripts of the interviews with Siri's neighbors, and I found a couple called Mia and Anton Blomgren. They lived only a few hundred yards from the Grandins; the two families used to hang out together, and they were members of the same golf club. Anton sounds a lot like Anders or Albert, wouldn't you say?"

Thomas nodded. The secret lover. This was a big step forward, and fit with their hypothesis: someone within their circle of friends, someone Petter Grandin also knew.

"Is he still married?" Aram asked.

Ida smiled and shook her head. "They divorced eight years ago, and they've both moved away."

Could there be a connection with Siri's disappearance? A heartbroken lover who couldn't grieve openly, and couldn't afford to be dragged into a police investigation because he was afraid of the repercussions for his marriage . . . But then the relationship with his wife collapsed anyway when the loss and all those suppressed emotions caught up with him.

Thomas found it easy to imagine the situation. "So where is he now?"

"He works in IT and lives in Lännersta. The couple has joint custody of their two sons."

"See if you can contact him—we need to have a conversation with him."

Ida tilted her head on one side. "Of course the quickest approach would be to ask Petter Grandin if Siri had an affair with Anton Blomgren—but maybe that's not a good idea?"

Aram shook his head. "I wouldn't have thought so."

"If we can speak to Blomgren, we might be able to break Grandin's alibi for that last weekend," Thomas mused. "When he claims Siri was alive. Ida, try and get ahold of him as soon as you can."

Aram linked his hands behind his head. "I can't figure out why Grandin would bury the body on Telegrafholmen. Why take the trouble to go all the way out there? It's quite a distance from Djurö."

"Twenty minutes by boat," Thomas said. "That's not far."

"And it wasn't a bad decision," Ida pointed out. "Ten years have passed without anyone finding her."

"If the council hadn't decided to start building, the body would never have been found," Thomas added.

Aram had to concede. "Grandin did say that he went to Sandhamn now and then."

Had he owned a boat ten years ago? One that was big enough to carry a corpse?

"Maybe someone had told him that no development was allowed on Telegrafholmen," Ida suggested. "He realized it was the perfect place to hide the body. Nobody would have seen him."

Thomas pictured the island. It was easy to moor on the far side, out of sight of Sandhamn. If Grandin had gone over during the night, there would have been very little risk of being spotted. A dead body was heavy, but he was powerfully built, and of course he'd been ten years younger. The spot where the bones had been found was on higher ground, but it was still pretty secluded.

Ida was right—Telegrafholmen was the perfect place to hide a body. Now all they had to do was prove it.

# Chapter 45

Nora knocked again, and a woman of about seventy appeared in the doorway. Lillian Eriksdotter smiled as if she vaguely recognized Nora but couldn't quite place her.

"Hello?"

Nora introduced herself and explained why she was there, but Lillian seemed reluctant to let her in.

"I'm a prosecutor," Nora added, hoping this would persuade the older woman. With a bit of luck, Lillian would draw her own conclusions, as Johanna had done, without Nora needing to elaborate. She pushed aside the knowledge that she was dangerously close to professional misconduct.

"Come on in—we'll have a coffee on the veranda," Lillian said, pushing back her graying hair. She led the way to the back of the house, where a thermos and a handmade ceramic mug were already set out on a small table between two pale-gray cane chairs. She fetched another mug for Nora.

"That business with Astrid was very sad," she went on when she'd sat down. "I remember it well. The police questioned me after she went missing."

"I've already spoken to Johanna Strand," Nora said, in case Lillian was wondering.

The mention of Johanna's name evoked a sigh. "Johanna lost her way when Astrid disappeared. She worked for me the following summer, but I had to let her go. She wasn't doing her job properly."

"In what way?"

"She was partying too much, and often arrived late for her shift. I tried to be patient with her—I sympathized with her, but in the end I couldn't keep covering for her. I had a restaurant to run. She's never really recovered from the loss. Johanna and Astrid were like sisters."

Nora took a sip of her coffee; it was strong and black, exactly what she needed this morning. "What do you remember of Astrid?"

"I liked her very much. She was a sweet girl, hardworking and conscientious. She had a good head on her shoulders."

Lillian leaned back, one hand resting on her knee. Nora could see a pale, narrow scar from meniscus repair surgery. She had the feeling that Lillian had more to say but wasn't sure how open she should be.

"I really appreciate anything you can tell me," she said.

"There was something . . . neglected about Astrid," Lillian admitted, with a quick glance at Nora. "I presume you know who her mother is? Monica Forsell. She lives behind Mangelbacken."

"Yes."

"This is just between us—but I expect you have a duty of confidentiality?"

Nora nodded, in spite of feeling extremely uncomfortable. She wasn't here in a professional capacity, but the more she could find out, the better. She wanted to see this through to the end.

"You have nothing to worry about," she reassured Lillian.

"Astrid wasn't happy living with her mother."

"What do you mean?"

"Things weren't great at home. Monica didn't always live up to her responsibilities as a parent. They argued often, and back then Monica had a boyfriend who wasn't easy to deal with. That didn't help."

"Zacharias Fahlman."

"You know who he is, of course? In that case, you also know that he's a man who likes a drink. I've seen him staggering home from the bar many, many times. He and Monica knew how to party, and that last summer it was worse than ever. There was a lot of talk in the village, as I'm sure you're aware."

Nora put down her cup. She was ashamed to admit that she hadn't had a clue. Ten years ago she'd been too caught up in her own problems to keep up with the local gossip, even though Astrid had often helped out with the boys.

"I felt sorry for Astrid," Lillian added.

"Did she get along with Fahlman?"

Lillian hesitated. "I don't know. Sometimes I got the feeling that Astrid really missed her dad. As far as I'm aware, Monica didn't exactly encourage the relationship. I certainly don't think Astrid saw Fahlman as a father figure. I got the impression she didn't like him much."

Nora couldn't help wondering if Astrid had left home, maybe to get away from Fahlman, then something bad had happened to her. But after her encounter the previous day, she'd begun to think there might be something else behind it.

"Zacharias was, or is, a hard man," Lillian continued. "He has no children of his own. He didn't seem very affectionate toward Astrid when I saw them together."

Something had been nagging at Nora—the cold look in Fahlman's eyes when he let his dog run at her, even though he could see how terrified she was, the total lack of empathy when they stood there face to face. He took no responsibility for the situation, in spite of her obvious distress.

"I'm sorry to ask you this," she said. "It might sound strange, but could something have gone on behind Monica's back?"

Lillian didn't even blink. "Astrid was a pretty girl, and her body was very . . . mature, if you know what I mean. She seemed considerably older than her seventeen years." She sighed. "However, I find it difficult to believe that Zacharias would do something like that. He's no angel, but I've never regarded him as a . . . predator."

"But it's not impossible?"

"You ask difficult questions." Lillian leaned forward and nipped a few yellowing leaves off a dark-pink pelargonium in the nearest pot. She held them in her hand and examined them closely. "To be honest, I don't know." She tossed the leaves away, and they landed on the pale sand, where several tall blades of grass were sticking up. "Maybe it would be better if you talked to someone else about that."

Nora decided to change tack.

"I believe Astrid had an admirer called Niklas—do you remember him?"

Lillian tilted her head to one side, a flash of interest in her bright eyes.

"I presume you mean Niklas Johansson."

"I guess so—I didn't know his surname."

"It can hardly be anyone else. He was very tall but skinny and kind of clumsy. He was very keen on Astrid."

Nora looked up. "Were they together?"

"I don't know." Lillian hesitated. "There was nothing wrong with Niklas. He was a nice kid with a lovely smile; he was good-looking in his own way. But he was very different from Astrid. She was outgoing, pretty, popular. Niklas was shy, as if he were always afraid of getting a beating."

"Sorry?" Nora was taken aback.

"Niklas's father was Nalle Johansson; he was the manager of the Sailors Hotel for a number of years." Lillian's face closed down. "Nalle was a hard boss. He certainly made the business profitable, but he wasn't too good at keeping up staff morale. Not many people dared to contradict him, and I assume it was the same in his own family. I guess Nalle wasn't afraid to beat the crap out of his son, if you know what I mean."

Nora was surprised at Lillian's frankness.

"Do you mean he actually hit Niklas?"

"I'm thinking of one occasion in particular." Lillian wasn't smiling now. "Niklas was carrying a case of wine, and somehow he dropped it in the middle of the floor in the restaurant. The bottles smashed, of course—there was a hell of a mess. Nalle happened to walk by just after it had happened. There was red wine everywhere—an expensive label—and Nalle went crazy. He slapped Niklas across the face right in front of me."

"Wow."

"To be honest, it was pretty shocking. I was Niklas's line manager, so I was responsible for him. Of course it was clumsy of him, but for Nalle to behave like that . . ." Lillian shook her head and her voice dropped. "The way he hit Niklas gave me the distinct feeling that it wasn't the first time."

"What did you do?"

"What could I do? Niklas was nineteen, almost twenty. He'd just left Tyresö high school; it wasn't exactly child abuse." Lillian sighed. "I spoke to Nalle afterward and said I didn't want it to happen again—not in my restaurant. I had no say over what went on within his family, but at work there are other ways of resolving conflict." She took out a packet of cigarettes and opened it, then stopped herself. "Do you mind if I smoke?" she said apologetically. "These old memories are upsetting me more than I'd expected."

"Of course not—it's your home."

Lillian lit a cigarette and took a long, slow drag, gazing up at the summer sky. The smell of smoke mingled with the heady scent of sweet peas.

"More coffee?" she said, refilling her own cup.

"Please." Nora held out her cup; the strong brew had revived her. "Tell me more about Niklas."

"I'm not sure what to say. As I said, he was a little timid, but very good with computers. He often helped reception with glitches in the system when he wasn't busy in the restaurant."

"How did he get along during the rest of the summer?"

"I don't really remember. The incident with the wine happened in July; I think he just carried on working as usual. We never mentioned it again."

"And his father?"

"So many questions." Lillian took another drag. "Both Nalle and Niklas left the Sailors after that summer, and I have to say I was pretty relieved. But thinking back . . ." Lillian frowned. "I didn't get to say good-bye to Niklas. He asked if he could finish a few days early—in the same week that Astrid went missing, actually."

Nora looked up. The same week? Had she heard correctly?

"It might just be a coincidence," Lillian went on. "We had dozens of temporary staff employed for the summer, and when I eventually realized that Astrid had vanished without a trace, that was all I could think about."

Nora tried to make sense of the equation. So Niklas had left at the same time as Astrid had disappeared. She didn't believe in coincidences.

Admittedly, Niklas sounded too gentle to constitute a threat, but domestic violence was often passed on from one generation to the next—she knew that from the bitter experience of Mina's case. Maybe Niklas hadn't been brave enough to stand up to his father, and had taken out his frustration on Astrid instead. Someone younger and smaller who couldn't hit back.

Although it didn't sound as if Lillian would agree with her.

"Do you know how I could contact Niklas or his father?"

"I've no idea. As far as Nalle is concerned, I'd rather not know, given the way he treated his son. With the benefit of hindsight, I wish . . ."

Lillian didn't complete the sentence. She stubbed out her cigarette.

"It's so sad about Astrid," she said. "I liked her very much. I'm sorry I can't be more helpful."

# *Astrid*

Astrid's phone vibrated in the pocket of her apron as she was heading into the kitchen with a heavily laden tray. Staff weren't allowed to use their phones while they were working, but she was curious.

She slipped into the bathroom and read the message. It was from Niklas. Did she want to go swimming at Norra Björkösund after work?

They'd seen each other several times lately, even though he wasn't the kind of guy she usually went for. There was something she recognized within Niklas, something that touched her heart.

He instinctively understood what things were like at home, without asking dumb or intrusive questions. She didn't need to pretend when she was with him. It was a relief to be with someone who got it, without a whole lot of complicated explanations. Even Johanna, with her kind parents who'd been together forever, couldn't really imagine Astrid's situation.

The only aspect she couldn't talk about was Zacharias—his revolting looks when Mom wasn't around, or when he thought she wouldn't notice. It was too much, too embarrassing. It wasn't her fault, but she still felt ashamed. She hadn't even mentioned it to Johanna.

Niklas didn't say much about his father. Astrid had eventually realized that Niklas had been on the receiving end of the tirade she and Johanna had overheard through the open window. People said that Nalle was a hard man with a short temper—especially when it came to his son.

Astrid was glad she worked for Lillian, and had nothing to do with him.

Niklas was waiting down on the shore when she finished at three. His red Jet Ski was by the jetty as usual. He looked good in his dark-blue T-shirt and shorts. His forehead was red—too much sun.

"It might be a bit rough out there," he said. "Is that a problem?"

Astrid shook her head. He was so nice, so attentive. He handed her a life jacket and helped her to fasten it with his long, slender fingers. Astrid almost laughed; she was perfectly capable of doing it herself. She wasn't five years old.

But she liked the way he took care of her.

They set off from the harbor, her arms wrapped around his waist, feeling the warmth of his body against hers.

He took the route between Telegrafholmen and Lökholmen, and continued toward Norra Björkösund. Astrid had brought some leftover food from the restaurant, while Niklas supplied a couple of beers. When they'd eaten, Astrid felt drowsy. She lay down on her towel and closed her eyes. Niklas blew gently on her face.

"Are you falling asleep? Shall I wake you up?" he teased.

Suddenly she felt the shock of cold water on her face and chest.

"What the hell are you doing?" she said, unnecessarily loudly.

She wanted to sound mad but couldn't keep up the pretense when Niklas made a funny face. He had a dimple in one cheek.

"Let's swim," he said, helping her to her feet. He held on to her hand for a second longer than necessary. She didn't want him to let go.

# Chapter 46

As soon as Nora got back home, she dug out her laptop. She'd hardly touched it this summer. She took it into the kitchen and sat down at the table. The August sun filled the room with light, apart from one corner that was in shadow.

She typed *Niklas Johansson* into the search engine and pressed "Enter."

There were thousands of Niklas Johanssons. She tried adding *Stockholm*, but there were still far too many hits, and she had no way of knowing which of them had had a summer job on Sandhamn.

Maybe she could trace him via his father, Nalle Johansson? She entered the name—almost nineteen hundred hits. Facebook was no help either; she'd be on the phone for days calling them all.

It was hopeless.

She got up and poured herself a glass of water, which she drank standing by the sink. Why couldn't he have had a more unusual name?

She tried again, this time adding *Sailors Hotel* after Nalle Johansson. Still no luck, just a long list of references to a former ice-hockey player in Eskilstuna.

Nora stared at the screen. Lillian had said that Niklas had gone to school in Tyresö; if his family lived there, it could hardly be the same person.

Then she noticed the hockey player's real name: Björn "Nalle" Johansson. How dumb was she? Björn was the Swedish word for *bear*, and Nalle—or *teddy bear*—was a common nickname.

With eager fingers, she tried *Björn Johansson Tyresö*, and in a second the screen was filled with interesting information. There was a local councilor by that name who was active in Tyresö; could it be the same person, even if he'd stopped calling himself Nalle in his official capacity?

She clicked on an article and studied it carefully.

> *Björn Johansson, leader of the Moderates in Tyresö, is pictured in the town square. He looks very pleased when we ask about the party's fortunes in recent years. He topped the list of Moderates before the 2006 election, and since then he has twice been elected chair of the local council. Johansson's aim of creating a business-friendly climate in Tyresö has been extremely successful. He has managed to attract many new companies to the town, and his efforts have been rewarded with the confidence of the voters.*

The accompanying photograph showed a well-built man of about fifty, with a firm chin and an alert gaze. He looked good and had kept his thick hair, peppered with gray. The age fit perfectly—he could easily be Niklas's father.

Nora did a little more research into his background, and within minutes she came across a reference to the Sailors Hotel.

*Bingo.*

Björn Johansson had indeed been the manager there. At last she was getting somewhere. Maybe she could track down a picture of Niklas, too? She googled Björn's family but found only an image of him posing with his blond wife. Annie Johansson was a trim woman with perfectly styled hair, but she looked pale and tired.

The photograph had been taken outside the white council offices in Tyresö. Björn was smiling broadly, enjoying the attention, while his wife looked much less comfortable. Her face was turned away from the camera, and she was leaning on her husband's arm. Her smile was stiff, her gaze fixed on some distant point.

Nora rested her chin on her hand and thought for a moment.

Niklas must be twenty-nine now; it was unlikely that he'd still be living at home. The simplest approach would be to contact Björn and ask for his son's number, but then she'd have to introduce herself, make out she was calling in an official capacity. She'd already done that once too often.

The alternative was to check the electoral register via the information service used by the Economic Crimes Authority. That would enable her to access Niklas's personal details and address. The database contained the children and parents of every single person registered in Sweden.

The only problem was that she wasn't working at the moment, so she had no official reason for logging in. But if she went in and out really quickly, nobody would notice . . . She hadn't been suspended, she was only off sick, for God's sake.

And yet she hesitated. What explanation could she give if someone asked why she'd done it? She ran her hands through her hair and plaited it into a short braid.

She wouldn't be breaking the rules of confidentiality. It wasn't as if she were planning to take a peek at someone's medical records.

Before she could change her mind, she typed in her password and began clicking her way through to Björn "Nalle" Johansson, residing in Tyresö, and his family.

# Chapter 47

Telegrafholmen lay silent and deserted when Thomas stepped ashore on Friday afternoon.

The police launch had moored at the concrete jetty on the western point. Thomas waved to his colleagues in the cockpit and set off toward the middle of the island. It was only a few minutes' walk along a narrow forest track to the spot where the bones had been found.

He was actually on his way to Harö for the weekend, but had decided to make a short stop on Telegrafholmen. He wanted to take another look around, even if he didn't have anything specific in mind.

The blue-and-white police tape was fluttering in the wind when he arrived. Staffan Nilsson's team had been over several times, searching for additional remains. Without success, unfortunately; they still had only fragments to go on, thanks to the strength of the blast.

He stopped at the edge of the forest. It was a natural glade, perfect for hiding a body. All the perpetrator would have needed was a spade. A spade Thomas would have liked to take a close look at.

If Grandin was the guilty party, then he was hardly likely to have kept it for ten years, but a search of his property would provide the answer.

Thomas ducked under the tape and made his way to the place where the grave had probably been, according to Nilsson's calculations.

The ground bore clear signs of the blasting that had gone on earlier in the week, with rubble and lumps of earth scattered everywhere. The rocky area farther away was still covered in a thick layer of gray dust.

He knelt down. The soil was considerably deeper here than on the rest of the island. He could understand why this particular location had been chosen.

He stood up and turned his head in the direction of Sandhamn. He could hardly see it from here; on a dark night it would be impossible for anyone over there to make out what was happening on Telegrafholmen.

Thomas tried to picture the scene. Some kind of light must have been required, but the beam of a flashlight moving around could have aroused suspicions.

He thought for a moment. The moonlight was especially bright in August—could that have been enough? He took out his phone and googled. There had been a full moon on Wednesday, August 9, 2006—only a few days before Siri disappeared, according to their hypothesis. If Grandin had murdered his wife during the weekend in question, then the moonlight should have enabled him to find his way.

In which case, he'd had nature on his side.

Thomas moved a few yards away to examine the scene from a different angle. The birds were singing behind him, and a bumblebee buzzed around a flower. He was still well hidden from sight.

This spot had been chosen with care.

The harsh sound of his phone ringing shattered the peace, and the birds flew away.

It was Susanna Alptegen.

"Sorry to keep calling you, but I wondered how the investigation was going?"

Thomas felt for her. She desperately wanted to know what had really happened to her sister, but unfortunately he couldn't conjure up an answer that would give her peace of mind, however often she called.

"We're doing our best."

"Have you arrested Petter?"

"As I told you yesterday—" Thomas began, but Susanna interrupted him.

"I couldn't sleep last night. All I can think about is Siri. How she died. If she suffered. Why I didn't do more when she disappeared. If only I'd told the police about my suspicions at the time . . ."

"We're doing our best," Thomas assured her again. "You have to try to be patient."

Susanna began to cry. "We don't even know exactly what he did to her. This is torture." She sobbed uncontrollably for a few seconds, then abruptly ended the call.

Thomas wished he could offer some consolation. A great deal pointed to Grandin's guilt, but the problem was that they had only circumstantial evidence to go on. Even if the National Board of Forensic Medicine confirmed that the bones were Siri's, they still had no concrete proof that Petter Grandin had murdered his wife.

Because the original investigation had accepted at an early stage that Siri had probably taken her own life, the forensic examination of the family home hadn't been followed up on. Nor were there any bloodstains or other evidence to point them in the right direction.

The current investigation would take as long as it took; there were no shortcuts. He couldn't give Susanna any assurances about Grandin's guilt, not at this stage.

He was about to put his phone away when it rang again. It was an internal number from the police station.

"Andreasson."

"Hi, it's Alireza from the main switchboard," said a young man. "I have a call from a woman named Johanna who wants to talk to you—it's about the discovery of the bones in the archipelago. Can I put her through?"

# Chapter 48

Thomas moved to a sunny spot as he waited for the call to come through.

"Hello?" said a woman's voice. "Are you the detective in charge of the investigation into . . . into what was found on Telegrafholmen?"

"I am."

"This might sound weird, but I'm wondering about one of your colleagues."

Thomas was used to taking calls from the public. It was always best to start with introductions.

"Could you tell me your name?" he said, trying to sound encouraging. "I'd like to know who I'm talking to."

"Oh sorry."

She didn't sound very old—probably under thirty.

"My name is Johanna Strand. I live on Sandhamn, and Astrid Forsell was a good friend of mine."

*Astrid Forsell.*

Thomas had been so busy concentrating on Petter Grandin over the past twenty-four hours that he'd hardly given the missing teenager a thought.

"I understand—what's this about?"

Johanna took a deep breath.

"One of your colleagues contacted me the other day."

None of the team had been asked to get in touch with Johanna Strand. Thomas had a vague memory of Astrid's friend coming up in the general discussion, but nothing more. Their focus had been on Siri Grandin.

"A prosecutor came to see me on Wednesday, that's why I'm calling you."

"Sorry, which prosecutor?"

No prosecutor was involved in the case—it was far too early.

"Nora Linde. She lives on Sandhamn, too. She questioned me about Astrid and her disappearance."

Thomas was doing his best to keep up.

"Nora Linde came to see you?"

"Yes, she wanted to know about Astrid and her relationship with her mother."

"You mean Monica Forsell?"

"That's right."

This didn't make any sense, but he didn't like what he was hearing.

"What did she ask you?"

"If Astrid had a boyfriend."

Thomas sat down on a flat rock among the trees. Had Nora decided to get involved in the police investigation on her own initiative? Why would she do that? She wasn't even back at work. And why hadn't she spoken to him first?

"That's why I'm curious." Johanna sounded embarrassed. "I thought it was odd for a prosecutor to turn up out of the blue at our summer cottage. Is that the way you usually work?"

A ferry sounded its horn in the distance. Three times—the signal that it was reversing away from the steamboat jetty on Sandhamn.

Thomas had a sinking feeling in his stomach.

"I contacted the Economic Crimes Authority," Johanna continued. "But they said that Nora Linde was off sick, so I thought . . ."

Thomas tried to gather his thoughts.

"Let me look into it—give me your number, and I'll get back to you as soon as possible. Thanks for getting in touch—you can leave it with me," he said, ending the call.

He sat there with the phone in his hand.

If what Johanna had just told him was true, and there was no reason to doubt her, then Nora was guilty of professional misconduct.

How was he going to be able to fix this without consequences?

# Chapter 49

There was no address on the line below Niklas Johansson's name.

Nora sighed. So how was she going to contact him? She was becoming increasingly convinced that Niklas was a key figure in her quest to find out the truth. Both Lillian and Johanna had confirmed that he'd been on Sandhamn with Astrid during that last summer, plus he'd left the island at almost the same time that Astrid had gone missing. That couldn't be a coincidence. There had to be a connection, she could feel it.

She really wanted to talk to him.

She pushed away her laptop and rested her chin on her arms on the table. Nothing was going right for her at the moment. She was trying to do something useful and getting nowhere, and Jonas still wasn't answering his phone.

OK, so she'd said the wrong thing, but it hadn't been that bad. He must realize that all couples fought.

Her anxiety over their quarrel had formed a hard lump in her stomach. She didn't want to believe that he was deliberately ignoring her calls, but all kinds of weird thoughts came creeping in when she couldn't get ahold of him. One minute she was so worried about him that she was almost in tears, and the next she was mad because he hadn't been in touch.

It was all such a mess.

Nora raised her head and stared at the screen. There was only one reasonable explanation for the lack of address: Niklas Johansson must have left the country, in which case, the electoral register was no help.

What were her other options, without contacting his parents?

There was a knock on the front door. It couldn't be Julia; she was at Molly's house, and Nora wasn't due to pick her up until later.

Another knock, then the door opened.

"Hello?" said a voice from the hallway.

It sounded like Thomas. Odd—they hadn't arranged to meet today. She got up and went into the hallway to find Thomas with one hand resting on the door handle.

"Hi," she said. She tried to give him a hug, but for some reason he pulled away. "What are you doing here?"

"We need to talk." His tone was unusually sharp, and there was a gravity in his expression that Nora found alarming. Had something happened to Elin? Or Pernilla?

"OK," she said slowly. "Let's go and sit on the veranda. Would you like a coffee? Or a beer?"

"I'm fine."

Nora led the way; she didn't want him to sit down in the kitchen and see the computer. The screen was still open; it was obvious that she'd been checking the register. She'd decided not to tell Thomas about her research until the time was ripe. Until she had something concrete to show for her efforts.

Thomas sat down on the sofa, and Nora chose the wicker chair nearest the window. The air was stuffy, even though the veranda door was ajar.

"Has something happened?" she said. "Is Elin all right?"

"What the hell are you doing?" he said, ignoring her question.

What was this about?

"Why have you been to see Johanna Strand?" he went on.

How did he know about that? He must have spoken to Johanna—that was the only possible explanation. She knew it was a little unethical in purely professional terms, but she'd done it for a good reason.

"Why do you ask?" she said, trying to sound casual, as if it were the most natural thing in the world that she'd dropped in to see Johanna.

"Don't jerk me around. We know each other too well for that."

His tone of voice took Nora by surprise. Thomas was mad at *her*.

"We talked about Astrid Forsell," she admitted. "But it's fine—there's nothing to worry about."

Thomas scratched the back of his neck. His once white-blond hair was now almost entirely gray.

"Johanna told me you introduced yourself as a prosecutor and questioned her about Astrid's disappearance."

Technically she hadn't shown Johanna her official ID, but Thomas wasn't going to be interested in that kind of detail. How was she going to explain this without getting herself into more trouble?

"She must have misunderstood. We just sat on the patio for a while, had a little chat. Nothing serious. I definitely didn't *question* her—I wonder what gave her that idea?"

It was unfortunate that Johanna had called Thomas. How much had she told him about their conversation?

The furrow between Thomas's eyebrows grew deeper, and his frustration was palpable.

"Don't you understand that by involving yourself in an investigation like this, you're guilty of professional misconduct?" he said. "It was sheer luck that the switchboard put her through to me. If she'd spoken to Margit or anyone else in the department, you'd have been in real trouble. The matter would presumably have been referred to your boss."

Nora looked away. Was this how Thomas behaved when he was interviewing a suspect? She knew he was a good detective with an impressive clearance rate, but she'd never expected to be on the receiving end of his interrogation technique.

She adjusted the little lace mat on the table between the wicker chairs.

"I don't know what you were thinking," he added.

Maybe it was time to come clean? Tell him not only about Johanna's experiences but also about Zacharias Fahlman and Niklas Johansson? Nora was pleased with the information she'd managed to acquire, even if the visit to Fahlman had been unpleasant. Thomas would see things in a different light if he'd just let her explain properly.

"Why don't you try listening to me?" she said. "I've found out quite a lot, and I really think it could be important to your investigation."

Nora was still hoping that Niklas Johansson would make the picture clearer. If she could just get ahold of him, the pieces of the puzzle would fall into place.

"Go on."

Thomas wasn't exactly brimming with enthusiasm, but Nora quickly fetched her laptop from the kitchen. To be on the safe side, she closed down the electoral register website; there was no point in giving him something else to be annoyed about. She brought up the file containing her notes, and turned the screen so that Thomas could see.

It took her almost ten minutes to tell him about Monica's relationship with her daughter and Zacharias Fahlman. As she moved on to her conversation with Lillian Eriksdotter, Thomas's expression darkened once more.

"Another sham interview?" he exclaimed, slamming the palm of his hand down on the arm of the sofa. "Seriously?"

"That's not fair," Nora replied, unable to conceal her own irritation. "I've spoken to a few people on the island who knew Astrid. If I hadn't done that, you wouldn't have realized how heavily involved Fahlman is. What if he's responsible for her disappearance?" She put down the laptop. "You ought to bring him in for questioning. He's a key player."

She hadn't even gotten to Niklas Johansson yet—a young man who'd experienced violence in his own home.

Thomas leaned forward.

"You cannot go around behaving as if you're representing the police. You, of all people, should know better. You're a lawyer, for fuck's sake. Don't you understand?"

In fact, she was a prosecutor. In Mina's case, she'd been appointed lead investigator, which meant that Thomas had had to report to her. Why was he being so unfair?

"You're always talking about how short-staffed you are," she said. "I'm only trying to help."

"Have you heard anything I've said?" Thomas had never spoken to her like this.

"Of course I have, but I'm wondering if you've heard anything I've said to you? I know exactly how an investigation works, in case you've forgotten!"

Why didn't anyone understand? Or was there something in the male psyche that meant they didn't want to understand? She gripped the arm of the chair.

"I'm only trying to help," she said again, speaking slowly and clearly. "A young woman might have been murdered. How do you think her relatives feel when nothing's being done? It's horrific."

Thomas sat up a little straighter.

"Enough, Nora. It's not true that nothing's being done. Our focus is on a different person, a woman from Djurö."

"Oh? And what have you found out?"

"Nora, please."

Suddenly, Thomas sounded less unreasonable, more conciliatory.

"Just tell me where you are."

"I can't."

"Is that all you have to say?"

"You just told me you know how an investigation works. At this stage, everything is confidential. I shouldn't have to explain that to you."

He was talking to her like a child again. She was so angry she couldn't sit still.

"Fantastic," she said, getting to her feet. "You have the nerve to come here and treat me like dirt, yet you can't tell me why I'm wrong. I've tried to make a contribution, but you won't give me any credit for what I've achieved."

"I—" Thomas began, but Nora wasn't having any of it.

"Get out! Leave me alone!"

# Siri

Petter carried the suitcases out to the car. The case of wine was already in the trunk; he came back for the thermal bag containing food supplies.

Siri watched in silence from the kitchen doorway. She'd offered to help, but Petter had rejected any attempt at reconciliation.

It was Saturday morning; they'd barely exchanged two words since the evening at the Italian restaurant. Petter had merely informed her that he intended to travel to the archipelago as planned. His brother might join him later.

"See you in two weeks," she ventured. "I hope you have a lovely time."

Petter looked at her, his face expressionless. Suddenly he put down the thermal bag with such force that it tipped over. Something inside clinked worryingly.

"You're such a fucking bitch," he said.

Siri stared at him. "What did you say?"

Petter's cheeks were flushed.

"Do you think I don't know what you're up to?"

"I'm not up to anything!"

"Secret phone calls, all that overtime at work . . ."

"What are you talking about?"

"I'm not even allowed to touch you." He came right up to her, his breathing rapid and shallow. "Plenty of women would be grateful for what you've got, but *you* . . ." He almost spat out the word. "You can't show the least bit of gratitude. We could have a fantastic life together, but you're prepared to destroy everything."

Siri was standing with her back to the wall; she couldn't move any farther away from him. She was trying to stay calm, but his tone of voice was upsetting.

"A fantastic life," he'd said. He knew exactly why they'd reached this point. Why they were so unhappy.

If only they'd been able to have a baby . . .

Siri pushed away the forbidden thought. It was too late, all doors were closed. Petter had flatly refused to consider adoption. And now it seemed as if he suspected she was cheating on him.

"Sometimes I wish I'd never met you," he said, his voice trembling with rage. "I wish I'd been able to have a family with someone else."

He could hardly have put it any more clearly. Someone else who could get pregnant with his child.

It was like a slap across the face.

Siri was overwhelmed by grief. She would never be a mother, and it wasn't her fault alone. How could he be so cruel after everything they'd gone through?

At that moment she almost hated him.

"How can you say that?" she whispered. "Do you think I enjoy living with you?"

Tears were pouring down her cheeks. She couldn't bear it any longer. The words came tumbling out.

"You're a horrible, vile person," she sobbed. "Sometimes I think I'd rather be dead than carry on like this. You've ruined everything."

The look in Petter's eyes was ice cold.

"Me! You fucking hypocrite," he said grimly. Then he grabbed the thermal bag and walked out, slamming the door so hard that the house seemed to shake.

# Chapter 50

Only a handful of passengers were waiting to disembark on Harö. It had taken less than ten minutes on the ferry from Sandhamn; Thomas was last in line.

Nora had been totally impossible. He'd gone there to help her smooth over what she'd done, but she'd refused to listen, in spite of the fact that she was in the wrong.

He nodded to a couple of acquaintances and handed over his ticket to the sailor on duty. His phone rang as he stepped onto the jetty. It was Ida. He pushed aside thoughts of Nora and took the call.

"The insurance company came through," Ida said immediately.

"Sorry?"

Thomas set off along the familiar narrow path through the forest that led to his house on the north side of the island.

"You wanted me to check if Petter Grandin used to own a boat." Ida sounded a little impatient. "I spoke to three insurance companies before I got lucky with Folksam. Grandin owned a Buster XL ten years ago."

Thomas had the same model—a good, robust aluminum powerboat, more than capable of tackling rough seas. Mooring a Buster on Telegrafholmen would be no problem, and there was plenty of room for the body of a murdered wife.

Ida went on: "According to Folksam, Grandin reported the boat stolen just over a month after his wife's disappearance."

"Stolen?"

It could be a coincidence—but once again, Thomas didn't believe in coincidences in a murder inquiry.

"Exactly. He claimed it had been taken from the marina on Djurö, not far from his home. He said he'd forgotten to check on the boat in the chaos after Siri's disappearance." Ida laughed. "As if that wouldn't have been one of the first things he should have done."

Thomas's brain was working overtime. An insurance claim might have been yet another of Grandin's attempts to cover his tracks. By first "forgetting" about the boat and then saying it had been "stolen," he had managed to make it vanish so that it was never examined by forensic technicians.

"So what happened?"

"It was actually found a few months later; it had run aground on an island to the north of Sandhamn. The theory was that a group of teenagers had stolen it and gone over to Sandhamn to party, but hadn't tied it up properly, so it drifted away."

"Did anyone examine the boat when it was found?"

"You mean as a crime scene? Not exactly. The insurance company handled it. Their assessor immediately concluded that the steering mechanism was wrecked, and the engine was beyond repair. They wrote it off."

Thomas could see the roof of his house by the water and turned off to the right. The forest had given way to lush meadows. There was a lot more greenery on Harö than Sandhamn; once upon a time there had been strawberry plantations on the island.

"One interesting point," Ida continued. "Apparently there was a dispute between Grandin and the company. Even though the engine was ruined when the boat was found, there was no sign that it had been hot-wired."

In which case, it had been started with a key. Who would have done that, apart from the owner?

"Grandin insisted that the keys must have been stolen, too. He said they weren't on their usual hook in the house, but he had no explanation as to why."

"So what happened in the end?"

"He pushed the claim hard, and eventually threatened legal action. Because Folksam couldn't prove that he was lying when he said the keys had been stolen, they paid out in the end."

Thomas wasn't surprised. Grandin seemed like a man who wouldn't give up. Particularly when insurance money was involved.

"Do we know where the boat is now?" he asked without much hope. The chance of the Buster providing any useful information after ten years was minimal.

"Not a clue."

Ten years was a long time. The insurance company had probably sold it as scrap to reduce their loss. From Grandin's point of view, it was perfect. He'd managed to get rid of a key piece of evidence by making sure the boat disappeared. Many important months went by while it was missing, and the police lost yet another opportunity to prove his guilt.

He couldn't even be sure that the investigating officers back then had known about the existence of a boat that ought to have been forensically examined.

"Well done," he said to Ida. "Do me a favor and give Aram a call. He'll be pleased to hear this."

"I've also tried to contact Anton Blomgren, Siri's neighbor, but he's away on business. He left for a trade fair in Berlin yesterday, and won't be back in Stockholm until Tuesday." She paused. "By the way, Margit came by to see how things were going."

Thomas had reached the house, and took out his keys. Maybe he should have stayed in town and worked over the weekend, but all this pressure to solve the case quickly was exhausting.

Margit was stressed because things weren't progressing as rapidly as she would like. She'd been on the phone earlier in the day when he passed her office, and judging by what he'd heard, the call had been about the case and the need to take it seriously, solve it with the least possible publicity.

However, the bones had probably been in the ground for at least ten years; Thomas couldn't wave a magic wand. Plus he'd worked overtime all week.

He was more concerned about the situation in which the relatives found themselves. He hadn't forgotten about poor Susanna, but there was nothing he could do to speed up the identification process by the National Board of Forensic Medicine.

"Everything's under control," he said to Ida. "You can pass that on to Margit."

# Chapter 51

The strands of spaghetti were coiled on Nora's plate like unappetizing worms. She'd let Julia choose what they should have for dinner, and as expected she'd gone for spaghetti Bolognese. At least it was simple; all Nora had to do was boil the pasta and open a jar of ready-made sauce.

She poked at the food with her fork. She and Thomas never quarreled, not like this. She still couldn't understand why he'd been so difficult. She'd only been trying to help, and yet he'd told her off. She'd done her best to explain, but he'd refused to listen, almost as if he were determined to misunderstand her.

"Mommy?"

Julia's voice brought Nora back to the present. She'd put down her knife and fork and was holding a piece of spaghetti in her fingers, red sauce dripping onto her plate.

"Don't do that!" Nora snapped. She immediately regretted it when she saw Julia's terrified expression. Her daughter dropped the spaghetti as if it were red hot.

It wasn't Julia's fault that Thomas was behaving like an idiot.

"Sorry, darling. I didn't mean to shout."

She took a swig of red wine, then reached out and placed her hand over Julia's.

"When's Daddy coming home?"

"The day after tomorrow, I think."

To be honest, Nora couldn't remember. So much had been going on over the past few days. Jonas still hadn't responded to her texts or called back.

He was her husband, and Thomas was her best friend, but right now she was utterly sick of them both.

She reached for the wine bottle and realized it was empty. She hadn't intended to drink tonight, but the argument with Thomas had upset her.

She got to her feet. There was another bottle in the pantry.

"Mommy's just going to fetch something. Stay there and I'll be back in a minute."

# Chapter 52

It was almost seven thirty, and still warm outside. The birds were singing in the trees, and the hum of Friday-night activity could be heard from the harbor area.

Johanna was sitting on the terrace with her parents, Irene and Stefan. They'd just finished dinner, and she was full and contented. It had been a pleasant evening so far.

Everything was going to be OK with the rent; Mom was in a good mood. Life felt good, better than it had in a long time.

She'd had dinner ready when her parents arrived on the evening ferry. She'd cooked spaghetti carbonara and served it with fresh sourdough from the bakery. She'd set the table outdoors, with a vase of wildflowers that she'd picked in the meadow.

"The news is on in a minute," her father said, heading indoors.

Johanna glanced at her mother. This seemed like a good opportunity to talk about borrowing some more money. Dad could help her out with a few hundred, but it was Mom who decided on the larger sums.

"I'll stay out here with you for a while," Irene said, scraping up the last of the sauce with her fork. "This is delicious—thank you."

Johanna shrugged. "It was nothing special. I just thought you'd be hungry when you arrived." She glanced at her wineglass; it was empty.

They'd shared a bottle of red, and that was just enough, according to her mom. If Johanna suggested opening a second bottle, it wouldn't go down well.

"Is everything OK, honey?" her mom asked. "You're very quiet."

She ran a hand over her short light-brown hair. She'd changed into jeans and a sweater as soon as she got here; that was part of the ritual, the switch from optician to archipelago resident.

"Kind of."

Johanna piled up the plates, the cutlery clinking in the summer evening.

"I need to borrow some money," she blurted out, her lips suddenly dry. It was always hard to ask, but she didn't know how she was going to pay this month's rent on her apartment without her parents' help.

Her mom frowned. "Again?"

That was all it took to make Johanna feel ashamed and embarrassed, as usual. She'd heard it all so many times—that she ought to pull herself together, get a degree, make something of her life.

It wasn't that easy. If it was, she'd have done it long ago.

She pretended she hadn't picked up on her mom's tone of voice. There was no point in explaining that she was dreaming of becoming a hairdresser instead of going back to studying economics. That would just make Irene snort with derision.

"Things are a little tricky at the moment," she mumbled. "It's hard to get another job in the summer. I promise I'll pay you back as soon as I can."

Irene carefully folded her napkin and placed it on the table.

"You'll be twenty-eight in the fall, Johanna. How long are you intending to carry on working in restaurants? As a waitress?"

She uttered the word *waitress* as if it were a piece of dog shit.

"You need to sort out your life, sweetheart," she went on in a gentler voice. "That kind of life might be OK right now, but how will you feel when you're running around after customers in ten years' time, when you're nearly forty?"

*When your friends have graduated and found well-paid academic posts.* Mom didn't need to say it; Johanna knew exactly what she was thinking.

It was unbearable. Johanna already went out of her way to avoid her old friends. Their first question was always the same: *What are you doing these days?*

"Please, Mom."

Johanna gritted her teeth. She didn't feel good anymore, but she couldn't afford to get mad. Instead she made a fresh attempt.

"Do we have to talk about that now? All I'm asking for is a loan so that I can pay next month's rent. Six thousand, no more. We don't have to go through the whole thing yet again. I'm desperate; otherwise I wouldn't have come to you."

"So when are we going to talk about it?" Mom's cheeks were flushed with anger. "You never want to have these conversations. You always avoid anything difficult."

"That's not true."

Mom brushed a few crumbs off the table. Her tone changed from reproachful to pleading.

"Your dad and I are just so worried about you. Don't you understand?"

It didn't matter. Johanna couldn't listen to another sermon.

"Can I borrow six thousand or not?" she said, picking up the plates and getting to her feet.

Mom shook her head. "We can't keep doing this. We can't keep giving you money when you're not prepared to take responsibility for your own life. I'm sorry."

"But, Mom . . ."

"If you go back to college, we'll support you financially—otherwise you're on your own. You're almost thirty, Johanna—it's time to grow up."

Johanna slammed down the plates with such force that the loaf on the breadboard jumped into the air.

"Seriously? You're going for blackmail?"

"We're trying to help you." Mom pursed her lips.

Johanna lost control.

"Fuck you—both of you! I'll manage on my own!"

# Chapter 53

The water in the little inlet by Thomas's jetty was calm and peaceful. It was almost eight thirty, and the sun was slowly sinking behind the treetops on Storön.

Thomas was sitting in one of the cane armchairs with a cold beer, but he'd taken only a few sips. He was still irritated, but was beginning to think he'd been a little too hard on Nora.

She was fragile this summer—that was no secret. The Mina Kovač case had taken its toll, and she wasn't herself; she was a pale shadow of the strong woman she'd been.

He'd hoped that a few weeks' sick leave would do her good, that a summer on Sandhamn would help her to recover, but instead she'd decided to play detective, meddling in things that had nothing to do with her, even though she ought to know better.

He'd gone to see her with the aim of setting her straight, but she'd more or less exploded and kicked him out.

Women. He'd spent the last year quarreling with his ex-wife, and now he'd fallen out with his best friend. How hard could it be? How could Nora *not* see that she was in the wrong? Why wouldn't she listen?

His phone rang. The sight of Elin's name on the display immediately made him feel better. She often called to say good night when she was with Pernilla, and Thomas was always grateful.

"Hi, sweetheart," he said, smiling in spite of the fact that she couldn't see his face. "How are you today?"

"Good, but Mommy says I have to go to sleep now."

"Then I think you should do just that. It's important to do what Mommy says."

They chatted for a few minutes, then Elin passed the phone over to Pernilla.

"Hi," she said in her warm voice. "Are you on Harö? Down by the jetty?"

She knew him so well. Knew exactly where he liked to sit at sundown. The last red and orange streaks colored the sky as if someone had swept a wide paintbrush across the blue. The wispy clouds were edged in pink.

In the distance he could hear the sound of a motorboat.

"Exactly right," he said. "I guess I'm a creature of habit."

"With a cold beer in your hand." Pernilla laughed. "It must be beautiful out there. It's way too hot here in town; the air in the apartment isn't moving at all. Elin's sleeping with just a sheet over her."

"Why don't you come out here tomorrow?"

The words took Thomas by surprise; it wasn't a question he'd planned to ask.

Pernilla was equally taken aback. "What, both of us?"

The thought of spending the weekend with Pernilla and Elin was infinitely preferable to sitting around brooding over the argument with Nora.

"Absolutely. The water's lovely and warm, perfect for Elin. She loves swimming by the jetty."

Elin had finally completed the traditional test—jumping off the end of the jetty and swimming back to the shore on her own. That meant she no longer had to wear a life jacket whenever she was anywhere near the sea. She was so proud of herself.

"Are you sure you want us both to come?"

"I'm sure." Thomas cleared his throat. "There's always the guest room if you feel awkward . . ."

Pernilla responded with a laugh that sounded reassuringly genuine. "I'm sure it'll be fine. OK, we'll catch an early-morning boat to Sandhamn."

"I can pick you up from Stavsnäs in the Buster if you like."

"No need—we'll take the ferry. You can fetch us from the steamboat jetty."

# Saturday, August 13

# CHAPTER 54

Nora was on the ferry heading for Stavsnäs. She'd chosen a window table in the stern, with her back to the other passengers so that she could hide her bloodshot eyes.

There weren't many people on board. Most would be heading out into the archipelago on a fine Saturday in August, rather than traveling into the city.

Her stomach had refused breakfast, but she was managing to drink a cup of coffee along with two painkillers. Her head had been pounding when she woke up. She wished she hadn't had to medicate herself on yet another morning, but at least she was beginning to recover.

Nora gave herself a shake. Last night she'd fetched an expensive bottle from the cellar, a present to Jonas, and opened it. She refused to have a guilty conscience just because she'd allowed herself a glass or two. She was so tired of all the men in her life trying to make her feel that way.

Julia was with Eva. Nora had asked if her daughter could spend the day at the Lenanders', because she had to check out something at the apartment in Saltsjöbaden. As usual, Eva had been happy to help, and had also lent Nora her car, because Jonas had taken theirs to the airport.

Nora was definitely in a more positive frame of mind than yesterday. Her gut feeling told her she was on the right track, that Thomas and his colleagues hadn't seen the full picture. He'd been talking about some woman from Djurö instead of focusing on Astrid. Presumably the police didn't know Niklas existed.

And she was the one who'd told Thomas about Zacharias Fahlman and his possible involvement.

It was important to look at the case from different perspectives, but her instinct told her to distrust Fahlman. He'd terrified her, and Johanna also seemed to be scared of him. Nora had no doubt that Fahlman had the potential to be violent.

The ferry reversed away from Hasselkobben and swung around so that the sun was shining on Nora's seat. She moved into the shade.

If only she could get ahold of Niklas Johansson. He was the unknown factor. Maybe he was the perpetrator? That was probably a long shot; Lillian had spoken well of him. However, Nora wasn't prepared to exclude him at this stage. It wouldn't be the first time a "nice guy" had shown violent tendencies. Some men were capable of the most heinous crimes against women.

Andreis Kovač was the perfect example. He had once behaved in a loving and gentle way; otherwise Mina would never have fallen for him.

Appearances could be deceptive.

Nora tried to imagine the course of events. Maybe the killer had persuaded Astrid to go with him to Telegrafholmen, then something had gone wrong and she'd died. It could have been an accident, but once disaster had struck, the body had to be hidden. Telegrafholmen was the perfect place, because it was uninhabited. Everyone in Sandhamn knew that no construction was allowed there.

Nora took out her laptop.

If Niklas was the guilty party, then it was hardly surprising that she couldn't find him on the electoral register. Presumably he'd fled overseas when he realized what he'd done.

She finished her coffee. She'd begun to understand what she had to do in order to achieve justice for Astrid. She must convince Thomas that he was heading in the wrong direction, and solve the case for him.

The only way to do that was to track down the real perpetrator.

She had to contact Niklas, which meant speaking to his parents. A face-to-face meeting would increase the chances of her getting answers to her questions, hence the trip to the mainland.

She'd even put on a smart blue jacket and pants, in spite of the warm weather. She wanted to look as if she were there in her official capacity.

Once the case was cleared up, the police would thank her.

She was already looking forward to an apology from Thomas.

## *Astrid*

Astrid was setting the tables on the eastern veranda when Lillian came to find her.

"Can you go to the storeroom and fetch a box of napkins—we've almost run out up here."

Astrid laid out the last of the cutlery. "No problem."

The linen room, where all the bedding, towels, tablecloths, and napkins were stored, was in the cellar of the hotel across the way. A glassed-in bridge connected the two buildings; there was no need for staff or guests to face the elements if the weather was bad.

Astrid hurried across the bridge and took the elevator down to the cellar.

The corridor was in semidarkness when the doors opened; the only light came from tiny windows just below the ceiling. She groped for the switch, but before she found it, she heard a dull thud from the storeroom. When she turned around, she saw that the door was ajar. Someone was already in there, but the light wasn't on.

She wasn't alone down there.

The sound of a hard kick made her inhale sharply. Then came another, and another. Something crashed to the floor.

Astrid knew she ought to do something, but she was paralyzed by fear. If the attacker went for her, no one would hear her scream. And she didn't have her phone with her.

It could be quite some time before Lillian realized she was missing.

Her feet refused to move.

She felt behind her for the elevator button; maybe she could go back up before she was discovered.

A bellow of rage made her jump.

Her eyes had begun to grow accustomed to the darkness. The storeroom door opened a little farther, and she pressed herself against the wall, hoping that whoever was in there wouldn't see her.

After a moment she leaned forward. A lone silhouette was furiously battering something—it looked like one of the square packs that had just been returned from the laundry.

Suddenly there was silence, followed by a despairing sob. Astrid recognized the voice. She took a couple of steps forward and cautiously called out: "Niklas? Is that you?"

He was sitting in the middle of the floor surrounded by packs of bedding. He was hiding his face in his hands, and his shoulders were shaking. Astrid dropped to her knees beside him.

"What's happened?" she whispered, placing a hand on his arm.

"Go away."

"Has someone hurt you?"

"Get out!"

Astrid hesitated. She couldn't leave him like this.

"I'm not going anywhere," she said, gently stroking his wrist.

Niklas looked up, his expression wild. His eyes were swollen and bloodshot, and he had an angry red mark on one cheek. Someone must have hit him hard.

"I don't want you here!"

He turned and punched the wall with his fist, breaking the skin.

"Fuck off!"

# Chapter 55

Thomas was waiting for Pernilla and Elin on the jetty at Harö. The M/S *Dalarö* was only a couple of hundred yards away.

It was another beautiful day, with just a few ripples on the surface of the water beneath a clear blue sky.

It took a while for Thomas to identify the unfamiliar feeling in his body. For the first time in months, his spirits had lightened. The thought of seeing Pernilla wasn't irritating or upsetting; instead he was almost . . . happy.

After all the arguments, there shouldn't be anything left to be happy about, but today every trace of frustration was gone. He was looking forward to the weekend with Pernilla and his daughter, to spending a couple of uncomplicated days together with everything the way it used to be.

He couldn't think any further ahead. He'd done that on so many occasions in the past, and been equally disappointed each time.

Instead he focused on planning dinner. There were perch in the freezer, caught earlier in the summer. With new potatoes, cold mustard sauce, and a good Riesling, it would be a delicious meal. They could eat down by the jetty, just like in the old days.

Pernilla had always loved having dinner outdoors in the summer, spending hours at the table as the sun slowly disappeared in the west.

M/S *Dalarö* docked, and the gangway was lowered.

Thomas could see Pernilla and Elin; his daughter was jumping up and down and waving to him.

"Hi, Daddy!" she shouted eagerly. "We've got a surprise for you! We've bought raspberries for dessert!"

Raspberries indeed. With fresh cream, just like when he was a little boy.

Pernilla came toward him carrying a blue overnight case. She'd put her hair up in a ponytail; she let it grow over the past twelve months, and it suited her.

"Hi, Thomas."

She stopped, as if she weren't sure whether to hug him or not. "You haven't changed your mind? About the visit, I mean?"

She sounded almost shy.

"Not in the least," he said as he reached for her case.

He definitely hadn't changed his mind.

# Chapter 56

The house on Fornudden in Tyresö didn't look particularly striking from the street. The yellow building sat high above the lake known as Drevviken, and the black tiles on the roof shone in the morning sun.

Nora assumed that the view from the other side was magnificent. It was a fitting residence for a local government politician from a center-right party. Björn Johansson's home was in a beautiful setting, but it wasn't lavish enough to arouse resentment.

She parked her car and got out.

The property looked as if it dated from the eighties. There was something about the apricot-colored brick and the steel-framed windows that made her think of shoulder pads and big hair. She'd been a teenager back then, dancing to Culture Club. It felt like a hundred years ago.

A sparkling clean Volvo stood on the drive, next to a smaller Toyota. Good—that meant they were home.

It wasn't hard to figure out who drove which car. She'd seen photographs of Björn Johansson, and his firm jawline had already given her a clear impression of the kind of man he was.

She rang the doorbell. She had no choice but to introduce herself as a prosecutor, even though she knew it wasn't a good idea. Thomas would be furious if he knew what she was up to now, but all her instincts told her that she had to speak to Niklas's parents in order to make progress. Besides, she had no intention of letting Thomas boss her around. Not after yesterday's quarrel.

The door opened after a minute or so. Nora recognized Annie Johansson from the picture online, although she had noticeably aged. Her hairstyle was the same, but the color was now more silver than blond, and there were shadows beneath her eyes. She'd kept her neat figure, but Nora thought she looked skinny rather than slender.

"Yes?" Annie said, frowning slightly. She was leaning heavily on a crutch.

Nora held out her hand. "My name is Nora Linde, and I'm a prosecutor." She made an effort to sound as authoritative as possible. "I have some questions about your son, Niklas. May I come in?"

# CHAPTER 57

Annie Johansson led the way into the generous living room with pale sofas, the cushions perfectly arranged. The whole floor was open plan, and huge windows made the most of the stunning view, just as Nora had imagined.

On the wide terrace, which extended along the entire length of the building, a man was sitting at a table reading the morning paper.

Björn hadn't aged as much as his wife. He looked fit and healthy, as if he worked out on a regular basis. His shoulders were broad beneath the white polo shirt, and his arms were tanned.

Compared with her strong, powerful husband, Annie appeared even gaunter.

Björn glanced up as they stepped outside. The sun was dancing on the surface of the water only a couple of hundred yards below them.

"This is Nora Linde—she's a prosecutor," Annie explained. "She wants to ask us about Niklas."

Björn's enquiring expression grew serious. "Niklas?"

Nora had thought about what she was going to say. Best to get straight to the point. She hoped the Johanssons would be willing to talk to her.

"I've been trying to contact your son," she began. "The electoral register doesn't give a current address for him, so I was wondering if you could help me. Does he live overseas?"

Björn took his time folding up the newspaper and placing it on the table. It was *Svenska Dagbladet*, of course—the center-right morning paper.

"Why are you looking for my son?"

Nora had hoped to avoid bringing up the discovery on Telegrafholmen, but that was impossible under the circumstances.

"It's in connection with the bones found on Telegrafholmen earlier this week."

Björn and Annie stared at her blankly. Annie inhaled almost imperceptibly.

"What are you talking about?" Björn said.

Nora didn't want to say any more than she had to, but she was going to have to explain. Could they really have missed the news? It had featured heavily in the tabloid press, the perfect story for the summer, when little else was going on.

"Last Monday, human remains were found on the island of Telegrafholmen," she said. "It's opposite Sandhamn in the archipelago."

Annie's eyes widened, and she lowered herself onto the chair next to her husband.

"Your son knew the girl we think was murdered and buried there," Nora added.

"Is Niklas a suspect?" Annie whispered.

"I'm afraid I can't tell you that, but we'd really like to get in touch with him."

Annie's face was chalk white.

"Shall I get you a glass of water?" Björn asked. He, too, had paled beneath his tan. Annie shook her head, and Björn gently stroked her cheek.

"You'll have to forgive us," he said to Nora. "We've been in Spain for two weeks; we got back late last night. We've only just unpacked; we knew nothing about this."

"We need to reach Niklas in order to ask him one or two questions," Nora said again. "Could you give me his contact details?"

Annie glanced at her husband. She was twisting her wedding and engagement rings around her finger, the diamonds sparkling in the sunlight.

"Niklas couldn't possibly be involved in something like that," she mumbled.

"I'm not saying he is. I just want to talk to him."

"I'm afraid we can't help you," Björn said, getting to his feet.

This was disappointing. Nora realized that the parents' instinct would be to protect their son, but she'd still expected them to give her a phone number at least.

"Why not?" Her tone was brusque. "We really do need to question him; it's very important for our investigation."

Björn spread his hands apologetically. "I'm afraid we don't know where Niklas is."

"I'm sorry?"

"Our son—" He broke off and took a deep breath.

"We hardly ever hear from him. He sends a postcard every now and then," Annie said, her eyes shining with unshed tears.

"It's OK, sweetheart," Björn murmured, placing a supportive hand on his wife's shoulder. Annie put her own hand over his, clinging to his fingers like a shipwrecked sailor clutching a life preserver.

"How long has this been going on?" Nora asked. Annie looked away. "How long?"

"Ten years," Annie replied tonelessly.

"Ten years," Nora repeated. This was too much of a coincidence. "Could you be a little more specific? What date are we talking about?"

"The middle of August."

Exactly when Astrid had gone missing.

"2006?" Nora said, just to be on the safe side.

Björn nodded.

"So what happened?"

Björn leaned on the fence surrounding the terrace, gripping the balustrade as if he needed extra stability.

"We were both working at the Sailors Hotel on Sandhamn back then. I was the manager, and Niklas worked in the restaurant. It was his last week before he finished for the season." His voice was filled with pain. He gazed out across the water. "He'd sent a text message to his boss, asking to leave early. When I went to his room in the staff accommodations, it was empty. He'd taken all his belongings without saying a word to me."

"You mean he . . . disappeared?" Nora hardly dared to believe her ears. This changed everything. Niklas had vanished at the same time as Astrid. He was the missing piece of the puzzle, just as she'd thought. Wait until Thomas heard this!

Björn was clearly upset.

"He'd gone away. We received a postcard a few days later; he said he was going to look for work overseas, and he told us not to try and find him. He'd be in touch when he was settled."

"And that didn't happen?"

Annie's eyes were filled with sorrow.

"Since then, he's only sent one card a year—on my birthday."

*Ten years. How terrible not to see your child for such a long time.*

"We haven't seen or spoken to him since then," Björn added.

"Did you report it to the police?"

"What good would that have done?" Björn sighed and rubbed a hand over his forehead. "Niklas wasn't a minor; he could do what he wanted. The police would have been powerless. We tried to get ahold of him through his friends, any contact we could think of, but it was hopeless. No one knew where he'd gone."

"And where did the postcards come from?"

"Different countries. The first one was postmarked in Sweden. There was no doubt that it was Niklas's handwriting, and he made it very clear that he wanted to be left in peace."

Annie was even paler now, almost transparent. Nora wondered how to ask the next question without hurting the poor woman. She was obviously finding the conversation extremely difficult.

"How come your son didn't want anything to do with you?"

"I've no idea," Björn replied. "He's the only one who can tell you that."

Annie's face crumpled. Her hand flew to her mouth and she stood up. "I'm sorry," she said, letting out a sob as she hobbled away.

Björn's jaws were working. "This split is a real tragedy for us. My wife is seriously ill—she was already sick when Niklas took off. That's what I've struggled with the most—the fact that he left his mom when she really needed him."

Nora could see the hurt in his eyes. He made no attempt to hide it as he continued: "We've kept it quiet because I'm something of a public figure within the local community. There's nothing to be gained by letting people into our private lives, and I don't want Annie exposed to gossip or harrowing questions."

Nora could hear suppressed sobs from behind the bedroom door.

"My wife grieves for Niklas every single day. I hope you'll respect the fact that we simply can't help you."

Björn came and stood next to Nora. He put his hand on her back and gently steered her toward the front door.

"My apologies. I have to take care of my wife—you saw how upset she was. She's suffering from chronic leukemia. This hasn't been easy for her."

He opened the door, and Nora set off toward her car. Suddenly she heard his voice again: "By the way, where did you say you work?"

Nora gave a start. She couldn't refuse to answer, even though it was the last thing she wanted to go into. She turned back.

"The Economic Crimes Authority."

"I'd like to see your ID."

Nora hadn't shown it to Annie; she'd been hoping to get away with it. Björn was looking searchingly at her, as if he sensed that he'd struck a nerve. He held out his hand. "Is that a problem?"

"Not at all."

She opened her purse, took out her ID, and showed it to him. He took it between his thumb and forefinger and inspected the laminated card.

"Can I ask why the Economic Crimes Authority is involved in a case like this?"

"I'm on loan temporarily," Nora said quickly. "Staff shortages."

"I see."

Björn Johansson's gaze burned into her back as she walked toward the car.

# CHAPTER 58

They'd finished dinner long ago, but Thomas and Pernilla were still sitting outside with a cup of coffee. Elin had played by the jetty for a while, then clambered onto his lap. Now she was dozing in his arms, her head resting on his chest. He loved the weight, the feeling of holding his daughter close. The sweet smell of a sleepy child.

"Is she heavy?" Pernilla said. "She's growing so fast—soon she'll be too big for your lap."

Elin was already eight years old. Thomas wished he could stop time, or at least slow it down. He didn't want to think about the fact that she would soon be a sulky teenager, a young person who cared more about her friends than anything else, and found her parents painfully embarrassing.

"It's fine," he said, stroking his daughter's soft blond hair.

"By the way, how are things with Nora and Jonas?" Pernilla asked. "I haven't spoken to them for ages—the summer went by so quickly."

*Good question.*

Thomas had managed to avoid thinking about Nora all day, and he had no desire to talk about her now. He was still angry because of their quarrel. He'd been prepared to cover for her, but he was beginning to feel more and more uncomfortable about the whole thing. Why should he make the effort if she was determined to ignore his advice?

There was no point in dragging Pernilla into it; this was something he had to solve on his own. Before it got worse.

"She's been off sick all summer," he said. "After that case back in the spring—the guy who was trying to get to his wife and son."

Pernilla was aware of what had gone on. "I know she took it hard—such a tragic outcome. She blamed herself, even though it wasn't her fault." She rubbed one eyelid with her index finger, her dark nail polish gleaming in the sunlight. "Typical female behavior—feeling responsible when something goes wrong, whatever the real reason behind the situation." She reached out and pulled up a few blades of grass. She gazed at them thoughtfully for a few seconds before adding: "We always think we can fix everything if we just try hard enough. Or make one more attempt."

That was certainly true of Nora. Right now she was hell-bent on investigating a case that had nothing to do with her. The fact that she knew this perfectly well merely served to increase Thomas's frustration.

Was she in some misguided way trying to make up for the Andreis Kovač fiasco? Was that why she'd gotten involved? But Nora wasn't like that, she was way too smart. Exhaustion and sick leave couldn't be the only reasons for her irrational behavior. There had to be another explanation.

Which unfortunately eluded him at the moment.

A gull came flying over the shining surface of the water before making a lightning dive. It disappeared equally quickly with something silver wriggling in its beak.

"Thanks for inviting us," Pernilla said. "I'm very happy to be here."

Thomas was happy, too.

It had been a peaceful, uncomplicated day, with no pressure. They'd spent most of their time relaxing by the jetty. Eaten a simple lunch, lingered over coffee with delicious vanilla donuts that Pernilla had brought with her from the bakery in Stavsnäs.

Dinner had also been a success. The three of them had worked together in the kitchen, and the fish Thomas had caught had gone down well. Even Elin had had a second portion. It was a long time since he'd felt so relaxed. It was almost like the old days; they were able to talk without any bitter undertones.

"Thank you for coming," he said. "This has been one of the best days of the whole summer."

Pernilla raised an eyebrow. She'd always been able to do that, raise one eyebrow at a time.

"Well, there you go," she said. "I'll take that as a compliment."

Her hair was loose, falling to her shoulders and framing her lovely face. In the soft evening light, Thomas could see the young woman he'd fallen for twenty years earlier.

"I'm not joking," he said with a smile. He adjusted his position on the chair so that Elin's weight was better distributed. She was fast asleep by now. Pernilla was right; he could tell how much she'd grown.

Pernilla yawned. "Maybe I should go and make up the bed in the guest room."

She gave Thomas a look that he found hard to interpret. Was it an invitation? Or a subtle reminder that they were no longer a couple, and would obviously be sleeping in separate rooms?

He had no idea, nor did he know what response was expected of him.

"Why don't you stay here for a while," he suggested instead. "I'll go and put Elin to bed if you pour me a glass of wine."

Pernilla sank back in her chair.

"Good idea," she said with a warm smile. "It's a lovely evening—it would be a shame to waste it."

# *Siri*

Mia called out just as Siri was unlocking the front door.

"Is everything OK between you and Petter?"

Siri managed to force a smile before she turned around to respond. Two weeks in the archipelago had done nothing to improve Petter's mood—quite the reverse. The chilly atmosphere between them was still there.

"Absolutely," she shouted back.

Mia glanced from side to side, then hurried across the street. Her hair was bleached by the sun, and her soft cheeks were covered in freckles.

"We haven't seen each other for ages," she said with a little shake of her head. "We've barely exchanged two words since Midsummer."

"Is it that long?" Siri murmured. The thought of the Midsummer party when Petter had gotten so drunk made her cheeks burn.

"Why don't the two of you come to dinner tonight? It would be good to catch up before the summer's over."

Mia and Anton enjoyed entertaining. Siri and Petter always celebrated Midsummer and New Year's with them.

Mia clearly had no idea of the real situation. Siri was desperately trying to come up with an excuse when Petter pulled into the drive, his eyes concealed behind sunglasses.

Mia smiled delightedly and waved at him, the bangles on her left arm jangling away.

"Perfect timing!" she exclaimed, opening the car door on Petter's side. "I've just invited you and your lovely wife over for dinner tonight!"

Petter opened his mouth, but Mia didn't give him the chance to speak. "Come in an hour. We'll have a barbecue—nothing special!"

She raised a hand in farewell and scurried away before they could protest.

"See you soon!" she called over her shoulder.

The smell of a freshly baked rhubarb pie met Siri and Petter at the gate. Mia had set the table on the wooden deck that Anton had built at the back of the house a few years earlier.

Siri allowed Petter to lead the way into the garden. Anton was at the barbecue, turning the meat. His fair hair was a little too long, and she could see the muscles of his back beneath the white shirt with rolled-up sleeves. She gave him a cautious hug, trying not to look at Petter, who was handing over a bottle of wine to Mia.

"Look, my favorite!" Mia called out to her husband.

She poured everyone a drink and told the boys to turn down the television. Siri could see five-year-old Pelle and eight-year-old Linus through the living room window watching a children's show.

Suddenly there was a yell, then a crash as Linus pushed Pelle off the sofa. A second later, Pelle came racing outside. He threw himself into his father's arms, sobbing loudly. Anton picked him up and stroked his hair, murmuring words of consolation, while Mia dealt with Linus. After a little while, Anton put his son down. Pelle still looked upset, but Anton managed to get a smile out of him. Order was restored.

Siri watched the boy as he trotted back to the living room. She knocked back her drink in a single gulp.

Mia returned, and they all sat down at the table, where pale-blue napkins matched the floral-patterned crockery.

"Help yourselves to salad," she said. "There's dressing in the white jug."

She chattered away as she passed around barbecue sauce and baked potatoes; she was her usual bubbly self. Siri admired her social skills; Mia could always find something to talk about. However, even she struggled this evening. Petter hardly said a word, and Siri could hear how stiff she herself sounded when she attempted to contribute to the conversation.

Anton brought over a tray of meat, then lingered by the barbecue, muttering something about the vegetables not being quite ready.

"So how was your vacation?" Mia asked. "You rented a cottage in the archipelago, didn't you?"

"Well now . . ." Petter said. He gave Siri an icy look. His jaw was tense and he was gripping his fork tightly. He leaned forward, shoulders up. Siri broke into a cold sweat, stress pulsating through her body. *Not tonight, please.* She wasn't ready for a scene, didn't want an argument in front of the boys. Where was Anton? She realized he'd gone into the kitchen to fetch something.

Mia glanced from Petter to Mia, confused by Petter's tone. Couldn't she see what was going on?

"Not great, then?" Mia said, raising her glass. "It's always a risk when you rent through one of those websites. Have I told you about the time we were supposed to go to Öland?"

To Siri's relief, she embarked on a funny anecdote. Siri tried to smile in the right places, and avoided eye contact with Petter. He was still staring angrily at Siri while Mia chattered on about the cottage on Öland.

Siri just wanted to go home. The situation was ridiculous, the four of them pretending that everything was fine. Four old friends with nothing to hide from one another.

Shame flooded her body.

# Chapter 59

The dark sea stretched out before Johanna. She'd curled up in a crevice down below Dansberget, with the lights of Korsö opposite. The rock was cold against the base of her spine, but she couldn't bring herself to move.

The lighthouse out by Svängen flashed regularly against the dark-blue sky.

What was she going to do?

Somehow she had to find the money for rent; otherwise she'd be evicted. The apartment was all she had. She couldn't lose that, too, not on top of everything else.

If she didn't pay on time, she knew exactly what would happen. She'd already been late more than once, and there was no more room for negotiation.

She swallowed, but the hard lump in her throat refused to go away.

She heard the sound of laughter up above—a group of young people who'd stopped to chat, presumably on their way home from the bar.

Johanna had been like that once, excited and giggly. She would cycle off with Astrid and a couple of boys, have a few beers on Kvarnberget as the sun went down. Sometimes they'd stayed there until it rose again.

She'd loved those light, carefree nights, the feeling of endless summer.

She'd been so happy back then.

Before it all went wrong.

A large motor launch shot past on its way out of the harbor. It was traveling way too fast, paying no attention to the speed limit of eight knots. It produced a substantial swell, and within seconds the waves came rolling in, crashing against the rocks and splashing Johanna's legs.

She shivered and pulled her cardigan more tightly around her. She shouldn't have come here. This place evoked too many unpleasant memories.

She had spent years avoiding Dansberget, but tonight, after the quarrel with her mother, she'd somehow ended up here.

She had to find the money, but there was no one left to borrow from; she already owed most of her friends.

Nor did she have anything to sell. Her old furniture wouldn't raise much if she advertised it online.

She owned nothing of value.

Or did she? The forbidden thought nudged at her.

She'd carried the secret for ten years. She was the only one who was still around, the only one who knew what had really happened that night.

Could she exploit that knowledge now that Nora Linde was sniffing around?

Did she dare?

What would happen if she threatened to tell the cops everything? It would be pure blackmail, no doubt about it.

She tasted the word, and became even more uncomfortable. The idea frightened her. She wasn't that kind of person, someone who put a price on her silence. She'd like to think that she hadn't committed a crime by keeping quiet for all these years, but extorting money from someone was a different matter.

What if Nora Linde found out what she was doing? Johanna could wind up in court.

She drew up her legs and rested her forehead against her knees. What should she do?

She'd never considered this course of action before, but the situation was desperate. However she turned things over in her mind, she couldn't come up with another answer. The secret was her only resource right now, and she had to use it.

If she could get the money that way, then all her problems would be solved.

There was no alternative.

For ten years, she'd kept quiet; maybe it wasn't so terrible if she thought about herself for once?

Johanna stared out into the darkness. The lighthouse continued to flash.

There was one person who couldn't afford for her to tell the cops what she knew. That person would risk going to jail for many years.

Johanna's only way out was to demand payment for her silence.

# CHAPTER 60

It was well after midnight. The last time Nora had checked her ancient clock radio, the figures had shown a quarter to one. Sleep still evaded her, even though the room was cool and the sheets freshly laundered.

She turned over onto her other side, stared at the roller blind moving gently in the breeze from the window.

She'd drunk almost a whole bottle of red wine; why couldn't she sleep? Her eyes ached with tiredness, yet her muscles refused to relax. She was simultaneously wide awake and exhausted.

A sleeping pill would help, but she was determined to stop taking them. That was why she'd allowed herself a little too much wine this evening; she couldn't give up everything at once.

Her mind was racing, living a life of its own.

Lillian's sad story. Zacharias Fahlman and Niklas Johansson—she hadn't figured out exactly how they were involved in Astrid's case. The suspicious look Björn Johansson had given her just before she drove away.

The quarrel with Thomas.

Jonas. He'd spoken to Julia while Nora was in town. She couldn't think about him right now; it was all too complicated.

She shifted her position in bed. She was certain that Niklas Johansson was the key, but was he the perpetrator or a witness? The fact that he'd disappeared at the same time as Astrid changed everything.

Another idea struck her: Was Niklas the person they'd found on Telegrafholmen? But no—he'd sent his parents a postcard every year, and apparently they were convinced that the handwriting was his. Therefore he was still alive.

She had to get ahold of him, but how?

Someone must be in touch with him. The only person she could think of was Johanna Strand, but she'd told Thomas about Nora's visit. Did she dare to contact Johanna again? There was no one else to turn to.

She decided to go and see Johanna the next day. Or rather later today . . . Ask if she remembered anything else about Niklas, anything that might help Nora to track him down.

She had to convince Johanna that she meant well. Her only aim was to solve the mystery of what had happened to Johanna's friend. Astrid deserved to have someone who was on her side, just as Mina had. That was why Nora was pushing the boundaries; she had to put things right.

She sighed and adjusted her pillow. It carried the scent of a fresh sea breeze; she'd hung the sheets and pillowcases down by the jetty to dry.

It was impossible to relax and get comfortable.

She'd become much too involved in Mina's case on a personal level, and now she was lying here. Nothing had turned out the way she'd expected, but she couldn't stop thinking about Astrid. Thomas wanted her to take a step back, but that was out of the question.

It wasn't a case of interfering in the investigation—she knew perfectly well that it was a police matter. However, she was absolutely convinced that Thomas and his team were on the wrong track, that they hadn't grasped the full picture. Astrid had presumably met a terrible fate ten years ago; even if she was dead, the case must be solved and the guilty party made to face the consequences of what he—or she—had done.

Nora clenched her fists beneath the covers.

Astrid's murderer must not be allowed to get away with it. She refused to let that happen. Whatever Thomas said, Astrid deserved justice.

She hadn't managed to protect Mina and see Andreis Kovač convicted, but this time she was going to get it right.

Emir Kovač's face came into her mind's eye, and her heart began to pound. She hated her body's spontaneous reaction, the fact that the mere thought of him terrified her. The nightmares that had plagued her all summer were deep-seated; she couldn't control her fear.

It would be so easy for someone like Kovač to break into the house . . .

*No. Don't think like that.*

Nora had never had a problem being alone on Sandhamn with the children. Only a few days ago she'd snapped at Jonas, told him not to worry about her.

And yet her stomach muscles contracted at the unwelcome memory of Emir.

She squeezed her eyes shut tight, tried to obliterate the image, but her heart was racing now. She placed the palm of her hand on her chest and pressed hard in an attempt to steady the beat. The fear of dying came flooding back.

If only Jonas had been at home, but his reassuring embrace was out of reach.

It was impossible to wipe out the hatred in Emir Kovač's eyes, the hatred that had haunted her for so long. It filled the room, it was as if he were standing right in front of her, his face contorted with venom.

His promise to take his revenge because she'd helped Mina when his brother, Andreis, was after her.

*I will rape your daughter and kill her before your eyes. Then it will be your turn. You will die slowly so that you will suffer for a long time, you dirty whore.*

The horrific words echoed inside her head.

Nora curled up in the fetal position and tried to take deep breaths, but there was no air. The covers were suffocating her; she kicked them off, but it didn't help. She ended up lying on her back, panting, shivering and sweating at the same time. Her mouth was so dry that she couldn't swallow, and her lips hurt.

In the bathroom cabinet, there was a box of the antianxiety medication she'd been given at the beginning of the summer. She knew she shouldn't mix alcohol and drugs, but she was having a full-blown panic attack. Her fingers were numb, the oxygen was running out.

*Enough.*

Nora staggered into the bathroom, opened the box of Stesolid, and forced down half a tablet.

She rested her forehead against the cool glass of the mirror, slowing her breathing as she waited for the effect to kick in. She put her wrists under the faucet until the cold water on her skin became so painful that she couldn't think about anything else.

After a while she managed to go back to bed. She wasn't sleepy, but her body felt calmer. Her pulse was no longer throbbing in her ears.

Would she be able to sleep now?

She began to count backward slowly from five hundred. Then she did it again with her eyes closed. Her muscles finally began to relax. She rolled onto her side and pushed her hand beneath the pillow—her favorite position. At long last she was dozing off.

A faint sound from downstairs made her open her eyes. She'd left her bedroom door ajar, just in case Julia woke and called out to her.

Was it her imagination, or had it come from the hallway? She propped herself up on one elbow, listening hard.

The seconds ticked by. Nothing.

There it was again. Louder this time.

# Chapter 61

The old wooden wall behind Thomas's head creaked. He turned so that he was lying on his back.

The summer cottage on Harö had originally been an unused barn that he and Pernilla had renovated early in their relationship. When Pernilla became pregnant with Elin, they'd made some changes to give them three separate bedrooms—smaller but much more practical.

And now each of them was in a room of their own.

Thomas glanced at the empty side of the double bed, where Pernilla could have been. He still thought of it as her side, even though they'd been separated since the previous summer, but Pernilla had eventually said good night down by the jetty and made up her bed in the room next to Elin's. Thomas hadn't protested; instead he'd lingered by the water, listening to the crickets chirping in the August darkness.

And now he was wondering what would have happened if he'd said something before Pernilla had gone up to the house. If he'd reached out and taken her hand, drawn her close, allowed himself to forget, just for a moment, all those harsh words they'd exchanged over the past twelve months.

She'd passed so close to him that he'd felt the warmth of her body, been aware of the scent of her favorite soap that was still in the bathroom.

It was too hot. The window was open, but it didn't help.

Thomas pushed down the covers, but kept them halfway down his chest, more for the comforting weight than the warmth.

Why couldn't things always be like this between them? Simple and uncomplicated, without the constant bickering.

By the time they separated, he'd been sick and tired of all the unspoken reproaches, the frustration when the least little thing was misinterpreted.

The counselor they'd been seeing had asked them to recall the good times in their relationship, the feeling when they first met and fell in love.

Thomas remembered the exact moment.

They'd spotted each other in a bar he'd gone to with Nora and her first husband, Henrik, when those two had just started dating. Nora had been head over heels in love, and Thomas had felt like the third wheel. Pernilla was there with two friends who only had eyes for each other, so she was in the same situation as Thomas.

They'd exchanged a glance and burst out laughing.

Things had moved fast. Before long they'd moved in together. They'd been so happy until sudden infant death syndrome took Emily from them.

That was the first time they separated; the pain drove them apart. However, they'd managed to find their way back. Been given Elin, and a second chance to love each other.

Could they do it again?

Thomas clasped his hands behind his head and stared up at the ceiling. He was probably letting his imagination run away with him. One enjoyable day had very little to do with reality. He was just fooling himself. They were incapable of living together, and that was that.

Why did it have to be so difficult?

He turned the pillow over, settled down again, closed his eyes, but he was still wide awake.

He heard something from the kitchen—the clink of a glass, the sound of running water. Pernilla must have got up for a drink.

Should he go and see if she was OK?

# Chapter 62

Nora tried to home in on what had disturbed her. Everything was distorted by the darkness. All she could hear now was her own breathing, rapid and shallow.

It must have been the wind, a branch lifted by a sudden gust. Probably the birch that grew much too close to the front porch. They'd talked about pruning it, but hadn't gotten around to it yet.

It was just her anxiety coming back to haunt her. Emir Kovač couldn't possibly be out there. She was imagining things.

But hadn't it sounded like the creaking of the wooden steps as someone approached the door? The squeak of the old iron handle, as if someone was cautiously pushing it down to see if the door was locked?

She heard something else—the unmistakable crunch of gravel. Someone was walking around the house, making their way to the veranda door, which was always left ajar in the summer to let in air.

Had she remembered to close and lock it before she went to bed? She wasn't sure.

She broke out into a sweat. This was no curious night stroller who'd taken a wrong turn. Kovač was here to kill her, just as she'd feared all along.

*I will rape your daughter and kill her before your eyes. Then it will be your turn. You will die slowly so that you will suffer for a long time, you dirty whore.*

She was overwhelmed by panic. The crushing sensation in her chest was worse than ever.

Nora pinched her arm hard, trying to remain calm. She mustn't lose control, not when she was alone in the house with Julia.

The pain helped. She breathed more easily, found the courage to open her eyes.

Another crunch from outside. There was no room for doubt; an unknown person was in her garden.

She tried to focus. If Kovač was about to break in, she had to protect Julia. Her daughter's safety was paramount. She couldn't let him get anywhere near Julia.

There was no point in calling the police; they wouldn't get here in time.

Who could she call?

Thomas? He was on Harö, at least fifteen minutes away. *Too far.* She might only have minutes. Eva lived a few hundred yards away. Her husband, Kalle, was a big guy—he'd be able to help.

Nora reached for her phone, but the screen remained dark when she tried to switch it on. The battery had run out before dinner; thanks to all the wine she'd drunk, she'd forgotten to charge it.

She was struggling to breathe. The charger was in the kitchen.

She pinched her arm again, even harder this time.

She felt the movement of the house as footsteps mounted the old wooden steps leading to the veranda. It was directly below her bedroom but couldn't be seen from her window.

She had to get up.

Nora swung her legs over the side of the bed and pulled on a pair of sweatpants. If he got into the house, she had to defend herself and Julia. Nothing else mattered.

She looked around in the darkness for a weapon.

There were knives in the kitchen, of course, but she daren't go downstairs. She tried to think—what was up here that she could use? Her hairbrush? The bedside lamp?

Scissors.

She crept over to the closet where she kept Aunt Signe's old needlework box. There must be a pair of scissors in there, long and sharp.

She dropped to her knees and could just make out the contours of the drawers in the box. She opened each one in turn and felt around until she found what she was searching for.

She grabbed the scissors and stood up. She was determined to protect her daughter. She had to do this, however terrified she was.

Silently she made her way to Julia's room.

## *Astrid*

It was three o'clock in the afternoon, and Astrid had just finished her shift. She was on her way out of the staff exit when Niklas called to her.

"Astrid—wait!"

They hadn't spoken to each other since the incident in the linen room, but there was plenty of gossip among the staff. Everyone was saying that Niklas had been beaten by his father.

Astrid had a strong feeling that Niklas had been avoiding her for the past week. They'd hardly spoken, even though they'd worked the same shifts.

She turned around, and he quickly caught up with her. He pushed back his brown hair; he seemed to be searching for the right words.

"Have you got time for a coffee?" he said eventually, pushing his hands deep into his pockets.

"Sure."

They each bought a coffee from the ice-cream kiosk by the children's play area and sat down on one of the benches on the promenade. The afternoon sun was warm, and it was good to relax for a while. Astrid's feet were aching, as they always did after a long day at work.

Niklas was leaning forward, both hands wrapped around his coffee cup. Without looking at Astrid, he mumbled something inaudible.

"What did you say?"

"I'm sorry I told you to fuck off. In the linen room."

The tips of his ears glowed bright red.

"It's OK," Astrid reassured him.

Niklas kept his eyes fixed on the ground as if the sand at his feet required his full attention. Astrid wondered if he was going to say anything else, explain what had happened, but when he didn't speak, she felt she couldn't keep quiet.

"Do you want to talk about it?" she said gently.

"It was a bad day, that's all."

"I see."

Astrid took a sip of her coffee, gazing out at the boats moored along the pontoons. A large yacht was just maneuvering into its space at the nearest jetty. She couldn't force him to confide in her. Some things were too difficult. As long as you didn't put whatever it was into words, you could pretend it didn't exist.

"It was my fucking dad," Niklas said after a long silence. "Maybe you've heard that already? I guess everybody knows. I've seen the way they look at me, like I'm some kind of freak."

The bitterness in his voice made Astrid's heart contract.

"He's crazy." Niklas's expression hardened. "He thinks he can discipline me now, even though he's never cared about anything except himself and his fucking career. And Mom."

"I understand."

Astrid understood more than Niklas could possibly imagine. The sense of powerlessness, of not being important to your own parent. Never coming first. Astrid knew all about that kind of pain, how it ate away at your self-esteem, little by little.

Just like Niklas, she stayed out in the evenings to avoid going home.

"I'm sure things will get better," she ventured. "Maybe you could talk to your mom?"

Niklas rubbed his eyes.

"She'd get upset. Dad's like a god to her—he can do no wrong in her eyes."

It was the first time Niklas had mentioned his mother.

"Mom's not well," he continued. "She has chronic leukemia. She can't work, and she mustn't get stressed. She can't cope with it."

He let out a bark of mirthless laughter.

"Dad bawls me out for that, too. I'm such a disappointment to them both because of my grades. I ought to behave perfectly all the time so that Mom doesn't have to worry about me. That's the only thing that matters."

"I understand," Astrid said again.

Niklas was clutching his coffee cup so tightly that his knuckles were white. His hair flopped over his forehead, hiding his face.

"I've only myself to blame. I should never have taken this job, then at least I wouldn't have had to work with him every fucking day."

Astrid wanted to give him a hug, make him feel better.

"I wish I didn't ever have to see the fucker again."

"Don't say that," Astrid protested. "You've finished school and you're over eighteen—can't you just leave home?"

"I will, as soon as possible. But right now I don't have any money. You know what it's like in Stockholm—everything's so expensive. Plus he's making me pay for the wine I dropped."

"Oh no!"

Astrid had heard about the broken bottles of red wine. It was a lot of money—at least two weeks' pay.

"If only I could figure out a way of getting ahold of some money, I'd leave tomorrow."

Niklas suddenly hurled his cup as far as he could. It hit the ground with a thud, coffee splashing in all directions.

Astrid stared at him, completely taken aback.

"I hate him! I'd do anything to get away from here!" He slammed his fist down on the bench. "Sometimes I think I could kill him!"

# CHAPTER 63

Julia was fast asleep when Nora silently slipped into her room to make sure she was OK. Her daughter was lying on her side with her face pressed against her favorite cuddly toy. She was breathing softly, steadily.

Nora sighed with relief, but she was still worried. The door couldn't be locked; the key had been lost long ago. Should she position herself on guard outside, or would it be better to stay in the room if someone was trying to gain access?

The only lock was on the bathroom door, but the pathetic little hasp wouldn't keep out a determined intruder. Plus she didn't really want to wake Julia. It would be impossible to get her to the bathroom without making a noise, and the child would realize that something was wrong.

Nora tried to calm down as she listened for fresh sounds from the veranda, but the shadows closed around her until she felt dizzy and had to lean on the doorframe.

If only she'd charged her phone, then she'd have been able to call for help. She should never have drunk all that wine. Or taken a sleeping pill.

They used to have a landline, but had canceled the contract the previous summer because they only used their cell phones. If she'd known . . .

Julia turned over and murmured something unintelligible. A strand of hair was plastered to her cheek, damp with sweat.

A sudden noise made Nora gasp, but it was just the roller blind flapping in the breeze.

Everything would have been different if Jonas had been home. Why had she quarreled with him? Their stupid argument seemed so pathetic and unnecessary right now.

If she and Julia made it through this night, she would fix things with Jonas.

Kovač could be there at any minute. If he got in through the veranda door, he would probably come straight upstairs. She and Julia were caught like rats in a trap.

She pressed her back against the wall, took deep breaths. She had to get through this. There was no one to turn to. Her fingers tightened around the scissors. Kovač might attack her, but she refused to let him touch Julia.

The thought gave her fresh strength.

Footsteps crunched on the gravel once more; had Kovač changed his mind? Was he heading back to the gate?

Nora was breathing with her mouth open. Was he going to leave without harming them? It was no good looking through Julia's window; the angle was wrong. She moved toward the stairs. She waited for a few seconds, then tiptoed down. From the last step, she could see the hallway and the front door. The banister hid her to a certain extent, but she still felt exposed, like a living target.

The crunching sound grew louder; he was on his way back to the house.

*Please, please make him go away.*

Nora wasn't sure if she'd only thought the words, or whispered them like an invocation.

Silence.

She held her breath, waited, with cold sweat trickling down her back.

A dark silhouette appeared behind the frosted glass in the door.

Nora crouched down, unable to take her eyes off the shadow. He was here, just yards away from her. He was standing outside her house, so terrifying that the hairs stood up on the back of her neck.

She knew he wanted to hurt her.

The shadow came closer, and Nora saw the figure raise its right arm, pointing at her as if he knew she was there.

He was aiming straight at her.

His brother, Andreis, had been armed when he'd attacked Mina, when he'd tried to kill her in front of their son.

The memories came flooding back with horrific clarity. It really was Emir Kovač out there. He'd come to kill her, just like in her nightmares.

Nora closed her eyes.

*He's going to fire,* she thought as the world exploded in a shower of broken glass.

# CHAPTER 64

When Thomas opened the bedroom door, he saw Pernilla standing at the sink. He'd assumed it was her; Elin didn't usually wake up during the night, and if she did, she'd call out to her daddy rather than get up.

Pernilla hadn't noticed him. Her silky nightgown clung to her curves. She'd always had a fondness for luxury nightwear; she never slept in faded T-shirts.

"I want to look good for you even when I'm sleeping," she'd said at the beginning of their relationship. Thomas could still recall the sensation of black silk against bare skin, how easily the fabric slipped off her body when they were together.

She turned and saw him.

"Did I wake you?" she said quietly. "I didn't mean to."

Thomas shook his head. "I couldn't get to sleep."

It was too dark to see the expression in her eyes, but something about her posture gave him courage. It was madness, but he couldn't stop himself. The wine and all those memories took over; he couldn't just say good night and close the bedroom door behind him.

He couldn't let this moment go.

He went and stood beside her. He could feel her hip bone against his, her flat stomach just touching his. Her perfume filled his head.

"You're so beautiful," he said, his voice thick with emotion.

Pernilla held his gaze as she put down her glass. She turned her face up toward him; he was inches away from her lips. She stood perfectly still for a few seconds, then reached up and stroked his cheek so gently that he shivered.

Was she still unsure?

The gesture was somewhere between a farewell and an invitation—impossible to interpret, like their conversation earlier in the evening.

He had to touch her.

He seized her wrist and pressed his lips to her palm. "I've missed you."

"I've missed you, too," Pernilla whispered. "So much."

Thomas's fingertips began to explore her body. He caressed her throat, her collarbone, her breasts, her stomach. He kissed her; his lips had longed for this moment.

She was soft and warm and she tasted so sweet. It was almost like the first time, even though they'd been together for many years.

Pernilla was breathing more heavily now. Thomas's body responded, strongly and intensely, with a desire that pulsed through his veins.

He slipped his hand beneath the silk, felt warm skin. Gently he moved her into the right position, leaning against the sink.

"Not here," she said quietly. "What if Elin wakes up and sees us?"

Thomas couldn't wait. "She's asleep."

Pernilla freed herself from his embrace, then took his hand and led him toward their old bedroom. "Come on—we've got all night," she said softly.

# Chapter 65

Nora couldn't hear a sound, but still she didn't dare open her eyes.

She was hiding within herself. As long as she kept her eyes shut tight, nothing bad could happen. She was safe.

The seconds passed. Had she been shot? Was she still alive? She knew it was essential not to move a muscle.

Was this what it felt like to die? Did everything simply stop? No pain?

After a while she noticed that her heart was beating. And she was breathing. It was hard work, but her rib cage was moving up and down, and she was getting enough oxygen.

Slowly she became aware of the silence. No raised voices, no one yelling. She was still waiting for something, but she didn't know what it was.

A blow, another shot? Warm blood trickling from a wound?

Nora had no idea how long she'd been crouching at the bottom of the stairs with her arms tightly wrapped around her body, but eventually she found the courage to open her eyes.

The floor of the hallway was covered in something that sparkled like snow crystals. It took her a moment to understand what it was.

The frosted window in the front door had shattered into a thousand pieces. There was a large gray rock in the middle of the broken glass.

Nora blinked, trying to grasp what had happened.

The door was still closed. By the light of the streetlamp, she could see that there was no one on the porch. Kovač had disappeared.

She was alone. No one was in the house, no one was about to attack her and Julia.

*Julia.*

Nora pulled herself to her feet. Her daughter was still sleeping upstairs, but Kovač could return at any moment. All he had to do was stick his hand through the broken window and unlock the door. He wouldn't give up so easily, she was sure of that.

The tears began to flow. She had to charge her phone, call for help. She couldn't face Kovač alone.

# Chapter 66

The shrill sound of the telephone sliced through the air only minutes after Thomas and Pernilla had crept into the bedroom. They were lying on top of the bed, limbs entwined. Thomas was like a thirsty man in the desert. He couldn't get enough of Pernilla's body, he had to explore every inch with his tongue.

The phone rang again.

He didn't want to tear himself away, not now, when they were finally back together, but he couldn't help glancing over at the nightstand. A call at this time of night usually meant bad news.

The display showed *Nora*.

The anger he'd felt after their quarrel gave way to concern.

Pernilla had also seen the name.

"You have to answer," she said, pulling down her black nightgown. "If she's trying to reach you at this hour, it must be important."

Reluctantly, Thomas reached for the phone. "Hello?"

At first nothing made sense, then he realized Nora was sobbing uncontrollably. It was impossible to comprehend what she was saying. He tightened his grip on the phone as he tried to calm her.

"I can't understand unless you speak slowly," he said several times, to no effect. A bead of sweat trickled down his forehead. Pernilla was sitting up, watching him with an anxious frown. The sound of Nora's sobs filled the bedroom.

"Please, Nora. Calm down," he tried again. He checked the time; it was almost one thirty. "Are you hurt? Has something happened to Julia? Or Jonas?"

Eventually she managed a coherent sentence.

"Kovač is here. Please come."

"You have to go," Pernilla whispered. "I'll watch Elin. Go!"

Keeping his phone pressed to his ear, Thomas pulled on his clothes. He spoke reassuringly to Nora while trying to get her to tell him what was going on. His body still ached for Pernilla, as if it couldn't understand the sudden shift in focus.

Was that the end of it? Would Pernilla be in her own bed by the time he returned from Sandhamn? He wanted to hold on to this feeling; he couldn't bear it if they went back to being like strangers again.

He pressed his lips to her forehead one last time before he left the room; the kiss was a mixture of an apology and a plea for a second chance later. She nodded in a way that he hoped was encouraging.

He closed the door behind him and ran toward the jetty and the Buster.

# Chapter 67

Nora stumbled back upstairs. She'd tried to avoid the broken glass, but had cut her feet anyway, leaving a trail of bloodstains.

She went into Julia's room and dropped to her knees beside the bed, resting her head on the covers. Julia was still asleep, totally oblivious to what had happened. Nora was grateful; all she wanted was for her daughter to be safe. Nothing was more important.

She was still clutching her phone; she'd managed to charge it for a few minutes, which made her feel better. If Kovač came back, then at least she could call Thomas again. She just had to stay calm until he arrived; when they spoke, she'd totally lost control, become hysterical.

Every fresh sound made her jump.

She was constantly listening for footsteps, a hand reaching in and turning the lock. She didn't dare close her eyes; every movement was an effort.

*Thomas will be here soon.*

She tried to cling to that thought, even though the tears weren't far away. She was determined not to panic again, but it wasn't easy.

Thomas had promised to come immediately, and she knew he'd never let her down.

Nora lifted her head and gently kissed Julia's forehead. Her delicate eyelids were closed, her mouth slightly open, her cheeks pink with warmth. Nora couldn't allow herself to break down while she was alone with her daughter.

Dizziness overwhelmed her again. She fixed her eyes on a point on the wall, but it kept advancing, then receding. She felt sick. Her whole body felt weird, light and heavy at the same time, as if it belonged to someone else. She had pins and needles in her arms and legs.

Emir Kovač had decided to avenge his brother. How could she have believed she was safe when he was after her? Why hadn't she spoken to Thomas, or her boss? Or told the counselor she'd been seeing?

The house shuddered. Nora knew exactly what that meant. Someone was mounting the veranda steps, heading for the door.

Kovač was back.

If it was Thomas, she'd have heard the boat, the throb of the Buster's engine as he moored at the jetty.

Her mind was racing. Presumably something had scared Kovač away just after he'd thrown the stone, maybe someone out walking their dog. It had given her a brief respite, but he'd been waiting for another opportunity.

Getting into the house now would be child's play. He could reach in through the broken window, be inside in seconds.

How could she have been so naïve? There was no escape.

Another shudder passed through the house. The sound of footsteps on the gravel told her that Kovač had gone back down the steps and was on his way to the front door.

Nora tried to open her phone to call Thomas, but she was in such a state that the numbers merged together when she entered the code. Her fingers were clumsy, refused to cooperate.

*Error,* the display informed her.

The footsteps came closer. Time was running out.

Nora entered the four numbers again. *Error.* She dropped her phone and looked around wildly.

Where had she put the scissors? She would have to face Kovač alone.

She crawled out of Julia's room on all fours, found the scissors on the chest of drawers. The cool metal felt cold and alien against her palm.

Footsteps crunched on the gravel once more.

# *Siri*

Siri went to bed before Petter got home. She was so tired in the evenings these days; she was already yawning by nine o'clock.

She was just falling asleep when she heard the sound of a car pulling up outside the house. It drove away as the front door opened. So he'd taken a cab. That wasn't good; it meant he'd been drinking again.

The thought stressed her out. Petter was always unpredictable when he'd had a few drinks. The atmosphere between them was horribly tense right now. She felt as if she were walking on eggshells; she kept out of his way as much as she could, and they hardly spoke.

Her guilty conscience tormented her, with the result that she became snappy and oversensitive. The fact that Petter's alcohol consumption had increased frustrated her even more.

It was a vicious circle, and things were getting worse with each passing day.

Siri turned over so that she had her back to Petter's side. She pulled the covers up over her shoulders and tried to slow her breathing.

With a bit of luck, he would get undressed and go to bed. Or sit down on the sofa to watch TV and fall asleep in the living room. Even better.

She listened, eyes shut tight.

Running water in the kitchen, then he went into the bathroom.

Suddenly the bedroom door flew open. He switched on the overhead light, with no consideration for the fact that Siri might be asleep. He sat down heavily on the bed.

"What are you doing?" she said, trying to sound as if she'd just woken up.

"What are you doing?" he repeated, slurring his words. He was definitely loaded.

"I was asleep," she mumbled. She really didn't want another quarrel, not now. She just wanted to be left in peace. She had to be up early; she had a meeting at eight.

"I was asleep," he mimicked her sarcastically. He got up and walked around the bed to Siri's side, planted himself in front of her with his legs wide apart.

He was scaring her.

"Can't we just get some rest?" she ventured, making an effort not to sound annoyed. "We can talk tomorrow if you like."

"What if I want to talk now?" He no longer sounded drunk; he was angry and aggressive. "To love and to cherish," he said grimly. "Do you remember the promise you made in church on our wedding day?"

"Please, Petter. It's really late."

"Where's the love now?"

He bent forward and tried to kiss her. He stank of booze. When he attempted to force her lips apart with his tongue, she felt sick.

"Stop it!"

Her protests were in vain. Petter started to tug at her nightdress, groping for her breasts with rough hands as he kissed her again.

"Leave me alone!"

When he refused to listen, she hammered his chest with her fists. "Get your hands off me!"

Petter stopped and stared at her, his eyes black.

"What the hell are you doing?" Siri whispered.

"Don't you dare blame me for this!" Petter inhaled sharply, then left the bedroom. He went into the guest room and slammed the door behind him.

Siri's entire body was shaking. She'd never seen Petter like that, so full of rage.

She couldn't stay in this house.

She would be safe with Anton. She longed to hear his calm, reassuring voice. She got out of bed and pulled on her robe, intending to run across the road, then stopped herself.

How would she explain her arrival in the middle of the night, half dressed, eyes red from weeping?

What would Mia say?

She couldn't do it.

Siri got back into bed, buried her face in the pillow, and sobbed out of sheer frustration.

# Chapter 68

Thomas crept toward the front door of the Brand villa. He'd already tried the veranda door, but it was locked.

There were no lights on; the windows were black rectangles in the night. He couldn't tell if Nora and Julia were still inside.

He stopped behind a bush and reached for his gun. He'd only just remembered to bring it with him; as always, he hoped to avoid using it. He stood for a few seconds, feeling the familiar weight in his hand. Carrying a gun made him both more courageous and more cowardly. It gave him a false strength he didn't really want to exploit, while at the same time it underlined the gravity of the situation, reminded him that he'd chosen a profession that could lead to death.

He adjusted his grip, focused.

Nora had said they'd been attacked, that Emir Kovač had turned up and tried to get in.

It didn't make sense to Thomas, but he didn't like the dark, silent house. Had Kovač come back since Nora's call? There was no way of knowing, and he didn't like uncertainty.

Something rustled behind him, but when he spun around, he couldn't tell where it had come from. It must have been an animal, maybe a cat. He stared at the Brand villa, listened for any sign of life.

The upstairs bathroom window was ajar, but the gap was too small for an adult male to get through.

He moved toward the door and immediately saw the shattered window, like a gaping wound with a few shards of glass still attached. Something must have struck it with considerable force. Thomas wasn't sure if it was a gunshot or some other form of projectile.

It reinforced the sense that he had to proceed with extreme caution.

Still not a sound from inside. Thomas pressed himself against the wall, gripping his gun with both hands.

He really wanted to call out to Nora, but that would reveal his presence to the intruder, if he was still around. He couldn't risk triggering a hostage situation. Better to keep going until he knew more.

The priority was to get into the house.

He crept up to the front door and tried the handle. The door was locked, but all he had to do was reach in through the broken window.

He checked his surroundings once more. No sign of life.

He couldn't wait any longer; every second could be critical.

He transferred his gun to his left hand and got ready to reach in with his right.

# Chapter 69

Nora was crouching on the bottom step. She had pushed open the narrow bathroom door, which concealed her from anyone standing outside but allowed her to see through the gap between the doorframe and the door itself.

Everything felt unreal; it was almost impossible to focus. When she tried to peer into the darkness, it was like looking into a thick fog, and she was finding it difficult to control her movements. She dug the scissors into her palm; her body had to obey her now. She couldn't afford to make any mistakes.

Suddenly she saw the shadow of a man, hesitating. The adrenaline cleared her gaze, but her whole body was shaking.

This was like a bad dream, but far, far worse than the nightmares that had plagued her all summer. Emir Kovač was here, determined to kill her for what she'd done to his brother.

Where was Thomas? Why hadn't he come?

The hand gripping the scissors ached, and her fingers were slippery with sweat. Emir Kovač was every bit as cruel and vicious as his brother, a brutal man obsessed with revenge.

He wouldn't hesitate for a second if he got ahold of her.

If she wanted to survive, she had no choice.

Nora raised the scissors to shoulder height, the point facing away from her like a dagger. Silently she prayed to God that it would be sharp enough to hurt him.

It was her or Kovač.

Her plan was to stab him in the throat as soon as he opened the door. She knew she would only get one chance; she had to make the most of it. He had to be seriously injured, and disarmed so that he couldn't counterattack. If she inflicted only a minor wound, thus angering him even more, she and Julia would be in grave danger.

There was no alternative. If necessary, she would have to kill him.

Was she capable of doing that?

The thought made her feel faint, but there was no time to think about it. He was standing on the porch, the light from the streetlamp behind him.

Nora peered through the gap, her stress level increasing by the second.

She had to hit her target with the first blow. Go in hard, without hesitation.

She saw a hand reaching in through the window, groping. The sound of the lock turning scraped against her eardrums. A click, and the hand was withdrawn.

Nora stared at the handle as if she were in a hypnotic trance. It was pushed down slowly. In seconds he would be inside. It was too late to pin her hopes on Thomas. If she were to survive, she had only herself to rely on.

She stood up and moved a fraction closer to the edge of the door, in Kovač's direction. He would have to walk past her hiding place; as soon as he came close enough, she would hurl herself forward, go for his throat. The step gave her a slight advantage; she could attack from above. The element of surprise was also on her side.

It had to work. She thought about Julia, and prayed for strength.

The door opened. He was here, inside her home, a dark silhouette creeping across the threshold and heading for her hiding place.

Nora thought she could make out the shape of a gun held in front of him in both hands.

Rage took her breath away, driving out every other emotion. He'd actually come back! He had no intention of leaving her in peace. Her jaws ached with the tension as anger replaced fear.

She hated Kovač with every fiber of her being, hated the fact that he had the power to do this to her.

Her heart was pounding. She wanted to hurt him, beat him and kick him.

Her fingers bent like claws. Kovač was going to regret the day he decided to come after her.

Nora raised the scissors and stabbed to kill.

# Chapter 70

An almost imperceptible movement made Thomas turn his head to the right. Instinctively he dropped the gun and raised his elbow to protect himself.

Too late.

A sharp object slashed the skin by his temple, continuing down over his wrist. Then someone jumped on him from behind and clung to his back.

Thomas lost his balance and crashed to the floor, which was covered in broken glass. He landed heavily on his side, his head hit the bottom step, and he lost consciousness for a moment. The impact knocked the breath from his body, and he felt a rib crack; the pain was indescribable.

He tried to grab his attacker, but the blood pouring into his eyes made it impossible to see. He hit out blindly in an attempt to defend himself and managed to land one kick, in spite of the pain.

The other person hit the wall with a thud.

"You bastard!" a voice groaned, and suddenly Thomas realized who he was fighting with.

"Nora!" he yelled. "It's me!"

Nora didn't seem to hear him. She was like a thing possessed, and kept trying to hit him even though she didn't stand a chance against his physical bulk and strength.

"Nora! Stop!"

Thomas twisted around and seized her wrist. He felt dizzy but managed to block her other arm with his upper arm as he tried to make eye contact.

She was still screaming and swearing.

Warm blood gummed up his eyelids; he couldn't blink it away. The room was spinning.

"Nora! It's me, Thomas!"

Everything went black.

# Sunday, August 14

# Chapter 71

Every muscle protested when Nora got out of bed and dragged herself to the bathroom. She closed the door as quietly as she could so as not to wake Julia.

Lowering herself onto the toilet was a huge effort. Her arms and legs hurt as soon as she moved. If she felt like this, what state must Thomas be in?

She still couldn't understand how she'd attacked him like a madwoman; the aggression had come out of nowhere. The fury she felt toward Kovač was like nothing she'd ever experienced before. She'd actually been prepared to kill him. She'd longed to hurt him, to see his blood.

The thought made her feel sick. She whimpered quietly. It was as if she'd become a different person, standing there with the scissors in her hand, ready to take him down.

She saw the box of Stesolid still sitting beside the sink. Could it have been the sleeping tablet she'd taken, combined with the red wine? She knew you weren't supposed to mix medication and alcohol, that was no secret, but she'd thought it was because of the risk of liver damage, not because it could turn someone into a violent aggressor. Was that the case? She ought to look it up, but knew she'd feel even worse if it turned out to be true.

She picked up the box and dropped it in the trash can, wishing she could do the same with the terrible events of last night.

Nora sat there on the toilet, head drooping. She ought to look in the mirror. Eventually she hauled herself to her feet and contemplated her bruised and battered face.

She looked terrible. One huge bruise started above her eyebrow and went halfway down her cheek. Her throat and chin were covered in tiny cuts from the broken glass on the floor.

With trembling fingers, she reached for foundation and loose powder. She couldn't let Julia see her like this.

She couldn't let anyone see her like this.

The tears began to flow, and she gave up. She'd just have to wear dark glasses and stay indoors for the next few days.

She sank down on the floor, leaned back against the wall, and closed her eyes. The tiles were cold beneath her legs. How was she going to get through the rest of the day when she felt this bad?

More tears.

She didn't want anything to eat, but maybe a big cup of coffee would avert a total collapse.

She pulled on her clothes and crept downstairs. There was a cold draft blowing in through the hole in the front door. She peeped into the guest room. Thomas was still asleep, thank goodness, but the sight of his bandaged face made her shudder. He'd regained consciousness after a couple of minutes, refused to let Nora call a doctor. Instead he'd taped up the wounds on his temple and wrist himself, washed down a couple of painkillers with a large brandy, then staggered into the guest room and fallen asleep immediately.

What the hell had she done? And how was she ever going to fix this?

# Chapter 72

When Nora looked into the guest room again in the afternoon, Thomas was still asleep, even though it was almost three o'clock. He was lying on his back, breathing through his half-open mouth. She thought there was something tormented about his expression.

He'd slept for almost nine hours. Maybe she ought to wake him, make sure he was OK? She couldn't help worrying because he hadn't been examined by a doctor. What if he'd suffered a concussion when she attacked him? Or even worse, a brain hemorrhage?

She remembered the thud when his head had hit the bottom step. He'd crashed down among the broken glass, with Nora on top of him.

He might not be asleep—what if he was unconscious due to internal bleeding? She found it all too easy to imagine a series of terrifying scenarios. She was struggling not to panic.

She'd checked on Thomas once an hour since this morning. At least his breathing was regular. Sleep was healing—maybe that was the best thing for him right now, exactly what he needed.

Nora shifted her weight onto the hip that hurt less. She was also on painkillers, and the bruise on her face was still throbbing.

She couldn't settle; should she call a doctor? She took out her phone and entered the code, then hesitated. Thomas had expressly forbidden her from bringing in a medic. After everything that had happened, she didn't want to go against his wishes. The situation between them was bad enough already; she couldn't risk another argument.

She stood there with the phone in her hand.

*Jonas.*

It was four days since they'd spoken, which was unheard of. He must be so angry with her, so disappointed. Yesterday he'd sent a brief message informing her that he'd be landing in Stockholm on Sunday night. He didn't usually come over to Sandhamn when he arrived so late.

Did he want to come over at all? She was no longer sure.

They would have to get together and talk at some point—but when?

Last night, when she thought Emir Kovač had come to kill her, she'd promised herself that if she survived, she would fix things with Jonas.

She'd tried to call him several times but had only left short messages; she hadn't apologized properly.

Before she could change her mind, she sent another message:

Sorry. I love you.

She couldn't expect a speedy response; he ought to be in the air by now, but at least he'd get her text when he landed. With a bit of luck, it would put him in a better mood.

There was a knock on the front door. Thomas didn't react; Nora left the bedroom and closed the door.

Did she have to answer? She really didn't want anyone to see her like this. Her sunglasses were upstairs, and the bruise seemed to be getting bigger by the minute.

Whoever it was knocked again, making her headache worse. *No.* If it was important, the visitor would come back.

A draft cut through the house as the door opened, then Julia called out: "Mom? There's a lady here who wants to talk to you."

Reluctantly, Nora headed for the hallway, coffee cup in hand. She'd drunk so much coffee during the day that she was trembling, but it was keeping her going.

Julia had already run back to her room, where she was playing with her dolls. Darling Julia, who'd accepted the explanation that her mom had tried to change the window in the front door and had hurt herself when the glass shattered.

Nora saw Johanna Strand standing outside. What was she doing here?

Johanna couldn't hide her surprise when Nora appeared. No makeup in the world could conceal her injuries.

"Are you OK?" she said, eyes wide as she took in the gap in the door. There were still fragments of glass on the ground at the bottom of the steps leading up to the porch. Nora might be able to fool Julia, but not an adult.

"What happened?" Johanna asked.

Nora wanted to tell her to go away, but Johanna came closer. "Can we talk?"

*Preferably not. I can't do this.*

Johanna didn't look as if she'd slept particularly well either. She had dark circles beneath her eyes, and the skin was puffy, as if she'd been crying.

Yesterday, Nora had intended to go and see Johanna one last time—now here she was.

That had to mean something.

She stepped aside. "Come on in."

# *Astrid*

The pink top or the yellow one? Astrid held up each in turn in front of the mirror in her little bedroom.

The pink one looked better with her hair, but the yellow one emphasized her breasts more. Yellow, she decided, with a white miniskirt.

Astrid dropped the clothes on her unmade bed and examined her body. She'd never been as pale as she was this year, but there was no time to lie in the sun; she was always working.

Finally she had a free weekend. For the first time since Midsummer, she could party on a Saturday night. She was going out with Johanna and Niklas; she'd been looking forward to it all week.

What time was it? They were due to meet at Johanna's for a few drinks in half an hour. She would have to hurry; she wanted to shower and wash her hair.

She slipped into the bathroom, turned on the shower, and enjoyed the sensation of the hot water flowing over her skin. She closed her eyes, increased the heat a little more so that the room was filled with steam.

A cold draft made her open her eyes. The door was ajar. Zacharias was standing there, openly staring at her naked body through the glass shower screen.

"Get out!" Astrid yelled.

"Sorry, I didn't know you were in here."

There was no lock on the bathroom door. Astrid had begged her mom to fit a catch, but she'd never gotten around to it.

Zacharias didn't move.

Astrid backed into a corner, trying to cover herself with her hands.

"Get out!" she yelled again. "Or I'll tell Mom!"

"What's the problem? I didn't mean to upset you."

Zacharias grinned but stayed exactly where he was.

"I mean it!" Astrid was on the point of tears but didn't want to give him the satisfaction of seeing her cry.

"Shall I pass you a towel? I can dry you if you like," Zacharias offered.

"Fuck off!"

"OK, OK. No need to overreact."

The door closed behind him. Astrid remained frozen to the spot until she heard his footsteps going down the stairs.

She sank to the floor and burst into tears. He made her feel so dirty.

# Chapter 73

Johanna followed Nora into the kitchen. She wasn't sure if this was a good idea; she'd lain awake all night worrying about it, and in the end she'd decided to come and see Nora.

The detective she'd spoken to hadn't contacted her again, so Nora's visit must have been legitimate. Before she dared to take the next step, demand money for her silence, she had to find out how much Nora actually knew.

She couldn't afford to end up in even more trouble.

"Coffee?" Nora pointed to the machine on the counter.

Johanna shook her head. Her stomach was already acting up; coffee was the last thing it needed. "I'm fine, thanks." She sat down at the table while Nora filled her own mug. It was difficult to take her eyes off the bruise on Nora's cheek—had she been in a fight?

Zacharias Fahlman's face came into her mind, but even he wasn't crazy enough to beat up a prosecutor. Was he the one who'd smashed the glass in the front door? The way he'd grabbed her in the bar the other night, his threatening behavior, had frightened Johanna. Since then she'd gone out of her way to avoid bumping into him again.

Had he tried to scare Nora, too, stop her poking her nose into his business? That sounded a lot like him.

What were the implications for Johanna's plan? She thought she knew, but took a deep breath in an attempt to slow her racing heart. She had no intention of revealing her identity; she'd already decided how to proceed, using an anonymous email address.

She'd spent most of the night trying to come up with different solutions, but kept coming back to the same conclusion: there was no alternative.

She *had* to get the money for the rent.

The sun was shining directly on Nora's cheek. It looked terrible.

"What happened to your face?"

"I don't want to talk about it." Nora's fingers instinctively touched the bruise. "What can I do for you?"

Johanna looked over at the window. She began chewing her thumbnail, even though the flesh was already sore.

Where should she start? *How* should she start?

A door opened in the hallway, and a tall blond man appeared in the kitchen before Johanna could speak. He was wearing jeans and a cotton shirt, but he was barefoot. His hair was tousled and he was unshaven. He looked as if he'd just woken up, despite the fact that it was late afternoon.

Johanna's mouth fell open. The man's face was battered and bruised, just like Nora's, plus he had a large dressing on his forehead and a white bandage around his wrist.

The man stared back, clearly surprised that Nora wasn't alone. He smoothed down his hair with one hand in an effort to make himself more presentable, but it didn't really help. He still looked as if he ought to be in the hospital.

Nora was the first to come to her senses.

"This is Johanna Strand," she said. "She lives on the island, over in Seglarstaden." She nodded in the direction of the man. "And this is Thomas Andreasson."

Johanna vaguely recognized the name. Where had she heard it before?

"He's a police officer," Nora added.

This must be the same Thomas Andreasson that Johanna had spoken to on Friday when she contacted the police to ask about Nora and her involvement in the investigation. Here he was in Nora's house, and he'd obviously been attacked, too. Did they live together?

They certainly knew each other—that was why he hadn't been in touch. He must have gone straight to Nora. Johanna found it hard to swallow; she couldn't trust Andreasson, even though he was a cop. She couldn't trust Nora either.

Coming here had been a mistake.

She got to her feet abruptly, the legs of the chair scraping loudly across the floor.

"Sorry," she murmured. "I have to go."

Nora stood up, too, frowning. "I thought you wanted to talk?"

"It's not important."

Johanna set off toward the front door, but Nora followed her.

"Was it about Astrid? Was that why you came?"

"Sorry, I really have to go. I shouldn't have come."

Nora touched Johanna's arm.

"Won't you stay for a little while?"

Johanna shook off Nora's hand and opened the door.

"Bye," she said over her shoulder, almost breaking into a run.

How could she have thought it was a good idea to come and see Nora Linde?

# CHAPTER 74

Thomas had settled down on the veranda. He was leaning back on the sofa, with a cushion tucked behind him to support his ribs.

Nora's cheeks flushed red with embarrassment.

Thomas was still pale, but he looked better. Nora's concern that he hadn't seen a doctor was beginning to subside. He was clearly exhausted, but at least he didn't appear to be dying.

Nora sat down in the wicker chair opposite him with a mug of tea. She had no desire for alcohol. They were behaving as if everything was perfectly normal, except of course they were both black and blue, and she was so ashamed of herself.

Sounds from the neighbors drifted in through the open veranda door. Last night she'd been terrified that the door wasn't locked.

"So how are you?" Thomas said after a while.

Nora grimaced. "I've been better. How about you?"

"Same." Thomas smiled wearily and pointed to the dressing on his forehead. "I feel like an old war veteran."

Nora relaxed. If he could joke, then he wasn't furious, although he certainly had every right to be mad at her. She took a sip of her tea and tried to breathe slowly. She mustn't feel sorry for herself. She had to pull herself together, however painful that might be.

"By the way, Pernilla texted a while ago wondering where you were."

"I just spoke to her and told her I was still on Sandhamn. She's taking Elin back to town with her."

"Good." This wasn't the time to ask why Pernilla had spent the weekend on Harö.

Silence fell. Nora switched her mug from one hand to the other; she couldn't look Thomas in the eye.

"Listen, I don't really understand what happened last night," she said, failing to keep her voice steady. "I don't know what came over me."

The distance between them seemed endless. Nora went and sat beside him, took his hand. "Can you ever forgive me?"

Thomas made a dismissive gesture. "It's over."

Nora sighed with relief.

"You thought I was someone else," Thomas went on. "It wasn't me you were attacking, it was an intruder. You were scared. I get it."

Nora's eyes filled with tears, despite all her efforts to stay in control. He was being so kind, but the fact remained: she hadn't recognized her best friend in the darkness, even though she'd asked him to come over.

"I really am sorry," she said, resting her head on his left shoulder. He let out such a groan that Nora gave a start. She immediately sat up, and her sore cheek collided with his chin. Now it was her turn to let out a yell.

"Sorry," Thomas said. "I've got bruises everywhere. For an amateur, you did a pretty good job. Have you taken up jujitsu recently?"

It wasn't funny. Nora tried to say something, but Thomas silenced her. He was the only one who was behaving like an adult; she was falling apart.

"Don't forget that there really was someone here before I arrived. We need to investigate." He put his arm around Nora and gave her a little squeeze. "And you and I need to talk."

He pushed her away a fraction so that he could look into her eyes.

"Why did Johanna Strand come here today? And why is Emir Kovač threatening you?"

Nora wiped away the tears; they refused to stop flowing. She winced when she touched the bruise.

"We're going to get to the bottom of this," Thomas said firmly. "Without getting mad at each other again."

# Chapter 75

She'd been crazy to go to Nora Linde's house. Johanna bitterly regretted her decision.

She was sitting at one of the long tables in the far corner of the bar, drinking a gin and tonic she couldn't afford. She was behind with all her payments; before long she would probably have a county court judgment against her.

Why had she decided to go and see Nora? Because she wanted to find out how much Nora really knew? Johanna ran her index finger over the surface of the table, aware that there was another explanation.

Because she wanted to confide in someone. Maybe in the hope of being persuaded not to do something stupid.

Before it was too late.

She'd kept the secret for ten years. He had no idea that she knew everything, and could expose him.

Johanna reached for her glass and took a big gulp, but it didn't make her feel any better.

He was a dangerous man. If you'd killed once, you could kill again, but she was desperate. There was no other way. She had to get her hands on some money, and soon.

A hundred thousand.

That would cover her rent for the next few months, plus the fees for her hairdressing course—the chance of a new life. She would be able to hold her head high, provide for herself pursuing a profession she enjoyed. No more begging from Mom and Dad.

A hundred thousand wasn't much to a man like him, but it was a lifeline for her.

Johanna took another sip, relishing the cool drink on her tongue. She switched on her phone, the screen gleaming in the faint glow of the candle on the table.

Quickly she created an anonymous Gmail account. He would never find out it was her. Almost feverishly, before she had time to change her mind, she wrote a few short lines—enough to convince him that she knew what she was talking about, that she was sitting on the kind of information that would put him in jail for many years if she passed it on to the cops.

A hundred thousand in cash. That was all she was asking for.

Her hand shook as she pressed "Send."

# CHAPTER 76

Thomas altered his position on the sofa, but it didn't help. He needed more painkillers. He really ought to go and lie down, but he didn't want to interrupt Nora's narrative.

It had taken her almost an hour to go through everything, from when she started looking into Astrid's case until today when Johanna unexpectedly appeared on her doorstep. She'd also summarized her visits to Lillian Eriksdotter and Niklas Johansson's parents, and she'd told him about Zacharias Fahlman.

Suddenly Nora broke off.

"You look terrible. You need to go and lie down."

She sounded more perky than before, as if her self-confidence had returned.

"I'm fine, but wouldn't say no to a couple of painkillers."

Nora disappeared, then came back with a box of white tablets and a glass of water.

Thomas took two. "Go on."

Nora had just reached an important point: the fact that Niklas Johansson had been close to Astrid, and had disappeared at roughly the same time.

"I'm almost done. I really do think that Niklas is the key. If only we could get ahold of him . . ."

She left the sentence hanging in the air, but Thomas was reluctantly impressed by her efforts. The new information about the existence of Niklas Johansson put things in a different light.

Nora might be off sick from work, playing the private eye, but there was nothing wrong with her ability to draw conclusions. She'd always had a sharp mind.

The investigation into Astrid Forsell's disappearance had taken a fresh turn.

"You told me you'd been concentrating on another case," Nora said.

Had he? Thomas couldn't remember.

"You thought it was a woman from Djurö who'd been found on Telegrafholmen." Nora took a deep breath as if she were gathering her strength. "I've told you everything—can't you be honest with me?"

Thomas opened his mouth to say that was impossible, that he was bound by confidentiality, as she knew perfectly well. But something made him change his mind. Nora was right; she'd put all her cards on the table. Maybe he should do the same. She was a prosecutor, after all, even if this particular case wasn't hers.

He'd already bent the rules by failing to report her involvement in an ongoing investigation, and he hadn't reported the events of last night.

He could hardly make things worse.

"You know I understand the need for confidentiality," Nora added, as if she'd read his thoughts.

Thomas wondered how long it would be before the painkillers took effect.

"This stays between you and me," Nora promised.

Two heads were better than one.

"OK, so we're looking at a woman by the name of Siri Grandin," Thomas began. "She went missing around the same time as Astrid."

Nora listened attentively as Thomas filled her in. From time to time she asked pertinent questions, as if she'd automatically slipped into her role as prosecutor. Thomas recognized the behavior; he was a cop whether he was at work or not.

But there was something else that was familiar. It took him a while to realize what it was. The spark in Nora that had been notable by its absence over the past few weeks was back.

After almost an hour, Thomas had finished his account, and the painkillers had worked their magic. His head no longer felt quite so heavy, and he was able to think clearly.

"Most of the circumstantial evidence points to Petter Grandin," he concluded. "It seems likely that he murdered his wife because she was planning to leave him. Plus she had a lover."

"But you still don't know if the bones belong to Astrid or Siri."

"We hope to find out this week."

Nora finished off yet another mug of tea.

"If we assume for a moment that it's not Siri Grandin but Astrid Forsell—where does that leave you?"

Thomas gazed out of the large picture window, across the peaceful inlet. The sun hung low in the sky over Harö.

"Where does that leave us . . . We have to start again. Petter Grandin is either a widower who just happens to have received a huge insurance payment on the death of his wife, or a criminal who will walk free if we don't find anything else. It's too early to say."

Could they have been so wrong about Grandin?

Thomas found that hard to believe, but going over everything with Nora had made him think again. Something happened when you told the story out loud. Even he could see the gaps, the lack of concrete evidence. However, there was still a lot pointing to Grandin.

At the same time, there was nothing wrong with Nora's instincts or the conclusions she'd drawn. Astrid's disappearance hadn't been resolved. There were too many loose ends, and he couldn't help agreeing with Nora that something wasn't right.

Maybe they'd been too hasty in putting Astrid's case to one side.

"Do you think there could be a connection?" Nora said. "After all, both women went missing around the same time."

"There's nothing to suggest that. Obviously we've checked."

They'd looked for links but quickly dismissed the idea. Siri Grandin and Astrid Forsell hadn't known each other. They had no mutual friends or other discernible points of contact.

On the other hand . . . Now he knew that a third person had gone missing in August ten years ago, someone who'd known at least one of the women. The question marks were piling up. There was another possibility they hadn't considered. Could there have been two bodies in the grave?

If that was the case, then they'd have to revise any conclusions they'd already reached.

It was only eight thirty, but it was already beginning to grow dark outside the veranda window. The archipelago's long, light evenings would soon be over. In a way, Thomas was pleased; maybe the fall would be better, a fresh start.

He thought back to Saturday evening, the time he'd spent with Pernilla just before Nora called. With a huge effort, he pushed the images away. His private life would have to wait. Pernilla and Elin had gone back to town; he might as well spend another night at the Brand villa and catch the first morning ferry into work.

"There's something wrong with the combination of Astrid, Niklas, and Siri," Nora said, tucking her legs beneath her.

"What do you mean?"

Nora turned her head from side to side several times, then massaged the back of her neck with one hand.

"I can't help wondering whether Niklas and Astrid are somehow involved in Siri's case. That could explain the timing." She put down her cup. "Maybe they ran away together because they didn't dare stay in the country?"

"Ran away together?" Thomas said. "Like Bonnie and Clyde?"

"I know it sounds far-fetched, but surely it's worth looking into? Three people going missing at the same time—it can't be a coincidence!"

She was right; Thomas didn't believe in coincidences. But a murder committed by two teenagers? That was going too far.

"Why would Niklas and Astrid want to kill Siri?" he objected. "A thirty-five-year-old council employee who was being unfaithful to her husband? What's the motive?"

Nora's shoulders slumped. "I don't know. That's for the police to find out."

Thomas suddenly realized how exhausted he was. Nora must be equally tired. They needed sleep, but there was still one topic they hadn't mentioned.

"The stone through your window," he said. "Are you sure it was Emir Kovač?"

Nora's face lost all its color. "Last night I was convinced he'd come to avenge his brother. He . . . He threatened me the last time I interviewed him. I've had nightmares about it all summer. I was absolutely sure he was outside the house—that was why I lost it."

"Why haven't you mentioned this before? You might need protection."

The question came out a little more sharply than Thomas had intended, but Nora should have realized the seriousness of such a threat. If only she'd told him, he could have helped.

Nora looked up at the ceiling as if she were searching for a reasonable explanation. She closed her eyes, sighed.

"You're right, of course, but Emir Kovač was much too smart to leave any evidence. No one else heard what he said, and the tape recorder was switched off. It would have been my word against his, and I just couldn't face that particular battle after everything that had happened."

"What did he say?"

"I can hardly bring myself to repeat it." Nora pressed her palms together in front of her mouth and took a deep breath. "He said: 'I will rape your daughter and kill her before your eyes. Then it will be your turn. You will die slowly so that you will suffer for a long time, you dirty whore.'"

Thomas inhaled sharply. No wonder Nora had been so scared. There was no point in criticizing her now because she hadn't reported the incident.

"Try to forget about Kovač," he said instead. "I'll take care of him." He made a mental note to check out Kovač's whereabouts as soon as he was back in Flemingsberg.

"I thought he wanted to punish me," Nora said. "I'm worried that he's done something to Mina and Lukas as well. I haven't heard from her in weeks."

"Have you tried to contact her?"

"Many times. I've called and texted, but she doesn't answer. I've thought about her so much this summer. I'd feel a lot better if I knew that she and her son were all right."

Thomas had had no idea that Nora was so worried about Mina, or that she was so frightened of Kovač. "Maybe Mina's gone overseas for a while to let things settle down. She's not your responsibility, Nora."

"It doesn't feel that way."

Nora's lower lip trembled. Thomas reached out and placed his bandaged hand over hers.

"It's OK," he said gently.

Nora closed her eyes briefly, holding back the tears.

Thomas swayed on the sofa, and Nora immediately got to her feet. "You must be worn out. Time for bed, I think."

Thomas nodded and followed her into the hallway.

"I have to go into work first thing tomorrow, but I don't like the idea of you and Julia being alone in the house. When is Jonas due back?"

Nora looked evasive. "Soon."

"Is there anyone else who could come and stay in the meantime? How about Adam?"

Nora's eldest son, who'd recently moved out, would be twenty-one the following weekend.

"Adam?" Nora sounded horrified. "I can't ask him to come if there's any danger!"

That was exactly why Thomas had mentioned him, but Nora had reacted as if her son was seven years old, rather than a young man who worked out and was considerably stronger than his mother. Thomas would feel much better if Adam was around.

"Well, could you go and stay with someone else?" he suggested. "Eva, maybe? At least until the glass in the door can be replaced."

Nora smiled faintly and pointed to his head.

"I'm perfectly capable of defending myself."

Thomas didn't think there was anything to smile about. There was no getting away from the gravity of the situation. If it was Emir Kovač or one of his henchmen who'd smashed the window, then Nora and Julia weren't safe here until the police had dealt with the matter.

He wasn't prepared to argue.

"Promise me that you and Julia won't stay here on your own."

"I promise."

# *Siri*

As soon as Siri opened her eyes in the morning, she felt the urge to vomit. She threw back the covers and ran to the bathroom. She just managed to open the toilet lid before the contents of her stomach came up. It was mostly bile, but she felt so bad that she could hardly stand.

Eventually she straightened up and rinsed out her mouth with cold water, gripping the white handbasin for support.

Siri caught sight of her face in the mirror. She looked terrible. This weird food poisoning had been going on for almost a week, ever since that embarrassing dinner at Mia and Anton's. Why hadn't she gotten over it by now?

A fresh wave of nausea sent her back to the toilet. The bitter bile seared her throat.

What the hell was wrong with her? Her breasts were sore and her belly was swollen. She seemed to have put on weight, even though she felt so bad.

Siri ran a hand over her belly. It was taut, maybe a little bloated. She moved back to the mirror and pulled up her nightshirt, exposing her breasts. They looked bigger, too, didn't they?

Slowly she began to process what all of this might mean, although it was almost incomprehensible.

When had she had her last period? It must have been several months ago. After all the IVF treatment, her body had gone into meltdown, and nothing had worked properly. She'd always been meticulous about keeping track of her cycle, but when they finally gave up on the IVF, she'd stopped.

Siri blinked in confusion. She and Petter had tried for so long to have a child. Could she really be pregnant? She closed the lid of the toilet and sat down, buried her head in her hands. Was it really possible? She couldn't take it in.

But if she was . . .

Siri stood up and took off her nightshirt. She positioned herself in front of the full-length mirror and scrutinized every inch of her body. Her belly was swollen, her breasts were bigger, her nipples looked browner than usual. She'd been getting up to pee unusually often during the night.

No way was she pregnant. And yet . . .

There must be a pregnancy test somewhere in the bathroom, left over from all those failed attempts. Siri rummaged through the drawers and eventually found a box. She ripped open the packaging and peed on the stick, then she closed her eyes and waited for those endless minutes to pass. When the time was up, she hardly dared look. She so wanted it to be true, but the disappointments of the past few years had killed her hopes.

It was probably wishful thinking, nothing more.

She already knew she was incapable of getting pregnant; she always carried that sorrow with her. Why should she believe something else just because she'd put on a few pounds?

She opened her eyes and saw two glowing blue lines on the slender white stick.

It was a miracle.

Siri's eyes filled with tears. She was going to be a mom—after all these years.

Her baby would have the best daddy in the world. There was no doubt about who the father was; she hadn't let Petter touch her for a long time.

She thought back to the other evening, Anton consoling little Pelle after the quarrel with his brother, the tenderness as he dried the boy's tears, the love between father and son.

Siri stared at her belly again. She pressed the palm of her hand against the soft skin, trying to detect any sign of movement, even though she knew it was much too early.

"Hi, you in there," she whispered, her voice almost breaking. "I'm your mommy."

She gently stroked the area around her navel with her fingertips, taking deep breaths. She was overwhelmed by a strange mixture of pure joy and absolute terror. She'd hoped for this moment so many times, and been equally devastated on every occasion when it became clear that nothing was going to grow in her womb.

Her happiness was on shaky ground. What if something happened, what if she had a miscarriage? What if the test was showing a false result?

*No.* Siri lifted her chin. She was pregnant, and nothing was going to go wrong. She had to have the courage to believe. Nothing could be allowed to take this happiness away from her.

Tears poured down her cheeks.

And just like that, everything had changed. They were going to be parents. It didn't matter what anyone else thought, or if Petter hated her for the rest of their lives.

Nothing was more important than this.

It would be fine, even if she had to endure dirty looks. No doubt her lover would have to put up with plenty of nasty comments about leaving his family.

It was the two of them against the world from now on.

Siri clasped her hands in front of her. She had shed so many tears lately. Today she was weeping with gratitude.

# Monday, August 15

# Chapter 77

The conference room where the morning briefing was usually held smelled stuffy when Thomas walked in. He was the first to arrive. There was only one early ferry from Sandhamn on weekdays, and it sailed more or less at dawn. He'd left the Brand villa without waking Nora or Julia.

One small consolation was that he didn't have to deal with his colleagues' curious glances at this hour. Neither his face nor his ribs had improved during the night; in fact, he felt worse. He hadn't shaved either, and his shirt wasn't exactly freshly laundered. He should have gone home and changed, but he hadn't had time.

Margit appeared in the doorway with her arms full of documents and folders, balancing a coffee cup in one hand. Thomas hadn't spoken to her since Friday evening, when he'd realized that the pressure to solve the case had been increased still further. The construction project had been suspended for a week now, and there was talk of a compensation claim if the police cordon wasn't removed soon.

"What the hell happened to you?" Margit said when she saw Thomas. "You look like shit."

There was never any need to worry that Margit wouldn't speak her mind.

"An accident. I slipped on a rock and fell."

The last word was true.

Margit came closer and inspected Thomas's injuries.

"Nasty. Have you seen a doctor?"

Thomas shrugged, but the movement made him grimace. Pain shot through his ribs, and he instinctively clutched his side. That was all Margit needed to draw her own conclusions.

"You haven't. May I suggest that you swing by the hospital after the briefing? You need patching up properly; otherwise you'll have to take a sick day and stay home. You can't walk around here looking like that."

Thomas was about to protest, largely out of habit, then he realized she was right.

"I'll go to the hospital."

If he was forced to stay home and do nothing, he'd go crazy. Besides, he couldn't stop thinking about Nora's theories. The investigation couldn't wait.

Aram reacted in the same way as Margit when he arrived; Thomas gave him the same explanation. When Staffan Nilsson and Ida walked in together, Thomas raised a hand before they had time to open their mouths.

"I wasn't looking where I was going, and I slipped on a rock in the dark. End of story."

"I didn't say a word," Ida said with a smile as she sat down. Today she had pink streaks in her hair.

"I hope you were sober!" Nilsson chortled and pulled out the chair opposite Thomas. He hadn't been that cheerful for weeks.

It was time to get started. Margit cleared her throat, and Ida raised her hand.

"Something to tell us?"

Ida nodded. "I went through Siri Grandin's calendar again. I noticed that she'd written down an appointment at a clinic on Odenplan a week before she disappeared." Ida leaned forward and folded her arms. "I contacted them and spoke to the doctor Siri saw. He's a gynecologist, and he still has Siri's notes."

Thomas began to suspect where Ida was heading.

"Guess what? Siri Grandin was pregnant when she went missing."

Nilsson let out a low whistle. "Are you sure?"

"Absolutely."

"What are the odds of Siri taking her own life when she'd just found out she was pregnant?" Aram said. "After all the years she and her husband had spent trying to have a child?"

"Very small," Thomas said.

"Was Petter Grandin with her when she saw the doctor?" Margit asked.

Ida shook her head. "He was almost certain that she was on her own. He said he'd never seen anyone so happy—that was why he remembered her even though it was ten years ago. Siri wept when he did the scan and she saw her baby on the screen. It was due at the beginning of March, so she wasn't far along—only seven weeks."

The pieces of the puzzle fell into place.

"Her sister said she'd put on weight over the summer," Aram recalled. "Now we know why."

Thomas thought for a moment. Petter Grandin hadn't said anything about a pregnancy. On the contrary—he'd blamed Siri's volatile mood on their inability to have children and their fractured relationship.

"Do you think Grandin was the father?"

"Doesn't sound like it," Margit said.

Aram drummed his fingers on the arm of his chair. "I suspect this was what triggered the murder."

"So Siri was expecting a baby with her lover," Margit concluded.

"Somehow Grandin found out, and acted in anger," Aram added.

The ultimate betrayal. After all they'd been through, Siri was pregnant by another man.

"I wonder if something happened during that last weekend," Aram went on. "If Grandin realized the truth before he went away, he could have killed Siri several days before she was reported missing." He leaned back and clasped his hands behind his head. "The conference he mentioned sounds like the perfect cover. By murdering Siri and hiding the body, then going off for a few days, he gave himself a watertight alibi. The police inquiry centered on a later date, because Grandin swore they'd been together all weekend."

"Excellent work, Ida," Margit said, and the young woman glowed with pride.

Thomas wished they'd had this information from the start, but there was no point in worrying about that now. And they still didn't have a cause of death . . . or confirmation that the bones found on Telegrafholmen actually belonged to Siri Grandin. It was easy to jump to conclusions, but until they heard from the National Board of Forensic Medicine, they had very little to take to the prosecutor.

He was still wondering how to raise the question of Astrid Forsell without revealing Nora's involvement. He'd thought about it all the way from Sandhamn to Flemingsberg. This morning's revelations strengthened the case against Petter Grandin, but he couldn't ignore the information Nora had given him.

"We've had an answer of sorts from the National Board," Margit said.

*At last.* Thomas couldn't suppress a surge of excitement. "Have they established the identity of the deceased?"

"Not exactly."

Margit's frustration was clear.

"They haven't finished the DNA analysis," Nilsson clarified, "but there's no doubt that we're dealing with a female skeleton."

"Siri Grandin, in other words," Aram said with satisfaction.

*Might as well take the bull by the horns.* Thomas cleared his throat.

"I think we should take another look at Astrid Forsell's disappearance."

# Chapter 78

Aram didn't bother to hide his skepticism.

"Why would we do that? Everything points to Siri Grandin, not least the fact that she was pregnant, as we've just heard."

Thomas went through Nora's observations without mentioning her name. He had to keep a certain amount of information to himself; otherwise it would be obvious that she'd involved herself in the case.

He placed particular emphasis on the fact that Astrid had felt threatened by Zacharias Fahlman. He talked about her dysfunctional relationship with her mother, and pointed out that Siri and Astrid seemed to have disappeared around the same time. Unlike Siri, Astrid hadn't been declared dead, but no one had heard from her in ten years, which was surprising. Teenagers who ran away from home usually contacted their parents sooner or later.

He didn't bring up Niklas Johansson or the fact that he, too, had gone missing; he had no way of explaining how he'd acquired that information. He would confide in Aram later before he looked into Johansson further.

Margit's gaunt face was twitching with impatience.

"I don't know what to say," she snapped. "Have you spent all weekend conducting your own investigation?"

Thomas did his best to look puzzled. Someone had certainly done exactly that—but not him.

"I was over there anyway, so I took the opportunity to talk to a few of the locals. I was just trying to save time."

"Before or after the accident?" Ida asked in a stage whisper.

Margit turned to Staffan Nilsson, whose notepad was covered in stick figures.

"When can we expect a definitive answer from the National Board? We can't move on until we hear from them."

Nilsson glanced at his watch. "Soon—hopefully today or tomorrow. I'm doing my best to chase them, but you know what it's like."

Margit frowned but didn't say anything.

Like Nora, Thomas found it difficult to believe that three people had gone up in smoke at the same time without there being a connection. He decided to turn the question on its head.

"Could we be looking at bones from two different women?"

Margit stared at him with the expression of someone who didn't want to be strapped with another case. "What are you talking about?"

Thomas turned to Nilsson. "Is there any chance that there could have been more than one body in the grave?"

"We haven't considered that possibility."

"Is it feasible?"

"Anything's feasible. You know that as well as I do."

Margit had had enough. "OK. If you want to spend some time on Astrid Forsell while we're waiting for the results from the National Board, that's fine by me. Just make sure this is cleared up soon."

She closed her notebook with a bang, then turned to Thomas.

"And get yourself to a doctor before you do anything else. It won't help anybody if you collapse on duty."

# CHAPTER 79

Nora was sitting in the kitchen at the Brand villa with the computer in front of her. She read the brief email once more.

It was from Jonathan Sandelin, her boss at the Economic Crimes Authority. He wondered, in carefully chosen words, what she thought about coming back to work next month, when her sick leave came to an end. Did she feel ready?

If she turned toward the microwave on the counter, she could see her bruise reflected in its glass door. It was even bigger today, the colors grotesque, but it should be gone within two weeks.

Was it time to go back?

The last few days had been traumatic. She didn't really know how to answer Jonathan's question, which was perfectly justified.

Last night she'd slept deeply, undisturbed by bad dreams, without the help of pills or alcohol for the first time in what seemed like months. All summer she'd slept so lightly that she'd woken at the slightest sound, but she hadn't heard Thomas leave this morning.

Her body no longer felt quite so stressed, and finally it seemed as if the gray fog that had permeated every aspect of her life was beginning to lift.

She was still embarrassed by the fact that she'd attacked Thomas, but at the same time, on another level, she was almost . . . proud. She'd defended herself and her daughter instead of collapsing in a heap. She'd trusted her own ability, although she had to admit that the combination of pills and booze had made her overstep the bounds.

She was also pleased that Thomas had taken note of the information she'd found out about Astrid and Niklas, and had shared her view of the situation. That gave her fresh confidence. Maybe she wasn't quite so worthless as she'd begun to believe during this dreadful summer?

She considered that thought for a little while; it felt good. Was it time to go back to work?

She had to make her peace with Jonas, too. He still hadn't been in touch, and that hurt her, particularly after the text message in which she'd apologized. Then again, maybe it hadn't arrived; it was worth sending another.

She picked up her phone and typed:

I love you and I really miss you. Once again, I'm so sorry. Call me!

# CHAPTER 80

Thomas caught up with Margit as she reached her office.

"One more thing," he said. "It's about Nora Linde."

Margit was one of the few people in the department who knew how close Thomas and Nora were.

"Nora? What's the problem?"

"Someone tried to break into her house on Sandhamn last night."

Margit had been brusque during the meeting, but now her expression softened.

"Was she hurt?" she asked, with genuine concern in her voice.

Thomas shook his head. "The only damage was to the property. The perpetrator smashed the glass in the front door with a large stone but didn't manage to gain entry."

"Has she reported the incident?"

"Not exactly."

Margit immediately smelled a rat.

Back in the spring, Thomas had allowed Nora to hide Mina Kovač in her former home on Sandhamn—against his better judgment. It broke all the rules on the protection of vulnerable individuals.

When there was a shooting at the property, he hadn't been able to hide it from his boss. Margit wasn't happy when she found out what had gone on. She'd really come down hard on Thomas, and had almost issued a formal warning.

"Why not?" she snapped. The softness was gone.

"It wasn't necessary."

"I'm sorry?" Her eyes narrowed.

"I went over and checked it out. Last night."

"You? In the shape you're in? Why didn't you send a patrol?"

"It seems that Nora has been threatened," Thomas said before Margit could fire off any more questions. "In connection with Andreis Kovač."

Margit raised an eyebrow.

"Nora thinks the younger brother, Emir Kovač, is after her," Thomas added.

Direct threats and attacks on prosecutors were still comparatively rare, but they had increased over the past few years. This was something that the police took extremely seriously.

"I'll get someone on it right away," Margit said. "I'll ask the maritime police to check on Nora today, and we'll find out where Kovač is." She took out her notebook and jotted something down. "Is that all? Nothing else you'd like to share with me?"

Margit clearly wasn't convinced that Thomas had told her the whole truth. She'd always had a well-developed instinct when it came to spotting bullshit.

Thomas shook his head. She'd go crazy if she knew what was really going on.

"OK." Margit went into her office and closed the door, while Thomas headed off to see Aram.

"We need to talk," he said to his colleague. "There's another person who seems to have disappeared at the same time as Astrid and Siri. We're going to Tyresö."

# Chapter 81

Thomas was sitting on a hospital bed carefully putting on his shirt after he'd been examined. The harassed doctor had already hurried away. A machine in the room next door was emitting regular electronic beeps.

He'd had an X-ray, and the results confirmed his own assessment. Nothing was broken, but several ribs were cracked. The doctor had also taken a look at the wound to his temple and said that while the dressing was reasonably competent, it should really have been stitched. It was too late now; he would probably be left with a scar.

That wasn't his biggest worry at the moment.

The pain in his side would get worse over the next few days before it got better, the doctor had kindly informed him. If Thomas had difficulty breathing, broke out in a cold sweat, or felt nauseous, then he must seek medical assistance. He'd been given a prescription for painkillers but had insisted that he didn't need to be signed off from work. He'd mumbled something inaudible when the doctor asked if there was someone to help out at home.

He ought to call Pernilla, ask her to look after Elin for a while longer. He was in too much pain to manage caring for his daughter right now.

He took out his phone; she answered right away.

"Hi, it's me," he said. "I need to ask a favor."

He explained the situation but didn't mention his injuries. Instead he blamed the case, said he'd be working flat out over the next few days.

"No problem—of course she can stay with me."

Pernilla's voice was so warm, so full of understanding, that he almost gave in and told her the truth. For a moment he considered taking a week off, dropping his guard, and asking if he could move in with her and Elin while he recovered.

When he thought about Pernilla in her silky black nightgown, he felt weak in the knees. Could they try to fix their relationship? Did they have the energy?

They'd already been through so many emotional storms. In many ways it was easier to switch off, let everyday life take over. They were getting along fine; was it worth taking the risk? He didn't want to give Elin false hope. Most kids whose parents were separated dreamed of Mom and Dad getting back together.

And yet he couldn't forget that moment in the kitchen when Pernilla had pressed her body against his.

"Thomas? Are you OK? You sound exhausted."

She knew him well enough to realize that something wasn't right.

Thomas closed his eyes, and his nostrils filled with the smell of disinfectant and sanitizing gel. He longed to have a proper conversation with Pernilla, to sit beside her, touch her. But Aram was waiting for him.

"I'll call you tonight and explain," he said. "Things are a little difficult right now."

He ended the call and gathered up his belongings. Aram was sitting in the sun by the main door. They set off toward the parking lot.

"So how did it go?" Aram asked as he unlocked the Volvo.

*Not great.*

"Cracked ribs."

"So you've been signed off work."

Thomas gave a wry smile. "I promised to take it easy."

"And the doctor believed you?"

Aram opened the driver's door. Thomas was grateful that his colleague was behind the wheel; the drive from Stavsnäs to Flemingsberg earlier that morning had been agonizingly painful.

They were off to Tyresö to see Niklas Johansson's parents; they'd already lost valuable time because of the hospital visit. Thomas rolled down the window to let in some fresh air as they headed for the freeway.

"Are you going to tell me what really happened over the weekend?" Aram said, eyes firmly fixed on the road. "You look as if you've been in a fight."

"I slipped on a rock."

"Sure you did."

Thomas didn't want to lie to Aram's face, but he didn't want to betray Nora either. He'd made that decision on Saturday night. He opted for a compromise.

"OK, so there was some confusion in the dark. A case of mistaken identity."

"You mean someone beat you up unintentionally?" Aram grinned and signaled to turn right. "Seriously? You're not exactly a rookie."

Thomas had to smile, too. There was a kind of humor in the situation. He would never have believed that Nora was capable of attacking an intruder like that.

"No—but you should see the other guy," he joked, and Aram was kind enough not to ask any more questions. Hopefully it wouldn't occur to him that "the other guy" was a woman. Poor Nora was also black and blue.

"OK, Tyresö, here we come," Aram said cheerfully.

# *Astrid*

The cigarette smoke drifting up from the kitchen confirmed that Mom was still sitting at the breakfast table. It was almost nine o'clock. Astrid was standing barefoot on the stairs in her robe, gathering her courage.

She'd spent several days wondering how to talk to Mom about what had happened in the shower. She'd done her best to avoid Zacharias; she hardly dared sleep when he was in the house, even if Mom was around.

There was no lock on Astrid's bedroom door either. She jammed a chair under the handle before she went to bed, but the feeling of unease never left her. Any sleep she got was restless and superficial, and she woke with tense muscles, always on edge.

She *had* to talk to Mom, make her realize that Zacharias had to go, that she had to call it quits with him.

The radio was on in the kitchen, music filled the house. Astrid gripped the banister as she tried to find the right words, the words that would make Mom listen to her.

It was always best to catch Mom early in the day, before she'd had a drink, when it was usually possible to have a normal conversation without it ending in a quarrel. Astrid had become an expert in assessing her mother's mood. She was volatile but sometimes open to persuasion.

*Please let this be one of those days.*

She went down the last few stairs and into the kitchen.

"Morning, Mom—did you sleep well?"

She did her best to sound normal. Mom often accused her of sulking, especially if Astrid mentioned the partying or the mess in the house.

Mom half smiled without looking up. She seemed to be OK. Astrid let out a long breath. She was so nervous that her armpits were damp with perspiration.

She poured herself a cup of tea and made two cheese-and-cucumber sandwiches. The counter was covered in crumbs, but she didn't wipe it down. Mom might take that as a criticism, and the opportunity would be lost.

Astrid sat down at the table, took a bite of her sandwich. It tasted of cardboard. Mom continued to smoke in silence. Her coffee cup was almost empty. Coffee and cigarettes were her usual breakfast; she rarely had an appetite before lunchtime.

There was no easy way of bringing up Zacharias's behavior, but Astrid had to say something. She was dreading it. She could never be sure how Mom would react.

"Zacharias was checking me out in the bathroom the other day," she said eventually, her voice rising to a falsetto in spite of her best efforts to sound calm.

Mom stubbed out her cigarette on a saucer. "What do you mean by that?"

"He came in and stared at me while I was in the shower."

Astrid blushed, even though it wasn't her fault. It was just so embarrassing to say it out loud—that her mom's boyfriend had seen her naked. Tears sprang to her eyes. She quickly blinked them away; she didn't want to appear too dramatic. Mom often accused her of exaggerating in order to get attention. She knew exactly which buttons to press to make Astrid feel bad.

"I don't want him to come here anymore," Astrid said, her voice rough with emotion. She looked at Mom, tried to hold her gaze.

Mom lit a fresh cigarette. There wasn't a trace of warmth in her expression. Astrid searched for some glimmer of understanding, some acknowledgment that she wasn't being unreasonable. Wasn't her demand an understandable reaction to unacceptable behavior?

It was Zacharias who was in the wrong, not Astrid—so why did she feel as if she were telling tales, like a little kid running to her teacher?

"What's this really about?" Mom said eventually. "Have you two been up to something?"

Astrid struggled to grasp what Mom meant. What was she supposed to have done when Zacharias surprised her in the shower? It wasn't as if she'd invited him.

"Like what?" she said. Her tongue felt thick and uncooperative.

"Did you ask him over when I wasn't here?" Two patches of red burned on Mom's cheeks. "Did you encourage him?"

Astrid was at a loss for words. She clenched her fists so hard that her nails dug into her palms, but that was nothing compared to the pain she felt inside.

Mom was taking his side.

That sick pervert who'd spied on her naked daughter in the bathroom.

Astrid hated her mom. And Zacharias.

Two months to go. In two months she'd be eighteen, although right now that didn't make her feel much better. She thought about Niklas. He was in a worse position—his dad hit him, in full view of other people.

"Do you want to sleep with him?" Mom asked.

"I . . . I . . ." Astrid couldn't speak. Why was Mom being like this? Astrid hadn't given Zacharias any encouragement. He was the one who'd stood in the doorway refusing to leave, even when she yelled at him.

The memory made her feel dirty all over again. How could Mom imagine she'd be interested in a pig like him? He was more than twice her age. A disgusting old man.

Mom took a deep drag on her cigarette.

"I'm sick of your lies," she spat. "Your constant need to be the center of attention."

Astrid recognized the argumentative tone, the way Mom deliberately misunderstood. She always went on the attack when she felt cornered.

"Listen to me!" Astrid wanted to scream. "I'm your daughter! Why can't you put me before him? Be on my side?"

"You can have any man you want," Mom went on. "You're young and pretty, yet you're determined to destroy my relationship with Zacharias. We've got a good thing going—why are you trying to fuck it up?" There was no affection in her eyes as she got to her feet, ending the conversation. "Are you jealous because you don't have a boyfriend of your own?"

# Chapter 82

Nora had regained her energy. The kitchen table had been transformed into an office, and she'd found an unexpected satisfaction in resuming her professional role.

She was determined to find the missing link, the connection between Astrid, Niklas, and Siri. It had to be there. She refused to believe that the disappearance of three people at the same time was a coincidence.

If only she had full access to the inquiry into Siri Grandin. She had only Thomas's account to go on, and he'd been exhausted when he was trying to give her the facts. Too many details were missing.

Julia came into the kitchen. She didn't seem particularly bothered by her mom's bruise, or maybe she'd already gotten used to it. Children had an amazing ability to adapt.

"Can I go over to Molly's?" she asked. "Her mom's baking pastries."

Nora tried to ignore her guilty conscience. "Sure, sweetheart. Don't forget your shoes."

Julia loved to go barefoot, but Nora was worried about the broken glass that could still be left in the gravel at the front of the house. The door had been fixed temporarily; a local carpenter whom Nora had known all her life had taken pity on her and fitted a sheet of plywood until she could order a replacement pane of frosted glass. At least the property was secure.

Julia ran off, and Nora focused on the screen once more. She'd googled Petter Grandin, and had spent a long time absorbing all the information she could find. There was a photo of him on the home page of the company he worked for. He still looked good, his reddish-brown beard concealing the faint hint of a double chin. He was a typical salesman; ten years ago he'd probably been quite attractive.

Nora studied his face. Was this a man who'd killed his wife? He was no different from any other middle-aged man, as far as she could tell. A little insincere, perhaps, but that wasn't a criminal offense.

On the other hand . . . Siri Grandin had had a lover, and jealousy was a powerful motive.

Nora decided it was time to leave Petter and move on to Siri.

Half an hour later she'd filled five pages with notes about Siri, her job, and her personal life. The Internet was fantastic, as was people's readiness to share every detail of their life on social media. She'd even found Siri's profile on Facebook. Ten years had passed, but it hadn't been taken down. The fact that it was still there was slightly creepy, as if the dead woman lived on in cyberspace. Maybe Petter hadn't thought of removing it, or hadn't known how?

Siri had only posted from time to time, but often enough to allow Nora to form a picture of her life. Slowly she scrolled through Siri's photos and updates. Thomas hadn't mentioned Facebook, so maybe the police hadn't checked it out during the initial investigation. If Nora remembered correctly, the platform had only started to be used widely in Sweden around the time when Siri went missing. She must have been an early adopter. And she hadn't used privacy settings; her photographs could be seen by anyone. Several showed her in various work-related situations. A large group of smiling people was captioned: "Pre-election conference!"

Nora enlarged the image; maybe there was someone of interest in the group. They were standing in front of a tall white building that looked familiar, but she couldn't quite place it. Nor did she recognize anyone in the picture, even though she examined each face carefully.

She carried on surfing and taking notes. If she was right and there was a connection between Astrid and Niklas's disappearance and Siri's, the link had to be here somewhere.

She turned her head from side to side several times. Her shoulders were aching and her neck was stiff. She got up to make fresh coffee, and as she took a white porcelain mug out of the cupboard, something clicked.

Suddenly she knew why the white building had rung a bell. She went back to the table and, with rising excitement, typed *Björn Johansson + Tyresö*. She scrolled through the images until she reached the photo of Björn and his wife, Annie, the one she'd found the other day.

It was taken in front of the same building—the council offices in Tyresö.

Thomas had said that Siri worked as a political secretary for the council. Nora had assumed he meant Värmdö council, because Siri lived on Djurö, but of course she could easily have worked somewhere else—Tyresö, for example, where Niklas's father had held a key local government post. It was some distance from Siri's home, but not too far. Both districts lay to the east of Stockholm; if Siri hadn't owned a car, she could easily have traveled by bus.

A smile spread across Nora's face.

There was a link between Astrid, Niklas, and Siri. Niklas's father.

She still hadn't quite worked it out. Were the teenagers involved in Siri's murder, or vice versa? Was it Astrid who'd been found in the grave, or Siri, or both of them?

However, the connection definitely existed.

*Wait until Thomas hears this!*

# Chapter 83

Thomas's cell phone rang as Aram turned onto the drive of Björn Johansson's house. They'd tried him at work, but had been informed that he'd left for the day.

"It's me," Nora said immediately. "How are you feeling?"

"Better," Thomas lied. "But this isn't a good time."

"I think I've found what you need—the link between Astrid, Niklas, and Siri. Just give me two minutes."

Aram had switched off the engine and undone his seat belt.

"Two minutes," Thomas agreed, nodding to his colleague.

Nora filled him in.

"So there you go. Siri worked in the same place as Niklas's father, and Niklas knew Astrid."

"I understand. Thanks."

Thomas slipped the phone into his pocket and clambered out of the car with some difficulty. He gazed at the house. Nora's information was interesting. Could Niklas have been introduced to Siri by his father, and have brought the two women together? Had something happened as a result?

It was all speculation, but he couldn't help thinking that no one had heard from Astrid or Siri for ten years, while Niklas regularly sent postcards to his mother, according to Nora. And Siri had left that postcard behind—but had she written it? Did that constitute another connection?

Aram waved to him. "Are you coming?"

Thomas joined him and rang the bell. The door was opened by Björn Johansson, in a white shirt with the sleeves rolled up. He was tanned, and had a half-eaten apple in one hand.

His smile vanished when he saw the two detectives. Thomas explained why they were there.

"Your prosecutor's already been to see us," Johansson said, clearly confused. "What's it about this time?"

Aram looked surprised. Thomas hadn't mentioned Nora's visit to the Johanssons; he'd kept it to himself, hoping that he wouldn't have to reveal her deliberate professional misconduct.

"We have one or two supplementary questions," he said quickly. "Can we come in? It won't take long."

Johansson led the way into the living room, which overlooked the lake. The broad glass doors stood wide open, letting in a faint breeze.

"It's about your son, Niklas," Thomas began, glancing discreetly around the room. Several photographs were on display—Johansson with his wife, Annie, and with well-known politicians.

Johansson sat down with his back to the water, allowing his guests to enjoy the magnificent view. At the bottom of the garden, they could see several motor launches moored at a long jetty; presumably one of them belonged to the family.

"As I already told the prosecutor, we no longer have any contact with Niklas. It's a great source of sorrow for both me and my wife."

Thomas could see that Aram was getting even more confused. It had been a mistake to keep quiet about Nora's involvement, but it was too late now. He couldn't exactly explain the situation in front of Johansson.

"So where do you think Niklas is?" he asked instead, hoping that Aram would save his questions until they were alone in the car.

"I've no idea. We haven't had any regular contact for many years."

"Did he ever say why he left?" Aram asked.

*Thank goodness he's not going to mention Nora,* Thomas thought.

"No."

"Did you file a missing-person report?"

"No."

"Why not?"

Johansson sighed. He turned his head and gazed out across the sparkling water, almost as if he'd forgotten the two policemen were there. Thomas tried to interpret his body language. How should a father react when his son broke off all contact?

Aram cleared his throat.

"I've already explained all this," Johansson said. "Niklas wasn't a minor. If he chose not to see us, there was nothing we could do about it. You can't force your grown-up kids to do things they don't want to do. Any power you have as a parent is gone the day they turn eighteen."

That was true, but according to Nora, Johansson had struck his son in front of other people—even though, by his own admission, Niklas was no longer a child.

"I can't give you a reason for what happened," Johansson went on. "My wife and I love our son—we always have."

He reached for a packet of cigarillos on the coffee table in front of them.

"When did you last see Niklas?" Thomas asked.

Johansson was in the process of lighting a cigarillo with an elegant silver lighter. The little flame flickered.

"Too long ago. Ten years."

"Can you tell us about the last occasion when you saw him?"

"I don't remember exactly. I'm sorry, I know that sounds strange, but it was a busy period. We were right in the middle of an intensive election campaign, and I was trying to do my ordinary job at the same time. I was traveling back and forth between Tyresö and Sandhamn. Niklas and I . . . we didn't get along too well that summer."

Thomas couldn't decide which was the most tragic—a son who simply broke off contact with his father, or a father who couldn't recall the last time he'd seen his son. Ten years was an eternity in some ways. No doubt there was a psychological pattern behind the way Johansson was handling his loss.

"What exactly do you mean when you say you weren't getting along?"

"I was very stressed, and Niklas wasn't doing his job properly. I'd arranged it, and I felt doubly responsible, both as the manager and as his father. I found it difficult to hide my disappointment when he failed to get his act together—for once." His fingers tightened around the cigarillo. "I should have been more understanding—he was only nineteen. I've given it a lot of thought over the years, but at the time I just got mad. I've regretted many things I did that summer, believe me."

"There was nothing to suggest that he was thinking of leaving?"

"No, but when we realized that he'd taken his clothes and his passport, we knew he'd gone."

Thomas tried to find a more comfortable position. It was hard to sit without his ribs causing him pain. "What about his laptop and his phone?"

"He took everything that was important. It was obvious that he wasn't coming back, and of course he sent a postcard to Annie, telling her that he was going to look for a job overseas. Since then she's received one postcard a year, on her birthday."

"Don't take this the wrong way," Aram said cautiously, "but did your son show any sign of mental instability, or any violent tendencies?"

Johansson stiffened. "What do you mean?"

"Did he have any mental health issues? Depression, outbursts of rage?"

"Niklas wasn't sick, if that's what you're driving at." Johansson took a deep drag on his cigarillo. "But he wasn't a strong person. He was weak, and that worried me sometimes."

Thomas thought back to what Nora had told him: according to Lillian Eriksdotter, Johansson hadn't hesitated to raise his hand to his son.

"Why did it worry you?"

"Life can be brutal and cruel. You have to defend your position. I wasn't sure if Niklas had the ability to do that. He was a good-looking boy, and his appearance took him a long way, but he could be much too . . . compliant." He tapped the ash into an elegant square ashtray and gave a faint smile. "Maybe he took after his mom."

The words were tender, but Thomas got the feeling that Johansson saw this as a flaw. Some fathers tried to bring up their sons in their own image.

The incident in the restaurant, when he'd hit Niklas in front of everyone, presumably wasn't unique. In which case, Johansson had just explained why his son felt he had to leave home. Thomas made a note to check with social services to see if there was any record of domestic violence ten years ago. Judging by the elegant façade, he thought it was unlikely—but it was worth looking into.

"Where is your wife, by the way?" he said. "We'd really like to have a word with her as well."

"Annie's resting. She suffers from a chronic illness, and she mustn't get upset."

"I understand. On a different matter—do you know a woman by the name of Siri Grandin?"

Thomas didn't take his eyes off Johansson.

"Siri Grandin? I don't think so. Who is she?"

"She was a political secretary with the council ten years ago," Aram said. "But she didn't belong to the same party as you."

Johansson's puzzled expression disappeared.

"Oh, you mean Siri Persson. She had a double surname, now I come to think of it, but she was always Siri Persson at work." He ran a hand over his thick hair, which was peppered with gray. There was sadness in his eyes. "She was the one who killed herself, wasn't she? I think she went out into the forest to die. It was a terrible business. It came as a total shock."

"We're looking into her disappearance," Aram said.

"That's why we want to get in touch with Niklas," Thomas added.

"But she took her own life." Johansson raised his chin. "Why would Niklas have anything to do with Siri?"

"Her body was never found, and now human remains have been discovered on Telegrafholmen."

"Telegrafholmen . . . That's where they found the body the prosecutor mentioned. But she was talking about a young girl."

"We're investigating a number of different leads," Thomas said. "We can't exclude the possibility that it could be Siri Grandin."

"You can't seriously think . . ." Johansson swallowed and tried again. "Do you really believe my son is involved in her death? Why?"

Thomas exchanged a glance with Aram. It was always a balancing act in a situation like this: how much information to reveal without compromising the investigation.

"I'm afraid we can't go into that at the moment, but we really do need to speak to Niklas."

Johansson was still holding the cigarillo between two fingers. The ash had grown into a long gray column that was due to drop off at any second.

"I'm afraid I can't help you. If I had any idea where Niklas was, I would tell you—but I don't."

# Chapter 84

Johanna was sitting on a sun lounger on the terrace, clutching her phone. The afternoon sun was low in the sky, and her elongated shadow reached the sandy ground beyond the deck.

She read the email one more time. The brief response was what she'd both hoped and feared it would be. He was ready to meet up and give her the money she'd demanded in return for her silence.

One hundred thousand kronor.

Relief flooded her body. This meant the difference between life and death.

Her parents had gone back to town the previous evening, thank goodness. The atmosphere had been tense ever since the quarrel on Friday; Johanna was happy to be alone. She'd avoided her mom all weekend, and barely said two words to her dad. They'd given her anxious looks as they set off to catch the ferry, but she didn't have the energy to worry about that. If they didn't intend to help her, then that was their problem. She'd found her own solution; she was going to show them that she could stand on her own two feet.

She would never ask them for money again.

She opened an ice-cold can of Coca-Cola, her fingers leaving clear marks in the condensation.

She read the email again. He was prepared to hand over the cash tonight, which was perfect. She ought to feel excited, but there was a lingering sense of unease.

He was a dangerous man.

She was well aware that in revealing what she knew, she was playing with fire. However, she couldn't see another way out.

Time to arrange the meeting. She decided that the promenade down by the harbor was the best place. She was going to tell him to put the money in a white plastic bag and leave it in the third trash can along from the steamboat jetty. If she sat in the ice-cream kiosk, she would have a clear view of the location without being too close. If she bought an ice cream, no one would take any notice of her. As soon as he'd gone, she would walk over and pretend to throw something away, then she would fish out the bag and get away from there as quickly as possible.

The handover would be at nine o'clock, when the sun had gone down and the darkness offered some protection.

She'd gone over her plan several times. It ought to work. It had to work. If she asked him to pay the money into her account, she could be traced. That mustn't happen. She also needed cash, and quickly. The rent was due; she couldn't afford to wait.

She typed in the instructions and pressed "Send." There. It was done. No point in brooding about it any longer. In a few hours all her problems would be solved. It would be worth a little nervous waiting.

*Everything will be fine,* she told herself.

She had a plan.

# *Siri*

The gynecologist's waiting room was decorated in soft shades of green. To be on the safe side, Siri had made an appointment at a clinic on Odenplan instead of with the doctor she and Petter usually saw.

Fear and joy bubbled away inside her, as they had ever since she realized she was carrying a new life.

A baby of her own.

She couldn't help worrying about a miscarriage, but she was doing her best to push away the thought. Hopefully an early ultrasound would reassure her. If she could see her child, then maybe the paralyzing fear that came over her at night would disappear.

"Siri Persson Grandin," the nurse called out.

She showed Siri into a consulting room and asked her to lie down. The friendly doctor chatted away to her as he prepared the equipment. He spread cold gel over her stomach, then moved the probe gently back and forth.

Siri watched closely. The tears had already begun to fall; she couldn't help it.

"There—can you see?" the doctor said after a little while.

Siri stared at the grainy image on the screen, and her heart exploded with love when she saw the peanut-shaped figure. Tiny but full of life. She began to sob; she tried to explain that it was pure happiness, nothing else, but the doctor seemed concerned.

"Sorry," Siri managed to say eventually. "It's so overwhelming. I can hardly believe it; I've waited so long for this."

The sobs took over again, and the doctor patted her hand reassuringly.

"It's too early to pick up the heartbeat, but everything seems fine."

Siri couldn't stop looking. It was almost too much to take in.

"I'd say you're in week seven," the doctor continued. "Does that make sense?"

Siri thought back. She knew exactly when the child had been conceived—one evening when his eyes had glowed with love and tenderness.

Was it really possible to be this happy?

"Bring your husband next time," the doctor said with a smile, glancing at her wedding ring.

Siri went cold all over.

She couldn't risk Petter finding out what was going on. He was already furious; sometimes she thought she saw hatred in his eyes.

If he realized she was carrying another man's child, he would kill her.

# Chapter 85

It was almost three thirty in the afternoon when Aram turned onto the 229. He'd been driving in icy silence for ten minutes.

Thomas was hoping against hope that his colleague wouldn't ask about the prosecutor who'd visited Björn Johansson.

No chance.

"Isn't it time you explained what the hell is going on?" Aram said when he finally opened his mouth. "What are you keeping from me?"

Thomas considered playing dumb, but Aram was way too smart to fall for that. Plus he didn't want to risk Aram telling Margit about the prosecutor who'd clearly questioned Johansson before they got there.

"What do you mean?" he said, playing for time.

Aram gave Thomas a weary glance. "You know exactly what I mean. Johansson said he'd already spoken to a prosecutor. We don't have anyone on the case. And your explanation as to why we needed to see the Johanssons today doesn't hold water either."

Aram switched lanes and passed a truck with overseas plates that was traveling five miles below the speed limit.

"For fuck's sake," he muttered.

"It's kind of complicated," Thomas began, rubbing his chin and feeling the stubble. He really needed a shower and a shave. Or even better—a bed.

"Am I supposed to guess?" Aram's tone was sharp, and he was drumming on the wheel with the fingers of one hand.

"Can this stay between us?" Thomas asked.

"That depends on the consequences."

Neither of them invariably followed internal guidelines to the letter, but Thomas could understand Aram's concerns.

"OK. Here goes."

By the time he'd summarized Nora's involvement, leaving nothing out apart from the fact that she was responsible for his cracked ribs, they'd turned onto Huddingevägen.

"Do you realize how serious this is?" Aram said when Thomas had finished.

"I guess so."

"We ought to report her."

"She meant well. She was only trying to help."

"That's no excuse for playing the cop," Aram said. "She's spoken to several possible witnesses without any authority whatsoever."

"It's not necessarily a disaster. She's given us useful information. Without Nora, we wouldn't have found the link between Astrid and Siri. Or Niklas Johansson, for that matter."

Aram refused to be pacified. His irritation filled the car.

"Neither you nor I can judge how much damage she might have done by interfering in the investigation."

They'd almost reached Flemingsberg. The last thing Thomas wanted was for the discussion to continue in the corridors of the police station, where Margit's sharp ears might tune in.

She was already on the warpath.

He made one last attempt to persuade Aram to drop it.

"I know we ought to report Nora, but I'd rather we didn't. She is a prosecutor after all—she knows what she's doing."

Aram pulled into the parking lot and found a space.

"I understand that, Thomas, but I'm not sure I'm ready to face a charge of professional misconduct just to protect your friend."

# Chapter 86

As usual, Nora had settled down on the veranda in the twilight. The sun was setting, the pink and red tones of the sky were reflected in the shimmering sea.

She longed for a few hours on her own, so when Julia asked if she could sleep over at Molly's, she'd said yes immediately.

It was still warm enough to leave the glass door ajar. She would be sure to lock it tonight. She'd promised Thomas that she wouldn't be alone in the house, but the more she thought about it, the more unnecessary it seemed to go somewhere else.

Emir Kovač wouldn't risk coming back now the police had been here—even he couldn't be that dumb. Thomas had also texted to let her know that they had people out looking for him; she felt perfectly safe. She couldn't imagine that anything would happen tonight, and she had no desire to explain the situation to an outsider. Eva would happily have offered Nora her guest room, but Nora didn't want to involve her.

She tucked her legs beneath her and watched a little wooden boat as it puttered by. It must belong to one of the older families on the island. It was a long time since she'd heard the sound of a two-stroke engine.

It was kind of embarrassing to admit it, but after the events of the last few days, it was a relief not to have to think about anyone else. She was still upset. She could feel the adrenaline in her body, and her brain was preoccupied with Astrid and Siri's disappearances.

Hopefully, Thomas would let her know how things had gone with Björn Johansson. She was desperately curious but didn't want to call and disturb him.

She longed for a glass of wine but was determined to resist. It was time to cut back on the booze. If she could defend her home against an intruder, then she was perfectly capable of controlling her drinking.

Then again, one glass wouldn't do any harm. The mild late-summer evening was made for a chilled rosé. Soon the autumn darkness would come creeping in, and everyday life would take over once more.

*No. No more booze.*

Nora took a deep breath and pressed her lips together. She'd made a decision, and she was going to stick to it.

Her phone buzzed in her back pocket. Jonas—at last. He was supposed to have landed last night; all day she'd been wondering why he hadn't contacted her. She felt a huge wave of relief. His silence had worried her; it wasn't like him at all. They usually spoke several times a day, but it seemed like an eternity since they'd been in touch.

She opened the message. A shard of ice pierced her heart as she read the words.

Staying in town for a while.

She read it again; she couldn't process what she was seeing. There was no tenderness, nothing about her apology, no indication that he'd forgiven her, just six little words that froze her blood.

Jonas was staying in town, what did that mean? He hadn't even said when he was coming back to Sandhamn. Back to Nora and Julia.

She'd never gotten such a cold message from him.

Was he going to leave her? Jonas, the kindest man in the world, who'd always been there for her. Was he so tired of her that he was never coming home again?

Nora tried to think logically, but it was as if a thick fog had descended on her brain. She couldn't even get mad; she was the cause of the problem. She'd lost count of the number of times he'd asked her to see a counselor this summer. He'd offered to go with her, if that would make it easier. She'd dismissed the idea over and over again, insisted that she didn't need any help, asked him to stop nagging.

Had she driven away the love of her life, the man who'd healed her after the terrible, painful divorce from Henrik?

Her eyes filled with tears. How had it come to this? What had she done?

She got up and staggered into the kitchen. The promise she'd made to herself was forgotten. She opened the cupboard, took a bottle of red wine from the top shelf, and unscrewed the cap.

Jonas had sent a cold, emotionless text. He couldn't even be bothered to call her, let alone come over to Sandhamn to talk things through.

Nora picked up a wineglass, but her hands were shaking so much that she dropped it on the counter. It shattered, and she stared blankly at the mess. It took a while for her to realize that she ought to gather up the pieces and throw them in the trash.

She poked at one of the larger pieces, but left it where it was. She took out an ordinary tumbler, filled it to the brim, and emptied it in one go. She refilled it and drank half.

Jonas didn't want her anymore. It was her own fault.

Thomas had been badly hurt. That was her fault, too.

No one could deal with her anymore—including herself. What the hell had she done?

Nora sank down onto the floor with the bottle in one hand and the tumbler in the other. She leaned back against the cupboard door and closed her eyes.

# Chapter 87

The ice-cream kiosk closed at nine, but Johanna got there a little earlier and bought a large cone with three scoops, which would last her quite a while.

"What flavors would you like?" asked the girl behind the counter.

"You decide," Johanna mumbled. "I don't mind."

The thought of eating made her stomach turn over, but the ice cream was part of her plan, her reason for being there if anyone spotted her.

When she tried to pay, she was so nervous that she dropped a hundred kronor note on the floor. She gave the girl a stiff smile and bent down to pick it up, her hand shaking violently.

"Sorry," she whispered. She couldn't meet the girl's eye.

Tables and chairs were set out on the wide wooden deck in front of the kiosk; Johanna chose the far corner. To the right lay the deserted play area, which was always busy with kids during the day. The promenade was a couple of hundred yards away, and she had a good view of the harbor and the third trash can from the left.

If someone went past she would look like an ordinary person who'd felt like an ice cream late in the evening.

To be on the safe side, she'd tied her hair back and pulled on a cap. A pair of ripped jeans and an unremarkable black top completed her outfit. From a distance she wouldn't be easy to recognize; she could be anyone.

Her stomach was churning. Five minutes to go, then he'd be here.

Johanna tried to watch the promenade without making it obvious. She licked her lips. The time was passing too quickly and too slowly. A part of her felt that she ought to stop this right now, not put herself in danger. Walk away.

It wasn't too late to change her mind.

Another part of her was thinking about the unpaid rent. If she didn't get the money, she was fucked. This was her only chance, if she wanted to keep the apartment and train as a hairdresser.

There was no alternative. This was her only way out, her ticket to a new life.

She checked her watch again. Three minutes.

The girl emerged from the kiosk to take in the trash can and the triangular sign showing the opening times. Then the lights went out, and there was a rattling sound as the gray metal shutter slowly came down over the doorway.

Johanna was all alone. She really wished the kiosk had stayed open a little longer.

If only she'd had some weed to calm her nerves.

The ice cream was dripping, covering her fingers in pink and brown stickiness. She'd forgotten all about it.

She licked it quickly, in spite of the fact that she felt sick with fear. She had to force herself to swallow. It kept on dripping. She wrapped a couple of white paper napkins around the cone, but in the end she gave up and lit a cigarette instead. The nicotine entered her bloodstream and made her feel slightly better.

She could hear laughter from the fish restaurant a short distance away. It was in the same row of shops, and was almost full. The waitresses were hurrying back and forth with laden trays. At least if anything happened, if he attacked her, there were people nearby. Admittedly she couldn't see anyone she knew, but she was pretty sure they'd hear her if she screamed for help.

The promenade was deserted, except for an elderly woman walking her dachshund.

Johanna craned her neck. He ought to be on his way by now.

He *had* to be on his way by now.

One minute past nine. Darkness was falling. The sun had gone down a while ago, but a pale strip lingered in the western sky.

Johanna took a nervous drag. Where the hell was he?

Someone was approaching from the steamboat jetty. It was a man, but she couldn't see his face.

He was striding along purposefully. He was heading for the third trash can, wasn't he? And he was carrying something white, she was sure of it.

Johanna held her breath.

He was there.

# Chapter 88

There was a ringing sound. It took Thomas a while to realize that it was his phone. He was in his apartment on Östgötagatan lying on top of the covers in his bedroom.

Silence.

He was sinking back into oblivion when the ringing started again. He wanted nothing more than to sleep, but he managed to get the phone out of his pocket and mumble, "Hello."

"How are you feeling?"

Pernilla's worried voice. He'd intended to call her when he got home, but he'd been so exhausted that he'd staggered into the bedroom and collapsed without even getting undressed.

"Sorry," he mumbled. "I should have called you earlier, but I fell asleep."

"Are you hurt?" She sounded tense.

"Not exactly."

"What does that mean?"

There was no point in prevaricating.

"I've cracked a couple of ribs, but it's not as bad as it sounds."

Pernilla inhaled sharply. "At Nora's house? What the hell happened?"

Thomas wanted to explain, but he just didn't have the energy. The painkillers had worn off, and he could barely think straight. "Can we do this another time?"

He was reluctant to upset Pernilla. There were other things he wanted to say to her, words he longed to whisper in her ear.

"Sorry," he said, his voice thick with emotion. "I'm exhausted. Can I call you tomorrow?"

There was a brief pause. Thomas hoped she wouldn't react as she'd done over the past year, with anger and irritation. He couldn't handle that right now.

When she spoke, her voice was warm and sympathetic. The old Pernilla, the one from Saturday night, was still there.

"No problem. Call me when you're feeling better."

# Chapter 89

Johanna was still sitting outside the kiosk, even though darkness had fallen. Just over half an hour had passed since the man placed what looked like a white plastic bag in the third trash can along the promenade.

He'd left as quickly as he'd arrived, and since then there had been no activity in the area.

Did she dare to go over there? She had to make a decision.

Johanna glanced in the direction of the fish restaurant; the laughter and the hum of conversation had died down a little. The place closed at ten; the diners were finishing their meals and beginning to leave. Soon there would be no one there.

It was high time to collect the money, and yet something was holding her back. What if he was lurking in the shadows?

*Stop it,* she told herself. There was no sign of him. The promenade was deserted; the woman with the dachshund was long gone.

She ought to go and pick up the bag before the restaurant closed; otherwise she would be all alone in the silent harbor area.

*I can do this,* she thought, and got to her feet. The two hundred yards to the trash can felt like a mile. As she drew closer, she looked around; no one seemed to be watching her or paying any attention to her. The barman at the fish restaurant called for last orders.

Johanna ran the last few yards and reached into the bin.

*There.* Her sweaty hand grabbed something that felt like smooth plastic. She quickly pulled it out—*yes!*

She peered into the bag and saw bundles of notes. The relief was so great that she swayed on the spot, and had to lean on the trash can for support. He'd left the money exactly as she'd demanded, and her life was about to change.

She was holding one hundred thousand kronor in her hands.

The thought was dizzying; she'd never had so much money.

She was so overwhelmed that she remained standing there for a couple of minutes before she came to her senses. She mustn't stay here a second longer. What if someone asked why she was rooting around in the trash, or what was in the bag?

Johanna set off toward Seglarstaden, clutching the bag tightly. Tomorrow morning she would catch the first ferry into town and pay off all her debts, then she would go and enroll in the hairdressing course. And she'd still have money left over.

Something bubbled up from inside her, something between a sob and a hysterical laugh. The laugh won; she'd done it! She'd gotten the money she needed, given herself a breathing space—and she'd achieved that all by herself.

It had gone well.

Mom should see her now—Mom, who thought Johanna was hopeless, and had no faith in her.

Johanna pressed the bag to her chest.

All her troubles were over.

# *Astrid*

The water below Dansberget shimmered white in the moonlight.

Niklas had gone home. He had an early shift on Monday, and had to get to bed. Astrid and Johanna were free, and could sleep in. They'd sat down on a rock at the bottom of the hill that used to serve as an outdoor dance venue. Johanna had brought a bottle of wine, but after all the drinks they'd bought with their staff discount at the bar, they were both pretty drunk already.

Astrid was lying on her back, gazing up at the twinkling stars. She thought about Niklas, and got a warm feeling in her chest.

The other night she'd slept with him for the first time. It had been wonderful; he'd been so gentle and caring, as if she were made of porcelain. Afterward he'd tucked the quilt around her so that she wouldn't be cold, and caressed her cheek with soft fingertips. She'd curled up beside him with her head on his shoulder, wishing she could stay there forever.

Home was unbearable, with Mom's suspicious glances and Zacharias's sickening grin.

She'd tried to stay away as much as possible, only going back to collect clean clothes. Tomorrow, Mom's vacation would finally be over. She was catching the first ferry into town, and Astrid would be able to go back to the house.

"Can I stay with you tonight?" she asked Johanna.

No reply. Johanna must have passed out. She'd probably been more drunk than Astrid realized. The drinks in the Sailors Restaurant bar were pretty strong.

"Need some company?"

Zacharias's voice made her jump. She sat up and saw him standing right next to her. This was the last thing she needed. What the hell was he doing here? Had he followed her?

"Fuck off," she muttered.

"Why do you have to be so crabby?"

Astrid gave him a dirty look.

"Are you still pissed off about that business in the bathroom?"

He came closer, and she could see that he wasn't exactly sober either. He was having some difficulty focusing, and he wasn't too steady on his feet. There were beer stains on his shirt.

"How was I supposed to know you were in the shower?"

"Yeah, right," Astrid said sarcastically. If Zacharias was intending to join her, she had to get out of here. She poked at Johanna with her foot. No reaction.

Zacharias slumped down beside her and offered her a cigarette.

"No, thank you," she said politely, wondering why she was bothering to be civil to this asshole.

He tilted his head to one side. He looked ridiculous. Why was he doing this? She just wanted him to leave—why couldn't he understand that?

"I saw you and your friend coming up here. I thought I'd come and apologize. You could at least be nice to me."

Astrid didn't reply. She glanced at Johanna, who still hadn't moved.

"We ought to be friends, you and I," Zacharias continued.

*Fat chance.*

She edged away until she was almost sitting on the heather. The ground was covered in pine needles.

"Do we have to quarrel all the time?" He shuffled along until he was so close that she could smell his disgusting aftershave.

Why didn't he leave? She drew up her knees, refused to look at him. If she didn't answer, maybe he'd get the message.

"Come on, Astrid. You're such a pretty girl."

He put his arm around her shoulders, drew her to him. Astrid immediately shook him off. "Don't touch me, you fucking pervert."

"What did you call me?"

"You heard."

"What the fuck?" Any hint of niceness disappeared. Zacharias's face was bright red, and his lips were nothing more than a narrow line. "Who the hell do you think you are?"

Astrid stared at him. The change of mood had taken her by surprise. She hadn't expected it; Zacharias could be difficult, but right now he sounded furious. The unpleasant atmosphere had become something much more frightening.

She'd never seen him so aggressive. For the first time, he really scared her.

"Leave me alone."

She tried to move farther away, even though the moss was damp beneath her skirt and the needles were sticking into her thighs.

Zacharias grabbed her by the wrist.

"You're nothing but a spoiled little slut," he hissed. "You don't get to speak to me like that!"

He was hurting her, and his rage was terrifying.

"Let go of me!"

His eyes were wide, the pupils dilated.

"I'll tell Mom!"

He didn't seem to hear her. His grip tightened as he pulled her close.

"You'll do as I say—apologize!"

She fought to free herself, but he was much too strong. She couldn't pry his fingers away, so she scratched his face with her other hand.

She drew blood.

He stared at her in astonishment for a second. Astrid was equally shocked.

The fury returned. "You fucking bitch! What do you think you're doing?"

The stench of alcohol was overwhelming. Before she had time to react, he grasped her hands so that she couldn't move. He threw himself at her and pushed her down with the weight of his body. He was heavy, she couldn't breathe, she panicked. She was lying on pine cones, they tore the skin where her top rode up.

He began to undo his jeans with his free hand.

Astrid was crying now. "Let me go!"

"This is what you wanted all along."

Zacharias was breathing heavily. She could see spittle at one corner of his mouth.

"Do you think I haven't noticed the way you walk around in your short skirts and tight tops? Showing off your tits? You're begging for it, anyone can see that."

His nails scraped the inside of her thigh. He fumbled with her skirt, yanked down her panties, his clumsy, insensitive fingers making the ordeal even worse.

"Get off me," Astrid whispered, but Zacharias wasn't listening, and it was hard to speak with him lying on top of her.

"Please . . ."

His sweat was dripping onto her face. She couldn't fight him off.

She stopped trying.

A silent scream, which would never completely go away, echoed inside her head.

Zacharias's grunts grew louder, but Johanna seemed oblivious. Her eyes were still closed.

Astrid fixed her gaze on the white moon and tried to pretend she was somewhere else, in a place where the burning pain in her belly didn't exist, where her body wasn't moving involuntarily with every agonizing thrust from Zacharias.

The tears poured down her cheeks as she stared up at the starlit sky, and her lips formed a futile cry for help.

"Mommy . . ."

# Chapter 90

As soon as Johanna arrived home, she locked the door behind her. Then she went into the kitchen and lit a cigarette, even though Mom didn't allow her to smoke indoors.

She took a long drag, then blew a perfect smoke ring. She was buzzing with excitement; she couldn't stop smiling.

Dad had brought a bottle of gin that weekend. Johanna mixed herself a strong gin and tonic with ice in a tall glass, and knocked back half of it in one go.

Tomorrow she would go into town and pay her rent, then she'd treat herself to a few grams of coke. Her smile widened at the thought that she didn't need to worry about the price anymore; she could afford as much as she wanted.

She could hardly believe it was true—she'd actually made him pay!

She topped off her glass and took it to her room. Just to be on the safe side, she pulled down the blind before pouring the contents of the plastic bag out onto her bed, scattering bundles of notes across the quilt. She couldn't take her eyes off them. One hundred thousand kronor in five-hundred-kronor notes. She counted them, just to make sure. The amount was correct, but she counted again.

Still correct.

She'd never seen so much money in her life.

She took another swig of her drink. It was the best gin and tonic she'd ever tasted. It didn't matter if she got drunk tonight; a celebration was definitely justified.

She gathered up the money and put it back in the bag, then tucked it away at the bottom of her underwear drawer.

Best to keep it out of sight.

Johanna took off her clothes and got into bed without brushing her teeth. The alcohol was taking effect, and the stress had left her body. She felt pleasantly tired and drowsy, just as she'd hoped.

She emptied her glass and placed it on the nightstand, then switched off the bedside lamp and adjusted her pillow. She stretched out contentedly. The money was safe. Tomorrow she would go into town and start a new life.

Everything was going to be OK. Finally.

# CHAPTER 91

The bedroom was in darkness when Johanna woke. She couldn't have slept for very long; there was no hint of the dawn outside the window. She was curled up on her side, facing the wall. It was a few seconds before she understood why she'd woken up.

She wasn't alone.

It was hard to see properly, but she was aware of another person's presence. Soft breathing.

He was standing at the foot of her bed.

Johanna tried to peek at him from beneath half-closed eyelids, but could make out only a tall silhouette.

Fear flooded her body. How had he gotten in? She knew she'd locked the door. If he'd broken a window, she'd have heard.

Then she figured it out. He'd been here the whole time, just waiting for her to go to bed. As usual, she hadn't locked the front door when she went down to the harbor. He would have been able to walk straight in and hide until she came home.

How could she have been so stupid?

He'd had plenty of time while she sat outside the ice-cream kiosk plucking up the courage to go over to the trash can.

Johanna caught a movement at waist height; he seemed to have something in his hand. A gun?

Her heart rate increased. Had the payment, the money in the bag, simply been a way of luring her out into the open?

She was terrified now. There wasn't enough oxygen, and her mind was racing. She broke out into a sweat, the sheets sticking to her skin.

There was nothing she could do. She was half naked and defenseless. He was twice her size.

He took a step forward, and Johanna couldn't suppress a whimper. He was so close that she could smell his breath, a mixture of alcohol and tobacco. The sour stench of sweaty armpits.

"Don't hurt me," she whispered.

"You have only yourself to blame," he said quietly. "You started all this. You forced me to come here."

It sounded as if he were trying to justify his actions. He looked around the bedroom.

"Where's the money?"

Johanna pointed to the closet in the corner.

"In . . . In my underwear drawer."

He was wearing a cap, pulled far down to cover his hair. Thin gloves. Black clothes that allowed him to blend into the darkness.

"How did you find me?" Johanna didn't recognize her shrill voice. She had to know, even if it was the last thing she did.

"You were the only one outside the kiosk. I saw the glow of your cigarette, and I realized it couldn't be a coincidence that you of all people were sitting there."

He raised his hand, and Johanna panicked.

"Wait!" she yelled, although it came out as a hoarse whisper. "Killing me won't solve anything—other people know it was you!"

He stopped in midmovement. Johanna stared at him, eyes wide with fear, heart pounding. She had to come up with something that would make him leave.

"Who have you told?" he hissed.

Johanna searched frantically for an answer. She sat up, and one last fragment of courage gave her strength.

"I'll tell you if you promise to leave."

"Who have you told?"

"Nora Linde." Saying the name made her feel a little safer. "The prosecutor here on the island who's investigating the case."

"When did you speak to her?"

"This evening. Not long before I went to bed."

The tears began to flow. She was prepared to say anything to get rid of him. *Please, please don't let him hurt me.*

"Is that the truth?"

"Yes," Johanna sobbed. "If anything happens to me, she'll know it was you."

"Where is she?"

"I'm not telling you."

He took another step forward. Johanna's resolve collapsed.

"She's at home, she lives by Kvarnberget."

He was so close that she could see his eyes shining with icy determination. There was no sign of hesitation, no hint of compassion.

No mercy.

Johanna shuffled until she felt the wall behind her.

"I've told you the truth, so now you need to leave," she whispered. "Please."

She realized what he was holding in his hand. A thick pillow in a pink-striped case. *From Mom and Dad's bed,* she thought. *That must have been where he was hiding. In their closet.*

He was going to kill her, and suddenly she wanted to give up. Maybe this was the punishment she deserved, because she hadn't helped Astrid on that terrible night at Dansberget ten years ago.

She'd lain there rigid with terror and pretended to be asleep while her best friend was raped a few feet away. If she'd been brave enough to intervene, then everything would have been different.

This was what she deserved.

At least now she wouldn't have to feel guilt and shame any longer. The regret that had eaten her up and set the course for her life.

A heavy weight pressed down on her nose and mouth. She couldn't breathe, she was so scared, she couldn't move.

The last of the air was forced out of her lungs. The world disappeared.

# CHAPTER 92

When Nora opened her eyes, she was freezing cold. She must have fallen asleep on the drafty floor; now she was shivering, her teeth chattering. The bottle beside her was empty, the glass tipped over.

She was pulling herself up with the help of the counter when she heard a noise outside.

At first she couldn't figure out where it was coming from, but then she realized that someone was messing with the sheet of plywood covering the hole in the front door where the frosted glass had been. She staggered to the kitchen door and peered into the hallway, trying to make her befuddled brain work. Was someone really trying to get in?

The sheet of plywood moved. It would be easy to remove; it was only tacked in place as a temporary measure.

Nora was finding it impossible to make sense of the situation. Thomas had told her that everything was under control, that Emir Kovač was under surveillance.

And yet he was here. Again.

Light seeped in through a gap between the wood and the window frame; in seconds he would be able to reach inside and turn the lock. Just as Thomas had done when she mistook him for Kovač.

*This isn't happening. It's impossible.*

She groped for her phone, but her pocket was empty. When had she last had it? On the veranda when she received that upsetting message from Jonas. She'd gone into the kitchen, and then . . . ?

She couldn't remember.

There was no time to look for her phone. Instead she stared at the door as if hypnotized, waiting for Kovač's face to appear.

Despair took over, followed by an unexpected feeling: relief.

Maybe this was for the best. Jonas didn't want to live with her anymore, and she'd injured Thomas, her best friend. She'd become impossible, an embarrassment, a burden to those around her. They'd all be better off without her.

There was a scraping noise as one side of the plywood came away from the door.

In spite of her dark thoughts, Nora couldn't simply stand here waiting for Kovač. Her feet moved of their own free will, running toward the veranda and the door that led out into the garden.

She stumbled down the steps and stopped on the last one, staring down at the gravel. Through the drunken fog, she realized it was impossible to get away without making a sound. She looked around for another escape route, one that wouldn't reveal her presence.

Her mind was too slow, she couldn't focus. Her ears were buzzing with a combination of panic and too much wine.

She couldn't head for the village without being heard. She was cut off from both the road and her nearest neighbors. In the opposite direction lay the water. Their boat was moored at the jetty, but she didn't have the keys with her.

*The rowboat.*

It was also bobbing up and down by the jetty. Julia had just started learning to row; she and Elin had been out in the boat the other week.

Could she manage to creep over there and get away?

She swayed where she stood, incapable of making a decision. She clutched the rail and listened. Silence. She couldn't tell if Kovač was in the house or not.

The night air was chilly and raw. Nora shivered in her thin top. She wanted to live, in spite of the fact that she'd hurt everyone she cared about. Everything had gone wrong, but she was determined to fight.

Where could she go?

There was no time to waste.

# Chapter 93

Nora stumbled toward the jetty in the darkness. She hadn't been able to avoid taking a couple of steps across the gravel, but hoped Kovač hadn't heard her.

She passed the woodshed and considered hiding inside but instantly dismissed the idea. If Kovač found her in there, she would be trapped. She couldn't take the risk.

When she reached the jetty, she realized that the old planks were damp, thanks to the evening dew. They were unbelievably slippery, and she only had socks on her feet. Plus she was still very drunk.

She glanced anxiously over her shoulder at the Brand villa. Thank God she'd let Julia sleep over at Molly's.

She crouched down and edged along. It might be dark, but she knew it would be easier to see her on the jetty; the reflection of the water made her a visible target from the house.

She couldn't undo the mooring rope. Jonas had tied it too tightly, and her clumsy fingers refused to cooperate. The whole time she was waiting for the sound of footsteps on the gravel, the ominous sign that Kovač knew where she'd gone.

The boat lurched as she tugged at the rope. Nora held her breath, hoping he hadn't heard the splash.

Still the knot refused to give. She was almost in tears, scrabbling with her nails, but to no avail.

She was concentrating so hard that she didn't notice the approaching shadow.

When she looked up, he was no more than twenty yards away. He'd almost reached the jetty when she met his ice-cold gaze.

Nora recoiled in fear and shock.

# *Siri*

The prospect of the weekend seemed unbearably long when Siri woke up on Saturday. She tried to stay out of Petter's way as much as possible, and did her best to conceal the morning sickness that had begun to plague her.

Petter was avoiding her, too. He barely looked her in the eye on the rare occasions when they were both at home.

The silence between them was heavy and bitter.

The other day he'd caught her weeping on the sofa. The whole complicated situation had overwhelmed her, but she couldn't tell him that. Instead she'd locked herself in the bathroom until she heard his car drive away.

Now they had two days together. She couldn't hide at work or on the golf course.

Siri was alone in the double bed; Petter had taken to sleeping in the spare room. She'd arranged to meet Suss at ten o'clock, just to get out of the house.

She longed to tell her sister her news. She needed someone to share her happiness with—and the worry that refused to go away, even though she was making an effort to be positive. Admittedly, Suss was absorbed in her own pregnancy, but if Siri told her that she, too, was pregnant, then maybe Suss would wake up and think about someone other than herself.

But first Siri had to talk to the father-to-be.

Joy fluttered in her breast. They hadn't had the chance to meet, and she didn't want to break the news over the phone or by text. The biggest revelation of her life had to happen face to face, but they'd both found it difficult to get away over the past week without arousing suspicion.

When Petter informed her that he'd be away at a conference from Monday to Wednesday, it sounded almost too good to be true.

She pulled the covers up over her stomach. Although the underlying melancholy was still there, she couldn't help smiling. It was weird, being so intensely happy yet unhappy at the same time. Even weirder that love could triumph over every pang of conscience, every moral principle.

She had arranged to see him on Tuesday. She would tell him about the child growing inside her, the little life they'd created together. Then she would confide in Suss and leave Petter.

Siri rolled over onto her back. For once she didn't feel sick. It was lovely to lie in bed instead of rushing to the bathroom to stick her head down the toilet.

She caressed the smooth skin of her stomach with her fingertips. When she was lying down, it was almost flat.

*Please let this pregnancy go well.*

She pushed away the unwelcome thoughts. The doctor had been very clear: the child was developing as it should. Everything was fine, there was nothing to worry about.

On Tuesday she would share her fantastic news. He would look at her with the same all-consuming love as always, but with twice the reason.

Tears sprang to Siri's eyes. He loved her in a way that no one else had ever loved her. He saw the true essence of her, and he made her shine.

It would be wonderful to feel his arms around her at last; they were going to be so happy.

She couldn't wait for Tuesday.

# Chapter 94

Time stood still as Nora stared at the man in front of her. He was tall and powerfully built, and she had nothing to defend herself with. She didn't stand a chance against his raw strength.

He was there to kill her; she could feel it with every fiber of her body.

Her fingers were still tugging at the knot, and suddenly it came undone.

Instinct took over.

In a single clumsy movement, she hurled herself into the boat and kicked hard. She saw him break into a run, but the boat had slipped some distance away by the time he got to the bollard.

Far enough to stop him from grabbing it.

She picked up one oar, then the other. Her strokes produced little more than hysterical splashing, but miraculously the boat was moving in the right direction.

Away from the shore. Away from him.

It had never been so difficult to coordinate a pair of oars, but the distance from the jetty kept increasing.

She'd banged her knee when she threw herself into the boat; something warm was trickling down her leg, but there was no time to stanch the bleeding.

*He's probably got a gun,* she thought. *In which case, he'll shoot me.*

*No.*

She couldn't allow herself to think like that. She had to get as far away as possible; anything was better than staying within reach.

Within firing range.

She'd almost passed the white northeastern buoy. A few more yards and she would be on the open sea.

Nora looked around desperately. Where should she go?

If she headed toward one of the other jetties, he could easily make his way there and wait for her. She couldn't possibly row faster than he could run. If she'd had a boat with an engine, things would have been different. Her arms were already aching with the effort; rowing wasn't something she did on a regular basis, and the amount of alcohol she'd consumed wasn't helping.

Tears of frustration trickled down her cheeks.

Why hadn't she taken Thomas's advice and stayed over with Eva? Why did she never, ever listen to anyone except herself?

Now it was too late.

She was alone in the night, and none of the neighbors were awake. No one knew she was in mortal danger. There were no lights on in any of the houses she could see; no one would hear if she screamed for help—and if they did, they wouldn't be able to tell where the cries were coming from. She had no navigation lights on board, not even a flashlight to signal SOS.

She tightened her grip on the oars, managed a few more strokes.

Was he still standing on the jetty? It was too dark to see.

She was getting more and more frightened.

She couldn't just sit here in the boat. The wind was blowing from the north; she would be driven back to the shore if she didn't keep rowing.

Nora glanced over her shoulder and saw the dark silhouette of Telegrafholmen looming up behind her.

It would be much easier to get away if she could reach the smaller island. She would be able to hide there until it grew light. Surely someone would help her then? Boats were passing all the time, and she'd be able to wave to the sailors on Lökholmen.

She set off with renewed energy. There was a concrete jetty on the western side. If she could make it that far, she'd be fine.

# Chapter 95

There was a constant ringing in Thomas's dream; he tried to ignore the shrill noise, but in the end he had to open his eyes. He realized his cell phone was demanding his attention.

Who was it this time? Why wasn't he allowed to sleep in peace?

He was lying on top of the covers, fully dressed, his muscles aching with exhaustion. It must be well after midnight; the sky was dark outside.

He switched on the bedside lamp and picked up the phone.

"Hello?" he mumbled groggily. "Who is this?"

"It's Margit. Did I wake you?"

"Yes."

The one-word answer was all he could manage.

"Sorry about this, but all hell seems to have broken loose on Sandhamn. That's why I'm calling you at this late hour; the duty officer just contacted us."

Thomas sat up. His ribs protested, but it couldn't be helped.

"What's happened?"

"It seems as if we have another homicide on our hands—a woman who features in the investigation into Astrid Forsell's disappearance. Her name is Johanna Strand."

Johanna Strand. Astrid's best friend, who had called him the other day and shown up at Nora's house. *Jesus.*

Thomas was suddenly wide awake.

"A neighbor heard the front door banging in the wind and went over to see if anything was wrong," Margit continued. "She called the emergency number a little while ago. But there's something else . . ."

Margit broke off, which worried Thomas. She wasn't the type to hesitate before delivering bad news.

"I asked the maritime police to check out Nora Linde's house, given what you told me earlier. It appears that someone's broken in."

"Is Nora hurt?"

"They couldn't find her."

"What?"

"The house was empty, and the front door was wide open. There was broken glass on the kitchen counter."

*Shit.*

"The veranda door was also open. I don't like to say this, but it's not looking good."

Thomas was already heading for the hallway to put on his shoes. When he bent down, he felt a searing pain in his side, as if someone had stabbed him.

"I'll get straight over there," he said, wondering where he'd left his painkillers. He pulled on his jacket, checked his pockets.

"The police helicopter will pick you and Aram up from the helipad at Slussen in a few minutes. I've just spoken to them."

"Thanks."

"Thomas . . ." Margit hesitated again. "Can you handle this? I know how much Nora means to you, but you're not well. You looked terrible this morning."

"I'm already on my way."

# CHAPTER 96

The helicopter throbbed across the dark archipelago. From time to time, the beam of a flashing lighthouse sliced through the night sky; otherwise the islands flickered by like black shadows.

Thomas adjusted his safety earmuffs. Adrenaline had temporarily conquered his tiredness. He glanced across at Aram, who was staring ahead, completely focused on their goal. They'd exchanged a few words before climbing on board, but it was hard to talk in the air.

It was almost two o'clock, and the sun wouldn't rise until about five.

Was Petter Grandin involved in this, too? So far they hadn't found enough evidence to arrest him. Thomas hoped that decision hadn't cost Johanna Strand her life.

The lights of the Sandhamn Sound appeared up ahead. Thomas had passed the red houses by the mouth of the Sound so many times that he could see them clearly in his mind's eye.

The pilot switched on the searchlight as he prepared to land. The helipad was by the customs post, right next to the restaurant. Thomas followed the white beam with his gaze. He saw a person in a rowboat approaching Telegrafholmen. It was impossible to make out who it was, but something about the boat made him think of Nora. Jonas had been teaching Elin and Julia to row not long ago; the shape looked familiar.

Who would be heading for Telegrafholmen at this time of night in Nora's boat?

He spoke to the pilot. "Can you turn around?" he asked her over the microphone. "Is it possible to shine the searchlight on Telegrafholmen?" He pointed to the island they'd just passed.

Aram turned to face him. "What are you doing?"

"Look!" Thomas exclaimed, pointing again. "There's someone down there!"

The helicopter wheeled around, and this time Thomas saw that the boat was empty—and there was a motorboat heading for the same mooring.

It couldn't be a coincidence.

"Take us down on Telegrafholmen!" he shouted. "Quick as you can!"

# *Astrid*

The old boathouse was damp and musty, and there was crap everywhere, but Astrid knew that no one would find her here.

She'd often sought refuge in the boathouse when she was little; it belonged to a neighbor who rarely used it. When Mom was mad at her, Astrid would sneak in and hide until it all blew over.

She was sitting on the floor with her legs drawn up, arms wrapped around her knees, staring at the old wooden wall. Trying to empty her mind of all the self-loathing and disgust that threatened to overwhelm her.

The shame wouldn't allow her to forget what had happened, not for a second. It flowed through her veins like poison, the pain increasing with each passing hour.

Her arms were covered in bruises, her thighs marked with deep scratches. Her vagina was sore, and it hurt to pee, but the physical pain was nothing compared to the way she felt about herself.

She'd lain there, perfectly still, without fighting back. She'd let him do exactly what he wanted, even though every repulsive second had been agony. A normal person would have screamed and fought him off, but she'd simply allowed him to carry on. Like a lifeless mannequin.

It was her own fault. There was no one else to blame.

*This will pass,* she'd thought in the darkness of the night, but instead it had gotten worse. She hated herself with an intensity that obliterated everything else.

*If only* she'd left as soon as she'd seen him. *If only* she'd yelled loudly enough to wake Johanna. *If only* she'd been a stronger person when she'd spoken to Mom. She should have demanded that Mom break up with Zacharias instead of folding as she always did when Mom turned nasty.

All these dark thoughts were tearing her apart, destroying her self-esteem like corrosive acid. That didn't stop her from going over them time and time again, increasing the underlying sense of fear and panic.

Two days had passed, but it seemed like an eternity. She'd called in sick on Tuesday. She could barely get out of bed, never mind go to work. The slightest touch from other people made her jump. There was no way she could behave as if everything were normal.

It didn't matter how much she showered, scrubbing her body until the skin was red, her scalp stinging.

She would never be clean again.

Astrid rocked back and forth in despair. There was no point in saying anything to Mom; she'd never believe her. Astrid had realized that after their conversation in the kitchen. Mom wouldn't stand up for her. Not against *him*.

There was no one on her side.

Mom was in town, working, but Astrid didn't want to go home. Zacharias had a key to the house; the very thought that he might show up kept her away.

She'd spent the last couple of nights at Johanna's, but had woken up screaming, over and over again, her face wet with tears and panic enveloping her body like a suffocating blanket.

Johanna had somehow understood what had happened, but Astrid was too traumatized to talk about it. If she acknowledged what Zacharias had done, she would never be able to get out of bed again.

She hadn't responded to any of Niklas's text messages or calls; it was impossible. She didn't have the words, she couldn't breathe. She deleted every message, rejected every call, and in the end it was easier just to switch off her phone.

A creak from the dilapidated door made her look up. Fear flooded her veins; she pressed her back against the wall, tried to make herself invisible.

The door opened slowly, letting in a strip of light. To her surprise, Niklas was standing there. He peered into the darkness, spotted her in the corner, and quickly came over.

Instinct told her to hide, somehow disappear before he could tell her that he knew about her humiliation.

There was nowhere to go. She turned her face away, into the shadows. She couldn't look him in the eye.

Niklas sat down beside her.

"Johanna told me," he said after a little while.

Astrid had a huge lump in her throat. "I can't talk about it."

He couldn't help her, no one could. Her life was ruined.

Niklas tried to take her hand, but she pulled away. "Leave me alone," she mumbled, her eyes fixed on the floor. His presence merely increased her pain, reminded her that she was broken and could never be whole again. Never be healed.

Niklas stayed exactly where he was, and Astrid didn't have the energy to tell him to go away again. Minute after minute passed, became half an hour, maybe longer. Time went by, and he simply sat there, his breathing matching hers, without the least sign of impatience.

Somehow she found solace in the fact that he seemed content to stay with her in silence when she'd told him to go.

She wanted to say thank you, but the words stuck in her throat.

He moved a fraction closer. To her surprise, she didn't mind; her body didn't immediately try to get away.

"Do you want to report him?" Niklas said in a softer voice than she'd ever heard him use. "If you do, I'll help you. I'll go with you to the police. I'm on your side—I always will be."

Astrid let out a long, shuddering sigh. Something unlocked inside her. She wasn't alone against the whole world.

She found she was able to speak to him.

"There's no point. No one will believe me, especially not Mom. There's no proof."

She sounded like a different Astrid, scared and pathetic. A few unwelcome tears trickled down her cheeks, and she dried them with the back of her hand.

"I just want to get away from here. I can't bear to see either of them again."

Niklas took her hand, and she let it happen. He squeezed it gently, as if he were trying to give her strength.

"I've got a plan. We'll leave together."

# Chapter 97

Nora jumped out of the boat as soon as the prow scraped against the rocks on Telegrafholmen. She cried out in pain when she landed on her injured leg. Her knee gave way, but she got to her feet and managed to pull the boat up, in spite of the numb feeling in her arms from rowing.

She'd just stumbled into the forest when she heard the throbbing of a helicopter up above.

If only she'd had something to signal with so that she could call for help, show that it was an emergency. She waved frantically, but by the time she emerged from the trees, the helicopter was already gone.

She was about to turn and head back when the sound of an engine reached her.

*A motorboat.*

Had he followed her?

*No no no.*

Nora pressed her knuckles to her mouth in an attempt to keep her nerves in check as she peered into the darkness. If it was anyone else, the navigation lights should be lit, and there would be no reason to worry. Regular boat owners often enjoyed a night trip, but if there were no lights, that was a different matter. It was a sign that he was coming after her, and didn't want to be seen.

It also meant that he'd realized where she was heading.

The noise grew louder. She couldn't tell which direction it was coming from, and there were no red or green lights to be seen. Everything melted together into an amorphous gray-black mass.

The sound changed. After all these years in the archipelago, Nora knew exactly why; the boat was slowing down, getting ready to come to shore.

Something glinted in the darkness, and suddenly she saw the outline of a motorboat, the prow pointing straight at her.

He was here. It couldn't be anyone else. He'd guessed where she was planning to hide, and had followed her to Telegrafholmen. This time she wasn't going to escape him.

She was stuck on an island without a single living soul nearby. No one would hear her cries for help.

Nora turned and limped into the forest as fast as she could.

# CHAPTER 98

Nora stumbled along the path. It was hard to see; she blundered straight into a thicket, the branches whipping and scratching her face.

Her cheeks almost hurt more than her knee, but she had to keep going. He couldn't be far behind; it didn't take long to moor a boat, and that was all she had in terms of a head start.

Eventually she reached the highest part of the island. It was a little lighter here, easier to make out shapes and outlines. The police tape fluttered in the wind.

Nora suddenly realized where she was—in the spot where the bones had been found.

Was this a cruel twist of fate? Was she going to be murdered in the same place? She was looking around for somewhere to hide when a deafening roar drowned out every other sound.

Nora gazed up at the sky.

The helicopter had come back, and seemed to be heading straight for her. Its lights were flashing, and she thought she could make out the word *Police*.

Was it really a police helicopter? Had someone realized she was in trouble and sounded the alarm?

It must have come to rescue her!

Nora waved hysterically, both arms high in the air.

A searchlight sliced through the night sky, showing the way through the forest.

Tears of relief sprang to her eyes.

"I'm here!" she shouted, crying and yelling at the same time, knowing perfectly well that they couldn't hear her. "Over here!"

The helicopter passed low over her head, holding a steady course for the landing area on the western point, where she'd just left the rowboat. Any minute now she'd be safe.

The helicopter lifted into the air.

Nora stared at it, frozen to the spot as it flew away over the trees and disappeared out to sea.

She was alone in the darkness once more. And she'd lost her few minutes of grace.

# CHAPTER 99

The pilot had changed her mind at the last second; the helicopter lurched and flew away from the island.

"What happened?" Thomas shouted.

"It looked as if someone was standing in the way."

"What?"

"I couldn't risk landing."

Thomas leaned forward, but he couldn't see anyone down there. However, there was a considerably larger motorboat moored next to the little rowboat now.

The helicopter sped away so fast that he only got a fleeting glimpse, but he was sure it was Nora's rowboat.

"I'm going to have to repeat the maneuver—sorry," the pilot informed him. She'd already had to go around again to try to land on Telegrafholmen instead of Sandhamn; it hadn't taken long, but Thomas had a feeling that every second counted.

"For fuck's sake!" Aram snapped. He thought they should be heading straight for Seglarstaden, where Johanna Strand's body had been found. The maritime police were waiting for them, as were the CSIs. This wasn't the time to get sidetracked. "We need to get to Sandhamn," he went on.

Thomas shook his head.

"Telegrafholmen!" he roared in a tone that brooked no opposition. "Look!"

Aram peered into the darkness; it was impossible to see anything.

"What am I supposed to be looking at?"

Thomas swayed as the pilot wheeled around once more. The seat belt dug into his side, and he braced himself with one hand, trying to protect his cracked ribs.

Aram's skeptical expression made it clear that he didn't agree with Thomas's new priority, but the helicopter was making for Telegrafholmen, the searchlight plowing a furrow of brightness through the night.

# Chapter 100

Nora forced herself to keep going, in spite of her failing strength. The soles of her feet were bleeding; her thin socks had been shredded by the rough ground, and the wounds from the previous evening had opened up. The pain in her knee had become a constant ache, increasing with every step.

She wanted to sink down and weep, but that wasn't an option. There must be a place on the island where she could hide, but the crevices in the rocks weren't deep enough, the vegetation wasn't dense enough.

If only she could keep out of his way until dawn, maybe he'd give up.

Up ahead she saw the construction workers' trailers. Could she hide in one of them, or would she be walking into a trap of her own making? Would he track her down easily, do what he'd come to her house to do?

The trailers were probably locked anyway, and she didn't have time to work out how to break in.

Nora's chest was rasping with every laborious breath.

*Please don't let him hear me.*

She tried to breathe more quietly, through her nose, but she couldn't get enough air without opening her mouth.

Through the wind, she heard the helicopter. There was no chance of it coming back. Whoever was on board hadn't seen her; it was hopeless.

She was on the point of giving up when she realized that the throbbing was getting louder. She looked up at the sky; unbelievably, the helicopter seemed to be returning to Telegrafholmen.

The searchlight was on.

Nora blinked back her tears. Had they seen her after all?

She followed the flashing lights, heading straight for the concrete jetty.

It was going to land. Nora inhaled sharply. It was actually going to land!

For a second it hovered above the trees, then it disappeared from view and the noise subsided as the rotors slowed.

The police had come to rescue her. She allowed the tears of relief to flow, then began to limp toward the helicopter.

Suddenly someone came rushing at her.

## *Siri*

Siri's heart was beating fast with joy as she moored the boat on the northern side of Telegrafholmen, the part of the island that couldn't be seen from Sandhamn.

She was the one who'd suggested the location. It wasn't the first time; it was too risky to meet on Djurö, where people might recognize them. There were rarely any visitors on Telegrafholmen, and she'd always loved the uninhabited island. Plus it was only twenty minutes from Djurö, and Siri was an adept sailor.

She'd stayed home for the past few days. The nausea had gotten worse; for the first time she'd called in sick and lied about the reason. In Petter's absence, it was a relief to lie on the sofa and dream about the future. She didn't often allow herself to simply rest and do nothing.

It was a beautiful, mild evening. The late-summer warmth still lingered, and there wasn't a cloud in the sky.

She wasn't the first to arrive; he'd already moored his boat in the usual spot. It didn't take long to make the crossing from Sandhamn.

Siri patted her belly and whispered, "Let's go and meet Daddy," even though she knew it was foolish.

She set off with the picnic basket. She could see him through the trees smoking one of his cigarillos.

"Hi, honey!" she called out as she waved to him. When Nalle turned around, she felt dizzy with love. His smile was the first thing she'd fallen for, the pure joy on his face whenever he saw her.

As if he couldn't get enough of her.

That was why she hadn't hesitated when he asked her to stay behind after a late meeting at work.

She loved being with him.

On that first evening his gaze had made her feel hot and cold at the same time. It had gone straight into her heart and awoken a longing for forbidden pleasures, his lips on hers, his fingertips touching her bare skin. They'd kissed as if it was the most natural thing in the world.

He opened his arms and Siri ran to him. He kissed her as intensely as he had the first time, and she felt a rush of desire, as she always did. The picnic could wait. She just managed to spread the blanket so they didn't have to lie on the ground.

Afterward she lay with her head resting on his chest, tracing a pattern over the smooth skin with her index finger. She'd intended to save her news until they'd eaten, but she couldn't hold back any longer. Siri propped herself up on one elbow so that she could see his face.

"I've got something amazing to tell you," she said with a big smile. She leaned forward and kissed him gently on the mouth. He laughed, misunderstanding the gesture.

"Again?" he murmured in her ear. "So soon?"

"We're having a baby," Siri whispered. "I'm almost eight weeks along."

She caressed her stomach and tried to kiss him again, but Nalle turned his head away. He freed himself from her embrace and sat up.

"That's out of the question," he said.

Siri thought she'd misheard.

"It's definitely yours," she said, in case he'd misunderstood. "It's our child."

"We can't have a baby together."

Nalle pulled on his sweater. An irritated frown spoiled his handsome face, and the soft lips she'd just kissed were set in a hard line.

"You must realize it's totally inappropriate at the moment. What if someone found out, right in the middle of the election campaign? How would that look? The prospective chair of the council having an affair with a political secretary!"

"What do you mean?"

"Besides which, I couldn't do that to Annie. She's much too sick."

The loving gentleness was all gone when he stood up.

"You told me you couldn't get pregnant. Did you lie to me?"

Ice spread through Siri's veins. Nalle had never spoken to her in that tone. She didn't recognize him; it was as if a stranger had taken over the man she loved.

"I thought I couldn't," she stammered, feeling an uncomfortable pressure in her chest. "I would never lie to you."

"No one must know about this. You have to get rid of it—you do realize that, don't you?"

He pulled on his jeans, tightened the belt without looking at her.

Siri picked up her own sweater and held it to her breasts. She stared at him in total bewilderment. Was he leaving? They were supposed to be having a picnic, toasting the good news with champagne.

"I think it's best if we don't see each other for a while," he went on. "Let things calm down. This has been great, but we need to take a break."

Siri was so shocked that she couldn't even cry. She'd risked everything for his sake, cheated on her husband and destroyed her marriage.

He picked up his jacket. "You can organize the abortion—I won't come with you. We shouldn't be seen together."

Siri finally managed to speak. "What are you saying?"

"Take it easy, OK?"

He sounded as if he were at work, dealing with some minor problem at the office. As if she were a difficult colleague.

He glanced at his watch. "I'm sure we can resolve this without getting hysterical. I have to go."

He turned and walked away. Just like that.

Siri sat there as if she were paralyzed for a few seconds, then rage took over.

She lost control of her body.

She saw herself pick up a stone and hurl it at him with all her strength. She picked up another, and another.

"What the hell are you doing? Are you crazy?"

Nalle yelled at her to stop, calm down. Had she lost her mind?

But when he continued to walk away, it was impossible for Siri to stop. She ran after him with another stone in her hand. She lashed out at his back and shoulders, desperate to hurt him.

He turned and grabbed her wrist, but she started biting and clawing at him instead. She wanted to see him bleed, see the pain in his eyes.

They crashed to the ground, rolling in the moss. She was determined to hurt him as much as he'd hurt her.

He was still yelling at her, but she couldn't stop, even though she knew she ought to think about the baby.

She was almost howling with pain.

Suddenly he was sitting on top of her with his fingers around her throat. He squeezed, but still she couldn't stop biting and lashing out. It was impossible, her hands refused to obey her, her body did as it wished. Hatred fueled her, drove her on.

He squeezed harder. She didn't stop.

Not until everything went black and the last of the air was forced out of her lungs.

Then she stopped.

# Chapter 101

For a second, Nora looked into Björn Johansson's eyes, then she acted instinctively and pushed him as hard as she could.

The adrenaline made her strong, but he was stronger.

He seized her arm, held on to her. She did her best to pull away, but got nowhere. She kneed him in the crotch, but still he didn't loosen his grip. Instead he used his free hand to grab her neck and force her down. Nora did her best to stay upright; she knew she would be in real danger if he got her on the ground, but she was no match for him.

She wound up underneath him, kicking and struggling. Johansson locked her arms with his upper body, releasing both his hands. He put them around her throat. She couldn't get any air.

Everything flickered before her eyes, her field of vision shrank.

The pressure increased.

*I'm going to die,* she thought, but somehow she managed to turn her head toward one of his forearms. With fresh strength born of desperation, she bit through fabric and flesh and muscle until she struck something hard. Her mouth was filled with the taste of blood. She felt sick, but refused to let go.

Johansson let out a roar and rolled off her.

Nora scrambled to her feet, coughing and coughing. She looked around for something to defend herself with, and saw a large stone.

She gasped for air. Her throat was in agonizing pain, but she was ready to fight.

Far away, she heard faint voices. One of them sounded like Thomas—was that a hallucination, brought on by the lack of oxygen? She couldn't tell. She tried to shout for help, but all that came out was a hoarse croak.

Björn Johansson was also on his feet now, standing in the middle of the path and blocking the way to the helicopter. He was clutching his injured arm, and his eyes were full of hatred.

"You fucking bitch—you'll pay for this!"

Nora raised the hand holding the stone. There was nothing she wanted more than to hurt him. He'd broken into her home, terrified her. Anger gave her fresh energy.

"Get out of my way!" she hissed. Johansson circled around her, like a boxer preparing to attack. Nora hunched her shoulders, ready to counter any onslaught.

"You don't stand a chance," Johansson said, his voice dripping with contempt. "Do you seriously think you're a match for me, after what I've done?"

Nora tightened her grip on the stone.

*Any second now.*

She longed to smash his face, destroy that supercilious look.

Suddenly, Thomas's voice came from behind her.

"Hands in the air or I'll shoot!" he yelled.

Nora didn't take her eyes off Johansson. Every muscle was trembling with tension.

"Second warning!" Thomas yelled again; he was only a few feet away.

Time stood still.

Slowly, Björn Johansson took a step back and raised his hands above his head.

"Don't shoot!"

Nora hesitated for a few endless seconds, then she dropped the stone. It landed on the ground with a thud, between her and Johansson.

The tension left her body as if someone had stuck a pin in a balloon. She fell to her knees and vomited violently.

## *Astrid*

Astrid was lying in the spare bed she used when she stayed the night with Johanna.

Someone tapped on the bedroom window. Astrid opened her eyes, got up, and looked out to see Niklas standing there. He beckoned to her. It was only a few hours since they'd parted company in the boathouse.

Astrid pulled on her robe and crept to the front door.

Niklas's face was ashen, his expression strained. His eyes were red and swollen; it was obvious that he'd been crying. It wasn't particularly cold, but he was shaking so much that his teeth were chattering. Astrid made him sit down on the edge of the decking. She grabbed a blanket from one of the garden chairs and wrapped it around his shoulders.

"What's happened?"

Niklas opened his mouth but looked totally bewildered, as if he'd forgotten how to speak. His breathing was so rapid and shallow that Astrid wondered if he was injured. She looked for signs of bleeding, but his clothes were intact and she couldn't see any injuries.

"Has someone hurt you?" she asked gently.

Niklas shook his head.

His lips were alarmingly pale, his eyes dull and lifeless. Astrid had no idea what was going on, but she was becoming increasingly worried. Only that afternoon he'd sat quietly with her in the boathouse; it was Niklas who'd given her the courage to get up and walk out of there.

Now he seemed to be as crushed as she was.

What was wrong? Something terrible must have happened during the evening.

Niklas took out a packet of cigarettes and tried to light one, but his fingers were shaking too much. Astrid did it for him. He took a deep drag, then another. He buried his face in his hands.

Astrid sat quietly beside him, hoping he'd be able to tell her eventually. Was it his mom?

"My dad . . ." Niklas said at long last. A shuddering sob passed through his body. Astrid waited patiently.

"I think . . . I think he's killed someone."

Astrid's eyes opened wide. "What?"

"I decided to talk to him this evening. I was going to tell him that I was leaving home, that I wouldn't be coming back to Tyresö with him when we finish on Sunday."

Niklas was speaking so quietly that his words were almost inaudible. Astrid leaned closer.

"I've sold the Jet Ski, so you and I will be able to afford somewhere to live."

He took a quick drag, then coughed.

"Someone said Dad was out in the boat, so I took the Jet Ski out for one last run while I waited for him to come back."

Astrid shivered and drew her robe more tightly around her body. Niklas's voice was a monotone, as if he were in a trance.

"When I passed Telegrafholmen, I saw my dad's boat moored in the inlet on the far side of the island. I recognized it right away; not many people have a Targa of that model. There was a Buster next to it. I was curious, so I went ashore."

Niklas's hand was still shaking; flakes of ash drifted down.

"As soon as I switched off the engine, I could hear a woman yelling hysterically. Then I heard Dad yelling back at her. It was crazy—they sounded as if they were killing each other."

His voice almost broke.

"I followed the sound, then everything went quiet. I hid behind a tree. That's when I realized what he was doing."

Astrid hardly dared ask the next question.

"What did you see?"

Niklas opened and closed his mouth as if he couldn't bear to go on.

"I saw my dad sitting on top of a woman who was lying on the ground. She was naked from the waist up, I could see her breasts. He had his hands around her throat. She wasn't moving."

He took a deep breath.

"He strangled her, right in front of me."

Johanna had appeared in the doorway. She came over to them and sank to her knees beside Niklas. She looked very shocked; she must have been listening.

"Did he see you?" Astrid asked.

Niklas shrugged. "I don't know. I turned and ran, jumped on the Jet Ski, and came back to Sandhamn. I've spent the last few hours trying to get my head around it all."

"You have to go to the police," Johanna whispered.

"He's my dad."

Astrid knew all about conflicts of loyalty.

"But you said he'd killed a woman," Johanna persisted.

"I can't do it."

"Why not?"

Johanna was almost as pale as Niklas.

"If Dad ends up in jail, Mom won't be able to cope." He stubbed out the cigarette in the sand with such force that it disintegrated. "Don't you get it?" He was almost crying now. "Dad could get a life sentence.

Mom can't manage without him; she's too sick. I can't do that to her. It would kill her."

Astrid could feel Niklas's pain. She tried to think, but her head was all over the place. A dog started barking in one of the houses along the road, then a door opened and closed. "What are you going to do?"

"I don't know." Niklas rubbed his forehead. "I have to get away from here. I can't stay and face him in the morning as if nothing's happened. I just can't."

Astrid sat up a little straighter. There was an obvious solution. In her despair after Zacharias's attack, she hadn't been thinking clearly; the answer had been there all along.

"We'll go to my dad," she said firmly. "He lives in Bergen. He'll help us."

She no longer felt paralyzed. Niklas had led her out into the sunshine this afternoon; now it was her turn. She took his hand and pulled him to his feet.

"Go and get your stuff—we'll catch the early ferry in the morning. We can travel to Oslo by train, then on to Bergen. They hardly ever check passengers' ID or passports on Swedish Railways; if we book our seats using false names, no one will know where we've gone."

Astrid turned to Johanna. "Can I borrow some money? I promise to pay you back—we just need enough for the tickets."

"I told you, I've got money from selling the Jet Ski," Niklas said quietly.

Johanna's bottom lip was trembling. "You're not coming back, are you?" Her voice was thick with tears.

Astrid shook her head. They would go to Norway, leave this crap country. No one would ever find them—not her mom, not Niklas's dad. She had no intention of saying one more word to her mother, or of setting foot on Sandhamn again. She knew with absolute certainty that she couldn't stay in Sweden.

Something deep inside her had shattered. It would probably never be healed completely, but maybe she could start the process in her father's country.

Together with Niklas, she was prepared to try.

She grabbed Johanna's arm.

"Promise you won't say anything about this. You can never tell anyone that we're alive or where we've gone."

Johanna stared at her, unable to hold back the tears.

"Promise me, Johanna! Whoever asks. Everyone has to believe that we've gone for good. We can't let anyone find us!"

# Tuesday, August 16

# Chapter 102

Nora slowly opened her eyes. Everything was white. The walls, the blinds, the sheets.

Then she realized. This wasn't her own bed. She was in the hospital; the helicopter had brought her here during the night. Vague memories of someone examining her throat and dressing her injured feet flickered through her mind.

How long had she been asleep? More than twenty-four hours? It was dark outside.

Her throat felt strange, as if it were badly inflamed. It was hard to breathe or swallow. Her feet and the rest of her body ached. There was an IV drip attached to her arm.

Someone was slumped in the chair beside her, dozing with his chin resting on his hand.

*Jonas.*

"Water," Nora croaked in a voice that didn't sound like her own.

Jonas gave a start. "You're awake!"

"I'm so thirsty."

He held out a glass with a straw in it, and Nora drank gratefully. She couldn't even manage to hold the glass herself.

"Thanks."

It was impossible to keep her eyes open. She sank back against the pillow.

"Julia?" she murmured, with a huge effort. She'd never felt as tired as this.

"She's still on Sandhamn, with Eva. There's nothing to worry about."

"Thomas?"

"He's fine, too. I guess he's at home, catching up on his sleep. It was a long night."

Jonas took her hand and caressed it with his fingertips.

"It's going to be all right, Nora. I'm so sorry I wasn't home when . . ." His voice gave way. "If only I'd been there when that guy showed up, then this would never have happened. I should have been with you and Julia."

Nora's eyes filled with tears. "I'm so sorry," she whispered. She wanted to apologize for everything, tell him he'd been right all along. She would stop drinking and see the counselor, listen to well-meaning advice, and never quarrel with him again—but she was too exhausted. Another time. She had to sleep.

She managed to squeeze his hand.

"You're here now."

# Wednesday, August 17

# Chapter 103

There was a gentle tap on the door of Nora's room. She was dozing but opened her eyes and saw Thomas with Pernilla behind him. She beckoned them in and did her best to sit up in bed.

"How are you doing?" Pernilla asked, holding out a bunch of flowers that she'd already found a vase for. Typical of Pernilla to be so efficient.

Nora smiled wearily. She was sleeping most of the time, but it was easier to breathe now, though her voice still sounded horrible.

"I think I'll be allowed home the day after tomorrow," she croaked. "They just want to check that my windpipe is OK before they discharge me." She grimaced. "I know I look terrible."

She'd seen herself in the bathroom mirror, and wished she hadn't. The bruise on her face was still huge, and Björn Johansson's fingers had left purple marks on her neck.

"How are you?" she asked Thomas.

He shrugged. "OK."

"He's taken off work for a week," Pernilla informed Nora. "He gave in eventually."

Thomas managed a wry smile. He pulled up a chair and sat down next to Nora's bed, his movements slow and cautious. "I've got some good news for you." He held out his phone and showed her a photo of a short-haired woman with a little boy in her arms.

It took a moment for Nora to realize who she was looking at. The last time they met, the woman had had long blond hair; now she was a brunette.

"It's Mina," she said. "Mina and Lukas!"

"They're absolutely fine. I have a contact at Interpol who helped me track them down. They're in Macedonia."

"Macedonia?"

"That's where Mina's father comes from, and they still have family there. It's a good place to get away from Emir Kovač."

"So they're really OK?" Every word was an effort.

"Yes. You don't need to worry about Mina anymore. Or Emir Kovač—we're keeping an eye on him."

Nora sank back onto her pillow, almost dizzy with relief. She'd been so anxious about Mina and her son.

"By the way, Kovač was never on Sandhamn. It wasn't him who broke your window—it was Zacharias Fahlman."

Nora blinked. "Fahlman?"

"We found his fingerprints on the door handle, and he's admitted to the crime. He'll be charged with criminal damage. We think he was trying to scare you off, stop you digging into his past. We're currently looking into whatever he's hiding. Presumably he was too drunk to think clearly."

Nora let out a long breath. Mina and Lukas were all right; nothing else mattered.

She couldn't keep her eyes open any longer.

"Thank you," she whispered, and fell asleep.

# Monday, August 29

# CHAPTER 104

It was pouring rain in Bergen. The Norwegian coastal city was notorious for its constant wet weather, and it was certainly living up to its reputation.

The plane had landed on time. Thomas and Aram had caught the shuttle train into the center, which took forty-five minutes, then paid a courtesy visit to the local police.

They took a cab to their final destination, a five-story apartment building in the suburbs. As soon as they got out of the vehicle, the damp air wrapped itself around them. There was no mistaking the proximity to the Atlantic; they could almost taste the salt.

Aram glanced around. "So here we are."

They set off up the stairs to the fourth floor and found the nameplate that said "Hansen." Thomas rang the bell, and the door was opened immediately by a young woman who seemed a little tense.

Astrid Forsell hadn't really changed, even after ten years. She still had long blond hair; her face had filled out, but she was slim and looked fit.

"Are you from the Swedish police?" she asked.

Thomas nodded. "May we come in?"

Astrid led the way into a light, airy living room with a huge window overlooking the water. A tall man about the same age as Astrid was sitting on a pale leather corner sofa with a child on his lap. The little girl was wearing a yellow-striped romper and a cardigan, and she had a pink pacifier in her mouth.

When the two police officers came in, he stood up and held out his hand. A white-gold wedding ring glinted on the third finger of his left hand.

"Niklas Hansen."

His voice was deep and steady. Only a couple of nervous blinks revealed that he found the situation difficult.

"We took my father's name when we came here," Astrid explained. Her Swedish had acquired a lilting intonation, sounding vaguely Norwegian.

Thomas and Aram sat down on the sofa. The apartment was spotlessly clean and tidy, in spite of the fact that the couple had a young baby. The glass coffee table shone, as did the open-plan kitchen. There was a clean smell, as if someone had just gone through the whole place with a lemon air freshener.

"Thank you for letting us come and talk to you," Thomas began.

Niklas swallowed and pressed his lips to his daughter's downy head. "We read the news online—that someone had been arrested for the murder of Siri Grandin. It was Astrid who persuaded me to call you when we realized it was my father."

Astrid had sat down beside her husband. She adjusted the baby's cardigan as the little girl gazed with interest at the visitors, her chubby hands waving happily in the air. She looked like her mom.

"We've stayed away and carried these secrets for far too long," Astrid said. "It hasn't done either of us any good. It's time to talk." She stroked Niklas's hand, her eyes shining with unshed tears. "My dad said we ought to speak to you. He told us you'd contacted him, but he wanted to let us decide what to do." Her voice faltered. "We haven't even been in touch with Niklas's mom—or my mom."

Thomas opened his notebook. Aram had already set up the tape recorder.

Given what Astrid had already told them, it seemed likely that Zacharias Fahlman would stand trial for his crime. It was the eleventh hour, but it wasn't too late. The statute of limitations for rape was ten years, which was the middle of August in this case, but the fact that Astrid had been under eighteen at the time of the assault made a difference. The time limit was calculated from her eighteenth birthday, in late September.

They still had a month to charge him, and had already brought in a prosecutor with vast experience with sexual offenses. Thomas knew she'd do her best to help Astrid.

The sun emerged from between the clouds, filling the room with light. The little girl let out a gurgling laugh.

When Astrid smiled at her daughter, the tension in her face eased slightly. She exchanged a glance with Niklas. In spite of the couples' obvious nervousness, Thomas could see that the love between them was strong.

He checked his notes.

The National Board of Forensic Medicine had completed the DNA analysis of the bones found on Telegrafholmen, establishing beyond all doubt that it was Siri Grandin who'd been buried in an unmarked grave.

Björn Johansson had admitted that they'd had a secret affair. When Siri told him she was pregnant, he'd panicked. There would have been a huge scandal if the news had gotten out, and his political career as a prospective chair of the council in Tyresö would have been ruined. The revelation had led to a huge quarrel between him and Siri.

The police had interviewed Johansson several times. His attorney wanted him acquitted or, in the worst-case scenario, charged with involuntary manslaughter, but absolutely not homicide.

Johansson insisted that Siri's death had been an accident. She'd slipped while they were quarreling and hit her head with such force that she'd died.

There were no grounds for a charge of homicide or even manslaughter, according to the attorney. His client had seen burying

Siri in secret as the only way out. Yes, he'd placed the postcard in the Grandins' mailbox in order to give the impression that Siri had taken her own life, but that didn't make him a murderer.

The bones, of course, provided no evidence as to how Siri had died.

Johansson also denied the murder of Johanna Strand.

He hadn't left any fingerprints at the scene; however, there were thumbprints on the money found in a white plastic bag. Again, it was a tricky case. There were no witnesses, but Thomas hoped that traces of Johansson's DNA would be found.

As far as the attempted murder of Nora Linde was concerned, his attorney cited self-defense—Nora had attacked his client with a stone. Thomas knew that a good prosecutor would have no problem demolishing that explanation; Johansson had been caught in the act.

He studied the young man sitting opposite him. If he'd understood the situation correctly, Niklas Johansson had stayed away for ten years in order to protect his mother, who was already seriously ill when her husband murdered Siri Grandin. Niklas had left the country to avoid testifying against his own father and destroying his mother's life.

Now he'd come forward voluntarily. Niklas was the only eyewitness, and his account completely contradicted his father's story.

Astrid could also testify; she'd heard his account only hours after the event.

Even if Björn Johansson couldn't be convicted of Johanna Strand's murder, Thomas thought that, with Niklas's help, they ought to be able to prove he'd killed Siri.

He caught Niklas's eye, and saw courage and resolve. The young man was determined to do the right thing, without letting family ties hold him back. At long last he was ready to reveal the truth about Siri Grandin's death.

"Go at your own pace," Thomas began. "We've got plenty of time. What really happened that evening on Telegrafholmen?"

# Acknowledgments

This is the tenth book in the Sandhamn Murders series, and no one is happier or more surprised than I am that there have been so many! Therefore, first of all, I want to thank all the loyal and enthusiastic readers who have made this possible.

I couldn't have done it without you.

As a writer, I have taken certain liberties. The construction work on Telegrafholmen began a year or so earlier than 2016. With nature conservation in mind, there was no blasting. I've invented the odd path or track on the island, but I take full responsibility for any errors that may have occurred. All the characters are pure invention, and any resemblance to persons living or dead is entirely coincidental.

Many kind people have helped me with this book. Warm thanks to Detective Inspector Rolf Hansson, who has patiently answered all my questions about police work, and to Gunilla Pettersson, who has once again gone through the entire manuscript with her sharp archipelago eyes.

My daughter, Camilla, provided invaluable assistance when I got completely stuck. Without our discussions around the kitchen table, I wouldn't have been able to progress. Thank you, sweetheart!

Madeleine Jonsson, my peerless assistant, has been a great support throughout the entire process, and has cleared up a number of research questions while maintaining her everyday tasks at the same time. Thank you so much!

My fantastic editor John Häggblom—who constantly pushes me and makes me a better writer—has tirelessly encouraged and supported me. I don't think you realize how grateful I am, especially this time. You're a rock, and this book wouldn't exist without you!

Karin Linge Nordh, my publisher for so long, was unfortunately only with me for half the journey. Thank you for everything over the years; your contribution to these ten books has been immense.

I would also like to thank Lina Rönning, Lisa Jonasdottir Nilsson, and everyone else at Forum who takes care of my books and is behind the Sandhamn Murders.

To the gang at Bindefeld—thank you for everything you do, you're the best!

Nordin Agency, led by the extraordinary Anna Frankl—I'm so grateful for the work we do together, and for your wholehearted passion for promoting my books all over the world.

Finally—I couldn't do any of this without my family. Lennart, Camilla, Alexander, and Leo, you are my everything. I love you so much.

*Sandhamn, September 25, 2019*
*Viveca Sten*

# About the Author

*Photo © 2016*

Viveca Sten made her author debut in 2008 with the crime novel *Still Waters*, the first book in the Sandhamn Murders series. It became an overnight success, and her books about inspector Thomas Andreasson and lawyer Nora Linde have now sold over six million copies worldwide.

The tenth book in the Sandhamn series, *Buried in Secret*, was published in October 2019. It, along with the other books in the Sandhamn series, still tops international bestseller charts today. Viveca Sten's novels are also the basis of a hugely successful TV series set on Sandhamn Island. An estimated eighty million people around the globe have watched the adventures of Nora and Thomas unfold on their TV screens.

Today, Viveca divides her time between Stockholm, Sandhamn, and Åre, a famous Swedish ski resort that also happens to be the setting for Sten's new crime series, the Åre Murders. For more information visit www.vivecasten.com.

# About the Translator

Marlaine Delargy lives in Shropshire in the United Kingdom. She studied Swedish and German at the University of Wales, Aberystwyth, and she taught German for almost twenty years. She has translated novels by many authors, including Kristina Ohlsson; Helene Tursten; John Ajvide Lindqvist; Therese Bohman; Theodor Kallifatides; Johan Theorin, with whom she won the Crime Writers' Association International Dagger in 2010; and Henning Mankell, with whom she won the Crime Writers' Association International Dagger in 2018. Marlaine has also translated *In Bad Company*, *In the Name of Truth*, *In the Shadow of Power*, *In Harm's Way*, *In the Heat of the Moment*, *Tonight You're Dead*, *Guiltless*, *Closed Circles*, and *Still Waters* in Viveca Sten's Sandhamn Murders series.